THE VAMPIRE LORD

BOOK TWO OF THE BLOOD AND VENOM SAGA

K. E. BEALE

CONTENTS

AUTHOR'S NOTE

And Content Warnings

This is the second book in the *Blood and Venom Saga* and should be enjoyed after reading *Book One: The Vampire and the Scorpion.*

The Blood and Venom Saga is a Dark Fantasy/ Paranormal Romance series that explores polyamorous LGBT+ (MMF) relationships, full of misdirection, heartbreak, and drama along the way. This series gets *dark*. (Please check the content warnings below if needed). But if you can trust me, I promise you'll get your 'happily ever after'... eventually.

The story is written in British English, so for my American friends, please enjoy our spelling variations of words such as 'realise', 'colour', and 'practise', as well as some of our quirky idioms and slang.

The Vampire Lord contains 'on-page' panic attacks, body-shaming/ bullying, cannibalism, gory violence, injury detail, limb loss, explicit sex scenes, imprisonment, abuse during pregnancy*, and substance abuse.

It also contains 'off-page' rape*, forced breeding*, domestic violence, child abuse, and references to torture, homophobia, and suicide.

* Not to the main character.

Future instalments may deal with other triggering themes. Reader discretion advised.

CHAPTER ONE

Ivan didn't let a simple thing like death stop him from tormenting me. Those few nights after Madigan and I had killed him—when I'd slipped into the abyss of unconsciousness—were the only moments of peace I'd been gifted before the monster crept into my nightmares.

His eye sockets were a mess of pulp, blood raining from the gaping holes and into my face. Into my eyes. My nose. My mouth. Until I couldn't breathe, the torrent unrelenting. Red streamed down his cheeks as his lips spread into that sickening leer.

"I'll admit it, Ava Monroe," he said, his cigar breath making my stomach writhe. "You've got guts." His hand was in my navel, groping inside me, his fingers worming through my intestines. He pulled. An eruption of blood and entrails.

I screamed, the sound echoing inside my head until my throat was raw. And he continued to pull, yanking out a trail of innards, landing in a heap beside me.

I couldn't move, lying flat on my back as Ivan pulled more and more, until I was certain I was empty, and yet, he didn't stop. My stomach splattered as it hit the floor—nothing left to pull—but that didn't stop Ivan. He reached inside me, closed his fingers around my heart, and wrenched the still beating organ from my rib cage. It sat thumping in the palm of his hand. God... I wished it would stop...

Ivan laughed as he shoved it down my throat, forcing me to swallow it until I was choking. But before the darkness took me into sweet oblivion, I retched, my heart still lodged in my throat, propelling itself back up.

And Ivan laughed harder.

I curled onto my side as my stomach contracted with a painful crunch, my heart landing in a splatter of blood, acid burning my throat.

I retched again.

My face peeled from the vomit-soaked pillow as I gasped for air, my heart rattling so hard it hurt. I propped myself up on one elbow, straining to see—eyes burning, watering—blind in the darkness. I jumped, almost tumbling out of bed, as a hand gripped my shoulder.

"Ava, it's okay. It was a nightmare." Latisha squatted beside my bed, the shape of her spiral curls just visible in the gloom.

With a soft click, Latisha switched on the lamp that had toppled from my nightstand, bathing the small camper bedroom with a soft golden glow. But it was of little comfort. My body shivered with a combo of adrenaline and cold, wet vomit coating the left side of my face. My short hair was wet too, the dark brown strands at the back sticking to my neck, and the white tuft at the front slick against my forehead. I drove my fingers through it, making it stand on end rather than endure the discomfort of having it against my skin. Only now, the sick clogging my hair coated my hand instead.

"Don't do that," Latisha said, taking my wrist and wiping me clean with some paper towels she'd brought with her. It was only now I spotted an empty glass on the floor beside the lamp, the carpet beneath a darker shade than the rest: the glass of water I'd set on my nightstand before going to bed.

"You were thrashing about in your sleep," Latisha said as she noticed what I was staring at. "I couldn't wake you. And when you knocked the glass, I fetched these to clean up." She raised the roll of paper towels.

I reached out, touching Latisha's arm. Warmth from her skin seeped through the silk of her blue-and-orange dressing gown. I squeezed. Her flesh was firm within the sleeve. Then I squinted into her face, searching for missing details or mistakes, but she was perfect. The long lashes that framed her eyes. Her plump, ruby lips—the same lips that once framed a soft smile, etching dimples into her cheeks. No smile now.

"Is this real?" I asked, my voice getting lost somewhere in my throat, escaping as a croak.

"Yes, this is real," she said. "You were having a nightmare. You're safe."

I pressed my lips together and wrinkled my nose to stop the tears that stung my eyes. "This is real," I repeated, more to myself than to her.

"Come on." Latisha took me by the arm, helping me out of bed. "Let's get you cleaned up."

After bundling into the shower and changing into some spare pyjamas, I took a seat in the living area of Latisha's camper while she zipped about the kitchen making tea.

"How are you feeling?" she asked, pouring boiling water into a teapot.

"Better." It was only half a lie. As well as being fresh and clean, I'd also washed away the fogginess of sleep and could now fully remember where I was, who I was with, and why I was there: as Latisha's familiar, it was custom for me to share her living space, her motorhome. But I still massaged my chest as my thumping heart tried to liberate itself from my ribcage. I shuddered, pushing the nightmare down, and instead focused on Latisha's glittering fairy lights, the reds, blues, and purples of her cushions and blankets, and the soft fragrance of last night's incense still in the air.

Real.

Safe.

I scrutinised Latisha as she brewed our tea, still looking for glitches, but her movements were as fluid and graceful as they always were. When she placed the tea tray on the table, I spotted a shot glass among the crockery, containing a sunny-yellow liquid I instantly recognised as Mollifier from its floral scent. Nothing better than a witch's potion to cure what ails you, and I wondered how long it would be until I learned how to brew them myself. Sure, I wasn't a witch yet—just a lowly shapeshifting familiar—but the day I wielded the same powers as my mistress and could defend myself from the horrors of the super-natural world couldn't come soon enough.

I knocked back the Mollifier and reclined into the sofa as its pleasant calming effect spread through my body, slowing my heart, relaxing my muscles.

Latisha didn't speak as she poured our tea and handed me a plate of toast from the tray, perhaps knowing I'd struggle to string words together. But after letting the Mollifier do its magic and a quick break-fast, I felt more like my usual self.

"I was dreaming about Ivan," I said at last, brushing crumbs from my fingertips and letting them fall onto the plate.

"I figured as much." Latisha eyed me over the top of her teacup before taking a sip. "This sort of reaction is... to be expected." She was choosing her words carefully. "Horrible, yes, but not unusual. I'd say you're only human, but that's not technically true, is it?"

I managed a half-smile and sipped my tea.

"It's only been two nights since..." Latisha's voice trailed off. Per-haps it was difficult to say, 'since a deranged vampire disembowelled you'. Instead, after a pause, she opted for, "Since you and Madigan freed our coven."

A grin split my lips—genuine this time. Yes, we *had* freed the coven from Ivan's rule. Me and my vampire boyfriend, though it sounded somewhat juvenile calling the one-hundred-and-thirty-something war veteran my *boyfriend*. Was partner better? Other half? Hmmm, I'd have to think about that.

Latisha's teeth grazed her lower lip as she stared into her teacup. "I was going to ask you to assist me and the other witches in some potion making tonight—"

"What potion?" I asked, keen to get my training underway.

"A sedation draught for Len to take on his trip to the Vampires' Nest. He'll need to keep Dominic in a subdued state."

Ahhh yes... Dominic, Ivan's most loyal henchman. I suppose, in a way, it's good he gorged himself on so much blood he's almost become a Brain Eater and needs to be taken to the Nest for trial. The sooner he's gone, the better...

But wait a second...

"What do you mean you *were* going to ask me to help?" I asked.

Latisha tilted her head, her lips pressed together, and I could almost hear her mind race with the best way to phrase whatever was rattling around in there. "It's not that I think you're incapable."

"You think I'm too traumatised?" I said, a flare of defiance rising in my chest.

Her brows pinched into an apologetic expression. "Well... I mean... If your nightmare is anything to go by—"

"You said yourself it was natural! And you know I'm a stress-vommer."

"A *stress-vommer*?" Her lips quirked with amusement.

"Yeah!" I couldn't help but smirk too. "Y'know, someone who vomits when they're stressed! Remember when I chundered after the ordeal with Austin?" I regretted mentioning Austin immediately; the memory of Ivan crushing him to death extinguished the brief flicker of solace, making my stomach tense again.

"Yes," Latisha said, her eyes narrowing like she'd somehow sensed my queasiness returning. "And it's also natural to need time to decompress and practise self-care."

"Please, Latisha. I can't sit around doing nothing. I need to keep busy, and as much as I *love* doing the laundry for the coven, it's not distracting enough. Pleeease?"

She stared at me, thinking, as I blinked my best puppy-dog eyes at her.

"Fine."

"Yes!"

"But," she said, raising a hand to curb my excitement, "just for tonight, and we'll see how you cope. Tomorrow, I want you to spend the night with Len instead."

"Not that I need much persuasion to hang out with Madigan"—I could already picture his perfect ass—"but why?"

"I'm hosting some demons."

"Demons?" The hair on the back of my neck rose as I remembered my one and only encounter with a demon.

Lascivious.

His golden, shimmering skin, dark blue—almost purple—eyes, and that sultry curve of his lips. But the most unnerving thing was my body's reaction to him. The hot tingling across my skin. Every inch of me yearning to be touched. And then the cold, clammy sweat that coated me as he departed, like a comedown. Neither sensation was within my control, and I suspected he made *everyone* feel that way, whether they wanted it or not. *Lascivious* was in control.

"Yeah, three of them." She scrunched the curls at the back of her head, glancing away from me. Though she spoke in her usual light-hearted voice, her body language betrayed her, leaving me with a heaviness in the pit of my stomach.

"Why?"

She drummed her fingers on the table for a moment before answering, "Well, do you remember I told you witches can gain extra abilities from demons?"

"Yes. For a price."

"Well, with the Hallows' return, I must be certain I can defend our coven. Right now, all I have is my glamour and standard potion making. I promised myself I wouldn't take any extra abilities. Not after last time. But..."

I raised an eyebrow, about to pry deeper into her past when she'd been leader of a different coven, and presumably, had been more powerful.

But Latisha clasped her hands and said, "That's enough chatter. If you want to help with the potion, we'd better get going. Grab my cauldron from the back, and I'll meet you in the woodland clearing."

"Wait. What? The clearing?" My tea and toast threatened to make a reappearance at the mention of where I'd watched Austin die, and later, fought Ivan in that ring of fire. "Why there?"

"I'm using it as my new Sacred Ground. You know, where witches perform their spells and rituals. Magic is stronger where blood has spilled."

An involuntary spasm shot through me. Though the clearing was no doubt better than the old shipping container Ivan had forced her to use, the idea of going back... *there...*

"Your magic is going to be pretty fucking strong then," I said grim-
ly.

I trudged towards where Madigan was working on an old, battered
campervan, easy to spot in the darkness of the showmen's yard thanks
to a couple of spotlights. My Doc Martens somehow felt heavier than
usual as I dragged my feet. My trip with the witches into the woodland
clearing could *not* have gone any worse.

The vampire emerged from the rear of the campervan, his spine
straightening as he looked through the darkness and directly at me.
Though I was still several feet away, his sensitive olfaction must have
announced my presence to him.

"Ava?" he called out, face flushed from his work, sweat dripping
from his dark hair onto his oil-streaked face. It still sounded strange to
hear him use my first name. I'd grown so used to 'Miss Monroe', that
calling me Ava was almost as intimate as kissing to us.

"Yeah, it's me," I said heavily as I lumbered closer, still shrouded in
the shadows of the night.

As I stepped into the light to join him, he strode towards me,
cupped my face in his oily hands, and stared at me with those haunted,
grey eyes.

"You smell of adrenaline and cortisol," he said, worry etched across
his sharp, handsome features. "And your heart is racing." I didn't
miss the way his eyes flicked to my throat for half a second. "What
happened? What's wrong?"

I took another step forward, breaking his hold on me as I wrapped
my arms around him and squeezed him in a tight hug. His body
stiffened at the display of affection, but soon, his muscles relaxed, and

he returned the embrace, resting his chin on the top of my head. I don't know how long we stood locked in each other's arms, but he seemed to know this was what I needed. No talking. Just him.

Only once my pulse had stopped throbbing in my ears did I release him. "Latisha wants us to use the woodland clearing as the Sacred Ground."

His dark brows furrowed as he nodded slowly. "I understand." He didn't need any further explanation, like he somehow knew *everything* that had just happened. Of course, he couldn't have known how one witch, Aurora, who'd once been so friendly she'd gifted me a topaz necklace, could no longer look me in the eye. Latisha had said grief did odd things to people, and Aurora was still grieving for her twin sister, Luna. She'd been killed during the carnage I'd caused by joining the fight between Ivan and Madigan.

"She doesn't *really* blame you," Latisha had said to me, but it sure as hell *looked* like she blamed me. I couldn't fault her. After all, I blamed myself, too.

And then, there was the way my head swam as I'd entered the clearing and caught sight of a ring-shaped scar of dirt and ash marking the earth. The flashback of burning branches forming the fighting arena. The scent of petrol, and blood, and burning flesh, and the sound of screams. *My* screams.

I shook myself before the memories could grip me like they had in the clearing.

For a moment, Madigan and I just stared at each other. It wasn't an uncomfortable silence. More like we didn't need words to communicate. There had always been a deep sadness behind Madigan's eyes I'd never been able to comprehend, but now, not only did I understand that sadness, I was certain it was now reflected in my own eyes, too.

A shared pain.

"Does it ever go away?" I said in a whisper, like it was a question my soul had asked.

Madigan bit his lip, perhaps afraid to answer. "No," he said after a pause. "But it gets easier."

Again, our eyes met as I searched for the words I wanted. What happened in the clearing was somehow... embarrassing.

"Were you sick?" Madigan guessed. It was a fair assumption.

"I was when I woke up this morning. I had this nightmare about Ivan. He was..." My words trailed off. I didn't want to relive the dream... or the reality. "And then in the clearing, it all came flooding back and I..." I didn't want to relive that either.

Madigan took both of my hands and looked directly into my eyes, so deep I thought he could see the heart of me. "Now, Ava, you listen to me. Don't go thinking you're weak or that there is anything *wrong* with you. I've seen fully grown men—soldiers—react this same way. My friend, he..." He paused, swallowing a lump in his throat before continuing, "He used to wake up screaming, fighting some invisible enemy that had followed him into his dreams. What you have been through is truly, truly terrible. But you survived, and you are going to keep on surviving. And I will be with you every step of the way."

"Every step?" I asked, glancing towards the campervan—the one he'd take on his long, *long* journey to the Vampires' Nest.

He sighed, his body deflating. "I promise I'll come back for you."

I managed a weak smile for him, and after a twitch of his lips, he offered me a rare, genuine one in return.

Putting on a brave face, I cast my eyes over the campervan again. "Are you really driving to the Nest in *this*?"

I circled the dilapidated machine. Rust coated the wheel arches and encircled the headlights, so it looked like it was crying, orange mascara dripping down its face.

"I'm not towing the caravan, and the motorhomes are too wide for the roads I'm taking." Madigan wiped his hands on a rag, and it was only now I noticed his tailcoat folded neatly beside a box of tools. He wasn't as concerned about getting his trousers or shirt messy, but to get oil on his tailcoat would have been sacrilege. Though I loved him in his suit, I enjoyed the novelty of seeing him roll up his sleeves, the first few buttons of his shirt undone to reveal his collarbone, covered in dirt.

"It should be fine," he said, stepping up beside me as I peered at the engine. "I was having some problems with the temperature regulator, but I think I've fixed it now."

"You *think* you've fixed it?" I teased.

Madigan narrowed his eyes, lips pressed together, but I could see how the corners of his mouth curled. "That's enough of your cheek."

"I didn't know you dabbled with mechanics," I said, inspecting the engine—not that I knew what the parts were. "Hell, Madigan, I didn't even know you could drive!"

"There are many things you don't know about me, and apparently, my name is one of them."

I had, in fact, thought about calling him Len, like everyone else did, but I secretly enjoyed having a name for him that only I used, and that it had become a running joke only made me like it more.

"Sorry, Madigan."

He snorted, suppressing a laugh. "Such impertinence." He rubbed his wrist in the search for a cuff that wasn't there after having rolled up his shirtsleeves, leaving behind a smear of grime. I'd never seen him so filthy or dishevelled—a side of himself he'd kept hidden away—lighting a fire in the pit of my stomach.

He ducked down into the rear of the van again, allowing me the perfect view of his backside. I bit my lip as my mind flooded with images of the one time we'd been intimate with each other, the fire within me spreading.

Madigan emerged once more, fixing me with a hard stare, squinting beneath his almost-permanent frown. He sniffed, a pink tinge on his pale cheeks barely visible beneath the oil. He could smell my arousal.

"Sorry," I said again, half smiling.

"No you're not."

"No, you're right, I'm not."

He grinned, and my insides melted again.

After slamming the door to the engine closed, he extinguished the spotlights, plunging us both into darkness. His vision remained unimpaired, while I was blinded. I gasped as his warm hands pinched my sides, pulling me into his body, his usual sweet scent masked by sweat and oil.

"It's a pity our time together is so short," he said against my ear. "But I hope to make the most of it, with your permission."

"Oh God, *yes*." Ignoring his filthy clothes, I wrapped my arms around him again, pressing myself into his lean body, and tilted my head upwards, searching for his lips.

They met mine, warm and soft. I drove my fingers through his wet hair, my other hand at the back of his neck, pulling him into me, making my heart flutter.

This. This is what it had all been for. All the suffering. All the bloodshed.

I clutched him tighter, like I was afraid that if I stopped kissing him—even for a second—he might disappear. And in return, his lips parted mine as he moaned into my mouth, his tongue sweeping against mine in a frenzied dance.

It was worth it. Every drop of blood spilled. Every tear shed. Even giving up my humanity and becoming a scorpion shifter. And as he kissed me, I almost forgot the horrors of my nightmare. *Almost.*

CHAPTER TWO

After another visitation from Ivan and waking to my own screams, I had to admit that Latisha was right—I needed time for self-care. On the plus side, it meant I could avoid demons and hang out with Madigan guilt-free.

Once again, I found myself in his rundown caravan, sitting at the tacky table with its peeling veneer, my butt growing numb on the rock-hard sofa. And yet, it never felt more like home.

"Ask Latisha if you could spend the next few nights with me," Madigan said, not looking up from his book, his long legs crossed on the table.

I let out a hiss through my teeth as I died—*again*—in the game I was playing on my ancient handheld console. The batteries would meet the same fate soon.

"I've only been living with her for three nights, and I'm already asking to move out." It's not that I didn't enjoy living with her. In fact, Madigan and I thought separate quarters would be beneficial after the previously forced living arrangements, but my new, little bedroom felt so... *empty*. Like it was missing something—or *someone*—important. I would clutch my pillow and think of him until my brain went quiet and I could sleep. Not that sleep brought comfort, of course.

"Besides," I said, "you're leaving in a few nights. I'll have to get used to being alone."

"You won't be alone."

"You know that's not what I meant." I stared at my pixelated avatar, but wasn't really focusing on the game, the words I *really* wanted to say racing through my mind, and when I died for the umpteenth time, they spilled out. "I want to come with you."

"You don't." He eyed me over the top of his book.

"I do!" I reached across to lower it—a move that made his features tighten, one eye twitching. I was walking on dangerous ground, but I couldn't work out if it was because I'd asked to leave with him, or because I'd interrupted his reading. Probably both, but I was in too deep now. "I want to go with you. If you ask Latisha—"

"I can't."

"Why not?"

"You..." His eyes darted from side to side, as though searching for the answer. "You don't know what it's like there."

My counter-argument was on the tip of my tongue, but a bang at the door almost made me leap out of my seat.

"Ava!" called a familiar voice. Trevor—the shifters' representative. He'd have been *my* rep if I hadn't become Latisha's familiar.

Madigan and I blinked at each other in bewilderment.

Trevor banged on the door again. Louder this time.

Dread coiled inside me as Madigan opened the door to reveal Trevor's lined, pale face, glistening with sweat. His thinning brown hair was sticking up from where he must have driven his fingers through it.

"Ava," he said, slightly breathless. "The demons are here. They have asked to see you. *Personally.*"

My knees shook as I ascended the steps to the enormous motorhome that had once belonged to Ivan, currently unused. I took a steeling breath as I gripped the door handle.

Why did they meet in this *camper?*

"You don't have to go in there, Ava," Madigan said behind me. He'd insisted on coming despite Trevor's assertion that the demons had asked for me to come alone.

"It's okay," I said, trying to convince myself as much as him, though my limbs tingled with adrenaline. "I'll be fine. Latisha's in there."

"I'm coming with you."

"I told you, you can't!" Trevor snapped, and the two of them began squabbling again.

I couldn't really hear them, my focus on the door handle still beneath my palm, growing sweatier with each passing second.

Demons create witches. This is why they want to see me. I'm sure of it. Time to get strong. Time to learn to defend myself. To defend... him.

I glanced over my shoulder at Madigan. "I'll be ok. I'll see you back at your camper when this is all over, all right?"

"Wait!"

But I opened the door and stepped inside.

The moment both feet had crossed the threshold, the door slammed behind me, and a putrid stench like rotting meat blasted through me. I gagged, clapping a hand to my mouth, pressure rising, my saliva turning sour. I spun, my heart stopping as the exit was replaced with a meat-coloured wall that throbbed in and out like it was breathing, emitting a wet squelch with each pulse. The door had vanished.

"Here she is," came the low, silky voice of the one demon I recognised.

Lascivious.

Summoning every drop of courage I had, I slowly turned to face the group sitting around Ivan's coffee table. Six of them. The witches, Latisha, Cassandra, Alex, and three demons—human-like in appearance, except for a few crucial details. Their features, already other-worldly, were further warped by the ominous red glow emitted by the lamps around the room—a far cry from the golden hue they once cast.

Lascivious looked just as I remembered him, lazily ruffling his coal-black hair, the buttons of his shirt straining across his muscled chest. He grinned.

"Don't just stand there gawking. Join us."

My courage bled out of me, and I stood rooted to the spot until he beckoned me with one finger. The foul stench engulfing the room morphed into something sweet and floral, a warmth creeping through me as his smile grew wider, and without a thought, I stepped towards them. No sooner had I taken that first step than the stench returned thick in the air, stealing my breath.

"What did you want her for, exactly?" Lascivious asked the demon sitting to his right, his tone becoming one of amusement, almost mocking. "She is not yet ripe."

I couldn't deny how my heart sank. Last time I'd met Lascivious he'd said the same thing. So, if they didn't want to make me a witch, what did they want me for?

The other demon sprang to his feet, lips splitting into a cheeky grin. His mop of obsidian-black hair covered one of his eyes like a millennial who never outgrew their emo phase, but his one dark, visible eye ran down my body, then back to my face, making my skin prickle with unease.

"Ahh, don't worry your pretty little head about that, Lasci. You never could think outside the box," he said, his grin growing unnaturally wide. He was only a couple of inches taller than me, and dressed entirely in black, save for a pair of bright pink—

"Doc Martens!" I blurted.

"Snap!" he said with a laugh, spotting the black pair on my feet. "Glad to meet another with taste."

"Interesting colour choice."

"Pet, I look fabulous." Besides his questionable haircut, he *did* look fabulous. His clothes, as dark and sleek as his hair, clung to a toned body, and his pale skin shimmered green-and-pink like mother-of-pearl. "I'm Mischievous."

He reached out a hand, and not wanting to offend a literal demon, I shook it. As soon as I made contact, ideas of trickery, disobedience, and fun flooded my brain, a sly smile creeping across my face.

"Enough of that," snapped the third demon in a voice that made me shudder and drop Mischievous's hand. It echoed like two people had spoken at once, one with a deep, gravelly tone, the other eerily high. When I looked at her, I expected to see a wizened old hag with grey wrinkled skin, limp, scraggly hair, and flesh almost rotting on the bone. At least, that's how I'd seen her through my peripheral vision, but when I focused on her, I couldn't have been more wrong. Her skin shone the same colour as Mischievous's, and her silver hair had an iridescent pink sheen to it. Though it was her facial features that struck me hardest. Narrow, dark-framed eyes with salmon-pink sclerae surrounding aqua-marine irises. No pupils. And her lips, as full as Latisha's, were the colour of red wine. The only thing more striking than her beauty was the aura of power she exuded. Indomitable and terrible. "I'm Sanguineous. Now sit your ass down and let us get on with our meeting."

I darted forward, perching on the arm of the sofa beside Cassandra and Alex, who, I noted, no longer resembled themselves. True, they were recognisable—Cassandra, with her mane of untameable blonde curls and Alex's short black bob—but it was like viewing them through a filter, their flaws erased, and their best features highlighted.

Glamour magic.

They must have struck a bargain with one of the demons, transforming them from shifters into witches.

Mischievous laughed again, shrugging, clearly not as intimidated by the female demon as I was, but he too resumed his seat. Though I noticed that the instant I averted my gaze from Sanguineous, her beauty withered, and out of the corner of my eye, she appeared as I'd first seen her: hag-like.

"I fulfilled my end of the bargain," Latisha said to Mischievous. "Ava is here, as you asked. Now fulfil yours."

"Yes, pet. I was coming to that." Mischievous extended his hand again, and when Latisha took it, a white light gleamed between their palms. "Keep in mind, this is not *full* invisibility. Simply an alteration of perception. Anyone searching for your coven will be unsuccessful, but should they hunt for something, or *someone* within it"—his visible eye flicked towards me—"you may not be so fortunate."

"I understand," Latisha said, releasing herself from him now the light between their hands had faded.

"And remember, it's time to renew when the nights live longer. Is there anything further I can help you with?"

"Not when you make such outrageous demands for *genuine* invisibility, no."

"Then it's my turn next, isn't it?" Lascivious leant back in his seat, crossing an ankle over his knee, hands resting behind his head. As he did so, I noticed the front of his trousers straining upward, and hurriedly averted my gaze back to his face, but that only made my heart flutter, a tingle spreading through my chest as he gave me a knowing smile.

Bastard...

"I'll do you a good deal, Tish," he said. "You've already assisted me in adding these to my collection." He nodded towards Cassandra and Alex, both of whom were staring directly at their demon master through infatuated eyes. "It's a pity I lost Aurora, but this is a clear net gain."

It was only now I realised Aurora was absent, but before I could question it, Lascivious said, "To regain your shifting abilities *and* have a healing touch, I would usually make two separate bargains. But as you've been such a good girl, I'll simply ask you to join me tonight, just as you did all those hundreds of years ago." His lips curled into a smile that made heat pool in my stomach... and then lower. "You know what I mean, don't you?"

I glanced at Latisha when she didn't respond. She was staring at Lascivious, and though she didn't have the same dreamy expression that Cassandra and Alex wore, there was an undeniable look of longing that, despite her efforts, she couldn't hide. She bit her lower lip as she nodded.

"Verbal confirmation, please?" Lascivious said, his smirk positively devilish now.

"Yes, I know what you mean, and I agree to those terms," Latisha said, her voice shaking as she reached out to shake Lascivious's hand.

He took it, but no white light appeared between their palms. Instead, he yanked Latisha towards him, put his lips up to her ear and purred, "Good girl. I'll give it to you after we're finished with our meeting, my dear little witch."

Latisha shivered, a gasp catching in her throat. It was only when he released her, she slid back down into her seat, her breathing slightly heavier than normal.

I tugged the sleeves of my hoodie to conceal my hands as I shifted in my seat uncomfortably. The heat coursing through me intensified as I watched the pair of them. It was like witnessing an intimate moment I wasn't supposed to be watching, making me feel dirty inside. And yet, I *wanted* to watch. Worse than that. I wanted to be a part of it.

"My turn," Sanguineous said through her echoing voice. Despite its distortion, I could hear the tone of excitement.

Latisha regained her composure the moment she focused on the female demon, fixing Sanguineous with a stony glare, clenching her fists in her lap.

"Now then, Latisha," Sanguineous said, "let's talk about the power of Fear. It's been a while since you had this ability, isn't it? Quite adorable. With a single look, you'll strike fear into the hearts of all that see you." Her wine-red lips spread into a smile that revealed pointed teeth. "Fairly harmless, unless they have a weak constitution, or you… get carried away. And with the amount of blood you have spilled, we all know you're not the weak little witch you'd like everyone to believe."

Latisha's eyes narrowed, lips pursing together, like she was holding in a snappy retort. Her shoulders tensed as she balled her fists tighter until her knuckles cracked. Even I flexed my fingers, like I was preparing myself for a fight.

Sanguineous continued, "I would normally expect a week's service in the fifth circle with me for a power like this. But as it's you, I'll simply ask you to kill a particularly vile human so that I may have a new toy to play with. I've picked him out already." She snapped her fingers, and a photo appeared between them. "Local guy. Likes to use his body as a weapon, if you know what I mean. He would be a perfect addition to the seventh circle, don't you think?"

"That, we can agree on. I'd happily take that assignment." Latisha took the photograph, her voice low with a malice I'd never heard from her before. She wrinkled her nose as she examined the photo, a dark shadow forming beneath her eyes. It hit me that if Lascivious could make those around him feel lustful, then perhaps Sanguineous could make people feel bloodthirsty.

"I'll grant your abilities when I have him in my possession."

"What will you do to him?" I asked before I could stop myself, an overwhelming desire to hear what terrible fate would befall him overpowering me.

All heads turned to face me. Latisha's eyes were wide, perhaps horrified I'd dared to speak. Mischievous and Lascivious both looked somewhat amused, but Sanguineous's smile widened yet further, splitting her cheeks, reaching her ears.

"Someone who uses their body as a weapon doesn't deserve to have a body at all. I'll remove a piece at a time. Fingers and toes to start. Nice and easy. Then limbs. Followed by... the *offending* piece. *That's* what truly breaks them." She let out a cackle, and despite myself, I felt my features twist into a sneer. "Then the lips, nose, and ears. That should entertain me for a century or two. I like to take my time."

"And then what?" I leant forward, gripping the edge of the sofa, knuckles white.

"Then the organs. You can't die in Hell, but he shall wish for it. And when he is nothing but pulp, rotting in the ground, his soul will bind to the trees of my Wailing Woodland. Still conscious. And every time we fell a tree, use it in a pyre, or craft it into something, he will feel that too. Who knows all the wondrous things he could become? Spoons, chopping boards, stools. Perhaps even a coffee table?" She brushed a speck of dirt from Ivan's table. I recoiled in my seat. There couldn't be someone's soul trapped in there... could there? But when I caught Sanguineous's eye, a secret side of me *hoped* there was.

I shook myself, my head almost spinning at the emotional whiplash the demons were putting me through.

"But Latisha," Sanguineous said, "you realise, for such a good deal, there is a minor catch."

"I thought there might be."

"I will leave Aurora for your disposal."

"Wait! No, that wasn't part of the deal."

"There is no *deal* regarding Aurora. She's a witch who has forgone her contract: an Unformed, for which there is only one method of disposal. I don't see why I, or my colleagues, should do it." She jerked her head towards the other demons. "Our business is concluded, and we shall take our leave. This pocket dimension will close, you'll be back within the human world, and an Unformed isn't something you will want to keep hanging around."

"Look, Tish," Lascivious cut in. "You're my favourite, so I'll make it a little easier for you. I'll give you back your shifting abilities now. Your healing touch will have to wait until the terms of our arrangement are"—he chuckled to himself—"*fulfilled*."

Latisha glared at him.

"But," he continued, "returning your shifting abilities should help you dispose of an Unformed. Perhaps my new witches will assist you?" He turned to Cassandra and Alex. "I'll give you both your shifting abilities and you can help your leader. All it would cost you is..." He leant forward and whispered into each of their ears. Their captivated expressions died, the colour draining from their faces.

"I don't think I need to shift anymore," Cassandra said, her voice shaking as she twisted her fingers together.

Alex nodded in agreement. "Me neither. Becoming a witch has already taken a lot out of me."

Lascivious's playful smirk dropped, replaced by a frown of genuine disappointment. "A pity," he said, turning back to Latisha. "Looks like you'll do this alone. My new witches have yet to grow a backbone." He held out his hand. For a heartbeat, Latisha beheld his hand with a grim expression, then grabbed it. Once again, light filled their palms as she acquired her power from the demon.

Lascivious's eyes fell upon me. "Be a dear and sleep in your vampire's abode for today."

Ice coursed through my veins. How did he know about Madigan? More importantly, how did he know we were *together*?

"Your leader will be very, *very* busy. Unless you are willing to assist her, I think you'll want to give her some privacy. It's no concern of mine if you watch, I suppose," he said with a shrug as Latisha flushed. He then stood, marched across the camper to where the door had been, and stepped *through* the pulsing wall, disappearing.

Mischievous was the next to rise. "Always a pleasure," he said, giving a two-fingered salute and heading to the wall that Lascivious had exited through. But he paused, turning back towards me. A trickle of sweat ran down my spine as he stood before me and took my hand, pressing something small into my palm, and as his skin brushed mine, his flesh grew hot, then cold. A tremor ran through me as he leant close.

"This is why I wanted to see you, little seedling," he said, voice low, his breath hot against my ear. I examined the trinket in my hand. It looked like it was supposed to be a brooch, except there was no pin. A flower, its petals made of rubies and stem of twisted gold, but the stone in its centre was what made me gasp. An eyeball with a crimson iris stared back, its focus always locked onto me no matter what angle I tilted it, like liquid core dice.

"There will come a time when you realise what you saw tonight wasn't so bad," Mischievous said, "and when you do, call on me. I'll be there to help." He winked before following Lascivious and disappeared through the wall.

"Until next time." Sanguineous stood, though I noticed she had some difficulty getting to her feet, like the chair she was sitting on had a wonky leg. "And there *will* be a next time." As she left, I squinted at what she had been sitting on. And gasped.

Aurora. Only recognisable by her large green eyes.

Her neck had stretched at least a foot, maybe two feet long, curled around a fleshy pink mass of meat and protruding bones, her clothes rolled and ripped from what must have been a brutal transformation. I scrambled back, breath leaving my lungs as I fell over the edge of the sofa, landing on my backside. But I couldn't rip my eyes from the horror before me.

Her fingers appeared glued together, and her shrunken arms resembled featherless wings. The ends of her shoes had burst from where her feet had expanded, now black in colour, toes elongated and webbed. Her face stretched outward until her nose and lips resembled an ivory-coloured beak. Ripped skin, pulled too tight across unnatural shapes and slipping away, revealed bone and muscles beneath, and they too seemed to bubble and melt. The mountain of flesh swelled, then deflated like a balloon. A dark brown, almost black liquid pooled beneath her. Now the scent of rotting meat made sense, becoming even more potent.

That was the final straw. I had no time to react as nausea washed over me. My stomach clenched, pushing vomit up my throat and splattering onto the carpet, Sanguineous's cackling laughter echoing in my ears as she disappeared through the wall behind her companions.

The red glow flooding the room lifted, replaced by the harsh brightness of electric lights, and the walls stopped pulsing, now decorated with beige-and-gold wallpaper.

But the putrid stench persisted.

Aurora—or what remained of her—stopped moving. Except for the slow rise and fall of her chest, that is. Alive but decomposing.

Gripping the arm of the sofa for support, I stood. I wanted to tear my sights from Aurora, but it proved impossible. Cassandra, too, had her glassy stare on Aurora, but Alex wrenched her by the shoulder to face the opposite corner.

"Don't look," Alex said, but Cassandra turned her head to glance back, tears spilling over her cheeks.

"B-but, Aurora…"

"You can't help her." Alex pulled Cassandra into a tight hug, now weeping herself.

Latisha's eyes flicked between me and Aurora, like she was trying to communicate something telepathically, but the message wasn't getting through.

"I'm sorry, Ava," she said, her voice heavy with burden. "It's best you don't watch. There is only one way to kill an Unformed, and I must end her misery."

She closed her eyes, bowing her head as she took a steeling breath, and when she opened them, saffron-yellow orbs blinked back at me. The hue of her ruby lips darkened until black, then stretched into a sharp, hooked beak.

I clasped my chest, my heart slamming so hard I thought each thump could be the last. "Latisha?" I asked, my voice weak, like she might not *really* be the mistress I loved. But I knew it was her…

Latisha pounced onto the heap of rotting flesh, sprouting feathers from the knees down, her feet now sharp talons as they erupted from her shoes. As she spread her arms, they elongated into wings that she curled around herself and Aurora's remains, shielding what she was doing from view. Though from the way her head bobbed down, then wrenched back, paired with a wet, ripping sound, I knew what she was doing. She was *eating*.

My stomach crunched again. And again. But I was running on empty, coughing up bile, saliva dripping from my lips. I turned my face, unable to watch. My eyes burned with the unrelenting flow of tears as one of the few people I thought I could trust performed the most revolting, gut-wrenching thing I'd ever witnessed.

But turning away wasn't enough. The sounds of ripping flesh, then the cracking of bone pierced through me. I wanted to run. With *all my heart*, I wanted to run. But my legs had turned to jelly. Useless. And all the while, Aurora emitted a low agonised moan that persisted until every scrap of meat was devoured, leaving only bones and a black soup.

I was in a nightmare again, but this time, I wouldn't wake.

CHAPTER THREE

My panting breaths misted in front of me, my throat burning as I marched up the row of campers, eager to put distance between myself and Ivan's motorhome. Or was it Latisha I was fleeing from? I didn't know; I wasn't controlling my body. Only driven by instinct. I had to escape, and there was only one person I could rely on.

The trinket Mischievous gave me weighed heavily in my pocket, thumping against my thigh with each hurried step until I reached Madigan's caravan.

"Ava?" His voice reached me through the noise in my head as I entered. He was already standing, tracks in his black hair from where he'd been running his fingers through it. "What happened? What did they want?"

I lowered myself down onto the single sofa that had once been my bed. My legs, that had moments ago forced me into a brisk pace, were now limp noodles.

Madigan squatted into my line of vision, resting his hands on my knees. "Ava, *what happened*?" There was an edge to his voice, barely concealed behind the concern.

At first, I was rendered mute. I just stared at him, his brows drawing into a scowl, and his charcoal-grey eyes darkening.

I swallowed, still unable to find my voice. Instead, I took hold of one of his hands, just to feel his skin on mine. Hot and rough.

"Did they... do anything to you?" he asked through a clenched jaw, clutching my hand in return, so hard it almost hurt.

I shook my head.

"To anyone else?"

"Latisha." It was the only word I could muster.

"Latisha? They hurt her?"

I shook my head again.

"Then what—?"

"She did something... *disgusting*."

Madigan nodded slowly, like he was trying to decipher what I'd just said. "I've heard the price of a demon's help is steep."

"That's not it—I mean, you're right—but that's not... that's not..." I *had* to tell him. If I didn't, he would never understand why I needed to leave the coven. "Latisha... ate... Aurora."

Whatever Madigan had been expecting, this wasn't it. His eyes widened, his mouth falling open. "W-what?"

"You heard what I said!" My voice grew thick as tears pricked my eyes. "Latisha *ate* Aurora!"

Madigan's hand drifted to his cuff and tugged. Once. *Hard*. "For... for what purpose?"

"They said Aurora was an Unformed. And Latisha became this... this... sort of..." I searched for the words to describe her, but my brain was refusing to cooperate. "Like a... harpy?"

Madigan let out a breath, and it was like his whole body deflated. "Aurora became an Unformed?"

"That's what the demons called her."

He nodded, eyes turning from mine to the floor. "I understand."

I watched him, waiting for signs of disgust or shock. But they never came. Instead, he adjusted his cuff from where he'd yanked at it, smoothing it between his thumb and forefinger.

"Well, I don't," I said after a pause, his reaction—or lack of—somewhat unnerving.

He tilted his head, licking his lips before saying, "An Unformed is a witch who has broken her contract with her demon. I've never seen one myself, but from what I've read, it's a wretched existence. One that hovers between life and death. A body that never dies, nor is it living. And their soul eternally trapped within. Unless freed."

"Freed?"

"Well, in a sense. Freed from their old body and taken into another."

I nodded, seeing where this was going. "By eating them."

"It's the only way. Though why Latisha resembled a harpy is a mystery."

"She regained her shapeshifting powers," I said, remembering her deal with Lascivious. "He said it would make it easier for her."

"Well, there you have it."

Somehow, this revelation offered little comfort. If anything, his matter-of-fact explanation only made me more uneasy, like I didn't belong here. In fact, I *knew* I didn't belong here. I shouldn't have meddled in this world of monsters.

Billy had known this. He'd tried to warn me when I asked for his help to become a shapeshifter..

"You don't know what you are getting yourself into."

Stupidly, I'd dismissed his concerns. And that wasn't the only warning he'd given.

"Pity about the demons that will hound you for eternity, but you can cope with that, right?"

"I can't stay here," I said before I could stop myself.

"What do you mean?"

"I mean, I can't be a part of this coven. I never should have become a supernatural—I can't handle it. And now there are demons and Unformed. And someone I thought trustworthy has turned out to be—"

"You *can* trust her. She did it for Aurora—to end her suffering. Everything she does is for our coven. To protect us."

"And you're certain of that?"

"I would trust Latisha with my life." He stared into my eyes. No hint of a lie. But when I didn't respond, he added, "And my afterlife, if it came to that."

I wasn't sure what he meant, but there was no doubting his sincerity. "Yeah... maybe you're right..." I said, but I wasn't convinced. "I still don't think I can cope here. I still want to leave. There has been too much bloodshed. Too much death. It's suffocating me."

"Then what do you propose?"

"I want to come with you to the Vampires' Nest."

Madigan let out a guttural sound in the back of his throat as he rose from his squatting position in front of me, closing his eyes and pinching the bridge of his nose. "Ava, we've been through this."

"No, we haven't!" I jumped to my feet too, glaring up at him. "You just saying '*No*' isn't a conversation!"

He slowly lowered his hand from his face, one eye twitching, jaw set. I thought he was about to lose his temper, but after a steadying breath, he said, "The Nest is no better. You'd be walking from one nightmare and into another. There might not be demons, but we have our own monsters."

"Soul Suckers and Brain Eaters?"

"Worse. Politicians."

I spluttered with laughter, surprising even myself that I could make such a noise after what I'd seen. Madigan, however, remained stony-faced.

"I'm serious. It's the time of the election, and they're always a messy affair. Sometimes literally. Our current Liege Lady once used her allure to seduce the competition and... but I digress. Ava, the Nest is *dangerous*. You're safer here with Latisha than with me in the Nest."

"Safer with demons, too?"

But Madigan narrowed his eyes, plainly saying he was done discussing it.

As per Lascivious's suggestion, I stayed with Madigan that day, sleeping beside him, his arms around me like a protective shield from the horrors outside. Horrors that shrieked, cried, screamed, and *purred* Lascivious's name over and over... and over...

Madigan's door swung open, sunlight pouring into the caravan. The vampire awoke with a startled cry. I sat bolt upright, seizing the duvet and instinctively covering him, exposing my nude body for the intruder.

"What the fuck are you—!" I started to say, the fury in my chest about to explode, but it was Latisha's panic-stricken face that looked at me, eyes wide, panting, sweat coating her dark skin.

"Shift, Ava!"

"What?"

"Shift! Now!"

I blinked at her, my mind numb, like the memories of the previous night and the sudden demand had short-circuited my brain.

She wants me to what?!

"Please!" she hissed in a whispered shout.

"Do it, Ava!" Madigan's muffled voice sounded from beneath the duvet.

Though my heart thrummed at the demand, I made the wish to shapeshift and instantly my bones snapped. There was only a split second I could scream before fire blazed through every cell of me, wrapping me in agony, until I collapsed where I sat, shapeless, suffocating beneath my own weight. What remained of my spine stretched behind me. Hands and forearms split into pincers. Shrinking, burning, tighter, *tighter*...

The world exploded into scent and vibration.

I was a scorpion.

I scuttled out of the bedsheets to the bedside counter. The hairs covering my body bristled as I registered my surroundings. Though my eight eyes were near useless, my other senses compensated, and I formed a picture in my head so vivid it was like I really *could* see.

Then—movement. A head slid into view around the doorway, topped with a police officer's hat.

Shit.

I froze, not daring to so much as *twitch*. In the unlucky event the copper noticed me, perhaps I could pass for some weird bedside ornament, instead of one of the deadliest scorpions on Earth. But he was more interested in the person hiding beneath the duvet.

"Are you decent?"

"No," grumbled Madigan. "Do you have any idea what time it is?"

"It's two in the afternoon." It was difficult to pick up on inflections when translating the vibrations in the air, but I still caught the officer's bemusement.

"And I work nights," Madigan said, peering from beneath the duvet, using it to shield his face from the sun's rays.

"I won't keep you long." The officer held up a piece of paper. "Have you seen this woman?" Though blind to the image, I could guess whose photo it was.

"Never seen her before in my life," Madigan said.

"Really? Your colleagues said that, too, but we have sources that suggest otherwise."

"You think I can hide someone in a place like this?" Madigan said, sweeping his arm around the caravan. "Maybe I have hidden her in one of the cupboards?"

"Okay, sir, there is no need to—"

"Get out." He threw a pillow across the caravan. "Look wherever you bloody well like, but she isn't in here!"

"You've seen all the campers now," Latisha's voice said from the doorway. "If you want to carry out a proper search, I must insist you get a warrant."

"Miss Abara, I'll return—" But Latisha closed the door, cutting him off.

Madigan groaned and shoved the duvet off, glowering. "Bloody sun. Ava, where are you?" His eyes scanned the bed, then landed on me. I raised a pincer in salute. With a sigh, he offered me his hand, and I crawled onto his palm. "Leave it a few minutes before shifting back again."

Following his advice, I waited until Madigan assured me the officer's voice had died away before resuming my usual form.

"The police still believe you're *missing*, then," he said, referring to when I'd joined the coven and someone had filed a missing person report. "Strange. They've never traced anyone back here before."

"Perhaps..." I swallowed. "Perhaps I'm wanted for Greg's murder." My stomach dropped at the thought of my ex-boyfriend; how Dominic had killed him and, out of desperation to save my own skin, how

I'd assisted. "They've ignored the disappearances in Kinwich for years. But murder is—"

The camper door burst open, and once again Madigan ducked beneath the duvet, snarling with annoyance.

It was Latisha, wearing an almost *frightening* expression. Her dark eyes were wide, brows drawn into a scowl, her lips a thin line.

"To my camper," she said in a crisp tone. "Both of you."

"I *can't!*" Madigan grit out.

Latisha made a noise in the back of her throat, flicking her curls.

"What's wrong?" I asked her. I'd never seen Latisha like this, and even after last night's shitshow, my heart ached. Was she angry with me?

"I'll bring Trevor and Alfred *here*, then," she said, not answering my question. "Get dressed."

After throwing on some clothes and waiting for the representatives to squeeze into Madigan's camper, Latisha explained what had happened, though her mood hadn't improved, and I found myself picking at the cuffs of my hoodie as she spoke.

"That officer was looking for Ava." She leant against Madigan's kitchen counter, arms folded. "He wouldn't tell me why, but he said he'll return with the warrant."

"We've never had trouble with the police before," Trevor said from the opposite end of the caravan, resting his forearms against his knees, leaning forward in his seat. "Did Ivan really have that much influence over them?"

"Some influence," Latisha said, "but whenever someone came snooping, it was usually *me* who sent them on their way."

"How?" I asked my cuffs, unable to meet Latisha's eye.

"My glamour," she said. Madigan made an uncomfortable noise beside me, but Latisha ignored him. "You've never seen me use it at full strength, Ava. But you've had a small experience with it, haven't you?"

I had, indeed, seen her use it a couple of times. One was a momentary flash when I'd first met her. The second was when I'd made her a dress. She'd said it became stronger when she felt beautiful, like it had leaked out without her intention.

"When I use it at full power," she continued, "I can make a mortal do anything I want. Especially those ruled by their... urges."

"So why didn't you use it this time?" Trevor asked.

"I *did* use it," she said. "That's the point. It should have worked. Especially after having struck that deal with Mischievous to cloak the coven."

"We've seen first-hand what Mischievous meant, haven't we?" I said, remembering what he'd said about how the ability worked. "The showmen's yard isn't invisible. The police aren't looking for the coven. They're looking for *me*." I managed a glance at her, and saw her looking right back, lips tight, but as she opened her mouth to respond, Alfred, the werewolf rep, cut in.

"You used your glamour at full force, and it didn't work on some random human?"

"Perhaps he's not so random after all," she said darkly. "I'm not saying I used my glamour and couldn't *quite* convince him to leave. I'm saying I used it full blast and it did nothing. *Nothing*! Like he was completely immune."

"This might be a stupid question," I said, "but what if... y'know... he isn't into women?"

"Are *you* into women?" Latisha asked with a raised brow.

No. I wasn't. And yet, when Latisha used her glamour...

I shrugged. I knew it had been a stupid question. "Then why—?"

"He's a Hallow," Latisha said bluntly, and a heavy silence filled the room.

"Tish," Trevor said after a pause, "you don't *know* that."

"Yes, I do," Latisha said, glaring at him, her folded arms locking tighter. "I'm the only one here who's met the Hallows—"

Madigan coughed and gave her a pointed look.

"Oh, all right," she snapped. "Technically, so has Len. But not like I have. I'm *certain* he's a Hallow and was using some sort of artefact to nullify my powers, or shield from them completely."

"They can do that?" I asked.

"Their artefacts give them all sorts of powers. But we don't know which ones they have, how many, or the number of Hallows currently in Kinwich. And if they have the police working for them—"

"We can't be sure they've infiltrated the entire police force," Madigan said, but Latisha waved a hand, like she was brushing the comment aside.

"It doesn't matter if it's the whole force or one individual. The point is, we have a Hallow with a warrant knocking at our gates. If we don't act fast, they'll search this place and find a lot more than Ava. For one, they'll find a half-rabid vampire locked in a container." Latisha straightened herself and looked at Madigan. "You must leave tonight."

"No!" The word slipped out before I could stop it.

"I'm sorry, Ava," Latisha said, and for the first time that night, she sounded like the protective, caring Latisha I was familiar with. "The sooner Dominic's gone, the better." She turned to Alfred. "How fast can we pack up?"

My insides squirmed as a ripple of panic washed through me. If the coven left Kinwich, how would Madigan find us again? Would I have to wait until next winter to see him?

"Not long," Alfred said with a shrug. "Twenty-four hours. Tops."

"Then that's settled," Latisha said. "We are moving on. Shifters and werewolves are to start work immediately. Len, gather the last of your things. You leave at sunset."

Madigan gave me a pained expression before nodding. "As you wish."

"Wait!" I jumped to my feet without thinking and grabbed Latisha's arm. "Let me go with him."

"Ava, no," Madigan said with a sigh. "I've already told you, the Nest is dangerous—"

"Latisha, the police are looking for me. Probably for murder."

Her brows drew together. "You can shapeshift."

"But you said yourself you don't know which artefacts the Hallows have," I argued. "And the police are searching for *me*. Not the coven. While I'm with you, I'm putting the entire coven in danger."

Latisha bit her lip, her frown deepening. She was resisting... but if I pushed a little harder...

"I will come back," I said, perhaps to convince myself as much as her.

She scrunched the curls at the back of her head, gaze dropping. I could feel the eyes of everyone upon us, waiting for Latisha's decision. She let out a long sigh, turning her head to Trevor.

"What do you think?" she asked him, but Madigan cut in.

"Latisha, you can't really be considering this!"

Latisha raised a hand, her eyes on Trevor, awaiting his answer.

Trevor blinked, then looked over his shoulder, as though searching for someone else she might be talking to. He ran his fingers through his thin hair before saying with a slight stammer, "I-I dunno, Tish. I mean... I suppose she has a point."

"No!" Madigan was practically shaking beside me.

"Alfred?" Latisha asked the werewolf rep.

"I agree with Trevor," Alfred said, his voice as stiff as his posture. "It doesn't matter if he was a regular policeman or a Hallow: Ava's presence complicates things. Our chances of remaining undetected increase if she's gone. At least, for a time."

"Latisha, this is madness." Madigan drew as close to her as the cramped caravan allowed. "You've been to the Nest. You know what it's like. Ava can't go. She's not... she's not..." When he turned his face to look at me, his eyes were glistening, his composure slipping faster than I'd ever seen before.

"Not what?" I asked. Though I spoke quietly, the room was so tense I could have shouted.

Madigan didn't answer right away, instead just staring back at me, jaw locked, until with a sigh, he said, "I'm just trying to protect you."

"Not. *What?*"

The silence that followed was so thick I could have choked on it, until he tugged on his cuff, and said, "You're not strong enough."

"I was strong enough to save your arse."

His whole body twitched, like I'd dealt him a physical blow. I would have regretted my words if it weren't for the impact they had on Latisha.

She nodded slowly, her shoulders slumping, like the fear and anger fuelling her were fizzling out, but then, she straightened her posture and clasped her hands together.

"All right then," she said, now facing me. "You will accompany Len to the Vampires' Nest."

Madigan shook his head. "This is utter insanity," he muttered under his breath. "Madness. Total lunacy."

Latisha ignored him. "Like it or not, we have a war coming, and we will need to recruit more coven members if we're to survive. If I let you accompany Len, it's with the understanding this isn't a holiday—you're on an official mission. You'll return with more recruits. Can you do it?"

I felt all eyes on me, but the only person I could look at was Madigan.

"Yes," I said. "I can do it."

CHAPTER FOUR

O nce the meeting was finished, I rushed back to Latisha's camper to stuff some essentials in a bag. Clothes, food, a torch, anything I could get my hands on that might be useful on our journey. It was only when my cheeks ached that I realised I was grinning. I couldn't remember the last time I'd been so giddy. No matter what Madigan had said about the Nest, it couldn't compare with what I'd experienced within the last few weeks. Hell, it couldn't compare with what I'd seen within the last twenty-four hours!

As I slipped the last items into my bag—a photo of my grandma and my games console—I imagined what it would be like travelling with Madigan. I'd never been on a road trip before, never mind a road trip with a boyfriend. Or a vampire. Or a vampire-boyfriend! My heart quivered, reverberating through every cell of my body.

And then, I remembered I wouldn't have him *entirely* to myself. There would be another travelling with us.

Dominic... Ugh...

I'd almost forgotten why Madigan was going to the Nest in the first place. But it didn't matter. After taking the potion Latisha had prepared, Dominic would be nerfed into oblivion—just sitting in the back of Madigan's campervan, drooling, about as dangerous as a loading screen.

I cast one last glance around Latisha's camper for anything I might have missed. When I'd first visited, I'd fallen in love with Latisha's home. Now, I was trying to escape it. But before the pang of guilt consumed me, I marched to the door... only for Latisha to open it from the other side.

"Ava," she said, stepping into the camper and closing the door behind her.

"Is everything all right?"

"Yes. I just wanted to speak with you before you leave." She scrunched her curls, her movements stiffer than normal. "I wanted to check if you were all right after... everything you saw last night."

"Yes!" I said far too quickly. "I mean, it was awful to see Aurora suffering, but I understand you did what you had to."

She raised an eyebrow, and I knew she could see right through me. I'd never been a good liar. Heat crawled up my neck as she took one of my sweaty hands in hers. "I'd like you to return."

"Of course I will."

"When you're ready." She forced a smile, and for a moment, it was like the horrors had never happened, and she was the Latisha that had supported me through my ordeal with Ivan. But then, the sound of Aurora's ripping flesh echoed in my head, making me squirm.

"I'm sorry," I said in a choked voice, the words unwilling to come out.

She squeezed my hand. "I know." And now, the corner of her mouth curled wryly. "I look forward to hearing of your adventures in the Nest."

"How will I find you if you leave Kinwich?"

Her smirk deepened; pretty red lips twisted to one side. "A familiar can always find their sire, provided they're in the same dimension.

Trust me on this." And she winked, before glancing out of the window towards the setting sun. "Come on, we'd better get a move on."

We left her motorhome and made for the campervan Madigan had been working on, weaving through the busy showmen's yard as the coven scrambled to complete their tasks. It was the most active I'd seen them all, working in unison, their shouts and commands carrying on the night air.

Madigan was already loading his suitcase into the van. A deep line formed between his brows as he squinted against the blood-red glow of sunset, shadows sharpening the angles of his thin nose and hollow cheeks. Though he wore his usual fine clothes, he'd added a huge heavy-looking coat that reached his mid-calf.

I blinked at him, almost doubting it really *was* Madigan. The coat had grungy badass vibes—not exactly his usual style, what with his fondness for three-piece suits and tailcoats—but he quashed my doubts when his grey eyes met mine and hit me with his trademark glower. He was still upset with me for refusing to stay behind like a good little liability, yet he still held out a hand to take my bag, ever the gentleman.

"Got everything you need?" Latisha asked him.

"All except the most important thing," he said, nodding towards a figure heading our way.

Alfred carried Dominic over his shoulders in a fireman's lift, then dumped the rabid vampire on the ground at our feet before dashing off to help a werewolf carry some heavy machinery across the yard.

I wrinkled my nose at Dominic. Skeletal. Bald. Skin ghostly white. His irises matched his pallor, with black pinprick pupils staring in different directions. Three deep scars adorned his face—marks I hadn't seen before—perhaps trophies from his wrestling match with the werewolves who'd locked him up. Though I preferred him in this docile, brain-dead state, being so close to Ivan's most loyal henchman made my skin tighten. This cunt-bag had murdered Greg... and forced me to assist.

"This," Latisha said, handing me a large, amber-coloured bottle as Madigan manhandled Dominic's unresponsive body into the back seat, "is what you'll need to keep him in this state." She then handed me a syringe. "Fill one of these and give it to him every twenty-four hours. If you're consistent, he'll remain like this, making it easy to administer the next dose. Leave it too long and Dominic will be back to his usual charming self."

"I understand," I said, getting into the passenger seat of the campervan as Madigan took the driver's. "And I won't come back without your recruits." My mission was perfect. I'd take my time recruiting for Latisha, and return when I was ready. *If* I was ready.

"With or without recruits, I'd like you back," she said with a knowing look.

Madigan started up the engine, and the van rattled into life.

"No seatbelt?" I asked him when I couldn't find the strap and buckle.

"Afraid not. She's a little too old for that," he said as he gave the dashboard an affectionate stroke.

"You'd better not drive like a lunatic."

"She wouldn't let me, even if I wanted to."

I cast my eyes over the showmen's yard one more time.

I was *leaving*...

The journey was long, though it felt even longer without Madigan talking to me, still sulking. I'd tried asking him about the Nest, but he met my questions with one-word or evasive answers, and in the end I gave up, amusing myself with my game until the batteries eventually died.

On the second night, we reached a quaint rural village, and Madigan pulled into a carpark. The building beside it was as historic as the rest of the village: timber frames, tiny windows, and a door only suitable for children and hobbits.

"We'll stay here," Madigan said, getting out. "Leave Dominic. He won't go anywhere."

"*The Halfway House,*" I said, reading the hanging bar sign, squeaking on its hinges in the breeze. I tried to hide my excitement—it might only be an inn, but after two nights' travel, it could have been a five-star hotel.

"It's the last warm bed you'll find between us and the Nest. Make the most of it," Madigan said.

"Are *you* going to warm it?"

He didn't answer, and after being given the silent treatment for way too long, something inside me snapped.

I marched up to him as he hauled the suitcase from the campervan. "Are you going to be like this the whole time?"

His nostrils flared as he regarded me, his lips pinched tight.

"Perhaps I really should have stayed behind if you're going to be such a stroppy bastard." Now I'd started on my tirade, it was impossible to stop. "Two sodding nights we've been on the road and all you've done is sulk! Do you hate having me here *that* much?"

His eyes widened, his expression unreadable, but still no answer.

"I see..." Tears burned in my eyes, but I refused to blink. I'd shed enough tears for fuckwit men. "Well in that case, you can kindly go fuck yourse—"

He dropped the suitcase, grabbed me by the upper arms, and pulled me towards him, his lips meeting mine in a kiss so passionate he stole my breath away. For a moment I stood stiff in his hands, barely able to believe the one-eighty our exchange had taken, but as he deepened the kiss, I melted, wrapping my arms around his neck and returning his kiss with equal enthusiasm.

"My apologies," he said, breathless as he broke away. "I've been a fool." His features twitched as he grappled with his emotions. "You're precious to me. I owe you so much more than my life and yet, here I am, taking you somewhere I know I shouldn't. I didn't really mean what I said. I *do* think you're strong. And you *did* save my... save my..." His cheeks flushed, and I couldn't stop the involuntary smirk, knowing which word had tripped him up.

"If you say it, I might consider forgiving your behaviour," I teased, revelling in his slight embarrassment.

The corner of his mouth twitched. "*Arse.*"

The giggle that bubbled out of me turned his curled lip into a full-blown smile, extinguishing the last of my flaring temper.

He brushed stray strands of my hair behind my ear. "Can you imagine taking the one good thing in your life and tossing it into a lion's den?"

His words were like a stab to the heart. Perhaps *I* should be the one apologising? "I hadn't thought of it like that."

"It was wrong to take my ill mood out on you, and I'm no longer your master; I have no say in what you do. All I can do is protect you to the best of my ability. Rest assured I would give my life for yours, if it ever came to that."

Our touching moment was ruined when my stomach emitted a loud rumble, and I gave him a sheepish grin.

"And perhaps I should feed you too," he said, picking up the suitcase and heading towards the entrance to the Halfway House.

"It still weirds me out that vampires eat people food."

Madigan had once told me that what humans '*knew*' about vampires—though based on a few truths—was mostly inaccurate. Unlike Brain Eaters, who at least resembled Nosferatu, Blood Drinkers like Madigan had normal teeth, ate regular meals, and didn't *immediately* burst into flames in sunlight. They even had a heartbeat. Good thing too—I never understood how Edward Cullen managed to get it on with Bella.

Madigan snorted. "Ah, yes. Because if there's one thing vampires fear, it's a nutritionally complete diet."

A man stood outside the pub as we approached. He rivalled Madigan in height but was built like a rugby player, dressed in a black suit, arms folded.

Odd place for a bouncer. Who knows, maybe the village's pensioners get rowdy on a Wednesday night?

The bouncer scrutinised Madigan, giving him a curt nod, then turned his eyes on me, frowning. My heart stopped, sending a tingle of panic through my limbs. I didn't have my I.D., and though I was twenty-two, I'd never managed to wiggle past a bouncer without one.

"She's with me," Madigan said.

To my amazement, the bouncer nodded.

"You're responsible for her," he said, and stood aside to allow us entry.

A blast of heat rolled over me as soon as I stepped inside. Madigan had to duck beneath the wooden beams stretching across the ceiling, the top of his head brushing the hops woven between them, filling the pub with a woody, earthy scent that complemented the bitter aroma of beer. Horse brasses decorated the bar, empty glasses hanging from above. Chatter hummed through the pub, occasionally broken by a loud drunken guffaw of laughter. A few tables and booths were taken, and one patron sat at the bar downing pints of ale, no less than four empty glasses surrounding the one he was nursing, foam caught in his long grey beard.

I claimed a booth while Madigan headed to the bar, returning with three drinks on a tray. Ale for him, vodka and coke for me, and a shot glass containing a thick red liquid I'd grown all too familiar with.

Madigan blinked at me, perhaps puzzled why I was squinting at him. Then a flicker of realisation crossed his face. "Oh," he said, taking the shot glass of blood, "this is a vampire pub."

"No shit," I said dryly, smirking.

"It's for vampires travelling to and from the Nest."

"Lurch out there isn't a bouncer, is he?" I jabbed my thumb towards the entrance.

"Well, I suppose he is, in a sense. But it's not age he's verifying."

"Am I... Am I safe here?" I cast a nervous glance around the pub. The last thing I needed was a patron deciding they'd rather take their blood from me than the barmaid.

"You're safe," Madigan said, wiping a trickle of crimson from his lower lip and placing the shot glass back on the tray. "Since becoming a shifter, your scent has changed. I still think you smell delicious, of course, but your blood has an uncanniness to it."

The word 'uncanny' transported me back to one of the few university lectures I'd paid attention in.

"Like the uncanny valley? When something is disturbing because it's almost human, but not?"

"Exactly. You might turn a couple of heads as you pass, but they'll lose interest when they realise you're not human."

Madigan's mood improved yet further after a hot meal and a couple more pints. I tried some of the ale myself, but wasn't a fan of its bitter tang, washing the aftertaste away with the sweet bubbles of my own drink.

"Shouldn't we feed Dominic?" I asked, as I threw my napkin onto my empty plate, the flavour of the salty meat and gravy still coating my tongue.

"He should be fine as long as we keep him hydrated."

"With water or...?"

"Yes, water. He could probably go a couple of weeks without blood, given the amount he's consumed recently. But I am not so fortunate."

"Would my uncanny shifter blood help in a pinch?" I asked.

Madigan fixed me with a hard stare. "In theory, perhaps. But I've never tried it, nor do I intend to."

"Suit yourself," I said with a yawn and a stretch, feigning nonchalance. I'd have given it willingly if it would have helped him—but was glad to keep it for myself, thank you very much.

"It's getting early." I rubbed my aching eyes, looking forward to a hot shower and a comfy bed.

"I'll speak to the barmaid about rooms."

I watched him leave, disappointed he'd donned a trench coat that hid *everything* from my prying eyes. So instead, I let my gaze wander. The old guy at the bar had chugged another two pints since I'd last observed him. Now, another joined him. He looked young—perhaps in his thirties—clean shaven, with a strong square jaw, and a crop of wavy auburn hair. Kind of... pretty looking.

His eyes met mine, and I was about to turn away, cheeks flushing, when something deep inside urged me to keep my sights locked on him.

He grinned. Dimples formed in his cheeks as he revealed perfect teeth, and the compulsion to keep staring only grew stronger as warmth spread through my chest, my mouth too wet. My mind clouded as I zoned in on his lips and wondered—just for a second—what they would feel like against mine.

Stop it...

Mustering all my willpower, I ripped my eyes off him and instead searched for Madigan, determined not to let my mind wander where it shouldn't.

"It's you..." The stranger's voice reached me, and though I knew I shouldn't give him a second glance... I couldn't resist.

But now, there was only an empty barstool. He'd vanished...

"Huh? What the—?"

Madigan landed on our table with a crash, sending glasses, plates, and cutlery flying as I let out a startled scream, jumping to my feet. The stranger stood over him, pinning him by the throat.

CHAPTER FIVE

For a heartbeat, my body stood immobile as my startled brain tried to process what was happening.

Madigan's face contorted, teeth bared, as he clawed at the hand around his neck. He let out a terrible gasping sound as he tried to draw breath, but as he beheld his assailant's face, his eyes widened, mouth falling open in shock.

Blood stormed in my ears, fury bursting through me as I snatched up a nearby chair and swung it in an arc, smashing it over the head of the stranger, who didn't even flinch as splintered wood showered over him. The stranger turned his face away from Madigan to glare at me, dark brown eyes crazed, lips peeled back in a snarl.

My raging-hot blood turned to ice as he surveyed me, and for a second, I thought he might drop Madigan and advance.

"Hiero!" Madigan gasped, his voice almost inaudible. "Hiero, stop!"

"Who are you?!" the stranger screamed, whipping his head back to Madigan. "Why do you look like *him*?"

"It *is* me!"

"No!" The stranger's knuckles turned white as he tightened his grip.

"Yes... Hiero... it's... me."

"Prove it!"

Madigan's lips moved, but his voice was trapped, strangled by the stranger's vice grip.

I seized another chair to strike again—for all the good it would do.

"*Prove it!*" the stranger demanded again, but relaxed his fingers on Madigan's throat.

Madigan sucked in a gasp of air, eyes flicking to me for the briefest of seconds, then returned his gaze to the stranger. "All right..." he said hoarsely. "How about when we last met, you didn't have this... this... *ridiculous* glamour?"

"That proves nothing."

"Or that I left the Nest to find a familiar?"

"That's..." The stranger flinched, struggling to maintain eye contact. "That's not exactly a secret."

"All right then," Madigan said, gritting his teeth, flushing scarlet. "Our first kiss was after you'd read Kipling's 'Recessional' to me, after *weeks* of tutelage."

My mouth fell open as I dropped the chair with a clatter of wood on stone, my fingers suddenly weak.

What did he just say?

The stranger released Madigan and stumbled back a step. His wild expression vanished, colour draining from his face as he said in a whisper, "*'Lest we forget'.*" He shook his head. "But... it's not... it's not *possible!*"

Madigan, who was coughing as he massaged his throat where the stranger had grabbed him, looked up through watering eyes and repeated, "*'Lest we forget'.*"

I blinked at the pair of them, looking from one to the other, unable to comprehend what I was seeing, what I was *hearing*, my pulse throbbing throughout my body, ringing in my head.

First kiss?! Madigan wasn't kidding when he said there was a lot I didn't know about him!

A moment of silence passed as Madigan and the stranger gawked at each other, both panting, Madigan still rubbing his neck, and the stranger still dumbfounded. It was only when the barmaid gave a loud cough, followed by a somewhat forced rumble of chatter throughout the pub, I realised everyone had stopped silent to watch the fight.

"Len?" The stranger stepped closer to Madigan. "Is that *really* you?" He raised a hand, reaching out to touch his face, and I waited for Madigan to recoil at the intimate gesture. He was not the touchy-feely type for anyone but me. But when he placed his hand over the stranger's, almost melting against his touch, it felt as though the ground beneath my feet crumbled away.

As though this was the signal he'd been waiting for, the stranger lurched forward, throwing his arms around Madigan and locking him into a tight hug, and the world seemed to turn itself inside out as Madigan returned the embrace in a public display of affection I'd never—*never*—seen from him.

"I thought you were dead," the stranger's voice was barely audible, his face buried in Madigan's neck, who stood a few inches taller.

Madigan's sights locked on me, peering over the stranger's shoulder as they hugged. It was difficult to read his expression, but his eyes looked as though he were silently pleading with me.

I tried to keep my face neutral. The events playing out in front of me were a total mindfuck, but I wouldn't jump to conclusions before Madigan could explain himself. I gave him a tight-lipped smile, which he must have found comfort in, as his body relaxed against the stranger's.

"A vicious lie," Madigan said, his voice still a little raspier than usual, "spun by my former coven leader."

"You joined a *coven*?" The stranger leaned out of the hug, examining Madigan's face for a hint of a lie or twisted joke.

"It's a long story."

"I have time."

Madigan glanced at me again as he tugged on his cuff, and now the stranger turned his attention to me as well, remembering I was there.

I shrugged. "Over drinks, I hope. And make mine a double."

After apologising profusely (and, what I suspected was a powerful use of his glamour), the stranger—named Hiero—convinced the barmaid to allow us to stay. Even after insisting she'd no longer serve us, Hiero *somehow* bought another round of drinks.

"So then, spill," Hiero said, wiping froth from his lips after he took a large swig from his pint glass. "Where have you been the last twenty-odd years?"

Madigan explained how he'd joined Ivan's coven. Some of it I'd already heard before; how Hallows had killed his former master; how he'd enlisted Ivan's help to track them down; how the price of his help was Madigan's membership. Despite the grim topic of conversation, I'd not missed the way Madigan gazed at Hiero, almost unable to take his eyes off him like he still didn't *quite* believe he was real.

"So *that* part is true, then?" Hiero asked. "Master Tobias is dead?"

"I am afraid so."

Hiero leant back in his seat, his chest deflating with a heavy sigh. Though he occasionally spoke with a hint of a posh accent like Madigan's, his mannerisms couldn't have been more different. While Madigan sat upright, like he had a pole pressed to his spine, Hiero sat more like me: casual and laid back. Perhaps a little *too* laid back, one arm draped over the back of his chair, his legs spread apart as he crossed an ankle over one knee.

His fashion sense was muddled too. He wore simple brown trousers, a white shirt, and braces, like he'd just walked out of the nineteenth century, but the first few buttons of his shirt were undone, teasing his pectorals like some supernatural thirst trap.

I caught myself staring, but no sooner had I done so, both men whipped their heads around to look at me. I blinked back at the pair of them, wondering what I'd done to provoke this reaction, when I remembered their sharpened senses would have picked up some telltale sign of arousal.

A skipped heartbeat.

A trickle of sweat.

My face burned.

"Well, this is awkward," I said with a half-laugh.

Hiero grinned, dimples forming in his cheeks again. Though he looked to be around the same age as Madigan, I noted the creases near his eyes, presumably formed by his infectious smiling.

"It doesn't have to be." Hiero raised an eyebrow with a smirk that seemed to raise the temperature of the pub by several degrees.

Before I even realised what was happening, a giggle erupted out of me. A *giggle*. Like a silly teen girl.

Madigan pinched the bridge of his nose and let out a sigh. "Please, Ava, he doesn't need encouragement." I might have believed his exasperated tone if it hadn't been for the curl of his lips.

"She can't help it," Hiero said, before turning that dazzling smile on Madigan. "No one can."

Madigan grinned—he wasn't even trying to hide it now. "I guess some things never change. Although, I must ask—your glamour—you're not a Soul Sucker, are you?"

Hiero maintained his smile, but the creases at his eyes flattened as he tilted his head to one side, and then the other, thinking. "Not a Soul

Sucker, no," he said at last, "but it's vitally important you keep that a secret. I achieve the glamour with Witch's Tears."

"But, *why*?" There was pain in Madigan's voice. "You don't need to use a glamour."

Hiero huffed through his nose. "Come on, Len. *You* thought the lopsided face was cute, but not everyone is so generous. But, for your information, I don't use a glamour to get laid. That's just a perk." He winked at me, and before I could stop it, another of those ridiculous giggles escaped from me. But then he returned his focus to Madigan and said seriously, "You know vampires associate beauty with power, and right now, I need our people to have confidence in me. You won't believe this, but I'm running for liege lord."

"You're *what*?!" Madigan's eyes looked ready to pop out of his head. "*Liege* lord? But you need a lordship to run for—"

"And I have one. It's been a long twenty years, hasn't it?" Hiero laughed into his ale, amused by Madigan's lack of composure.

The two of them spoke of politics—something about '*merit-based reform*' and '*a citizen advancement program*'. A whole load of buzz words that meant a whole load of nothing.

I got another round of drinks while they rambled, letting my mind drift elsewhere.

I wonder what else I don't know about Madigan. I knew he had an ex-wife, but an ex-boyfriend? Did not *see that one coming...*

I struggled more than I'd like to admit to keep the mental images PG, but I couldn't bear the mortification of being caught by their vampiric senses again.

"Now then," Hiero said with a clap of his hands, snapping me out of my thoughts. "Len, I can't continue flirting with this delightful companion of yours without a proper introduction. Actually, I prob-ably could, but it wouldn't be polite, would it?"

"Since when have manners been a concern of yours?" Madigan scoffed.

"Good manners would have been to introduce me yourself about half an hour ago," I said, making Madigan's cheeks turn scarlet. I held out a hand to Hiero. "I'm Ava."

But rather than shake my hand, he brought it to his lips and kissed my knuckles. "Len's familiar?"

"No!" I yanked my hand from him with an incredulous laugh. "Not anymore, anyway. I'm his missus."

Hiero's eyebrows shot upwards, so high they almost disappeared under his mop of auburn waves. "I see I'm not the only one whose circumstances have changed."

Madigan's blush deepened.

"In any case," Hiero continued, "it's a pleasure, Ava. I'm Hieronymus Blackford, but please, call me Hiero." He flashed me another gut-melting smile. "Nice hair, by the way."

I snorted, fingers habitually brushing the white patch at the front. "Thanks. I get that a lot."

"Is it your first time travelling to the Vampires' Nest?"

"Yeah. I'm not a vampire. I'm a shifter."

"Ahhh, a shifter. I wondered what was... *off* about you."

I glanced at Madigan, just long enough to spot the tug at the corner of his mouth. Yes, he was thinking it too. *Uncanny.*

"Tell me," Hiero went on, oblivious to our inside joke, "what brings a shifter to the Vampires' Nest?"

"I'm recruiting for our coven. The Hallows have returned, and our numbers are low. We need more members to fight back against them."

Hiero's smirk vanished, replaced by a stony glare that even his glamour couldn't make pretty.

"The Hallows?" His voice lost its playful tone, becoming deeper and dangerous, not dissimilar to Madigan's when wrestling with his rising temper. A tone that never failed to raise the hairs on the back of my neck.

Hiero narrowed his eyes at Madigan. "The same Hallows that killed *you*?" There was something accusing about the way he asked the question.

Madigan bristled. "The same Hallows that murdered Master Tobias."

Hiero's lips twisted to one side as he leant back in his chair, his eyes darting between us.

"You're certain they're Hallows?" he asked after a moment's thought. "No offence, Len, but after believing the Hallows murdered you and learning *that* was a lie, it makes me question... well... everything."

"They had a demonic artefact, and there's only one group of hunters with access to such things. They disappeared for a time after I—"

Madigan stopped mid-sentence and glanced at me, a sudden expression of panic on his face, like he'd said something he shouldn't have.

"After I... joined the coven," he said, though I was sure he was censoring himself.

A smile slowly crept across Hiero's face, a flicker of satisfaction in the depths of his dark brown eyes.

"What a coincidence," he said. "I'd made plans to exterminate the Hallows myself. Plans so complex they've taken twenty years to execute." He shared a meaningful look with Madigan. "But they say revenge is a dish best served cold, don't they? I shall escort you to the Nest. You *will* find your recruits. And we *will* destroy the Hallows."

CHAPTER SIX

When Madigan and I had first set off on our journey, it hadn't even crossed my mind that we might bump into someone from his past—never mind an ex. So having one sleep in our room at the inn was a total brain scramble. Fate had a twisted sense of humour.

The next night, the vampires bought blood shots from the bar and settled the tab while I force fed Dominic his potion through the syringe. They weren't long, but the minutes dragged as I waited in the campervan. Dominic was shit company at the best of times, and his dormant state was only marginally better.

With nothing to do, I simply sat and glared at the unresponsive vampire, as though it was *his* fault Madigan and Hiero had buggered off and left me alone with him.

Finally, Hiero opened the door, giving me a charming smile that—as handsome as it was—only annoyed me. He'd already ruined what would have been the only opportunity for Madigan and me to share a decent bed. I suppose, technically, we *had* shared the bed—Hiero had slept on the floor—but it wasn't *sleeping* I'd had in mind.

"Your mate looks ill," Hiero said, squeezing in beside Dominic.

"He's not my mate," I said, keeping my voice as even as possible. "He's a near-rabid vampire we're escorting to the Nest for trial."

"Not a romantic road trip, then. Or is he a part of some kink you share?"

"Ew! No!" A laugh rose out of me, unbidden, and I hated myself for it.

"Hey, don't knock it until you try it. Polyamory and harems are normal at the Nest."

"I'm not knocking anything," I said with a shrug. "It's Dominic I object to specifically."

"Ahhh, so you're saying you'd try it?"

Madigan made grumbling noises from the driver's seat, and I'm sure I heard him say *'incorrigible'*, causing a twinge of annoyance to shoot through me. Madigan spoke about *me* like that.

"I'm saying, you do you," I said, refusing to let my jealousy take over as I joined Madigan in the front, taking the passenger seat.

Polyamory had never occurred to me—I had enough trouble keeping down *one* romantic partner, let alone multiple. It sounded like hard work. And complicated. Still, it probably had its perks. Least of all the amount of *physical* attention everyone got.

I focused on the road before my thoughts ran wild.

As we drove into the night, Hiero sat forward in his seat, leaning over the back of the bench Madigan and I shared, his head between ours.

He gossiped for hours, and the more he spoke of people and places I'd never heard of, the more my stomach hardened with the strain of keeping my insecurities bottled up.

Is this the real *reason Madigan didn't want to bring me? Had he planned on reuniting with Hiero all along?*

I chewed the inside of my cheek as I gazed out the window. It was impossible to admire the countryside, the darkness cloaking it, and all the while, Hiero and Madigan pointed out various spots, speaking of their beauty. All I could do was take their word for it.

They were right beside me, but I'd never felt more isolated.

I glanced at the pair, Hiero laughing at something Madigan had said, and the corner of Madigan's mouth spasming in the worst attempt of a suppressed smile I'd ever seen. My stomach knotted, and I turned to the window again.

Wherever we were, it had steep hills, deep valleys, and narrow, winding roads unsuitable for *any* motor vehicle, let alone the campervan and its shoddy suspension. Without a seatbelt, I almost hit my head on the roof during a rough uphill stint. The poor battered old van nearly died before we reached the top. Madigan worked down through the gears as it violently chugged onward, slower and slower, and almost came to a halt as we reached the peak. I was going to ask about the stench of burning rubber, but to my surprise, we cruised down the other side without a problem, and I noticed the gleam in Madigan's eyes as he gave the dashboard another of those sentimental touches.

"Shouldn't be much longer," he said, pointing at a spot in the distance. "That's the farm over there. That's where we'll shelter next."

I squinted through my window, but all I could see was my reflection glaring back at me.

Once we arrived and I got out to stretch my legs, I soon realised the farm had long since been abandoned. All that remained of some barns and stables were their timber frames jutting into the air.

The farmhouse was the only building with its roof intact, though the windows had lost their panes. The wooden front door slowly creaked open, its hinges screaming in protest, then *banged* shut with a sudden gust of icy wind. I shrank inside my coat. As glad as I was to avoid another night in the campervan with Dominic, the farmhouse wasn't a great alternative.

I poked my head through an empty window, making out the shapes of broken chairs and a table, then recoiled at the scent of wood rot.

"It will soon feel like home once supper is on the stove," Hiero said as he headed inside, the front door slamming behind him.

I prayed the door had a lock, or I could kiss goodbye to any sleep with it banging all day. And I doubted the farmhouse did, indeed, have a functional stove. Though I found my trepidation of entering the farmhouse vanished after Madigan followed Hiero. I told myself it was to escape the frosty night air, but the idea of them being alone together had my teeth grinding.

Once inside, my eyes soon adjusted to the darkness. The entire ground floor consisted of one room. Up one end was a decrepit kitchen with a black metal stove I recognised from a history textbook. Still, at least it *was* a stove.

The rest of the room was a living area, littered with musty blankets, sleeping bags, and cushions. Some may have been usable, but I wasn't desperate enough to scavenge when we had our own in the campervan. There was also a decaying wooden staircase, but several of the steps were missing, making the upstairs area inaccessible. Not that I intended to explore up there. I'd played too much Silent Hill for that.

"Nice! The storeman's been here recently," Hiero said, rifling through a cupboard. "You're lucky. With so many vampires returning, the rations get used faster than we can replenish them."

"This is one of many rest spots near the Nest we stock with food and firewood for travelling vampires making their way home," Madigan explained, noticing my look of bewilderment. "This is probably the largest. Most are simply caves or derelict shacks."

"It's also the most popular," Hiero said as he grabbed a basket of firewood and dumped it in front of the stove. "Did you notice all the other abandoned cars out there?"

I hadn't, and the feeling of otherness surfaced again. Sure, the *vampires* could see the cars swallowed by the night—but not me.

"Shame there's no Husks, really," Hiero continued, oblivious to my discomfort as he added kindling to the firebox. "The storeman is usually pretty good at making sure there's at least one at each rest stop. But as I said—it's been busy. We're fortunate to have the place to ourselves."

Hiero kept talking as he lit the fire, but my mind was elsewhere, lingering on something Madigan had once told me.

"To become a Soul Sucker, a Blood Drinker must suck the soul from another being's mouth, leaving their victim an empty, yet obedient husk."

"A Husk is someone who's had their soul drained, aren't they?" I asked, and my skin erupted in a fresh wave of goosebumps that had nothing to do with the cold.

"That's right," Hiero said. "They're useful to feed from. Of course they need replacing after a while—"

"I think," Madigan interjected, "we should move on from this topic of conversation."

I turned to find him watching me with a knowing expression. It was one of the few times I was glad he could *'smell my mood'*, as he called it.

"Perhaps I might take Ava for a walk to the moth field for a change of scene." Though he spoke to Hiero, his eyes remained locked on me.

"Moth field?" I asked but no one offered an explanation.

"Sounds good," Hiero said. "This won't be hot enough to cook on for a while, so take your time." He cracked a cheeky grin. "Besides, it's probably the most romantic spot for miles."

Madigan straightened himself, strode towards me, and dipped his head in a gentleman's bow that coaxed a smile from my lips.

"Miss Monroe, would you like to accompany me on a short walk to one of the local beauty spots?"

His use of *'Miss Monroe'* was all the convincing I needed. I doubted I'd get much out of visiting a beauty spot in the dark, but his company—*alone*—was exactly what I needed.

"I'd love to."

Madigan held out his arm, which I linked my own through, and began our walk. Though I could make out various shapes in the darkness, I was relying on Madigan to be my eyes, reminding me of our walk through the woodland behind the showman's yard to his secret spot: the place we'd shared our first kiss.

I tensed at the memory. He'd been the one to break away, hesitant to get close. Had he been thinking about Hiero even then?

"What *exactly* is the relationship between you and Hiero?" I blurted before I could stop myself. We'd only just left the farm and already I'd lost control of my mouth.

I cringed, preparing for a scowl, but Madigan only huffed a small laugh through his nose. A *laugh*. A ghost of a laugh, sure, but a laugh nonetheless. I'd take it.

"If truth be told, I'm not entirely sure myself. I suppose you could say we first became close during the war."

"I'll never understand what it was like to experience all that." I didn't like asking about his service. It reminded me of his outburst when I'd naively suggested I could help him with the trauma he'd suffered during *'some war'*. Even thinking those words made me wince.

"I should hope not. I'd not wish it upon anyone. But when Master Tobias saved us after the explosion—"

I gasped, the penny finally dropping: Hiero's reaction to Master Tobias's death; the comment of his glamour hiding a lopsided face. "Your dearest friend who took shrapnel to the face. That's Hiero, isn't it?"

"That's right."

"Do you... do you love him?"

"I..." Madigan tilted his head in thought. "I suppose so. After a fashion. But it's been a long time since we were together, and I... I've grown affection for another." He looked down at me, one eyebrow raised slightly.

Ask him if he was coming back for Hiero, said an unhelpful inner voice. *Ask him if that's the real reason he wanted you to stay behind.*

I knew that voice well. It had insisted Greg had cheated on me. Spoiler alert: he hadn't.

I opened my mouth—words dancing on the tip of my tongue—and closed it. Just in time.

The corner of Madigan's mouth curled. "Ask it."

"Ask what?"

"The question on your mind."

A breath caught in my throat. *How did he—?*

"I'm not a mind reader, as you well know," he said, the curl of his lip now a rare full-blown grin that melted me from the inside. "But I can sense the stress in you. The flood of hormones. The racing heart. And after everything that's happened, you must have many questions."

I swallowed, my restraint bleeding out of me.

"Were you really going to come back for me?" I gabbled the words so fast I was surprised he could understand me at all. "Did you want to leave to be with Hiero?"

We stopped walking, and Madigan placed a hand over the one I'd linked through his arm, rejuvenating my numb fingers.

"For twenty years I dreamed of reuniting with Hiero," he said, his eyes meeting mine, and though he was calm, there was a slight strain in his voice, like he was trying not to show weakness or pain. "Twenty years of living in fear. Hoping I might see Hiero again was all that kept me going some nights. But those nights are past. You are my future. I don't deny I'd hoped to see Hiero upon my return. For closure. A proper goodbye. But I had every intention of returning to you. I swear it."

My heart fluttered. How could I ever have doubted him?

"I'm sorry," I said, feigning a laugh. "I shouldn't have accused—"

"It was a fair question, and one you feel better for asking, no?"

I nodded. "I was worried I might scare you off or something."

He smirked. "I don't scare so easily."

He led me through fields and valleys until we came to a pine forest. Trees stretched into the sky, merging with the inky blackness of the night.

"It isn't much further." He guided me through the forest, pine needles and cones crunching beneath our feet, until we reached a vast, open field.

I gasped.

The moon illuminated it like a spotlight, reflecting off the field's crimson surface; a surface that seemed to... *move*. Rippling like water. Like blood.

"What is this place?" I asked, a chill rippling down my spine.

Madigan released me, advancing until he reached the edge of the blood-red field, then looked back and extended his hand.

I stared at him in hesitation. He raised his eyebrows, wordlessly tempting me to join him.

I took his hand, and together we stepped into the field. No sooner had I set my foot down, the field shimmered from red to white, as a cloud of moths fluttered upwards. I took another step, then another, moths pirouetting up into the sky, wings glinting in the full moon's glow.

"What are they?"

"We call them blood-moon moths. Thousands of years ago, vampires were at war with each other. So much blood was spilt here, it permanently altered the moths that used it as their breeding ground." One moth flew up, landing on Madigan's lapel. The tops of its wings were deep red, but as it fluttered, I glimpsed the cotton-white underside before it flew away with the others.

"They don't seem to have a breeding season anymore," he mused. "They're here all year round. It's curious. Most animals that encounter vampire blood become monsters or die. And yet these..." His voice trailed off as he admired another moth fluttering past his face, more at peace than I'd ever seen him.

"I've never seen anything like this," I said, awestruck. "They're *stunning*." We reached the middle of the field, moths swarming around us, the moonlight reflecting off their wings like a glitter ball.

"Miss Monroe," he said with a bow of his head, then brought my hand to his mouth, kissing my knuckles. "Would you care to dance?"

I had to stifle a laugh. "I don't know how. Not *properly*, anyway."

"I'll teach you. It's straightforward. Just follow my lead." He placed my free hand on his shoulder, then clasped my waist and pulled me tight into his body.

I became hyperaware of my breathing, which had suddenly become difficult. With each breath, my breasts pressed to his firm chest, blood burning my cheeks. Madigan let out a small laugh through his nose. He could sense my reaction, which only made my face burn hotter.

"We'll keep it simple," he said in a low voice, his lips against my ear. "Two steps back, then feet together, then two steps forward, and feet together. All right?"

"Yes," I whispered, gripping him tightly to save myself from falling flat on my arse should my feet get tangled.

I followed his instructions. Clumsy at first, but after some practice I got into the flow of the movements. Moths flit around us, as though they too were dancing, and I gazed up into Madigan's face. He was still smiling at me; a smile that reached his eyes. Tender and real.

Fuck, I want you...

But before I could say the words aloud, Madigan's lips were on mine. Smooth. *Perfect.*

My arms wrapped around his neck, pulling him tighter against me as he nipped my lower lip, making me gasp. And in that second, he deepened the kiss, his tongue snaking into my mouth, and swept across my own.

I drove my fingers up into his hair and tightened my grasp until he moaned, revelling in his scent, his taste, his hands squeezing the soft flesh of my hips, and the way his breath caught as his cock stiffened, pressing into me.

"What is this spell you have on me, Miss Monroe?" he whispered against my mouth. "You make me feel... *powerless*. A slave to my desires."

"Tell me what you want to do." I needed to hear those desires. And re-enact them.

"I want to rip these clothes off you."

He tightened his hold on me, taking fistfuls of my clothes, pulling the fabric tight across my skin.

"I want to kiss your neck."

He lowered his head, brushing burning kisses against my skin.

"And across your collarbone, down to your breasts."

One of his hands slid to my ribcage, directly below my breast, like he knew how much I wanted him to reach a little higher and cup it.

Instead, he swept his thumb teasingly along the underside, extracting a soft moan from me. "Your nipples would already be stiff when I start to suck them. And as I play with your body, you would become wet—like you are right now."

"I'm not."

"You are."

I was. And *aching*.

"And then what?"

He grabbed me, lifting me off the ground, wrapping my legs around him, and said in a throaty voice against my ear, "Then, I'd slide myself inside you."

He pressed his hips hard against mine. His cock felt even bigger now it was grinding against my swollen clit.

"I'll make love to you until you can't help but make those moaning noises. You know which noises I mean, don't you? The noise you make when you cum—and you *will* cum. And every vampire will hear when you do."

The aching in my pussy was almost unbearable, his words sweet torture.

His hands trembled, like it was taking all his willpower not to rip my clothes off, and despite the cold, I *wanted* him to. I wanted him to see my naked body illuminated by moonlight. To see how my nipples peaked for him. How wet I was for him.

"Did you want to make love to me? Or did you want to *fuck* me?" I asked in a whisper.

"Miss Monroe..." The grip on my clothes constricted, uncomfortably tight.

"Or maybe *I* might kiss all the way down *your* chest." I dropped a hand from his shoulder, sliding it between us, down his lean torso. "Down your stomach and over your hips. Every. Last. *Inch* of you."

His mouth scorched as he sucked my neck, needier than before. His teeth grazed my skin...

"All the way down to your *very* stiff cock." I cupped the bulge in his trousers, making him gasp. "And take you in my mouth."

In a movement too fast to conceive, Madigan had me on my back, buried in the grass. His lips were on mine, then traced my jawline and down my neck as his hands clenched, ready to tear my clothes open.

I fumbled with the front of his trousers, desperate to free his cock. First the button. Then the zipper, his heavy erection springing forward at the slightest release of pressure. I traced my fingers beneath the waistband of his boxers, the coarse hair beneath tickling my fingertips, and was about to free his cock... when his hold on me suddenly slackened, and he sat upright, looking around, eyes wide.

"Don't stop!" I protested, but he took no notice.

"Can you smell burning?"

"*No!*" I sniffed. I genuinely couldn't smell anything, but even if I *had*, I'd have let the world burn.

"We need to get back—now," he said in a forceful tone, adjusting himself back into his trousers in an instant.

"Fuck, are you kidding me?!" The ache between my legs was now a painful throbbing.

"I'm serious." He extended a hand, and for a moment, I considered swatting it aside.

Our eyes met.

My heartbeat thrummed in my ears.

And with a sigh, I took it.

He yanked me to my feet before marching at a brisk pace, forcing me to jog to keep up with his long strides, ignoring as I muttered darkly about giving a girl blue balls. His pace quickened, until I was almost running and wheezing for breath, night air burning my throat.

"Come *on*, Ava!" he snapped, his grip on my hand pinching as he tugged me along, my pace lagging.

As we emerged from the pine forest, I made out a small orange light atop a hill. Madigan froze, mouth tight, eyes unblinking.

"Is that... the farm...?" I asked, clutching at my heaving chest, my lungs on fire as they begged for breath. Madigan looked at me, frowning, only now realising how exhausted I was.

"Yes." Though he kept his composure, I'd seen him do this enough times to know he was hiding his panic. "If I go ahead, could you catch up?"

"Yes," I said, grateful for the excuse to slow down.

Madigan nodded and set off so fast he became a blur as he disappeared into the darkness. I followed behind at a power walk, suddenly aware of the vast open space I was in, completely alone. I followed the orange light, growing larger and larger, until the waft of smoke caught in my nose and throat; a scent that constricted my throat as the image of a ring of fire surrounding Madigan and Ivan flashed into my mind, and it became even harder to go on. My legs wobbled, my feet suddenly cumbersome, like my body was screaming at me not to take another step. But I persisted.

When I reached the farm, there was no mistaking the source of the fire.

My mouth fell open.

The campervan was trashed: windows smashed in, engine ripped out, tyres slashed, consumed by a blaze that spread to one of the dilapidated barns.

I made a beeline for the farmhouse. Cooking equipment and half-prepared food scattered the floor, along with a puddle of dark liquid I recognised instantly as blood.

"Ava!" Madigan appeared in the doorway, his hair slick against his forehead, sweat trickling down his face, chest heaving with laboured breaths. "Has Hiero come back?"

I shook my head.

He drove a hand through his wet hair, eyes drawn to the pool of blood. "I've lapped the farm three times now. There is no sign of him anywhere."

"Can you smell him?"

"The smoke is too overpowering. And it's not only Hiero who's missing. There's no sign of Dominic either."

CHAPTER SEVEN

Madigan held his trench coat over his head as we marched through the pine forest, the closest thing he had to shelter from the sun already peeking over the horizon. From the way he flinched, you'd think it was a scorching forty-degree day, not a morning so bitter it made my limbs ache from shivering. I was already regretting our romp in the grass.

I'd had a spare coat in the campervan. Hoodies too, and more woolly socks. All gone up in flames, along with our sleeping bags and food rations. I kicked myself for not keeping Mischievous's weird trinket on my person instead of my bag; so much for all that help he'd promised. And it stung to think of my handheld console as nothing but a melted lump of plastic and charred circuit boards now. Sure, I'd got it second-hand at a car boot sale for only a tenner, but it had been *mine*. I'd given up most of my possessions when I joined the coven. Now I had nothing, save for the clothes on my back and boots on my feet. But nothing hurt more than losing the photograph of my grandma, tucked *safely* in a hoodie pocket.

I kept this to myself. What would Madigan care about a photo when his best friend (if that's what he was) was missing?

I'd suggested staying at the farm until the following night, but Madigan had insisted we leave.

"Far too dangerous," he'd said.

"But the campervan has burnt out."

"That's not what concerns me. Someone ambushed Hiero, and I'm not prepared to let them do the same to us."

"How do you ambush a vampire? Shouldn't you be able to hear or smell someone creeping up on you?"

"Not if we're distracted."

Those ominous words stuck with me as I hurried behind him, half-jogging to keep up.

We continued past the moth field and deeper into the pine forest, the density of the trees providing cover, but soon we reached the other side. Beyond were more hills and valleys, a vast sea of green with no shade.

"Accursed sun," Madigan said through a clenched jaw.

"We need to find somewhere for you to shelter until nightfall."

"I know of a shepherd's hut nearby. Look. There in the distance." He pointed towards a hill. Squinting, I made out a tiny brown speck on the horizon among the sprawling frost-kissed grass.

"That will take *all day* to reach. Can you survive that long in the sun?"

"Not walking at your pace, no. At my speed, I could reach it within... an hour? Perhaps two?"

"So, go on then. I'll catch you up."

"I'm loath to leave you behind while there's someone dangerous lurking about." He stared at the speck in the distance, running a hand over his mouth and letting out a humming noise as gears in his mind worked overtime. "I'll have to carry you."

"What, like a piggyback?"

He let out an irritated huff, either our situation or the sun itself wearing his patience thin. "No. If you shift, I can carry you in my pocket."

"Seriously?"

But as he fixed me with his signature scowl, I raised my hands in surrender.

"All right, all right. I'll shift. But"—I grabbed his arm and gave him a pointed stare—"you must look after my clothes *and* Doc Martens."

He huffed through his nose. "Very well."

"I mean it." I raised my eyebrows, refusing to back down until he understood how serious I was.

At first, he simply stared back with narrowed eyes, but his expression softened, and with a slight bow of his head, he said, "You have my word."

I gave his arm a soft squeeze, and with one last parting glance, I shifted.

After the world had blown up to an impossible size and the burning pain throughout my body eased, I allowed Madigan to pick me up and slide me into his coat pocket. There was a moment of comfort as I settled in the warm, dark space, surrounded by his scent, but that comfort was short-lived as he sped off and I was jostled about like a teddy bear in a washing machine.

If I'd been human, the motion sickness would have struck me in an instant. Up was down. Down was up. And I clung onto the walls of his pocket with my hooked feet, counting down the seconds until it was over.

Fifty-eight, fifty-nine, sixty. That's ten minutes.

It was a great idea in theory. But in practice...

Fifty-eight, fifty-nine, sixty. That's... wait. Was that twenty or twenty-one?

It wasn't much longer until I lost count all together. Time stretched on, and on, until I became disorientated. Just how long *had* it been? He'd said it would only take an hour or two, but it felt more like three hours had passed. Maybe four...

Or had it been longer? Half a day? A *whole* day?

No, don't be ridiculous.

Just as I felt like I was losing my grip on reality, I came to an abrupt halt as something slammed into me, and the world went still. I stood frozen in place, my limbs refusing to work, until a low anguished groan vibrated through my surroundings, making the hairs on my body prickle. I scuttled out of Madigan's pocket and onto firm ground, desperate to free myself from my scorpion prison. No sooner had I made my wish than I found myself kneeling on the floor, naked and shivering.

I grabbed Madigan's coat from where he'd dumped it on the ground and draped it over my shoulders. "Well, that was horrible. Are you all right?"

Madigan was also on his knees, hands braced on the ground and taking long shuddering breaths, sweat dripping from his hair. His exposed skin was scarlet, and there was something about the wheeze with each inhale that suggested his laboured breaths weren't simply from running.

He didn't acknowledge my question, and dragged himself towards a pile of straw before collapsing into it.

The shepherd's hut was barely standing, one of its stone walls crumbling, another nothing but rubble. There was no door, only the wooden beams of the doorway. The floor was solid stone with only that pile of straw for comfort, its earthy scent dominant in the chilly air. What wouldn't I have traded for those dirty sleeping bags from the farmhouse now. The hut's remaining walls might protect from both the sun and wind, but offered nothing against the cold, and I snatched up my clothes from where Madigan had dropped them and threw them on.

"Is there anything I can do for you?" I asked, watching the way Madigan's chest heaved as he lay on his back, one arm draped over his eyes.

"I... just need... to rest..."

Resting sounded good to me, my transformation back and forth already sapping my energy. I left Madigan laying in the straw as I searched every inch of the hut for a hidden stash of supplies, hoping it was one of the rest stops Hiero and Madigan had talked about, but found nothing but broken glass and old bones.

I monitored Madigan throughout the day as the sun inched across the sky and towards the horizon, yet his breaths remained ragged and his skin crimson. In fact, I could have sworn his wheezing was becoming raspier.

"Madigan?"

"Mmm?" He winced as he let out that small noise.

I paused before asking the question that tied my insides in knots.

"Do you need blood to recover?"

His silence was all the confirmation I needed.

"Where can I get some?"

"Rest stops... like the farm. Some might... contain Husks... if I'm lucky."

I bit my lip as my mind raced. How the hell would I get Madigan to the next rest stop in this state? If I knew where the nearest one was, perhaps I could bring a Husk back here? But I *didn't* know where the next one was, and even if I did, there was no guarantee there would even be a Husk.

'If I'm lucky'... Luck hasn't exactly been on our side so far.

I glanced out the doorway as the last rays of sunlight died. Darkness descended, and cotton-white specks floated in the air, lower and lower, settling on the ground.

Snow... Just what I need.

A chill ran through me that had nothing to do with the dropping temperature. It was no good sitting around and waiting for him to recover. I needed to act.

"Does animal blood work?" I asked.

"No... it doesn't."

"When we were at the Halfway House, you said shifter blood works in theory."

He didn't answer.

"Well?" I pushed, making him flinch, which in turn made him hiss in unmistakable pain.

"Yes, in theory..." He shook his head. "But I... don't want to."

Another glance through the doorway, the falling snow already coating the grassy fields and growing thicker with every passing second.

"I think we should try," I said.

"No."

"Shouldn't it be my choice?"

"Shouldn't it be *mine*?" In defiance, he removed his arm from his eyes and propped himself on one elbow to glare at me. Though he was clearly trying to put on a brave face, he couldn't hide his flinch of pain, nor how his skin cracked around his eyes and lips.

The hut gave a low *creak*, and we glanced at the rotting wooden roof, and then at each other. I knew what he was thinking, because I was thinking it too. Could this decrepit hut withstand the weight of the snow piling above it?

"It isn't safe here," I said, keeping my voice calm, though my heart was rattling my ribcage as I imagined clawing myself out from beneath snow and debris, like a zombie rising from its grave. "And I can't carry you to the next rest stop."

Madigan's eyes flicked to the doorway, squinting into the darkness, snowflakes dancing wildly through the pitch-black beyond, before returning to me. Glassy. "I don't want... to hurt you."

"You won't."

His features twitched. "What if... I can't stop?" His question came out as a whisper.

The hut creaked again, dust and splinters raining from a jagged crack running through a beam above us.

"I'd stop you. I'd shift. Please t-try?" I couldn't tell if my teeth were chattering from the cold or from the icy grip of fear itself. "I don't want to die here."

I could see the moment his resolve broke. "Promise me... you'll shift... if I take too much. *Promise me.*"

And as the hut let out a third creak, I said, "I promise."

Before he could change his mind, I snatched up a shard of glass and slashed across my forearm, blood beading on the cut. Like a man possessed, he sprang from the pile of straw and pounced before my eyes even had time to widen. His hot mouth clamped over the wound and sucked. *Hard.*

I'd expected pain from the cut, but it never occurred to me it would hurt when he drank from me. But it did. With each draw of blood, I held back a cry of pain. Once. Twice. Thrice. But on the fourth draw I couldn't stop myself.

"Ah! Easy."

But he didn't let up. If anything, he sucked harder, his grip on my arm pinching tighter.

I tugged my arm. "Easy, Madigan. That hurts."

He stopped only to come up for air, blood dripping down his chin and coating my arm—more blood than I'd been prepared for, the scent of iron making me feel sick. But then Madigan took my arm in his mouth once more.

I yelped as he sucked too hard, yanking my arm, meaning to break free, but couldn't, his hold too strong. "Okay, stop it now." My voice wavered as panic surged in my chest. "I said *stop!*"

But he didn't.

This is why he made me promise...

It was like a blow to the heart as, for the second time, I made the wish to shift, falling into darkness and agony, before shifting back again, ice-cold air burning my naked body.

Madigan blinked at me, his eyebrows drawn together in confusion, like waking up from a deep dream. Already his usual complexion had returned, and the cracks in his skin healed.

I grabbed my clothes. "What the hell?! I told you to stop!"

Madigan's eyes widened in horror. "You did?"

"Yes!" I examined my arm—more out of habit than anything. Of course, the slash had healed when I shifted, but my flesh still tingled, like it could remember what had happened.

"I couldn't..." Madigan drove his fingers through his damp hair. "I couldn't hear you." I could practically see the weight of shame upon him, unable to look at me, and my flaring temper fizzled out. After all, he *had* warned me. "I'm never doing that again. *Never.* It felt like... it wasn't enough. Like human blood, but diluted, and I... I needed *more.* I don't think I would have stopped if you hadn't..."

I'd seen Madigan face death before. But never had I seen him so... *afraid.*

More dust fell from the roof as one wooden beam groaned, long and loud, beneath the mounting snow.

"Shift again, Ava!" Madigan grabbed his coat and pulled it on. "Now!"

But my brain, exhausted by shifting, cold, hunger, and emotional burnout, didn't understand the request.

But I... I haven't got dressed yet...

Before I could so much as blink, Madigan whipped me up in his arms, and we shot out of the hut and into the snowstorm, as with one final groan, the hut collapsed in on itself, nothing but lumps of wood and stone hidden beneath snow.

I shook violently as Madigan pulled me against his body, wrapping his coat around me as far as it would go, as we stood out in the open, defenceless against the blizzard.

CHAPTER EIGHT

My feet felt like they were on fire, submerged in the snow as I clung to Madigan for heat.

"F-f-fuck me! It's f-f-freezing!"

I turned my head, opening one eye, but I couldn't make out a bloody thing except snow shooting through the air. Beyond that... nothing... Only the ink-black abyss and white carpet, flakes skittering off its untouched surface.

"You need to shift, Ava," Madigan said, calling out to be heard over the howling wind.

"M-my c-clothes..."

"Under my arm." Sure enough, Madigan had grabbed my clothes and boots at the same time he'd snatched me up. "After all, I gave you my word."

I didn't know if I should laugh or cry. It didn't really matter—I was incapable of doing either—consumed by the cold, and shaking so hard my bones rattled.

"You *need* to shift," Madigan said again. "I can carry you in my pocket to the next rest stop. You won't survive out here otherwise."

He was right. I closed my eyes, gripping him for inner strength and with the last of my dwindling energy, I shifted. As though the transformation wasn't agonising enough, my body seared as I landed in a heap of snow.

My stinger spasmed, but that was the only movement I could manage, and a jolt of panic shot through me. The cold was too much. I couldn't sense Madigan either, the fine hairs covering my body prickling as I tried to make sense of what was going on, but the snow impeded me. That is, until it melted away as his giant fingers from above scooped me up and lifted me into the air.

Relief washed over me as he dropped me in his pocket again, and finally, I could move my limbs, heat bringing them back to life. I was so glad to be somewhere warm that I didn't even mind being jostled about again as Madigan set off.

Like before, time became meaningless, stretching on and on until I couldn't tell if Madigan had been travelling for minutes or hours.

I could have wept with relief when my world finally stopped shaking and I could scuttle out of Madigan's pocket and into what I thought might be a cave. My suspicions were confirmed as I shifted into my human form, my muscles screaming with the effort of it.

Madigan sank to the floor beside where he'd dropped my clothes and boots, his face flushed, and his body heaving with each exhale. He winced as he stripped off his coat and draped it over me, which I accepted without argument, disappearing inside it as I buttoned down the front.

I dragged my near-unresponsive limbs, crawling towards him, unable to stand. I wanted to hold him. To speak to him. But I hadn't the strength to form sentences. Instead, I leant forward, pressing my forehead to his, and simply breathed with him. My eyelids ached, but I had this nagging feeling that if I closed my eyes, they might never re-open.

I don't know how long we sat like that, my mind blank, my body in survival mode, but soon, my numb extremities tingled. Only then did I realise how dry my throat was, and the deep gnawing in the pit of my stomach. I was dehydrated and starving, but I didn't even have the energy to panic. That in of itself was a huge red flag.

Madigan sat upright after catching his breath, though his once flushed cheeks were now the colour of chalk, and dark smudges beneath his eyes made his face appear skull-like.

"I smell blood," he said, his voice gravelly.

"I need water. And food." My lips didn't want to move, slurring my words like I was drunk.

He closed his eyes, his nostrils flaring as he took a deep inhale. "At the back of the cave. It will be warmer there too. I'm afraid you must wait for your clothes to dry before you can wear them again."

"Don't care. Need food."

With a groan, I used the wall for support as I got up. All I wanted to do was sleep, my body almost broken, but some deep-rooted survival instinct forced me to my feet.

I kept one hand on the cave wall as we walked deeper into the gloom. The surface was uneven, and I almost tripped a couple of times, my feet heavy and my legs aching. *Every* inch of me ached. I was even too weak to appreciate the pretty glowing mushrooms lighting the way. Instead, I kept my head down, focusing on putting one foot in front of the other, knowing in the back of my mind that if I didn't, I would be in dire trouble.

Madigan grabbed my shoulder, his grip painful.

I wanted to swat his hand away, or at least cry out, but all I could muster was a low moan.

"Shh, I hear something," he whispered.

He stepped in front of me, keeping me behind him as we crept closer to... whatever Madigan had heard.

Approaching a bend, we slowed our pace further, keeping flat to the cave wall, and peered around the corner.

I put a hand to my mouth.

A body lay on the ground. Not moving. And around it, three skeletal humanoid creatures—naked and ghostly white—attacked the corpse with sharp teeth and long claws, screeching at each other in anger, their only method of communication. Their skin was leathery, ears pointed, and heads bald. I needed no explanation of what these creatures were.

Brain Eaters...

Two of them were eating the carcass lying at their feet as the third dragged another body closer. It held the corpse in its hands, then opened its mouth. Wider. And wider. Its jaw clicked as it dislocated, wrapping its lips around the head.

Crunch.

The Brain Eater bit down, the skull of its victim cracking, their head a bloody pulp. The monster clawed at the wounds left by its fangs, digging in deep with its nails, and then with another crunching, ripping noise, opened its victim's head like an egg, their brain splattering to the floor. Dropping the corpse, the rabid vampire began to eat, lapping at the gooey, rubbery substance at its feet.

The crunch of bone made me want to hurl, and my mind was blasted with the memory of Austin being crushed to death beneath a wooden board and the *snap* of his spine. My stomach tightened, and I compressed my lips as a sour flavour coated my tongue.

No, no, no. Please, not now...

But I knew that taste all too well, along with the feeling of maggots crawling up my throat.

I pressed my hand harder to my mouth, begging myself not to.

I gagged.

A heartbeat.

A held breath.

And the Brain Eaters snapped their heads upwards. Pearly-white eyes fixed on us as their lips peeled back to reveal sharp teeth. Though their humanity had long since disappeared, they seemed to *smile* at us.

Then pounced.

Madigan shoved me to one side and rushed forward, colliding with one Brain Eater and knocking them into another. But the third leapt into the air, and before I could blink, it crashed on top of me.

The face of death leered from above, its mouth growing wider and wider. I tried to push the monster off me, but it took every drop of strength just to raise my arms. One hand on its shoulder. One on its neck. Jaws snapped from above. Saliva dripped. Fangs inched closer. *Closer.*

"Ava!" Madigan shouted from a million miles away.

A trickle of blood ran down the side of my face as the Brain Eater's upper fangs grazed my forehead, its putrid breath engulfing me as I stared into the abyss of its monstrous throat.

My arms shook, my biceps on fire, the last of my strength seeping from me.

Shift... please... But I knew I couldn't.

This was it. This was the end. I couldn't fight it any longer, and I let out a final whimper.

"Hey!" Another voice. Familiar.

The Brain Eater looked up, and with a *whoosh,* its head flew from its body. Blood burst from its neck, dousing my face, filling my eyes, nose, and mouth. A hand seized me from the back of my lapel, yanking me to my feet, the body of the decapitated Brain Eater falling away.

Wiping blood from my eyes, I stared into the face of my rescuer. *Hiero.*

He grinned at me, then, with another swing of the bloodied axe in his hand, decapitated a Brain Eater gnashing its teeth at Madigan, pinned against the cave wall. The remaining Brain Eater shrieked with unmistakable rage before darting to the back of the cave. Hiero launched the axe after it. A wet *whack* as it hit its target, then a *thunk* as the body hit the ground.

I gasped, my lungs drinking in air, then sank to my knees, my body heaving with each breath as my mouth turned sour again, and my stomach contracted.

"Lovely," Hiero said with a dry laugh as I coughed up a burning yellow bile. "Does she always do that?"

"She is predisposed to it, yes," Madigan said through a clenched jaw, his tone dripping with annoyance. "Where the hell have you been?!"

He marched up to Hiero, fists clenched at his sides, and for a moment, I thought he was about to punch him. But instead, he wrapped his arms around Hiero and pulled him into a tight embrace, burying his face in his neck.

"Sorry, guys," Hiero said, though he sounded more amused than sorry. "A couple of Brain Eaters ambushed me while I was making supper. Next thing I know, I'm waking up at the back of this cave. Full of bodies. Some fresh. Others... less fresh..."

The idea of a stack of corpses piled up at the end of the tunnel twisted my already sore stomach, but Madigan was unfazed, immediately heading to the back and returning with food and water. He handed me a bruised, mushy apple, but I was so ravenous I ate it, core and all.

Thank fuck for these rest stops. I didn't want to think about what would have happened if there hadn't been supplies.

Only after making sure I'd eaten did Madigan scavenge among the body parts, setting upon a severed leg like a fly on shit. After several wet, sickening gulps, Hiero smacked it out of his hands.

"That's enough," he said in a firm tone that was the utmost contrast to his usual jovial, carefree inflection.

Though Madigan glared up at his former lover, he wiped the blood from his chin and stood upright, colour returning to his face.

Hiero retrieved the axe from the Brain Eater's back. "I'll get a fire going. Lucky I found this with the other supplies." He tossed the axe up into the air, catching it by its handle. "Just been sharpened too. Better keep it in case we find any more of these bastards," he said in a casual voice, like we were discussing a round of Fortnite instead of a near-death experience.

"What happened to Dominic?" Madigan asked, examining one of the Brain Eaters.

"Dominic?"

"The Brain Eater we were escorting to the Nest."

"No idea. Isn't he with you?"

"No. By the time we reached the farm, he'd disappeared, and the van burnt down."

Hiero shrugged. "Maybe the Brain Eaters that attacked me were trying to rescue him or something?"

Madigan's hand drifted to his cuff as he shook his head. "No. That can't be it."

"Why not?" I asked, my voice rough. Though Madigan appeared to be making a rapid recovery, I certainly wasn't.

Madigan cocked his head to one side, running his thumb down his jawline in thought. "That's not how Brain Eaters behave. It shows a level of intelligence they do not possess."

A moment of silent thought before Hiero said tentatively, "Perhaps someone is thinking on their behalf?"

"*What?*" I asked, not bothering to hide my growing irritation at his cryptic words. "What do you mean, '*thinking on their behalf*'?"

Madigan and Hiero shared a look before Hiero said, "Well, Soul Suckers have a low-level psychic ability. They can control creatures without a mind of their own. Such as Brain Eaters, or Husks."

"But they can only follow simple commands, such as to eat, sleep, or attack," Madigan said, narrowing his eyes. "Could they *really* start a fire? They certainly wouldn't conceive of rescuing someone."

"Normally, I'd agree with you. But what if the Soul Sucker giving the commands had the crown?"

I opened my mouth, but seeing what I was about to ask, Madigan said, "The Vampires' Crown is worn by the liege lord or lady. It amplifies their psychic ability, allowing them to control any number of mindless beings. It's also how they communicate with vampires who have left the Nest. Recently, the Liege Lady sent out a message to all vampires reminding them of the upcoming election and to return to cast their vote."

"And perhaps that same liege lady is growing concerned about her position? Concerned enough to command an attack on her opposition," Hiero said, folding his arms.

"Though I wouldn't put it past her, that still wouldn't explain how she would have commanded them to set a fire, release Dominic, and kidnap you." Madigan bowed his head, pinching the bridge of his nose. "As powerful as the crown is, can it give commands that complex?"

"Who cares?" I said, and both vampires whipped their heads around to fix me with incredulous stares. "It's great a little sip of blood fixes you right up, Madigan. But I'm not so lucky. Have you both forgotten that I nearly just *died*?" The last word echoed throughout the cave.

Madigan's mouth dropped open. "My apologies. Hiero, get a fire going. This is a discussion for another time."

I cleaned the blood from my face and hair as best I could as the vampires got to work: Madigan making a bed with the cave's supply of furs and cushions, and Hiero building a fire. Meanwhile, I fought off the sleep trying to claim me until I could settle among the furs with Madigan and Hiero.

Warm. Safe. Glad to be with them. *Both* of them.

CHAPTER NINE

Despite my exhaustion, I slept poorly. I snuggled into Madigan, seeking his body heat, but the chill from the hard stone floor made me shiver so violently it hurt, and a creeping sense that I would never thaw out gnawed at me. That is, until Hiero lay beside me. He tensed, like he was waiting for the command to back off. But I didn't. And he nestled closer. So close, his hot breath caressed the back of my neck.

If it hadn't been for the dream, I wouldn't have known I'd slept. As pleased as I was that it wasn't *Ivan* visiting me in my dreams, it was still awkward waking up beside Hiero when it had been *he* who'd visited me instead. To my relief, he'd not been as violent or cruel as Ivan. Quite the opposite. He'd been friendly. *Too* friendly.

I forced the dream to the back of my mind, hoping it would sink into the depths of amnesia. I couldn't bear the idea of Hiero's smug grin if he discovered I was fantasising about him, consciously or otherwise.

After a breakfast of soggy fruit and a dose of blood for the vampires, we resumed our journey to the Nest. Though not as tiring as the last leg, it was still made unpleasant by the slushy snow and the damp lingering in my boots, numbing my toes almost instantly.

As we walked, the vampires discussed the mystery of Dominic's whereabouts and who started the fire. It was one of the rare occasions I didn't mind being excluded from the conversation, having nothing to contribute. But after a night of travelling and settling down in another abandoned hut—sturdier than the last—I'd grown tired of the same conversation, now going around in circles.

Fortunately, the following night, their discussion changed, and I listened intently while they reminisced.

"Private Turner never recovered from his public flogging. On a mental level, I mean," Hiero said, tending to a small fire as we prepared for another day sheltering in a miserable cave. Both vampires were more subdued than usual. Neither the hut we'd stayed in nor this cave contained Husks, much to their disappointment.

"I don't think *I* recovered, either." Madigan looked gaunt as he relived the memory, dragging a palm over his face, eyes turned downward.

"Good thing we weren't caught, or we'd have suffered the same."

"Don't." Madigan raised a hand to silence his friend. I'd seen him do this before; he'd done it to me when I'd been his familiar, and the simple gesture had always been so authoritative I'd obeyed. Hiero, on the other hand, ignored it.

"What?" Hiero raised an eyebrow. But Madigan's focus wasn't on Hiero. His gaze was locked on me. Hiero followed it, his eyes narrowing slightly before flicking back to Madigan. "You're not embarrassed of me, are you?"

Madigan flushed. "N-no! Not embarrassed. It's just... a little awkward."

It took me a few seconds to glean what they were talking about, but then realisation struck me: by '*getting caught*', they were referring to their relationship during a time when homophobia ran rampant.

"Don't mind me," I said with a wave of my hand. "I realise you had a life before meeting me, Madigan. It's only awkward if you make it awkward."

Hiero grinned widely, making his cheeks dimple, and for a second, heat crept over me, a flash of that dream rising to the surface of my mind.

"See, Ava doesn't care." Hiero turned to face me. "You're pretty open-minded for a human."

"I'm a shifter, not human. And of course I am. It's the twenty-first century."

Hiero snorted. "From my experience, it makes no difference what year it is. Humans don't change."

"Is that *your* prejudice talking?" I said, smirking.

Hiero raised his eyebrows, mouth open, unable to retort with anything but a stammering, "U-uh."

Madigan threw back his head with a roar of laughter. The sound, so beautiful yet foreign, made both Hiero and me stare at him. "She's got you there," he said, wiping a tear from his eye once he'd calmed down.

My stomach squirmed with an odd combo of satisfaction and angst as Hiero said in a voice that failed to hide his irritation, "Yes, she has. Can't argue with that. I see why Len is fond of you. He's always enjoyed a challenge."

Madigan massaged his cheeks from his outburst. "A challenge. Yes, that's certainly what you *both* are. Honestly, Ava, I've never seen Hiero rendered speechless before. Looks like he's finally met his match."

"Not many shifters have the nerve to talk to vampires like this." Hiero poked the fire with a stick, sending a jet of embers upward, reflecting in his dark brown eyes.

"You've met a lot of shifters, then?" I countered.

His focus locked on me through the flames, a devilish grin spreading his lips, displaying his perfect teeth. "Not many. But enough to know they shift in a life-or-death situation. Why didn't *you* shift when the Brain Eater was about to bite off that pretty little face of yours?"

I flushed. "Well, after shifting three times without eating or sleeping I—"

"Three times?" Hiero wrinkled his nose. "That's it?"

"How many times can *you* shift, Hiero?"

"That's not really my thing, is it? If you want a display of vampiric power, I'd be more than happy to oblige. But shifting is what you're meant to be good at, right?"

"My guy, I've been a shifter for about a week."

"So, you can't even shapeshift into a hybrid yet? What even are you? A mouse?"

"Hiero." Madigan's mirth vanished as quickly as it had appeared, his voice quiet but dangerous. "Back off. I mean it."

But Hiero waved a hand dismissively. "Ava knows I'm only messing, don't you, Ava?"

I gave him a thin, sly smile. "I'm a scorpion, actually. And yes, I know you're only joking. Only an idiot would piss off a scorpion shifter, and you can't be *that* dumb."

I kept up the charade that it had only been banter until I had a moment alone.

As the vampires set up the blankets for another day's rough sleeping, I took myself off and wished with all my might to do something other than simply shifting back and forth. Billy, the spider shifter, could sprout multiple limbs from his torso, so surely, *I* could too. But no matter how hard I focused, wished, and prayed, my form remained the same.

Perhaps I needed a shifter or witch to guide me, and for the briefest of seconds, I wondered if I'd made a mistake leaving the coven behind. But when Hiero's laugh carried from within the cave, I pulled myself together.

Imagine if I had stayed behind, and the two of them had reunited and...

I grimaced at the idea of them being together without me.

No, you're definitely where you're supposed to be.

But I couldn't shrug off the nagging doubt that if I was going to level up in this bizarre world of supernaturals and magic, blagging it wouldn't work.

A hand shook me awake. My neck clicked as I rose from my position nestled against Madigan. Again, Hiero had slept behind me, and though I hated to admit it, it was something I could have got used to, despite our earlier tension.

I rubbed bleary eyes to find Hiero crouched beside me.

"Wakey-wakey," he whispered.

"Eggs and bakey?"

Hiero had already re-lit our fire, a couple of animals roasting on spikes. Meat wasn't usually what I craved after waking, but after several days since a decent meal and vomiting multiple times, I salivated as soon as the smell wafted me.

"It's rat, actually," Hiero said, his nose scrunching.

"Mmm, my favourite."

I jostled Madigan to wake him, but he took longer to stir. Leaving him to get up in his own time, I joined Hiero, who held out a skewered rat towards me. At first, I merely grazed the meat from the bones with my teeth, but once the sweet, nutty flavour coated my tongue, I lost my squeamishness and devoured the creature.

Madigan emerged from the cave, dark shadows beneath his eyes, and his skin sallow.

"It's all right, mate," Hiero said. "We'll reach the Nest tonight and get some blood inside you. That'll perk you right up."

Madigan nodded, lowering himself beside me and rubbing his temples. Though he ate the food presented to him, he didn't pick the bones clean as Hiero and I had done, but rather nibbled at it.

I scrutinised Hiero. "How come you don't look so"—I paused, picking my words carefully—"tired?"

Hiero swiped his lower lip with his tongue before answering, "A potion: Witch's Tears. Without it, I'd look as tired as Len. I *am* as tired; I just don't look it."

Though concerned for Madigan's welfare, in their weakened state, the vampires moved at a lethargic pace, and I kept up without exhausting myself.

Before long, we discovered the remains of a drystone wall, sitting out of place among the trees. And then another. And another. The further into the forest we explored, the more walls appeared, until there were so many, they appeared to be the ruins of a settlement reclaimed by nature. I whirled about, looking at the strange structures with fascination.

"What used to be here?" I asked.

"According to our records," Hiero said, "it used to be a human village."

"Your records?"

"Yes, I can show you, if you like? They're down here." Hiero pointed to a circular structure: an old well. I peered down into its depths.

"Hilarious," I said with a roll of my eyes.

"No, I'm serious." Hiero flashed me one of those infuriatingly handsome smirks. "This is the entrance to the Vampires' Nest."

I looked at Madigan, who nodded.

"Not what you expected?" Hiero asked.

"Not exactly. I was expecting perhaps a grand metal gate or something."

"There *is* a gate, and it *is* grand. But first, it's down the well."

My stomach twinged. I wasn't afraid of cramped spaces or the dark, but the idea of jumping down the well made my chest tighten. "How far down is it?"

"I wouldn't jump," Hiero warned me. "You'd break your legs. We'll climb down. Think you can manage that?"

I felt as though I grew a couple of inches taller as I said, "Climbing is *easy*." Glad for the excuse to put Hiero in his place after calling me out, I shifted.

"Will she be all right?" Hiero's voice vibrated above me as I scuttled along the forest floor to the well and began the descent.

"Yes," Madigan said. "You shouldn't underestimate her. Come on, let's go down."

My hook-like feet made it an effortless task for me, and my scorpion senses allowed me to 'see' as I crawled. It was, indeed, deep, the distance appearing to stretch further now I was so tiny.

I shifted once I reached the bottom to find the vampires waiting for me, Madigan holding my clothes towards me, and Hiero wearing a cheeky grin. His eyes flicked downward for a moment before returning to my face.

"Cold?" he asked in a tone of mock innocence.

"Hiero!" Madigan gave him a backhanded slap across the arm, his weakness breaking down the last of his composure.

Though I could handle Hiero's ribbing, having Madigan come to my defence on this occasion ignited a fire within my heart. And yet, though I tried to lie to myself, part of me *liked* the moment I felt Hiero's eyes on me.

It's his glamour making you feel that way... probably.

I covered myself with my clothes. "Pervert. Turn around while I get dressed."

Once I was decent, we headed into a tunnel, Madigan taking me by the hand, and leading me through the darkness.

"Ah, here we are!" Hiero's voice echoed ahead. "I knew we'd find one eventually." A scraping noise, and then a burst of light as Hiero held a torch aloft, the familiar scent of burning wafting down the tunnel.

"You may have some trouble adjusting to the light—or lack of—in the Vampires' Nest," Madigan said. "But you won't be in *total* darkness."

"Come and look at this, Ava!" Hiero interrupted, beckoning me with a wave of his arm. "You wanted to see the records. Here they are!" He held the torch to the wall, and at first, I didn't understand what he meant, but as I drew closer, the markings scrawled onto the stone—not too dissimilar to cave paintings—became clear. Tiny figures in different colours, some red, some black, and some white.

"What is this?" I asked.

"Our history. Look." Hiero pointed at the figures. "These white ones are the Brain Eaters." A huddle of white stickmen beside a pile of black stickmen. The image of the Brain Eaters clawing at the dead bodies flashed into my mind, and I squirmed as a ripple of dread ran through me. "And the red ones—over here—are the Blood Drinkers."

I glanced at Madigan standing a few feet behind us, examining another of the markings. "Where are the Soul Suckers?" I asked.

"They don't appear until later." Hiero jerked his head down the tunnel and we walked further, and soon a stickperson painted in purple appeared, surrounded by red and white figures on their knees.

"The first Soul Sucker was treated as a god, or so we believe. But soon"—he gestured to another painting in which the purple and red figures stood side by side—"our people learned Soul Suckers are merely a different type of vampire. Not superior. Not a god. Just different." He then added in a low voice, "But that doesn't stop them from winning every damn election."

He chewed his lip for a moment, side-eyeing me, and I could practically see the secret he was trying to keep bottled up rise to the surface before it spilled.

"Just between us, that's another reason I take the Witch's Tears for my glamour. Our people have grown so used to having a Soul Sucker as their liege lord, I think I stand a better chance if everyone believes I am one."

"They don't know you're a Blood Drinker?"

He shook his head.

I frowned, squinting at Hiero as though seeing him for the first time. "I won't tell anyone."

"Thanks. I appreciate it." He smiled, the corners of his eyes creasing, and dimples forming in his cheeks.

Damn, that smile...

"But don't expect the teasing to stop," he added, giving me a nudge with his elbow. "It's in my nature."

"Of course. Just don't dish out what you can't receive back."

We walked further, and soon Hiero pointed out images of more black stick figures surrounded by walls. "These are the ruins. It looks like there was a settlement built upon the Nest's entrance. Our scholars have theorised that it was set up by our people: a sort of human farm. Others think it was built as a residence for our familiars. And some believe we had a mutually beneficial relationship with human settlers. They gave us their blood, and we offered protection from various threats. But for whatever reason, the settlement was abandoned, and over time destroyed. It does, however, prove useful in finding the entrance to the Nest."

"You've certainly been studying," Madigan said, joining us, eyebrow cocked as though suspicious. "How unlike you."

Hiero smiled again, though it wasn't the charming, almost seductive smile I was getting used to. His lips were too thin, and his eyes flinty.

"When you left, I found I had a lot of free time on my hands," he said, his voice tense, before plastering on his usual grin and taking me by the arm. "Now, if you look over here..."

He guided me further down the tunnel, Madigan following behind in silence as Hiero explained what each painting meant, and the further we walked, the more detailed the paintings became, changing in style until we reached modern events laid out like a comic strip.

"This last one is Liege Lady Franziska." He pointed to the image of a beautiful woman with raven-black hair, blue eyes, and a beauty spot just above her lip. "This was painted when she won the last election. And here"—he pointed to a blank spot on the wall beside her—"is where my painting will go when I win."

The walls remained blank from that point onward, but it didn't stop Hiero from talking at length about the vampires' history—the famous battles against the Hallows, other supernatural hunters, and even other supernaturals themselves—until we reached a heavy wooden gate, twice my height, set into rock. He slammed his fist into the gate twice, and a square peep hole slid open. A pale, feminine face peered through at us.

"State your name and purpose," she said, sighing, unable to hide her boredom.

"Hieronymus Blackford. I am returning from my expedition."

The sound of the guard flicking through paper reached me through the door. "Yes, no problem. Who is with you?"

"Leonard Madigan and Ava Monroe. Len is a returning vampire. Don't bother looking for his name. He left twenty years ago and has lost his house and possessions. But he's returned to vote, as is his right."

"And the other one?"

"Ava is a shifter. She's come to speak with the Liege Lady at my request."

"A shifter?" The guard's voice picked up, her boredom turning into curiosity. "Here to speak with the Liege Lady?"

"At my request," he repeated.

"You... you vouch for her, Hiero?" The use of his nickname suggested the guard had only been pretending to not know him—or at least, was just doing her job in asking for his name.

"I do."

The guard paused, her voice an indistinct murmur as she spoke to someone else, perhaps asking for their opinion.

I swallowed, playing with my fingers as I awaited an answer, the prospect of turning back just as daunting as heading into the Nest itself.

My heart leapt as a loud scraping noise issued from the other side, and the gate lifted. Two guards stood in a small room, but I couldn't glimpse them clearly as we stepped inside, the gate dropping and plunging us into darkness. A heartbeat before a second portcullis lifted ahead of us with a clicking sound.

Clutching Madigan's arm, I stepped into the Vampires' Nest, and *gasped*.

CHAPTER TEN

The cavern was immense, the vampires' civilisation built into an abyssal pit. From our position atop a steep flight of stone steps, I could almost make out the entire city. A low amber light from a monumental clock tower set in the very centre cut through the darkness, its face glowing a deep orange, flickering as if made of fire. And beneath the face, a symbol of a crescent moon shone so white it could have been reflecting real moonlight. The tower, like the architecture surrounding it—colossal mansions and what was unmistakably a palace—appeared to be made of black stone and metal, twisting into serpentine structures. And surrounding them all was a city wall that rivalled Kinwich's, though *this* city wall wasn't in ruins.

The buildings outside the wall were nothing more than shacks, only marginally better than the shepherd's hut we'd stayed in; at least these had four walls and a roof. Though admittedly, I doubted they'd remain that way, already rotting and ready to collapse. I figured the wall was to keep the peasants out of the wealthy city centre.

Perhaps vampires and humans aren't so different.

Madigan squeezed my shoulder. "Welcome to the Vampires' Nest." He couldn't hide the strain in his voice. As jaw-dropping as the Vampires' Nest was, it was anything but welcoming in appearance.

I could have stood there for hours, just taking it all in—everything from the hum of voices emanating from below, to the musty scent of decay and damp stone. But Hiero had already started down the steps before looking back and jerking his head, encouraging us to accompany him into the city, and before nerves could start twisting my guts, I followed.

We'd barely reached the first row of shabby huts when we found ourselves weaving through narrow alleyways, my boots squelching in thick muck stinking of ammonia. It was darker now, the clock tower's light unable to reach us in these little rat runs, and I bumped into Hiero as he came to an abrupt halt to allow several vampires to pass.

"Careful now," Hiero said, smirking down at me over his shoulder.

"I can't see too well." I squinted back, his features only illuminated by a flicker of candlelight from a nearby window.

He took my hand, just as Madigan had done when guiding me through the woodland, and my stomach gave a traitorous flutter.

"Then I will be your eyes," he said silkily.

My muscles tightened as a couple of passing vampires turned their heads, nostrils flaring as they caught my scent... but they lost interest and continued on their way.

The tension eased, and I felt Madigan's warm presence behind me as he said, "Uncanny, remember?"

I flashed him a smile before Hiero set off again.

The bodies of other vampires slid past mine as the alleyways became busier, and soon I was gasping for air, the scent of body odour thick in my nose, rough wool and leather brushing past my face.

We rounded a corner, and again Hiero came to a sudden stop, pressing his body against a wall to allow another group of vampires' passage. He pinned me to the wall too, pressing just below my ribcage, though he would feel my heart reverberating through my body all the same; he may as well have placed his hand on my chest.

He glanced down at me again as we waited for the horde to pass. "Hanging in there?"

I nodded. "Just about."

"It won't be much further."

Soon the alleyways widened, and though it wasn't the posh side of town, at least there was room to breathe. I could almost ignore the rats skittering across my boots and the stench from the slimy ground, which I suspected was a concoction of more than just mud.

As we arrived at a town square, there was finally enough space to have a proper look at the other vampires. All dressed completely differently. Some, like Madigan, appeared like they'd stepped out of Victorian England, whereas others wore jeans or leather, like I was examining a muddled timeline of fashion trends throughout the twentieth century. Even the way they spoke was a cacophony of accents and languages. One vampire spoke as though reciting Shakespeare, yet bellowed his words in the manner of a football hooligan.

"He does that on purpose," Hiero said when I asked if he knew him. "Yes, he is from the era, but he can speak modern English if he wants to." He then raised his voice, and said to the vampire, "Evening's Greetings, Edward!"

"Evening's Greetings!" Edward doffed his hat with a sweeping bow.

I forced myself to keep a straight face. Everything about him—from his speech, to his clothes, and even his pointed beard and moustache—was so stereotypical it seemed forced.

"Ah! I see thou art not alone." Another bow. "Kinsmen, mayhap? Come they to lend thee succour? Or peradventure to witness the Battles of Blood?"

"Friends, aye," Hiero said, attempting Edward's style but with all the fluency of a tourist reading from a guidebook. "Uhh... I do wanteth their support, but... erm... these guys hath come to... uhh... speaketh to the Liege Lady."

"Then I shall not delay thee. Go forth, and may fortune favour thy cause!"

As we moved on, Hiero lowered his voice again. "Daft old codger. Still, he likes me."

He led us to a building beside the town square: timber-framed and leaning slightly to one side. I squinted, just able to make out 'The Lucky Lantern Inn' in faded gold paint above the door. Despite the three floors it boasted, figures poured outside, squeezing past each other for entry. Hiero approached someone with their back to us standing in the doorway. He put a hand on their shoulder.

"Room for one more? Well, three more, actually." He tossed his head back towards me and Madigan.

"Lord Blackford! Yes, take my place." The vampire nudged the guy in front of him. "Move, it's Lord Blackford." The next vampire in the crowd scrutinised Hiero with a sceptical expression, then their mouth dropped open, gawking. Without a word, he too moved aside.

Hiero parted the crowd of vampires all the way to the bar, Madigan and me following.

I was blasted with sound the moment I crossed the threshold. Laughter, rowdy chatter, and the thunk of metal tankards against wooden tables. Almost muffled out entirely was the crackle from the fireplace, framing an enormous black iron pot, its lid rattling as something bubbled inside, the scent wafting from it making my mouth water.

"Two blood shots, please," Hiero said to the barkeep, raising his voice to be heard over the babble and setting a column of silver coins on the bar. "Got any rooms?"

"Afraid not, Lord Blackford," the barkeep said, his brows drawn and voice wavering. "We've been booked for weeks. Even the barn is full. With the Battles of Blood coinciding with the elections—"

"It's not a problem." Hiero brushed aside the barman's apology with a wave of his hand before quirking an eyebrow at Madigan and me. "You'll just have to stay with me." He flashed us dazzlingly white teeth before turning back to the barman. "What's on the menu tonight?"

"Mutton stew, Lord Blackford. But if there was anything specific you wanted—"

"Mutton stew is fine. Right, you two?"

"I'll eat anything," I said as my stomach gave a rumble. Madigan nodded in agreement.

"Three, please." Hiero placed more coins on the bar. They were unlike anything I'd seen before, reminding me of chocolate coins sold at Christmas. I touched one to see if it was real, and immediately noted the weight.

"What sort of currency is this?" I asked.

"Our own," Hiero said cryptically, but when he noticed my frown, he huffed and said, "Look, don't expect me to explain the exchange rate or anything; that's not my area of expertise. But if you're really interested, I'll take you to the Blood Bank after this to get your money exchanged."

"Must we?" Madigan asked, and there was a stiffness in his voice that piqued my interest. His eyes bored into Hiero as if trying to send him a silent, urgent message, his shoulders tensing.

"What's wrong with the Blood Bank?" I asked, my sights flicking from one vampire to the other to see which would crack first.

"Do you want to tell her, or shall I?" Hiero asked, his voice so innocent it immediately aroused suspicion.

Madigan hesitated, then said at last, "I will, but after we've found a table."

The barman set down two shot glasses filled with the thick red liquid I'd grown well accustomed to, and the two vampires knocked them back.

Madigan let out a refreshed sigh, a little colour returning to his cheeks, and the darkness beneath his eyes seemed to lighten. "Ahh, I needed that." He licked his lips, eyeing the drop remaining at the bottom of the glass.

"Would you like another?" Hiero asked. "It's been a while since your last."

Madigan bit his lip. I couldn't tell if his exhausted appearance was from the lack of blood or the journey itself. And it was only now I registered how filthy he was, red and brown smeared across his skin and clothes. I must have looked a state too, but no one gave us a second glance.

"*One* more," Madigan said at last.

The barman, who'd been listening, poured another shot for them both and said, "If you can find somewhere to sit, I'll bring your meals over."

Though still covered in dirt and blood, Madigan perked up after the second shot, resembling the handsome, healthy young man I'd always known.

Hiero led the way as we searched for a place to sit. Rather than individual tables, there were long benches lined with mismatched chairs and stools, at which vampires sat in clusters of about four or five. Some even perched *on* the benches to sit with their friends. I only now realised that nearly everyone was male, only spotting two women among the crowd.

"Where are all the girls?" I asked Hiero.

"You don't find as many female vampires. And those that exist tend to live on the other side of the wall."

"Why's that?"

"Franziska favours them for high-ranking positions or her personal guard. Of course, there are exceptions. Some prefer a simpler life, and others like to travel, but most do well for themselves. Even those who work in the Lover's Sanctum can usually afford a home in the inner circle."

A group of vampires at the end of one bench saw us approach and, after seeing Hiero, got to their feet, wooden chair legs scraping against the stone floor.

Hiero, smiling pleasantly and giving them a nod of thanks, took a seat. Following his lead, I took the chair opposite him. But Madigan stood at the foot of the bench, his spine rigid, eyes darting between Hiero and the vampires that had given their seats, as though waiting for them to change their minds and demand them back. It wasn't until Hiero kicked the stool beside him and jerked his head towards it that Madigan joined us.

"This is too bizarre," he said as he lowered himself down.

"Things were different when you were last here, weren't they?" Hiero laughed.

"Well, yes. We were nobodies back then."

"You're still a nobody, Len," Hiero teased. "It's all right, I haven't let the power go to my head. I still remember who my friends are."

They gazed at each other, a moment that lingered just a little too long.

I drummed my fingers on the table. "Sooo... about this Blood Bank, then?"

Madigan sighed, his shoulders slumping. "Very well." He closed his eyes as he took a steeling breath. "The Blood Bank itself isn't the problem. In fact, it's integral to our survival in the Nest. As well as exchanging money, it sells empty vials and needles for blood harvesting, and handles the distribution of blood to establishments such as this to ensure there's enough to go around. At least, in theory."

I couldn't stop the snort of sceptical laughter. "*In theory*. Isn't that always the case with valuable resources?" Vampires and humans had a lot more in common than they'd like to admit.

A line etched between Madigan's brows as his eyes dropped to a spot on the table, glazing over like he could see into the past.

"When I left the Nest twenty years ago, it was to find a familiar. There were blood shortages. Prices inflated, and on our wages, Hiero and I *needed* a familiar. We couldn't regularly afford vials from the bank or shots from the bar. But there was... an accident."

My stomach twisted, already predicting how this story would turn.

"Her name was Roz." His voice cracked as he spoke her name. "I didn't know her well. Certainly not as well as I should have, given how long she was in our service, but she was pleasant enough. Far too sweet to meet the fate she did. We'd run out of harvesting equipment, and Hiero had to work."

I caught how Hiero shifted uncomfortably in his seat, but Madigan continued.

"So, I kept Roz with me. We'd lost our previous familiar to kidnappers—sadly common in the Nest—and I wasn't prepared to lose another."

"I guess when there are blood shortages, it's a bad time to be a familiar," I said, the tightening in my stomach now spreading up to my chest.

"Exactly," Madigan said, nodding gravely. "Perhaps I should have left her at home. Maybe she'd have been kidnapped. Maybe not. We will never know. But I brought her to the Blood Bank and—" He swallowed, his Adam's apple bobbing. "I don't blame my people for what they did. They were blood-starved, and there's no reasoning with vampires when they become a mob."

He paused, fists clenching until his knuckles turned white.

"I clung to her hand as if I stood a chance of saving her. Like if I held on tight enough, she wouldn't be ripped apart. But it's the sound of her fingers snapping like dried twigs in my fist that still haunts my dreams some nights. I wonder if her death would have been swifter—less painful—if I had just let her go."

I touched his forearm, and he turned to face me, eyes glassy but focused.

"We don't need to go to the Blood Bank," I said, offering a smile that I hoped would be reassuring.

"And you don't need to worry about blood shortages anymore," Hiero said. "Or even prices, for that matter. They've halved since you were last here."

Madigan narrowed his eyes. "How?"

"Greater supply, thanks to yours truly. Why do you think I'm so popular? That's how I earned my lordship, actually."

I caught the flicker across Madigan's face—was it disbelief? Or admiration? But before I could acknowledge the pang of envy, three bowls of stew were set down before us, the familiar scent from the iron pot now wafting tantalisingly close.

"Good timing," Hiero said, rubbing his hands together in a display that didn't quite mask his relief at the interruption.

My lips stung as I licked hot, salty gravy from them; I'd not realised how chapped they'd become. The meat was tough and the vegetables sloppy, but after surviving on rats it tasted delicious, and I wondered if I could blag Hiero to buy me another bowl.

Hiero and Madigan continued discussing what had changed since Madigan had last been here. As interesting as it was to listen in, there was so much hubbub I found myself easily distracted.

A group of vampires beside us were engrossed in a card game I'd never seen before. It didn't take long to pick up on the basic premise—summoning creatures and casting spells—but they would barter between turns, putting up more of those silver coins, small vials of blood, or even little trinkets as bargaining chips.

One of the few women sat behind me, no less than five men vying for her attention, occasionally topping up her flagon.

"Got in last night," said another vampire from the table directly behind Madigan and Hiero. He was talking with two others in loud voices that carried over the din of chatter. "It was a long journey. I kept getting distracted, y'see."

"Women again, Boris?" asked one of his companions.

"I'm irresistible. What can I say?" He glanced over his shoulder to the female vampire behind me, allowing me a glimpse of his face.

The instant I saw his eyes, a prickling blaze swept through me.

His features practically shimmered with beauty. Those entrancing eyes were forest green, almost too vivid to be real. Black stubble framed a chiselled jaw, a darker patch in his cleft chin.

But it was his lips that *demanded* my attention.

I *knew* it was a glamour; I *knew* he had to be a Soul Sucker. But I couldn't tear my gaze away, no matter how much I wanted to.

I'd been around Latisha and the witches—and now Hiero too—long enough to recognise a glamour. And occasionally they had given me a quick flash of its power. But never had I encountered it being used so deliberately, *forcefully*, like this. Even the demon, Lascivious, hadn't used his glamour in such a direct way, simply exuding it, like it was too much for him to contain.

The female vampire behind me couldn't have spotted Boris, too many suitors keeping her occupied, and so never made that fatal eye contact, as I had.

It wasn't until Boris turned to face his friends that I caught my breath, the glamour losing its grip, and the heat spreading through me turned deathly cold.

My face burned as I realised Hiero and Madigan were watching me, having stopped mid-conversation. I couldn't bring myself to catch Madigan's eye, though I noticed he and Hiero wore identical drawn expressions.

"The last one I had was a screamer," Boris said, continuing his conversation, unaware he now had an audience. "Shame she was so flimsy, really. Humans are just so *breakable*." The way Boris laughed made my skin crawl. I clenched my fists in my lap, every muscle in my body tensing.

"That's why I prefer a nice vampire girl," said his companion with a wave of his hand. "Werewolves aren't bad either, if you can stand the smell."

Boris made a disgusted noise at the mention of werewolves. "It's *because* humans are breakable that makes them fun. Once you've broken the pelvis, they can't do anything to stop you."

My blood rang in my ears and my nails cut into my palms as I fought the queasiness now churning inside me.

Madigan reached for my hands beneath the bench, taking them in his own. Our eyes met, and in that moment, I knew he understood what had happened—that it wasn't my fault. I squeezed his hands.

"This girl," Boris continued, "lasted a long time—I'm talking *hours*. Wasn't 'til I ripped her legs off that she finally died."

Boris's companions broke out into sniggers of laughter.

My stomach lurched, the mutton stew threatening to make a reappearance.

"That's fucking *evil*," I said under my breath.

Madigan's grip tightened, his eyes darkening as a muscle worked in his jaw.

Chair legs scraped the floor as Hiero sprang to his feet and slammed Boris's head down on the bench. A glass smashed. Broken shards ripped the side of Boris's face with a crunching, grinding noise that set my teeth on edge.

Boris's companions jumped to his defence, but froze upon seeing who had attacked him.

"L-Lord Blackford!" Boris managed to choke out.

"Boris," Hiero growled in his ear. "That's not a conversation for the dinner table."

"What the fuck do you care?" Boris snapped, unfazed by the broken glass, but was unable to push Hiero off him.

"We can't survive without humans. You ought to show them a little more respect." Hiero slackened his grip, and Boris's stool clattered to the floor as the Soul Sucker squared up to Hiero.

"Respect?!" One side of his face was a terrifying mess of blood and glass, but Hiero didn't so much as flinch as Boris snarled, "They're cattle! Barely able to think for themselves, motivated by simple, primitive urges. Pull some shit like this again, Blackford, and I'll withdraw my support. You've already lost my vote. Don't lose my business, too."

"You think I need you?" Hiero sniggered, his lips curling into what would undoubtedly be an infuriatingly smug expression. "You wouldn't be missed. In all honesty, I envy people who don't know you."

The chatter in the inn had stopped, all eyes on Hiero and Boris.

The two stared at each other, Boris swaying like a snake trying to hypnotise its prey, while Hiero stood straight, firm, his cocky smile still set in place.

"Good luck with your operation, Blackford." And with that, Boris and his cronies pushed through the crowd and out of sight.

Silence constricted the inn, all eyes on Hiero, and it was only now his smile faltered. He cracked his neck from side to side before taking a steadying breath.

"Barkeep, for the next hour, all drinks are going on my tab!"

The silence shattered as everyone broke out into cheers and fought their way to the bar.

Hiero took his seat opposite me. "Sorry about that." He swept his auburn hair with an air of nonchalance that was almost convincing.

"That temper of yours will get you in trouble," Madigan said, shaking his head.

"You're not wrong, actually. I was bluffing when I said he wouldn't be missed. I need more Soul Suckers to support the business. Boris might have the personality of a demented baboon, but he served a purpose."

"Is there nothing I can do?" Madigan asked.

"Afraid not. I need Soul Suckers for their Husks."

"How did you overpower him like that?" Madigan asked, eyes narrowing with suspicion.

Hiero flushed. "Well... it's not just Witch's Tears I take to blend in. A strength enhancer. A speed enhancer—"

"How do you *afford* all that?"

"That's nothing. You should see my house."

I was about to ask Hiero if he'd get me a stiff drink when the crowd parted once again to allow another vampire through, and my jaw dropped as I caught sight of her.

She had to be over six feet tall, had broad shoulders and thick, powerful biceps that she must have worked *hard* for. Her curly brown hair was tied back, the loose strands pinned with a pink hair clip decorated with a sparkly-eyed kitten. But that was the only splash of colour on her.

She wore the same uniform as the guards at the portcullis: tight grey trousers, boots, and a black leather tunic that had clearly been altered to accommodate her large bust and narrow waist.

"Lord Blackford," she said, approaching, before snapping her heels together and giving a small bow of her head.

"Myla Stone." Hiero returned the gesture. "What can I do for you?"

"The Liege Lady has requested your presence in the throne room immediately." Her brown eyes then drifted over me and Madigan. "All three of you."

CHAPTER ELEVEN

Myla led us towards the city wall, weaving through the narrow streets, all those in her path side-stepping out of her way. Hiero walked alongside her, chatting conversationally, while Myla responded with one-word answers. I walked behind with Madigan.

"Where are they taking us?" I asked him in a low voice.

"The Shadowfort, where the Liege Lady resides. But I never thought she would summon us so quickly."

The city wall was even more impressive up close. Set inside it was an enormous wooden gate, perhaps not as large as the portcullis defending the Nest's entrance, but not far off. Myla opened it using a crank that looked like it should take two average-sized men to turn, allowing us through.

Hiero continued walking alongside Myla, paying little attention to his surroundings, but Madigan's pace slowed as he looked around, his mouth dropping, grey eyes widening in awe.

The difference between this side of the wall and the other was remarkable. Gone was the mud and who-knows-what-else coating the ground, replaced by cobbled stone. The houses—more like miniature castles—were three or four stories high, decorated with twisted black metal like the clock tower. But their grandeur was diminished by the palace standing in the centre, stretching so high the tips of its turrets were lost in the inky darkness of the cavern. Golden light streamed from arched windows, bathing the world outside in a warm glow. I rubbed my eyes, the light almost irritating after the gloom.

The Shadowfort. A fitting name.

Guards stood outside the palace, dressed identically to Myla, but even stood to attention they couldn't compete with her height. After a quick word from Myla, they stood aside, allowing us through a pair of ebony doors.

"Just follow the red carpet to the throne room. I'll meet you back here," Myla said, holding a door open for me.

"There's no need for that." Hiero clapped one of Myla's thick arms, making her nose wrinkle in response. "I'll escort them back to mine once we're finished."

Myla's lips twisted to one side as she regarded him. "It was a direct order from the Liege Lady."

Hiero's smile didn't waver, but the creases at his eyes slackened as he said with forced politeness, "Well, we mustn't go against a direct order, must we?"

Though I could hear Hiero and Myla's exchange, it was like it was happening half a world away, my mind consumed by the magnificence of the Shadowfort. If I'd thought the outside was impressive, it was nothing compared to the interior. The entrance hall reminded me of Kinwich cathedral: intricate carvings adorned the ceiling; spiralling columns stretched so high they made me feel giddy; and braziers cast a soft glow that lefts corners in shadow.

The castle was deathly silent, save for the soft pad of our footsteps on the velvet carpet leading to another pair of double doors, and I became hyperaware of how pristine it was.

"Should I take my boots off?" I asked, looking back along the stretch of carpet, scuffs of brown already noticeable. I spoke in a whisper, though my voice carried throughout the entrance hall, the space so dead and empty.

"Nah, Franziska's a big girl. She can cope with a little dirt," Hiero said with a dismissive wave.

"Won't it make a bad first impression?" Madigan asked, eyeing the trodden in muck.

"What? You think the Liege Lady cleans her own carpets or something?" Hiero lay a palm on each door. "Or are you stalling for time?"

He pushed them open before I could answer, and my breath froze in my lungs.

The red carpet seemed to span for miles, climbing up a flight of stairs and onto a circular, suspended platform where another guard stood waiting for us. A second flight of steps branched from the platform to a majestic throne made of the same twisted metal that decorated everything else. But the room was so expansive, and the throne so distant, I couldn't clearly see the person sitting upon it.

With a nudge from Hiero, we stepped forward. Although my heart jolted with every muddy footstep, I preferred walking on the carpet than the polished floor—so dark and shiny it looked like the carpet floated over a black abyss, and my stomach gave a horrible lurch.

We started up the first flight of steps.

The guard's crisp voice echoed throughout the throne room. "I present Lord Hieronymus Blackford and his companions, Leonard Madigan and Ava Monroe."

We reached the top of the steps. My heart was thumping so hard against my ribs it felt like it was about to burst free. Blood throbbed in my ears, and I suppressed a shudder as a cold bead of sweat trickled down the back of my neck and along my spine.

"Well, well," said a second voice. The Liege Lady's. Soft, almost musical, with a subtle, underlying tension that left my mouth dry. "Lord Blackford, thank you for escorting our guests."

Hiero strode to the centre of the circular platform to address the Liege Lady.

She reclined on her throne, leaning on one of the arms. Her dark, purple-blue dress peaked over her crossed legs, the tip of one shoe poking out beneath the ruffles of her midnight underskirt. Ivory skin contrasted with her raven hair, worn in forties-style curls. Her painting had not done her beauty justice.

"You're very welcome, my liege." Hiero dipped into a deep bow. Though unable to see his face, I could almost hear his charming smile in his voice.

The Liege Lady tilted her head and looked directly at me, smiling with scarlet lips.

"Step forward," she said with an outstretched hand.

I did as I was bid, stepping to Hiero's side.

"It's been many years since I hosted another supernatural within these walls. My name is Franziska Revay, but I think it would be more appropriate to refer to me as *my liege* while you're here."

"Yes, my liege," I said with a bow of my head. Her pleasant expression and demeanour did nothing to reassure me. On the contrary, it reminded me of Ivan. I shivered, subconsciously putting a hand to my stomach.

"Very good," she said, sinking back into her throne. One hand drifted to trace her red-nailed fingers over something sat on a plinth beside her. Something bone white, with edges so sharp it looked like it could draw blood. Her crown. "My sources tell me you're here on some sort of recruitment drive on behalf of your coven's leader."

I was about to respond when the sound of the double doors echoed throughout the throne room. Before I could so much as twitch to see who'd entered, Franziska's voice rang, "Uh-uh, eyes on me, Ava." Perhaps it was my imagination or the way her voice reverberated, but there was a dangerous edge to her tone; one that didn't match her sweet smile.

I locked my gaze on her. Though distance blurred the details of her face, a tingling sensation pulsed through my body. My every instinct told me to rip my eyes away. But I couldn't. Her glamour had ensnared me.

"You're recruiting for your coven?" she prompted after a few seconds of silence.

"Yes, that's right," I said, louder than I intended, but I had to concentrate, blocking out the sounds of those approaching from behind.

Franziska beckoned them forward, but her eyes never left mine. "Continue. State your case."

"Well, my mistress, Latisha Abara—"

"*The* Latisha Abara?"

"Uhhh... yes?" How many witches called Latisha Abara could there be? "She asked me—and my partner, Madigan—to speak with you on her behalf."

"Hmm, yes, I've heard of your partner. Friend of yours, isn't he, Lord Blackford?"

"Slightly more than that, my liege," Hiero said, raising a shoulder, smirking.

Franziska's smile widened. "How delightful. Continue, Ava."

I took a deep breath. Despite her glamour, I was growing impatient at the interruptions. But before I could speak, Franziska's guests reached the platform.

I caught them in my peripheral vision. Two women—vampires—dressed in the guard's uniform. They had something with them. Something leashed on a chain, but I couldn't see what it was, my sight pinned on the Liege Lady.

But Franziska allowed herself a glimpse. No sooner had she lowered her gaze, her hypnotic grip on me faltered, and I chanced a glance at what the guards had brought with them.

It wasn't one being. It was three. Leashed like dogs and stripped bare. Men. But these, I suspected, were no vampires. All were skeletally thin, ribs visible with each breath.

"Eyes on me, Ava," Franziska repeated, and now I was certain I'd not imagined her threatening tone.

I snapped my focus back to Franziska, concentrating on each and every word as I forced them out.

"My mistress, Latisha, was visited by her demon, Lascivious. He said the Hallows have returned, and are recruiting in our city, Kinwich. She sent me here to ask for your help. We're recruiting for our coven so we might get rid of them."

"The Hallows, you say?" she asked with mild curiosity. This was not the response I'd been expecting. Almost everyone I'd met trembled at the thought of the Hallows.

Her sights drifted from me once more, down to the prisoners. "Thank you, Sonia, I'll be right down."

A guard nodded and gripped the chains more tightly, making the metal links clink.

"Yes, the Hallows: the hunters that kill supernaturals," I said, gritting my teeth, my temper creeping to the surface again during her momentary distraction. Then, there was a hand at my shoulder—Madigan's—and it seemed to absorb my irritability, reminding me to keep my cool. "According to Lascivious, they're building their numbers, and once they have, they're coming for *all* of us. That includes you."

Franziska tilted her head to the other side, pretending to give what I'd said consideration. She didn't return her gaze to me, more interested in the prisoners. I couldn't tell if her rudeness was a relief or not.

She let out a melodramatic sigh. "The problem is, if what you say is true, it would be better for my people to remain here. You've seen for yourself how difficult it is to locate the Nest. The Hallows would never find us, nor breach our defences."

"That's not certain," Hiero said, folding his arms. "True, they haven't found us in the past. But that's because they were busy fighting the covens. The most notable being the coven of Kinwich. Who knows what would have happened without the Witch Queen and her army?"

Franziska pursed her lips, her pleasant façade slipping, and I could practically feel the crackle of annoyance in the air around her.

"That makes no difference," she said with a shrug. "This is still the safest place for vampires, and I won't send them to fight someone else's war."

"Some of your people live within covens," Madigan said, stepping forward. "Such as myself. Do we not deserve your protection? We will cast our votes within weeks. Don't you think that's something we'll consider?"

Franziska's lips were now so thin their crimson paint almost disappeared. Evidently, she wasn't used to people arguing back. "I would suggest those within covens abandon them and return to the Nest. Where you belong."

"Covens can't be abandoned!" I said, my voice rising, echoing throughout the hall. I focused on her forehead instead of her eyes, unwilling to be caught in their trap again. "Do you have any idea what we went through trying to leave Ivan's?"

"I'm aware." She traced a finger over her crown again. "I'll admit I was shocked when I could no longer feel his consciousness. It's a great disappointment the coven of Kinwich is no longer ruled by a vampire. But I suppose it's hardly surprising with the great *Latisha Abara* taking over. Almost makes your treachery seem worthwhile, doesn't it, Leonard?"

Franziska rose to her feet. "You're fortunate I won't hold your crimes against you. I understand in the human world it's kill or be killed. But it's for that exact reason I shall not assist you. I'm not sending my people to their death."

"Your people will see your cowardice for what it is," I said through a clenched jaw.

"My people care about one thing, and one thing only. *Power.*" She hitched up the long skirts of her dress and descended the steps towards us, her beauty blossoming into something almost oppressive as she drew closer.

Her features sharpened into focus. The beauty spot above her lip. The gloss of her raven hair. The contrast of her scarlet lips against flawless porcelain skin.

I kept my eyes from hers, unwilling to be lost in their ice-blue depths. But it didn't matter; her glamour bled through every pore of her, growing more potent with each step.

My cheeks burned as I found myself wondering what those lips of hers would taste like—how they'd feel, where I'd let them roam.

"And to be powerful," she said, "all I need is... one. Simple. Thing." She marched up to the three prisoners kneeling on the floor. All three raised their heads, eyes glued to her.

"A kiss."

The nearest prisoner got to his feet. Without a stitch of clothing on him, his arousal was painfully visible, but if he was embarrassed, he showed no sign of it. She cupped his face in her hands and, standing on tiptoes, leant up, and planted her lips on his.

For a second, their lips remained pressed together in a kiss that might have passed for sweet—until Franziska moaned, a sound that resembled hunger, not passion. She parted her victim's lips with hers, her tongue darting into his mouth.

Whether it was her glamour or my own morbid curiosity, I couldn't tell, but I couldn't avert my eyes, my heart dancing in a wild frenzy of fear and lust.

And as she broke away, what looked like a speck of golden light veiled in grey smoke drifted from the prisoner's mouth. The speck hovered between their lips as more of that smoke poured from him, which Franziska drank in like vapour.

"Help me!"

The voice was so quiet I thought I'd imagined it. But then I heard it again—distorted and echoing.

"Please, help me! Make her stop!"

I had to do something. But my body wouldn't move. Not my legs. Not my arms. Not even my fingers. I was stuck. And I couldn't look away. Almost as much a captive as the prisoners.

Franziska drew in the golden speck with the last wisps of smoke.

"I don't want to go! I don't want—"

She snapped her jaws closed. And swallowed.

The prisoner hung his head as his eyes glazed over.

Empty.

Franziska turned her face to me, and if I'd ever thought her beautiful before, now she was positively devastating.

An ache bloomed between my legs as I imagined all the things I both wanted and feared from her, yet a single tear tracked down my cheek. She might have hijacked my body, but my soul saw her for what she was: the living embodiment of a Venus flytrap.

And I was a fly.

"I'll forgive your rudeness," she said, smirking. She knew what she'd done to me. *Every* vampire in this room knew. "I have great respect for your mistress and do not wish to cause further divisions among the supernaturals. But while I remain liege lady, vampires will never, ever, be conscripted into someone else's war."

CHAPTER TWELVE

I sat on the stone steps leading to the Shadowfort, Madigan beside me, as Hiero and Myla bickered. Myla had tried to direct us to the portcullis the moment we'd crossed the entrance hall, but Hiero wasn't having it, insisting he take us to his manor. They argued back and forth, squabbling over semantics. But I was only half-listening, too caught up in my embarrassment to pay them much attention.

Madigan remained silent, sitting beside me with his hand resting reassuringly over mine. It was only when the tang of copper coated my tongue I realised I'd been biting my lower lip, already sore from the cold.

"Did Franziska specify *when* to take them back?" Hiero asked Myla with a smug tone.

"As soon as their business was concluded."

"Well, their business *isn't* concluded."

"Looks like they're finished to me." She gestured to where we sat. "They came for the Liege Lady's help. The Liege Lady said no."

"Len is here to vote."

"We both know that's not true."

"Do we?"

"Of course we do!"

And on they went. All the while, my eyes burned with tears I refused to shed. I'd lost enough of my dignity already. I wouldn't give Franziska the satisfaction of making me cry. Not that she would know or care. But *I* would.

"We can go home if you want to," Madigan said in a low voice so the others wouldn't hear.

I faced him—the first time I'd managed eye contact since my encounter with Franziska. I hated—*hated*—how Soul Suckers used their glamour. A method of control. Humiliation. Manipulation. I winced as Franziska swept through my mind again, the events replaying on repeat.

"Dominic is missing," Madigan said, his brows drawn into their usual frown. "And Myla is right. We asked the Liege Lady for her help. She has refused. Perhaps it's best we cut our losses and head back."

"You didn't mention Dominic to Franziska."

He gave a one-shouldered shrug. "There seemed little point. We can't very well have a trial for someone who isn't here. In fact, we may not even need a trial now. For all we know, Dominic could be a fully-fledged Brain Eater. He might even have been one of the Brain Eaters Hiero killed in that cave."

"You think so?"

He made a non-committal noise. "I wouldn't rule it out. It's not like I know how to tell them apart. And since Hiero woke up in that cave, it stands to reason that someone relocated him there. Why not Dominic himself? He was the last person with him, after all."

I slowly nodded, allowing the information to settle before I picked it apart.

"It's just a theory," Madigan added, perhaps noticing the critical pinch of my eyebrows.

It was as good a theory as any. I certainly didn't have any ideas. As far as I was concerned, Dominic was no longer my problem. But did that mean our mission was over? Already?

My gaze drifted to Hiero.

"Don't you want to vote?" I asked.

Madigan watched Hiero square up to Myla, then turned his attention back to me. "It's not my priority. I'm more concerned about you."

"Hmmm..." I didn't know what else to say. It felt wrong to speak my thoughts aloud; he was *right* to be concerned about me. My heart was racing, my usual fight-or-flight response opting for freeze instead, as the image of that smoky essence leaving the prisoner's mouth and entering Franziska's dominated my mind. "I never thought I'd see someone lose their *soul*. And that it's done with a kiss is just... is just..." Words failed me.

"Repulsive," he supplied, his grip on my hand tightening. "Truth be told, it's not *really* a kiss."

"Sure as hell looked like one to me." The way Franziska's tongue had slid inside his mouth made me recoil.

"Well, yes, Franziska enjoys playing with her food, but strictly speaking, it doesn't *require* a kiss. It is simply a name we have adopted since the soul is drawn from the mouth. It's a cruel name, romanticising a terrible fate."

"So, a Soul Sucker can kiss someone properly if they want to?" I glanced at Hiero again, still bickering with Myla.

"Yes," he said, "but remember, *any* vampire can steal your soul. Blood Suckers included—that's how Soul Suckers are created in the first place. Though admittedly, Blood Suckers don't have a glamour to assist them. That's why Soul Suckers are so dangerous—they use their glamour to make their victim *want* to kiss them, and then..." He didn't need to finish. I'd seen for myself what happened next.

"I'd not realised how powerful a glamour can be."

He sighed heavily. "I had not thought to warn you. Sometimes I forget how ignorant of our world you are."

I narrowed my eyes.

Colour flushed in Madigan's cheeks as he added in a hurry, "I don't think I articulated that particularly well. What I meant to say was—"

"It's fine. I mean, you're not wrong."

A heartbeat of silence followed, waves of awkward embarrassment radiating from him, until he said, "I've not told anyone this before, but I've been... *affected* by a powerful glamour, too. I'd been about to flee Ivan's coven—a death sentence, as you well know. But Latisha convinced me to stay."

"She *convinced* you, did she?" I allowed myself a smirk. He was trying to make me feel better by sharing his experience, yet couldn't bring himself to speak the blunt truth of it. How very like him.

The corner of his mouth twitched. "I think you have all the details you need."

My smile dropped. "Wait... Latisha used her glamour the same way Franziska used hers just now?"

"To stop me fleeing the coven, and thus, spare me a fate similar to Austin's, yes."

Austin's name hit me like a slap.

I grimaced.

His blood pooling. The snap of his spine. Ribs jutting out of a bloody mess—

"Nothing *happened* between us, you understand," Madigan added. "I told her to stop. She obliged."

I blinked, his words clashing with the gory images still stalking through my memories.

Oh! Right. Latisha's glamour.

Only then did it click: Madigan must have interpreted my wince as jealousy.

I shook off the waking nightmare, refocusing.

"I suppose the ends justify the means," I said stiffly, though the more I learned about Latisha, the warier I became. "You know what? I think we should stay at the Nest a little longer."

Madigan's brows shot upward. "Really?"

"Franziska might not want to help, but that doesn't mean we can't recruit other vampires ourselves, does it? We need to take down the Hallows. That's the most important thing. Right?"

He tilted his head, regarding me with critical eyes. He'd smell a lie, but I wasn't *lying*. Everything I'd said was true. But he didn't need to know I was stalling; I'd return when I was ready.

"If that's your wish," he said at last, and I gave him the most confident grin I could muster.

"Hiero!" I called, and he and Myla stopped mid-argument to turn their heads. "We're staying. We still have business here. Madigan wants to vote, and I can't leave without him."

Myla opened her mouth to protest, but I cut her off.

"We'll leave after the election. You can escort us out personally, as per your orders."

Myla huffed, returning her glare to Hiero. His self-satisfied smile became sickening as she drew close to him and hissed, "Fine. But if I get in trouble for this, *I'll kill you*."

She turned on her heel, and I could have sworn the ground shook with each of her stomping footsteps as she stormed off.

"Does she really mean that?" Madigan asked, cocking an eyebrow.

"Almost certainly," Hiero said, though if he was worried, he hid it well, a huge grin spread across his face. "But never mind her. I want to show you my home. We've wasted enough time already."

I feigned excitement on the short walk through the quiet cobbled streets towards Hiero's manor, set apart from its neighbours in the shadow of an industrial-looking building—a structure that felt oddly out of place.

"What's that?" Madigan asked as he noticed it, and judging from the twitch of his eye, disapproved.

"My factory," Hiero said as he skipped up the steps to his front doors. "What you see is merely the upper levels, but it's a maze below ground. You'd get lost wandering around on your own." He unlocked the doors. "Come in. Mi casa, su casa and all that."

Hiero's entrance hall was larger than the entire ground floor of my student housing. On this floor alone I counted six doors, as well as an enormous staircase to a landing that boasted three more. The walls and banisters were made of a rich, dark brown wood that shone like it had been freshly varnished, glinting in the light of flickering candles sat in sconces. One wall displayed a framed set of floor plans that I made a beeline for; I'd easily get lost in a house this size.

"Ballroom," I said, frowning as I deciphered the swirling calligraphy in blood-red ink. I *hoped* it was ink. It felt rude to ask. "Billiard room. Library—you live in the Cluedo house."

"You have a library?" Madigan asked, his voice brightening.

Hiero laughed. "I knew you'd like that. On the second floor. The others don't go there, so you can use it as you please."

"The others?"

"Talia and Xander. Didn't I tell you about them?"

I glanced at Madigan for answers, but he shook his head, staring blankly.

"No?" Hiero said in surprise. "Must have slipped my mind. Well, they work in the factory. Talia is a... I suppose... a scientist. And

Xander... well... I guess you could call it production. But they live here because we're *together*"—he winked—"if you know what I mean."

"You're in a relationship with your employees?" I asked, giving Madigan a nudge with my elbow. "Not very *professional*, is it?"

The corner of Madigan's mouth twitched as he suppressed his smile at our inside joke.

Hiero shrugged. "Fuck being professional. I can do what I like. We all can. We're not bound by the social stigmas of humanity. And they're not exactly employees, anyway. More like business partners."

He rang a small golden bell sat upon a marble table, and another vampire appeared from one of the many rooms. From his clothes and stance, I guessed he was a butler.

"Yes, Lord Blackford?"

"Take my guest's coats," Hiero said, shrugging off his own and handing it to the butler. "And have a room prepared for them. They're staying for a while. Oh, and you two"—he turned his attention to Madigan and me—"boots off. No mud on *my* carpets, thank you very much. Cassius will get them cleaned for you."

"You have staff, too?" Madigan asked as we removed our coats and shoes.

"Of course," Hiero said with a frown, like he'd asked a stupid question. "How else would a house this size stay clean? Come on, I'll give you the tour."

Though I'd studied the floor plan, it wasn't long before I was lost within the mansion. The corridors were long, narrow, and looked identical, the only things differentiating them were the paintings hanging on their panelled walls.

"There are secret passages around the place." Hiero knocked on a panel and it swung inward on hinges. He reached into the crevice and pushed a button, causing the wall opposite to click as it opened, the magnet or latch that kept it closed now released.

I peered into the pitch-black passageway. Perhaps Madigan or Hiero could see into the void, but I certainly couldn't.

"That leads to the billiard room," Hiero said. "Always useful if you're after a sneaky drink; it has its own bar. I'll show you the passages I know of, but I'd advise against looking for more. Some lead into a network of caverns and you'd be lost for years—I'm not exaggerating, either."

"You don't need to tell me twice," I said, wincing. "I'm going to get lost in the *house*, never mind caverns."

After the tour, we wound up in the lounge; a large square room, complete with roaring fireplace, leather sofas, and a drinks trolley.

"Help yourself," Hiero said, slumping into an armchair.

I immediately poured myself a drink.

"What's the matter?" Madigan asked. I looked up from what I was doing to see him take a knee beside Hiero's chair, their eyes now level. "I know that look."

Hiero ruffled his auburn locks with a sigh before turning his dark brown eyes on Madigan with an expression that made my stomach tighten.

"I've let you down. I thought Franziska would help when you told her about the Hallows. But I should have known she'd refuse. I asked for help when I thought the Hallows had killed you, Len. She wasn't interested in fighting back then, either. But I thought if someone else—a different supernatural—confirmed the Hallows' return, she'd change her mind." He snorted a sarcastic laugh. "How stupid."

"You've not let us down." Madigan placed a hand on Hiero's knee, and lightning shot through my chest. "Ava and I will find recruits ourselves. We don't need her help, do we, Ava?"

"No," I said, and knocked back my drink. The amber liquid scorched my throat, and I let out a spluttering cough. And then another. And another. Until my eyes streamed.

Both men stared at me, Hiero bursting into fits of laughter.

Even Madigan chuckled, hiding his mouth behind his hand. "You don't drink whisky like that."

"I'll... drink it... how... I like," I said between coughs.

Though they laughed at my expense, I couldn't resist grinning along with them. Hiero's laughter was infectious, and Madigan's had always been a secret addiction.

"All right," Hiero said, leaning forward in his seat, his mood rejuvenated. "To find eager fighters, the best place to start is the training ground. With the Battles of Blood coming up, it's heaving with the most vicious of our kind."

"What are the Battles of Blood?" I asked, recalling how the mad, old vampire, Edward, had mentioned them earlier.

"Every five years we hold a tournament: the Battles of Blood or Battles of Souls, fought by Blood Drinkers and Soul Suckers respectively," Hiero explained. "It's an outlet for those who are more"—he paused to find the right word—"*rambunctious*. It keeps them from getting into fights if they have something to work towards. The only thing vampires love as much as sex is violence."

"*Most* vampires," Madigan muttered, more to himself than to us.

"If there's anyone who will help you fight, it's them," Hiero continued. "In fact, I sponsor one of the favourites to win. I can introduce you tomorrow."

I nodded. Though my insides clenched with nerves, we were now back on track. We had a plan.

"And if that fails," Hiero said, fixing me with one of those smiles that had me melting inside, "you can simply wait until I win the election. Wiping out the Hallows will be my first priority. When I win, I will give you an *army*, and that is a promise."

I tried to memorise the route as Hiero led us to our room, but after a few turned corners, I was hopelessly lost again. As we reached the top of a spiral staircase, the butler we'd seen earlier emerged from a door at the top.

"Sir," he said, eyes widening as he saw Hiero. "It's ready if you would like to inspect it?"

Hiero stepped up to the butler, grinning. "Thank you, Cassius." He then leant forward and whispered something into his ear that made the butler blush.

"Th-thank you, sir," Cassius said, his voice catching before hurrying down the stairs, brushing past me as he went.

Hiero was still grinning. "He fancies me," he said with a one-shouldered shrug of false modesty.

"You flirt with him," I said. "Of course he fancies you."

"I flirt with you too," he said, raising an eyebrow, his smirk forming those dimples in his cheeks; an expression as handsome as it was infuriating.

My face burned. "Yeah? Well, you'll have to try harder."

"What about you, Len?" He ran a hand through his auburn locks. "Do I need to try harder with you, too?"

Madigan coughed into his fist, then tugged on his cuff. "Absolutely not. You flirt more than enough with everyone." He turned to me. "He needs no more encouragement."

"Wise words," Hiero said with a laugh. "Now then, this is your room." He jabbed his thumb over his shoulder towards the door

Cassius had appeared from. "It's one of the best rooms here with an en suite. I'll admit we are a little short on staff these days, so you won't be able to have food brought to your room but—"

"We are more than capable of feeding ourselves," Madigan said.

"Of course, but should you change your mind, Chef prepares meals at seven, midnight, and six for Talia, Xander, and myself. I'll let him know those numbers will increase."

I couldn't believe what I was hearing. "You have your own chef?!"

Hiero simply grinned in response, and opened the door, stepping aside to let us through. "Get some rest, and I'll see you at six." And with that, he closed the door behind us.

My breath caught as I surveyed the bedroom.

A semi-circular room prevailed a majestic four-poster bed furnished in dark grey and burgundy. Fat, fluffy cushions begged to be touched, illuminated by dark red candles perfumed with winter berries.

I stood frozen. It felt like a crime to step into luxury while covered in dirt and grime, and I was glad I'd left my boots downstairs.

Madigan had no such problem, striding across the room. He removed his tailcoat, tossed it onto a chaise longue, and stretched, accentuating his lanky frame.

"Forgive my rudeness," he said, heading straight for the door to the en suite, "but I *must* wash." He ran his fingers through his slick, dirty hair.

I nodded, still frozen to the spot, and it was only when he disappeared and I heard the splash of running water that I took my first tentative step, though the feeling I was intruding still hung over me.

In an attempt to settle in, I pulled off my socks, flexing my toes to feel every fibre of the soft carpet against my aching soles. Almost *too* soft. And the candles too sweet, and the lighting too sensual. *Too perfect.* And my presence tainted it. Coated in dirt and blood.

Madigan had the right idea.

I followed him, the splashing water growing louder and a cloud of steam engulfing me.

The walls of the en suite glittered gold, and against one, two glass panels seemed to twinkle with starlight, the shower between them. The faucet was so wide, it could cover three or four people. No door; only steam hindered my vision, Madigan's blurred figure shrouded, but not obscured.

He had his back to me, but like he could sense my eyes upon him, he turned, jumping slightly. He did nothing to cover himself. Instead, his gaze locked on mine.

I removed my hoodie, dumping it on the damp floor. And then my top.

"There's a bathtub around that corner," Madigan said, pointing towards a section of the room hidden by steam.

"The shower will do just fine." I wriggled out of my jeans and kicked them aside.

His eyes remained on me as I removed my bra, unblinking. "It's... uh... quite hot in here."

"I like it hot." I dropped my knickers.

A spray of water struck my skin, almost blistering, as I joined him in the shower and stood directly beneath the jets of water. And sighed. The tension building within me seemed to escape on my breath.

Like walking through fog and into rain, now I saw Madigan clearly. For a heartbeat, he simply stared at me, his eyes raking down my body. And I stared back, taking in the way water droplets cascaded down his shoulders, between his pectorals, down his toned abdomen, to the V of his hips.

Our eyes met again. He was frowning, but not with anger or annoyance. I'd seen that frown enough times to read it. It was the same frown he'd directed at me when he'd been my master, and though I'd not realised it at the time, I now recognised it was an expression of restraint.

I closed my eyes, turning my back on him and my face up to the faucet, relishing in the sensation of near-scalding water crashing over me and through my hair.

My body twitched as I felt Madigan's fingers tangled in my hair from behind, and then relaxed, melting at his touch.

"What's wrong?" he asked, his lips close to my ear. He could read me as easily as the books he cherished.

"I... don't know..." How could I put into words all the turmoil inside my head? "I think I'm just... anxious? Like I don't belong somewhere this fancy. But I don't belong out *there*, either, in the mud and squalor, without electricity, and vampires from all over the world; all over *time*."

His soft laugh rumbled through his chest, vibrating behind me, and my head lolled against his hand as he massaged my scalp. From the warm foam now sliding down my neck and shoulders and the scent of lemongrass, I knew he'd applied shampoo.

"Culture shock," he said, his fingertips now moving in circles.

"Yes!" Now he'd said it, it seemed obvious, and the rest of my jumbled thoughts came tumbling out. "Hiero's cool, but I didn't think I'd even *meet* one of your exs—let alone stay with him and actually *like* him. And don't even get me started on the mindfuck that is Franziska."

"I understand. If truth be told, I'm finding everything somewhat disorientating as well. Not everything here is as I remember or expected." He rinsed the remaining suds from my hair, and his hands drifted down over my shoulders, the pads of his thumbs pressing into my taut muscles, releasing a sigh from my throat. "But I will not abandon you. I said I was yours, and I meant it. And when we leave this place, it will be together."

I leant back, the softness of my body meeting the firmness of his. There was a sensation of absence—emptiness—as he removed his hands from my shoulders, only to return with something cold and slippery sliding from his palms, over my shoulders and down my chest, the fragrance of lemongrass thickening.

A second of hesitation.

I reached up to wrap a hand around the back of Madigan's neck, tilting my head back against his chest.

"Touch me." The words hissed from my lips before I could stop them, and immediately his palm slid from my shoulder to one breast, slick with soap, lathering at his touch. His other hand slipped too, creeping down my stomach, as the firmness of his erection pressed to the small of my back, making my breath hitch.

"Tomorrow," he said, as his thumbs rolled over my stiffening nipples, "we will resume our duty. We will meet with other vampires and persuade them to come with us. But you need not fear; I will stay with you. I can be your constant within this foreign world."

And then his mouth was on my neck, hotter than the cascading water, planting kiss after kiss from the spot beneath my ear, down, down to my shoulder, and his hands continued to work, though I must have been clean by now.

I opened my eyes. I wanted to *see* what he was doing. It looked so erotic—the way he spread white foam over my breasts and flicked my nipples—I *almost* felt a twinge of shame before being flooded with the need for more.

I spun to face him, pressing my hands to his firm chest, rising and falling with each breath, his heartbeat thrumming beneath. I traced my fingertips through the valleys of his muscles until I reached the smattering of scars on his left side.

"Can I touch you here?" I asked, gazing into those grey eyes, my fingers hovering over the spots the shrapnel had devoured him.

His features twitched, his mouth opening, then closing again. Then nodded. And I pressed my hand to his skin, my thumb tracing through the grooves. He let out a gasp, like I'd hurt him, and I withdrew my hand, but he grabbed my wrist and returned my palm to his side.

"I want you to touch me." His voice was so quiet it was barely audible over the sound of rushing water. "All of me. All my flaws."

That last word hurt. So much my eyes stung. "Not flaws. Just history."

His face twisted with emotion again, and now I wondered if he was holding back tears.

"Just history," he repeated, perhaps trying to convince himself. "And you, Miss Monroe, are my future."

He took hold of my waist and pulled me flush against him, leaning down to press his soft lips to mine, his cock hard against my belly. I moaned against his mouth, taking his face in my hands and kissing, sucking, nipping at his lips in return.

"Oh, Miss Monroe, the things I want to do to you…"

"Do it," I said against his mouth. "Do all those things you want. Do *more*."

He swallowed, the last of his restraint fizzling out, his grip on me tightening. "Do you mean it?"

"Yes. Tell me what you want. *Anything* you want." I brushed a hand over his scars softly. "I want to make you feel as beautiful as I see you."

His cock gave a sudden twitch against my stomach.

"Because you are."

His mouth claimed mine, stealing my breath before I'd even drawn it, and even as he wrangled me from the shower and fumbled for a towel, our lips remained locked together. I giggled as he swept the towel up my back, then ruffled my hair, and as I did, his tongue darted into my mouth. Hot. Sticky. Wrestling mine into submission. Until a soft moan escaped me.

Without warning, he swept me up in his arms, and before I could so much as blink, he'd rushed from the en suite and dropped me on the bed.

My skin barely had time to cool before he was on top of me.

I tangled my fingers in his damp hair as his mouth took me once more, his tongue dancing with mine. Then a hand snaked between my legs, making me jump.

"Shhh," he said against my lips. "Relax." His fingers traced upwards with a featherlight touch, reaching the apex of my thighs before drifting back downward again, making me writhe with frustration, my core throbbing with anticipation.

Madigan buried his face in my neck and let out a low growl. "*Fuck*, you smell divine." His fingers tickled upward again, teasing me until I squirmed.

"The endorphins. Your sweat. And of course..." He traced a finger between my labia and let out a groan as my body trembled. "Already so wet."

"I'd forgotten what a tease you are," I gritted out, clenching the bedsheets as my hips tilted upward, begging for a firm touch. But Madigan withdrew his hand to grip my inner thigh.

"Even your thighs are wet. You've made quite a mess." The corner of his mouth curled into a smirk.

My cheeks burned as the ache between my legs became painful. Was he seeing how far he could push me?

"Please stop," I gasped.

"*Stop?*"

"No, don't *stop*! I mean, stop teasing me. It... it hurts." My hips gave an involuntary spasm.

"Is this what you need?" He slid a finger against my swollen clit, slowly making a circular motion, drawing out a strangled cry from me.

He'd already wound me up so tight that within seconds I felt the rush of an oncoming orgasm, getting closer, and closer, until...

"But what about what I need?" Madigan asked, withdrawing his hand, and I couldn't stop the growl of frustration that slipped out. He was going to *pay* for that one.

With a deep breath, I looked up at him through my eyelashes. "Oh, I'll give you what you need." A threat or a promise—I wasn't sure.

Like he knew what I was going to do, he shuffled back until he stood by the side of the bed, presenting himself to me, his cock standing upright, commanding my attention.

I sat at the edge of the bed, gripped the base of his cock, and flicked the tip with my tongue. His shuddering gasp sent another pulse through me. I did it again. And again. And with each stroke of my tongue, his cock gave a violent twitch; each moan I extracted from him more desperate than the last. Until I wrapped my lips around the head and sucked. He drove his fingers through my hair, tilting his head back, and let out a long, breathy moan.

I bobbed my head, working my way down his shaft and up again, tracing my tongue along the underside of his cock.

"M-Miss Monroe," he gasped. "Where did you learn to do this, you naughty little thing?" His fingers tightened, his body going stiff, and I knew he was close.

I should stop. Torture him like he tortured me.

But I wanted him to lose control. To lose himself to me. I cupped his balls as I quickened my pace, and he braced himself against a bedpost with one hand, the other holding a fistful of my hair.

"Y-you're too g-good at this," he stuttered. "I'm... I'm going to—"

His balls tightened as he came, hot liquid hitting the back of my throat, and he let out an agonised groan. The sound of him coming undone drove me wild, wetness pooling on the bedsheets where I sat.

He relaxed his grip, withdrawing, but still leaned against the bedpost, legs shaking, chest heaving, dishevelled hair slick to his forehead.

He was a mess. And *I'd* done that. I couldn't help but smile, somewhat proud of myself.

His gaze flicked to my mouth as he ran his thumb across my lower lip. "You have a very dangerous mouth, Miss Monroe." A devilish expression crept across his face. "Allow me to remind you of mine."

Next thing I knew, he had me on my back, my knees spread apart, and I gasped as cold air struck my heat. He left a trail of kisses down the inside of my thigh to my pussy, sliding his tongue between my lips and flicked against my clit. Just once.

I screwed my eyes tight shut. They burned.

No... Those couldn't be tears... Could they?

"*Please*," I begged. "Don't tease me again."

He sucked on my clit, releasing it with a *pop*.

"You want to cum?" he asked, looking up at me from between my knees.

"You know I do!"

He grinned wickedly. "Then you should say so. *Explicitly*."

I let out a whimper. I knew I should have tortured him when I had the chance. "You're... you're *evil*."

His smile widened. A look that made me wetter. He wouldn't give in.

"Fine!" I snapped. "I want you to make me cum. I want you to use that perfect mouth on me. I want you to suck, and flick, and rub my clit until I lose control. *And* I want you to clean me up afterwards."

His body quivered, and though I couldn't see, I was almost certain he was nursing another erection, the idea of it making my inner walls spasm.

"As you wish." And then his hot, wet mouth was on me. His tongue rolling over my clit as he slid two fingers inside me, pressing against a spot that had my back arching, a squeal escaping my mouth.

He raised his head. "I'm sorry, that's not what you asked for, is it? I'll just—" He moved as though to retract his fingers.

"Don't you dare! Please, let me cum. *Please*!"

And as tears stung my eyes, he pressed that spot again as he flicked his tongue against the sensitive knot of nerves. Slowly building speed. Faster and faster, until I teetered on the edge. I gripped the bedsheets, hips bucking, as a wave of pleasure surged through me, my core tightening around his fingers. Lights sparked behind my eyelids, tears leaking from the corners. Pulse after pulse crashed through me, until my body gave out, and I lay gasping for breath.

My eyes still shut, I felt him crawl beside me, wiping the tears that had tracked down my temples. "A-Ava?" his voice wavered. Worried. "Are you all right? Did I hurt you?"

"No," I half laughed. And when I opened my eyes, more tears flowed. "That was... that was..." I shook my head, the word I wanted just out of reach. Nothing could describe the intensity; the power; the ecstasy. And all I managed was a lame, "That was... *amazing*."

I took his face in my hands, studying every detail. The crease be-tween his brows. The flecks of silver in his grey eyes. The way the corner of his mouth twitched.

I love you.

I opened my mouth to say it. And hesitated. "Madigan?"

"Ava?" He held my gaze. Fuck, he was *gorgeous*.

I love you.

"I'm glad you're with me," I managed.

A short exhale of laughter through his nose as he brushed my cheek with his thumb. "And I you, Miss Monroe."

CHAPTER THIRTEEN

I t took a good fifteen minutes to find the dining room for breakfast. If it hadn't been for Madigan, I wouldn't have found it at all. He paused a few times to get his bearings, then led on.

"How do you know where you're going?" I asked, pulling at the fabric of the hideous flowery top Hiero's butler had delivered to our room. Grateful as I was for the clean clothes, the note from Hiero stating he'd buy me new threads more to my taste was an immense relief.

Madigan made an uncomfortable noise. "I grew up in a manor house similar to this."

Strangely, we'd never talked about his childhood before. Then again, at over a hundred years old, Madigan had a lot of history to cover. I'd figured he'd come from a wealthy family from his mannerisms and way of speaking, but having it confirmed made me realise how little I really knew.

"That must have been nice," I said stiffly, unable to relate. Grandma's wages had just been enough to scrape by. And my mother's income... well... I still don't know where she got the money. But I could guess, and let's just say she didn't pay tax. Most of it went on her boyfriend, while I survived with hand-me-downs and peanut butter sandwiches for breakfast, lunch, and dinner. Or spaghetti hoops if she was feeling fancy.

"You'd be surprised." His tone matched mine, but before I could question him further, he opened the dining room doors.

Three figures looked up from the enormous spread—everything from eggs, bacon, and sausages to cold cuts, cheese, pastries, and fruit—sitting on elegant dishes across the long table. The smell was incredible.

Hiero sat at the head of the table and got to his feet as we entered, his lips spreading and eyes shining.

"Evening's Greetings!" He strode towards us and shook Madigan's hand, then took hold of mine, kissing my knuckles. Perhaps I'd grown used to seeing him tired, dirty, and blood-stained, but he appeared even more handsome than I remembered, effortlessly suave in his braces and slightly unbuttoned shirt, his auburn hair gleaming like polished copper in the firelight. "How did you sleep?"

"Great, thanks." My cheeks flushed as he looked up at me from his bowed stance, my knuckles still mere millimetres from his lips. I didn't fancy sharing that I'd woken up thrashing as Ivan invaded my dreams, nor that I'd kicked Madigan hard in the chest as he wrestled with me, my tortured mind *certain* he was one of Ivan's minions after my blood. Though Madigan had assured me it hadn't hurt—and I had no reason to doubt him, he was a vampire after all—I still felt a twinge of guilt somewhere around my navel.

"You must have been exhausted," Hiero said, a dimple forming in one cheek as his mischievous smirk twisted to the side. "It was a long journey. But you still had the strength for *fun* afterwards. No wonder Len likes you."

"What do you mean?" I asked, but as his smirk became a full-blown grin, his brown eyes twinkling, I knew what he was implying. And so, it seemed, did Madigan, his cheeks flushing crimson. "Were you *listening?*"

"The house isn't soundproof, you know." Hiero put a hand to his chest, as though I'd wounded him. "And vampires have excellent hearing."

"Our room is up a flight of stairs," I said as I eyed him with suspicion. "It's not like you would have been passing by."

"Maybe I wanted to deliver something to your room?"

"*Were* you delivering something?"

His tongue darted out to skim his lower lip as he thought about his answer.

"No."

He winked, and heat spread through my chest.

Madigan, still blushing, let out a sigh and pinched the bridge of his nose, muttering something inaudible.

"Allow me to introduce my partners." Hiero gestured to the others in the room. "Talia and Xander."

"A pleasure," Madigan said with a nod, likely glad of the change of topic.

Neither Talia nor Xander responded, the pair of them glaring in our direction, the room thick with a heavy silence. Even Hiero must have felt the tension, pulling out a chair for me some distance from the others.

I forced a smile and lowered myself into the chair, focusing on the various foods laid out for us, but I felt their eyes on me like there was a spotlight shining down where I sat.

As beautiful as the display of food was, my stomach was suddenly tight and my mouth too dry, but not wanting to be rude, I helped myself to a Danish and set it down on the small plate in front of me.

"She's a skunk-head," said Talia in a nasally voice. "I thought the woman who stole your lost love would be prettier."

It wasn't *what* she said that made me bristle—I'd heard all the hair-related insults before. It was that she talked about me like I wasn't there, or too simple to understand her. I was back at school again, ignoring the mutters and whispers from the girls sitting behind me that started as cruel jibes, and became balled up pieces of paper thrown at the back of my head. But I wasn't a schoolgirl anymore. I looked up from my Danish and fixed Talia with my darkest glare.

"If you're going to talk shit, say it *to* me. Or at least come up with something original." My insides knotted as I stared her down, focusing on her small freckled nose instead of her eyes, already feeling the pull of her glamour, though her twisted, bitter expression tainted her beauty.

She had long ginger hair, three braids over one ear tight to her skull, and looked like she might be a little shorter than me. She leant forward on the table, displaying her cleavage in a way I was sure was deliberate.

Hiero laughed, and not the roar of laughter I'd become accustomed to. It was forced. Wrong.

"Ava didn't *steal* anyone's lost love," he said, walking from our end of the table to theirs, resting his hands on Talia's shoulders. His smile was as strained as his laugh.

"We're glad to see you're alive and well," said Xander, his gaze on Madigan. He had short black hair, pale, pointed features, and couldn't have been much taller than Talia. If it wasn't for the fact that he, like Talia, was a Soul Sucker, I could have snapped him in half.

"Where have you been for the last twenty years?" he asked. "Trying to get back to Hiero, I hope. That's what loyal friends do, and according to Hiero, you were much more than that. Much, *much* more."

Madigan was still standing at the foot of the table, his flinty eyes on Xander, his lips razor thin. As haughty as Talia and Xander were, their venomous glares were nothing compared to the glowers Madigan was capable of.

"It must be difficult for you both," Madigan said in a voice so low that goosebumps erupted over my arms. "You had Hiero all to yourselves, and now here I am, swanning back into his life." He placed a hand over his heart and said in a tone that *almost* sounded sincere. "I am truly sorry. I did not intend to make you feel threatened."

"We aren't threatened by you," Xander snapped as he sprang to his feet, his nose wrinkled into an ugly expression that even his glamour couldn't fix.

From the way Madigan's mouth twitched at the corner, I could tell he was incredibly pleased with himself. I bit my lip to contain my mirth.

"Think it's funny, do you?" Talia said, her blue eyes on me. "You think provoking a superior vampire is clever?"

"Now, now." Hiero's knuckles whitened on her shoulders. "No one here is superior to another."

"That's odd," Xander said, now turning his glare on Hiero. "That's not what you said to us. Isn't this entire operation based on Soul Suckers' superiority over Blood Drinkers?"

Entire operation? I looked at Hiero for clarification.

But colour drained from Hiero's face. "Xander." The light-hearted tone of his voice had vanished now.

"In fact," Xander continued, his voice rising so that it echoed throughout the dining room. "Isn't his supposed *death* the reason for—"

"Xander!" There was no mistaking the danger in Hiero's voice now. "That's enough. We will discuss this later."

"But—"

"I said *later.*"

For a moment, Xander and Hiero stared each other down as my pulse thrummed in my ears.

"Fine," Xander said. "I'm done here, anyway." And he stormed off, knocking his plate of half-eaten breakfast to the floor with a smash.

"I'm done too." Talia wriggled her shoulders until Hiero released them, and followed Xander, slamming the door behind her.

Hiero gripped the back of Talia's chair, his shoulders slumping as he let out a long breath. "Sorry about that," he said, his voice light, but unconvincing.

"No," Madigan said. "It is I who must apologise. It had not occurred to me that my presence might cause difficulties for you." He ran his fingers through his hair.

Hiero waved a dismissive hand. "It's nothing. They're just protective of me. I'll admit the news of your death broke me and... well... they were there to pick up the pieces. But I should speak with them both properly. This wasn't the homecoming they were expecting. I'd promised them souls to take, and instead I've brought them my ex and a shifter. Though having said that, shifters aren't immune from a vampire's kiss, so make sure you watch out for them, Ava."

"You think they would try to kiss me?" I asked. From the looks they had thrown my way, I figured my *life* was in danger, not my soul.

Hiero grinned at me, flashing his perfect teeth. "Not while I'm around."

A tingle rolled low in my belly, and when I zoned in on his lips, I told myself it was the pull of his glamour.

"Now then," he said, straightening himself, and grabbing a shiny red apple from a bowl and biting into it with a satisfying crunch. "Eat up. We have a busy day ahead."

With my appetite abandoning me, I picked at the Danish while the guys piled up their plates, chatting again about their various escapades.

Though their stories usually brought me entertainment, there was something about the sour exchange with Talia and Xander and the phrase 'stealing his lost love', that dampened my interest. It was difficult hearing of their long intertwined history when Madigan and I hadn't even known each other for a month. And yet, when I gazed absent-mindedly at him, the words that had almost escaped me yesterday reemerged at the forefront of my mind.

I love you.

No. Don't be ridiculous. You can't love someone after a month...

Or can you?

I rose from my seat once I'd eaten most of my pastry, eager to leave before I started overthinking. "I have to pee."

"See you in the entrance hall in fifteen minutes," Hiero said through a mouthful of bacon. "Don't get lost!"

"I won't," I called back as I left, though I sounded more confident than I felt.

If I stick to the ground floor, I should be okay.

But I wasn't.

Within seconds of venturing through a couple of twisting hallways, I couldn't even find my way back, let alone the nearest bathroom.

Just as the creeping sensation of panic tightened in my chest, the sound of footsteps carried towards me, and I let out a small sigh of relief.

"I wasn't lost," I said, before Hiero could round the corner and tease me. "I was having a look round—Oh."

Talia stepped into view, blocking me from taking the next corner. She really was disgustingly pretty when she wasn't sneering, with those perfect blue eyes, perfect skin, and perfect braids in her perfect hair.

I forced a pleasant expression. "You don't know where the nearest loo is, do you?"

She didn't answer, and footsteps approached from behind, making the hair on the back of my neck rise. I didn't even have time to gasp before Xander rushed me. One of his arms wrapped around my middle, pinning my arms to my sides. His other hand grabbed my chin, fingertips pinching into my lower jaw and forcing my head to tilt upward. His palm compressed my throat, making it difficult to draw breath, let alone scream.

"Gerroff me!" I tried to twist myself out of his grip, but he was so strong it felt like I was encased in cement.

"I can't reach with her head pointing up like that," Talia said, taking two agonisingly slow steps forward. My already rapid heart pounded harder—so hard the beat crashed through every cell of my body.

"How about this?" Xander asked. My knees buckled beneath his weight as he forced me down, manipulating me like I was a doll.

My lungs fought for breath as he wrenched my head up to face Talia, now exuding a soft, glowing aura that steadied my heart and told me she was safe. *Inviting...*

I snapped my eyes shut before the last of my rational brain submitted, as Xander's hold constricted around me like a python.

"Let me go!" But the heel of Xander's hand against my throat choked my words.

Talia's hot breath brushed my lips. I clamped them together, so tight they turned inward into my mouth, and I bit down, using my teeth to keep them in place.

Then a cold thumb and forefinger pinched my nose.

The squeak of panic was muffled in my throat as I kept my lips locked together, holding my breath until my lungs ached, my trachea tugging. Tears leaked from the corners of my eyelids as my extremities tingled, my strength fading, my brain growing foggy.

Images swam through my mind, like watching a reel of my greatest highlights. Grandma teaching me to use her sewing machine. Laughing with my friends from the theatre society. Madigan's lips on mine. And travelling with Hiero...

"Why didn't you shift when the Brain Eater was about to bite off that pretty little face of yours?"

I fell through the air, not even acknowledging the pain of shifting before landing in a heap of clothes, and for a few glorious seconds, I felt air sweep under my abdomen and oxygen flood through me.

I scuttled from the clothes as my killer instinct drove me towards Xander, my stinger ready to strike, when something came hurtling from above—something round and colourless and almost impossible for me to focus on until...

It landed on top of me. *Over* me. And I realised with a sinking feeling what it was.

A glass jar.

"Told you it would work." The vibrations of Xander's voice were difficult to translate, distorted by my glass prison. "Pass me the lid."

I wouldn't let them capture me, but if I took my human form, they would simply overpower me again.

What do I do?

What do I do?!

One side of the jar lifted, and something like an enormous porcelain-white tile slid across the ground, forcing me to retreat, until I had no choice but to let it slide beneath my feet.

It's paper. Fine. If you want to play stupid games, be prepared for stupid prizes.

I waited until Xander lifted the jar into the air before shifting into a human again, showering him in broken glass. He might have possessed impossible strength, but the shock of the explosion and having a naked woman land on top of him knocked him to the ground.

Before either could respond, I scrambled to my feet. "*Madigan!*" I screamed so loudly my throat stung. "*Hiero!*"

I darted to the end of the hallway—back the way I'd come—but tripped over Xander and crashed into the wall.

"*Madigan!*" I screamed again, waiting for the Soul Suckers to pounce. I couldn't outrun them. I couldn't fight them. All I could do was yell and pray they'd get here in time. "*Hiero!*"

The sounds of laughter reached me through my adrenaline-drunk brain, and I turned to face the Soul Suckers, waiting for the end. They would be upon me in a microsecond, grab me and force me down again...

Except they didn't.

I blinked at them, only now realising it was *their* laughter I heard. They were both doubled over, cackling like they'd seen the funniest thing on Earth. Xander had both arms wrapped around his middle, like he was holding himself together, a tear tracking down one cheek. Meanwhile, Talia was leaning against a wall for support, pointing at me. First at my legs, then worked her way up, creasing with more laughter as her eyes fell upon each part of me. My stomach. My breasts. I covered myself with my hands, my eyes stinging, face burning, feeling smaller and smaller with each howl of laughter.

Hiero tore through the adjoining hallway, Madigan hot behind him, and as soon as I saw them, tears cascaded down my face; whether they were tears of anger, humiliation, or relief, I didn't know.

"What *the fuck* is going on here?" Hiero's face was twisted with rage.

"I was reclaiming my outfit," Talia said with such forced innocence it was obvious she'd been up to no good. She picked up the clothes from where I'd dropped them as Hiero whipped his head back to look at me. Unlike the last time I'd shifted in front of him, his eyes didn't roam my body. No playful mischief in his expression. Instead, his face paled as his sights locked with mine, then turned back to his partners.

Madigan stepped in front of me, removing his jacket and placing it around my shoulders. He didn't speak, but I noted how his hands shook, his jaw clenched so tight it was a wonder his teeth hadn't cracked. All the while, Hiero screamed at the others—I couldn't even make sense of what he was saying—the air thick with more curse words than even I could have conjured.

"It was only a bit of fun," Xander huffed.

Madigan's nostrils flared as he fumbled with the buttons to cover me, and for a moment I thought he was about to round on the Soul Suckers, his temper about to burst from him. But as a growl rumbled in his throat, I took hold of his hands. His cold, grey eyes met mine, and I gave the smallest shake of my head. He might be a vampire, but interfering with squabbling Soul Suckers was idiotic, if not fatal.

He pulled me against his body. "This will *not* happen again." His voice was so low I almost didn't hear him. He turned his face to the Soul Suckers, but Hiero was already coming to the end of his tirade.

"Fuck off the pair of you!" he said with a flick of his wrist. "Keep to your section of the manor. Stay away from Ava. Don't look at her. Don't talk to her. Don't even *breathe* the same air as her! Do you understand?!"

"Fine," Talia said, knocking into Hiero's shoulder as she passed him, Xander following. True to their word, they didn't so much as glance my way as they passed, though I noticed their surly expressions.

Hiero turned to us, out of breath, his face red from his rant. "I am so *sorry*, Ava." He sounded it, almost like he too was fighting the urge to cry. "I never thought they'd do something like that. They can be hard work, but never... not once have they... *Ugh*...” He shook his head, ruffling his hair. “I’m so sorry.”

“It’s not your fault.” I couldn’t look him in the eyes yet, my embarrassment lingering. Sure, I’d been overpowered by vampires before, and body shaming wasn’t exactly new to me, either. But the sound of their laughter still rang in my ears, snuffing out my confidence.

“No, it *is* my fault,” Hiero said. “You are under my protection; it’s my duty to keep you safe.”

Madigan squeezed me tighter as he bit out, “Be sure that you do.”

Worms seemed to wriggle in my stomach as Hiero fetched me new clothes, and we prepared to head to the training grounds. The last thing I wanted was to face more vampires, let alone recruit them. But as I dressed, my humiliation mutated into determination, and I vowed to make those cunts pay for what they did to me. Whether I had to wait to be tutored, or I taught myself, I *would* become a scorpion hybrid. I *would* defend myself. And I *would* produce a venom so toxic even Soul Suckers would writhe at my feet and beg for death.

Until then, I could work on my strength and stamina, and where better to start than the training ground?

I was ready.

CHAPTER FOURTEEN

The training ground was unlike anything I'd ever seen. A vast cavern split into two sections. One was unmistakably a gym, though certain pieces of equipment like the treadmills and stationary bicycles had been modified to accommodate the sheer power of the vampires using them, and the weights were comically large. A shiver ran down my spine as I recalled the trapezium-shaped weights Ivan had used to execute Austin, and I focused instead on the second chamber. Luckily, it was this chamber that Hiero marched into.

It held enormous boxing rings, some holding five or six fighters at a time, and though most fought hand-to-hand, some used weapons—albeit rubber variants of the genuine article. Shouts, grunts, and the occasional *thwack* of a weapon rang throughout the chamber.

"Will they use these kinds of weapons in the Battles of Blood?" I asked Hiero, as one vampire swung a rubber sword at another with a staff.

"No. The training ground is for exactly that: training. But in the tournament, it's the real deal." His brown eyes widened with glee. "Not all contestants survive. Especially in the Battles of Souls. But they're usually over so quick you can't see what happens, so it's not as exciting as the Battles of Blood, where you see everything in its gruesome glory."

Madigan frowned, folding his arms. "I don't recall you being this macabre before. Far from it, actually." He appeared particularly uncomfortable, his nose wrinkled against the scent of sweat, and as usual, looked out of place in his brand-new suit.

Hiero's smile faltered. "I've fully embraced vampire culture." He arched an eyebrow. "Perhaps it's time you did the same?"

Madigan's eyes narrowed, but before he could retort, the cavern erupted into cheers and applause.

A vampire—a female with long red hair tied into a ponytail—emerged from a tunnel. She smiled and raised a hand to give a modest wave to her supporters.

"That's Krysten, but everyone calls her Red," Hiero said. "She's the one I'm sponsoring and a favourite to win." He waved a hand and shouted, "Hey, Red! Over here!"

Red spotted Hiero and waved back to acknowledge him before striding towards us. She walked with her head high, confident, like she owned the very floor she walked on.

"Lord Blackford," she said with a slight nod of her head, a hint of an Eastern European accent in her voice I couldn't quite pinpoint.

She was around my height, but unlike me, was incredibly fit, with shapely legs in tight brown trousers, and displayed her toned delts and biceps in a white vest top. Now she was close, I noted her heterochromia: one eye blue, the other green. I tried to keep myself from staring at a deep red scar on one side of her face. It ran down her forehead, narrowly missed her eye—the blue one—before continuing down one cheek, and I made a mental note to ask Hiero how she got it. I wouldn't risk offending her; vampire or not, she looked like she could knock me out. Hell, she looked like she could knock out *anyone*, given the self-assurance in her stance: her hands on her hips, feet shoulder width apart, occasionally flicking her ponytail.

"I keep telling you, call me Hiero." He reached out to take her hand and brought it to his lips, but before he could plant the kiss there, she whipped it back, smirking.

"And I keep telling you to behave yourself."

"Never. Please, allow me to introduce my friends. This is Len and his companion, Ava. She is a shifter from a witch's coven, here to recruit fighters in their war with the Hallows."

Red raised her eyebrows. "The Hallows?"

"A group of supernatural hunters," I said.

"Yes, I know who they are." She squinted at Hiero. "This isn't a joke, is it? Or a part of your campaign?"

"Of course not," Hiero said, his voice rising in indignation. "You really think I'd lie about that sort of thing?"

Red's lips twisted to the side as she regarded me. My spine stiffened.

"Where is your coven based?" she asked, tilting her head to one side.

"Kinwich."

"Interesting..." She nodded, the corner of her mouth curling. "It's funny you should come today, Ava. I've been wondering what I'll do after the Battles of Blood are over. After I've won them, of course." Her eyes shifted from me to Hiero and back again, like she still didn't believe this wasn't one of Hiero's pranks. "And you're certain they're Hallows? *Real* Hallows? Aren't they meant to be dead?"

I explained for what felt like the hundredth time that Lascivious had confirmed their return.

Red's eyes seemed to glint with hunger as a smile spread across her face. "*Yes*, Ava. This is exactly what I've been looking for! I thought I might die if I had to wait until the next Battles of Blood to break some bones—with perfect form, you understand. I'm not a barbarian. Can you wait until the Battles are over?"

I blinked at her, hardly daring to believe my luck. "We're staying for the election anyway—"

"Perfect! Oh, I can't wait to let Myla know. Is there anyone else you've asked?"

"You're the first. Except for Franziska. But she refused to help."

She hissed in a breath through her teeth, wincing. "Yes, well, inter-species aid is always a divisive subject in politics."

Before she could explain, a gathering of vampires around one arena let out a roar. A pair of fighters circled each other, one with a bloody mouth, the other with a cut above their eyebrow.

"Oh no..." Red said with a groan, rolling her eyes and began shoving through the crowd to reach the fighters.

"Oh yes!" Hiero bounded after her, pulling me along with him, his eyes alight with excitement.

The vampire with the bloody mouth bull rushed the other, smashing him into the ground. The onlookers cheered as he bashed his foe's head in, again and again, until his knuckles bled.

"Jason, stop!" Red shouted above the hollering crowd. "You'll get suspended! Stop!" But the vampires who'd cheered for her moments ago now ignored her as she elbowed her way to the front, too caught up in the bloodshed.

Red leapt over the barrier, marched up to Jason and grabbed his shoulder to wrench him back. But without even looking at her, Jason shoved her aside, his wild eyes locked on his enemy.

He continued his assault, his victim's face now a swollen, bloody mess, a few of his teeth scattered in a crimson pool beside him. And still, Jason went on pummelling, his fists slamming down with a wet crunch.

Until the tip of a staff nudged his ear.

"I said, *stop*." Red pressed the rubber weapon against the side of his face.

The crowd fell silent, the only sound a grotesque gurgling as the vampire on the ground drew in laboured breaths.

Jason slowly turned his head to look sideways at Red, pressing his cheek against the staff in defiance, one bloody fist still raised and ready to strike.

"Do you know who this is?" Jason asked Red, his voice shaking. "Do you know what he did? To my familiar?"

"I know what he did," Red said.

"Then you know why I must do this."

"If you want to kill him that badly, wait until the Battles—when it is legal."

A beat of silence as Jason stared down into the ruined face beneath him. Then drove his fist down.

Before it could connect, Red jabbed at his head with the staff. He yelled, and brought his hand back to cover his ear, but Red struck that too. He toppled to the side, giving his victim enough time to scramble away as Red closed in on him.

She twirled the staff as Jason staggered to his feet, dazed by the impact. She could have struck again if she'd wanted to, but instead, leaned into a defensive stance, eyes laser-focused.

Once his head had cleared, Jason whirled on the spot, searching for his target, but his victim had vanished into the crowd. He let out a snarl, his eyes bulging.

"Look what you've done!" He charged at Red—the same move that had sent his previous opponent flying. But Red sidestepped, tripping him with her staff and sent him sprawling to the ground. She couldn't hide the gleam in her eyes as the crowd erupted into cheers and laughter, and she gave her staff another one-handed twirl as she waved to the crowd with the other.

Meanwhile, Jason lurched to his feet again, lips peeled back in a snarl. And Red, still humouring the crowd, hadn't noticed.

"Red, look out!" The words burst from me on their own.

Without looking back, Red spun her staff, and Jason ran directly onto the end, nearly impaling himself. He fell, winded, flat onto his back.

Only now did Red turn to look at him, the tip of her staff pointing down at his face. "Are you going to stop?" she asked, not even out of breath.

Jason raised his head as he glared up at her. For a moment I thought he'd continue fighting, but he leant his head back and closed his eyes, his chest juddering with each ragged breath, then gave the smallest of nods.

Red withdrew her staff and offered her hand, which Jason accepted, hauling himself to his feet.

Now without the promise of bloodshed, the crowd dispersed. Or perhaps it was because the broad, muscular form of Myla was striding towards us.

I shrank inside myself, feeling exposed now there was no longer a thick crowd to hide in, almost expecting her to single me out and march me from the Nest. I stumbled back a step, bumping into Hiero behind me.

He put a hand on my shoulder. "You're all right. You're with me."

I looked for Madigan, who stood a little way off from us, arms folded, watching with a disapproving scowl. He really *was* an odd-man-out within the Vampires' Nest. While the others were thrilled by violence, he was repulsed.

But Myla walked straight past us and joined Red as Jason hurried away.

"What was that about?" she asked, squinting at Jason's retreating form.

Red shook her head. "Nothing of interest, I assure you. Just two silly boys having a scrap."

If that was a scrap, I dreaded to see the Battles of Blood. I wanted to slink away before I caught Myla's attention, but Red's eyes had already lit up as she clutched Myla's thick arm with one hand and pointed her staff towards me with the other.

"Myla, this is Ava. She has an interesting proposal that will solve the problem I was talking to you about."

"We've met," I said stiffly.

"Nice to see you again." Myla inclined her head. "When I'm not guarding our liege lady, I'm Red's personal trainer."

"Myla." Red cut short the pleasantries. "I know what to do after the Battles are over. The Hallows have returned, and Ava is recruiting vampires to come back with her and kill the lot of them." I didn't know whether I should smile or wince at her eagerness to fight.

"So I've heard," Myla said, giving me an awkward sideways glance.

"What do you think?" Red asked, bouncing on the balls of her feet, gazing up at Myla with large eyes, like a child pleading for sweets. "You said you missed killing vampire hunters, and now we have a chance to wipe out the greatest hunters of all time!"

Myla gaze shifted again towards Hiero and me, her lips tight before turning back to Red. "You know I can't leave the Liege Lady."

"But what if she doesn't win? *Then* would you come? I'll go alone if I must, but it won't be half as fun without you."

Myla swallowed. "That would be decided by the liege lord." And when her eyes darted towards Hiero again, I noticed how her eyebrows tweaked upward. Could that be a spark of hope?

"I'd send you to fight them, Myla," Hiero said with a shrug. "It would be a crime to keep a warrior such as yourself from the glory of dismembering the Hallows."

Myla smiled. She *actually* smiled. A pretty smile so bright it matched the glittery unicorn hair clip she was wearing today.

"You're not *really* considering it, are you Myla?" said an unfamiliar voice. It came from a passing vampire, his shirt draped over one shoulder, flaunting his muscular chest as he approached. He was dark-skinned and wore his cornrows in a tight bun at the base of his neck. He would have been handsome if it hadn't been for his scrunched nose and curled lips, like he could smell something dying.

"Ugh... Max-fucking-Morningstar," Red said under her breath. "All the arseholes are out tonight."

"It's Max *Strider*—only my fans call me Morningstar, Red."

"It's Krysten—only my friends call me Red, *dupek*." I'm not sure what Red had called him, but I gathered it was no compliment.

Max's sour expression worsened, and he looked towards Myla instead. "As one of the Liege Lady's guards, I'm surprised you've not heard the news." He stood in a similar stance to Red: feet wide, shoulders back, but while her posture exuded confidence, his oozed arrogance.

"What news?" Myla asked, narrowing her eyes.

"That a shifter is spreading a bunch of bullshit." He directed his look of disgust at me.

"It's not bullshit." I stepped forward, but Hiero took me by the shoulder and pulled me back against his body.

"Easy," he muttered in my ear. "He's not one to mess around with."

Max ignored us and turned his attention back to Red and Myla. "Can you imagine how embarrassing that would be? Leaving the Nest to kill some pathetic humans, probably still at their mother's teat and pretending its some big victory? Though in your case, Red, it probably would be."

Red flicked her ponytail, snorting through her nose, unfazed. "I don't respect you enough to be insulted by you. Run along now. You'd better get practising if you don't want me to spank you in front of everyone."

He shoved into her shoulder as he pushed past her, strutting towards the other chamber.

"Such a charmer," Red said to herself, laughing slightly.

"What's his problem?" I asked, watching him leave.

"He's bankrolled by the Liege Lady," Myla said, folding her arms. "She's likely asked him to spread the word that the Hallows don't exist and leaving to fight them would bring great shame."

An uneasy weight settled in my stomach. That's the last thing I needed. I was counting on the vampire's bloodlust to persuade them to come with me.

"You know," Myla said, toying with her hair clip in thought. "The vampires are more likely to trust you if you become familiar with them. You could train with Red and myself, here in the training grounds. Perhaps if they see you preparing to fight, they might take you seriously. Besides"—she couldn't hide her coy smile—"I've always wanted to train a shifter."

I gaped at her, hardly daring to believe what I'd just heard. I'd been wondering how I was going to train when I'd not even set foot inside a gym, but now the personal trainer of one of the best fighters the vampires offered had just suggested I train with them!

"Hells yeah!" I said, earning looks of amusement from both Myla and Red at my sudden enthusiasm. "I mean, I have no idea what I'm doing—"

"Do we have time?" Red asked Myla, an eyebrow raised. "The quarter-finals are next week."

"We'll make time," Myla insisted. "Come on, when am I going to get another opportunity like this?" She clasped her hands together like she was begging and blinked puppy-dog eyes at her pupil.

I raised my hand slightly, like I was in school. "I'm sorry, but what's the big deal about training me?"

Myla's eyes lit up with excitement. "I have a theory about shifters. You guys heal each time you shift, right?"

"Yeees," I said, a little apprehensive.

"Do you know how muscles grow?"

I suddenly regretted all those times I'd bunked science and P.E. "Refresh me."

"They grow when they *repair*." Myla was positively shaking with excitement now. "Obviously that takes time when you're a human, but if yours repair every time you shift—"

"Ahhh, I get it," I said, nodding. I glanced at Madigan, who'd been listening intently. "Is that how it works? I just thought my body reset to the way it was."

He looked taken aback, the question catching him off guard. "I... I am not the right person to ask. But perhaps I could research it?"

"We *are* researching it!" Myla said. "Don't bother with the stuffy old books. I'll monitor your progress, and training, and diet, and—Oh! I've got so much to organise!"

She rushed off before anyone could stop her.

"I guess we're doing this, then?" Red said, folding her arms, though I noticed how she smiled at Myla's retreating form.

"I didn't mean to get in the way," I said.

Red waved a dismissive hand. "Nah, you're good. Besides, what's the point of getting stronger without someone to teach you combat?" She winked at me, and gratitude swelled in my chest. "See you here tomorrow. Similar sort of time?"

"Perfect!"

With a parting nod to Hiero and Madigan, Red followed Myla.

"Sooo," Hiero said, and I could already tell from his sly tone that a teasing remark was headed my way. "You really *don't know* if your body heals or resets after you shift?"

"Oh, piss off." I gave him a playful nudge, but even his taunts couldn't pierce through the excitement building inside me. Perhaps I didn't need to rely on witches to make progress after all.

CHAPTER FIFTEEN

"I'm stuck!" My legs trembled as I tried to stand, the weight across my shoulders crushing me down like a human concertina.

"You can do it. Just one more." Myla's strict order came from above—I couldn't see her, my eyes screwed tight, my face burning with exertion. "Keep your back straight, engage your core, and—"

I let out a strained cry as I attempted to complete the squat, my thighs and glutes screaming with effort. But it was no good. I'd reached as far as I could, and just when I thought my knees would buckle, the pressure eased as Myla assisted me with the last rep.

"That's enough for today," she said, lifting the barbell from my shoulders. If she hadn't drilled into me that training to failure was a good thing, I'd have beat myself up more than I already was.

A couple of weeks had flown by and if I had, indeed, made progress, I certainly couldn't see it.

Myla seemed to read my mind—or perhaps my mood—as she said, "You're doing better than you think."

"*Really?*" I would have fought the issue harder, but I could barely breathe.

"Oh yes!" She scribbled something on her clipboard. "Trust the process, Ava. You might have an advantage over humans, but you were never going to become a bodybuilder overnight."

I let out a huff—the only sound I could muster.

"Go shift and shower. We still have a couple of hours before Red's semi-final match, so you could ask some of the others about joining your coven, if you want?"

I shook my head. So far, every attempt to recruit had been met with a flat refusal and a smug look from Max as he watched from a distance. Usually, I'd have trained with Red in hand-to-hand combat after my session with Myla, but with her upcoming semi-final match, we'd had to postpone. A shame—I could have done with the confidence boost. I was far more adept at combat; my form had started out shoddy, my only experience being the scuffles I'd had in my human days. But at least it *was* experience. Weights and cardio were alien to me.

"I think I'll head back to Hiero's," I said when I'd finally caught my breath.

"No problem. I'll see you at Red's match. And don't forget to eat!"

I forced a smile. There was little chance of that, my hunger almost insatiable after training and shifting. Whenever Chef served dinner, I'd devour anything in sight, an almost animal savagery about me, no mind and all instinct. Though I was less certain that would be the case today, my stomach coiling at the prospect of watching another of Red's matches. The quarter-final had been something of a free-for-all, with sixteen vampires entering, and only four making it through to the next round. After Max *Morningstar-to-his-fans* had gouged out the eye of another competitor, I'd retreated, wiping my hands like they were still coated in the remains of Ivan's eyes. I'd had another nightmare that night.

"I can't believe Red has to team up with that absolute griefer," I said, scowling at Max as he replaced the weapon he'd been practising with in the rack before heading to the showers. The semi-finals were a two-vs-two, and fate had paired the rivals together.

"All the more reason to be there to show our support." She held out her clenched fist, which I bumped with my own before slinking off.

My post-shift shower and snacks usually lifted my mood. Not this time. Not even when I prettied up in the new outfit Hiero had gifted me. I couldn't shake the nagging doubt that my training wasn't making the slightest difference. Maybe my body really *did* reset back to square one, and all of this was for nothing. On my rest days, I'd experimented with my shifting—trying to summon extra limbs or turn my hands into pincers—but still no luck.

If only there was someone who I could ask.

Latisha's face flashed through my mind, and the pretzels I'd just consumed felt like they had tangled together inside me.

Perhaps Madigan's suggestion of researching wasn't such a bad idea.

It was a sign of how desperate I was that the idea of pouring over some dusty, old tomes didn't fill me with dread.

I headed upstairs and towards the library. After spending a couple of weeks here, I was finally learning my way around.

I wasn't surprised to hear Madigan's voice growing louder with every step as I approached. *Of course* he was in the library. I was about to enter... when he said something that rooted me to the spot.

"What did Xander mean? At breakfast, when we first met. He said my death was the reason for... what?"

I held my breath. I too had been curious about what Xander had meant, but had been so preoccupied I'd almost forgotten about it.

Crouching, I squinted through the crack between the door and the wall.

Madigan sat on Hiero's desk, one long leg raised, his foot resting on the wooden arm of a chair. And in the chair, facing him, was Hiero.

"Everything," Hiero said after a pause. "I knew I must become liege lord the night Franziska refused to avenge your death." His voice was heavy, more serious than I'd ever heard him before. "She won't fight the Hallows until they are at our gates and it's too late to stop them. She's weak. I will *not* let that happen." Hiero lowered his head, laughing slightly. "But I'll admit it was less nerve-wracking when I believed you were dead."

"What do you mean?"

"Before, I was just running for liege lord to build an army for myself. But now, I'm building it for you. And Ava, of course. If I fail, it won't just be myself I'm letting down."

Madigan sighed. "I'm sure we'd find a way. Red has said she'll come with us. Myla would have to remain a guard but... but I'm sure we'd find others."

"How many?" Hiero's voice grew louder. "Five? Ten? Not enough if the Hallows have returned. You know this, Len!" He stood, now able to look down on Madigan. "You've been reading nonstop about the last time they declared war on our existence. It took an army and a Witch Queen to wipe them out. And even then, some still survived. They killed Master Tobias!"

Madigan slowly rose from the table. He was only a couple of inches taller than Hiero, but he fixed him with the same stony glare he gave me whenever I overstepped the mark, and like me, Hiero flinched beneath it.

"You needn't remind me of the Hallows' crimes," Madigan said in a low voice, soft but dangerous. "I was there. I heard everything they did to him. I saw his remains."

Hiero swallowed, but maintained eye contact. They were mere inches apart.

"How did you survive?" Hiero asked, his voice almost disappearing, emotion constricting his vocal cords.

Madigan didn't answer right away. For a heartbeat, they just stared into each other's eyes.

"I'd rather not discuss it," he said at last, backing into the table with a bump, but Hiero lent forward, resting a hand on the table, so close their bodies almost touched.

"Tell me," Hiero said in a whisper, so quiet I almost missed it.

Still no answer. He merely stared back at Hiero, his chest heaving, and now I was sure it wasn't Hiero's eyes Madigan was staring at. It was his lips.

"I-I have something for you," Madigan said, plunging a hand into his pocket. A glint of silver.

"I don't want it yet."

"But you told me to bring it back."

"And one night, I shall accept it." Hiero's lips were millimetres from Madigan's. "But not now. Not yet. I need to know you have a reason to come back to me."

Each pound of my heart seemed to thrum through my body like an aftershock. Fire surging through my veins. My mind wild with panic, fear, and jealousy. But what broke me was that I wasn't sure which of them I was jealous of. That, and the thrill sparking between my legs.

What was *wrong* with me?

I knocked on the door as I marched in, just as Hiero raised his hand to... to do what? I'd never know. Would he have placed it on Madigan's chest? His cheek? Or run his thumb across his lips?

Hiero drew back, colour leaving his face, while Madigan flushed scarlet, his hand instantly reaching for his cuff and tugging.

"Sorry for interrupting," I said, pretending not to notice their flustered reactions, though of course, they would both sense mine, my heart still raging against my ribs. "I was wondering if you were coming to Red's match?"

Hiero swept his hand through his locks, grinning, but it was the least convincing smile I'd ever seen him wear. "Of course. I was just looking for Len." He turned back to Madigan. "Are you ready?"

But Madigan didn't respond. He was staring at me, blinking more than usual. "Ava. You look... different." A grin slowly crept across his face. "Simply"—he shook his head slightly as he struggled for the word he wanted— "*divine.*"

I'd been so distracted by what I'd walked in on, I'd forgotten I'd glammed up after my shower. The coiling envy within my stomach eased, replaced by a flutter of butterflies. I gave my skirt a small swish, suppressing the urge to give a stupid girlish giggle at the compliment. "Do you like it?"

Madigan strode past Hiero and took one of my hands in his. "It's beautiful. But not half as much as you."

I glanced at Hiero, who was now watching the pair of us with an expression difficult to read. But as he caught my eye, he captured his lower lip in his teeth, a hunger glinting in his dark brown irises that sent a spark through me. Was it unease? Or arousal?

Perhaps both.

In a bizarre twist of fate, my racing thoughts served as a welcome distraction during the semi-final. Fortunately, it was over swiftly, sparing me the gore-fest as one of Red's opponents yielded, lying on his back with Red's dagger at his throat.

I could see why she was a favourite to win, darting through the air faster than I'd ever seen Madigan move—and he was probably the fastest *anything* I'd ever seen. She was proficient with several weapons, spears, staffs, and tridents being her speciality, though had also shown her prowess with a sword and dagger. Good thing too, as halfway through the match, Max had turned on her, perhaps to wipe out his greatest competition, but she'd floored him with a throwing technique that I made a mental note to learn myself. Watching her, I realised she'd been using kid gloves during our sparring matches.

We ended up in the Lucky Lantern—Hiero's suggestion—to celebrate. Though I wondered if he, like me, was using it as an excuse to silence the demons dancing through his mind.

As my second shot of vodka warmed my throat, I tried to convince myself it was to numb my creeping insecurities around shifting and failure to recruit, but all I could think about was how close Madigan and Hiero had been. Hiero's lips. Madigan's hitched breaths.

What would have happened if I'd not interrupted? Would Madigan have stopped him? Or not? And if not, how did I feel about that?

Red and Myla can't have noticed anything was wrong as they chatted away about Red's upcoming final match against Max. I tried to focus on what they were saying, and not that Hiero and Madigan were now sitting as far apart as possible at our little table.

Occasionally I caught Hiero staring at Madigan, then hurriedly nod at whatever Red or Myla had said, though I could tell he too wasn't listening.

"Ava?" Red's voice yanked me from my thoughts.

"Sorry?"

"I said, I've had an idea that might help you with your recruitment."

"Oh, yes! Go on?" I stared into her mismatched eyes, determined to focus. Though recruitment hadn't been my priority recently—I'd been far too distracted for that—I didn't want to be rude to someone offering help. Especially Red, after she'd already gone out of her way to train me.

"When I win the finals, I'll make an announcement that I'm coming with you to fight the Hallows. Just about every vampire will be there, and the Battles tend to get them so riled up they'll be looking for a fight."

"You'd do that for me?"

"Sure!" She gave a nonchalant shrug. "It's no big deal, really. It just occurred to me last night that some celebrity endorsement might help your cause. Especially after defeating *Max*."

"We would both be grateful for that," Madigan said as he draped an arm over the back of my chair in an almost *possessive* manner. "So, what is your strategy to defeat Max? Are there any new rules for the final match?" He joined Red and Myla's on-going discussion of the finals with such force, that if I'd not known him better, I might have thought he was as excited to watch as every other vampire. But I *did* know him better, and his off-behaviour made my spine stiffen.

Instead of sitting at one of the long tables, like when we first arrived at the Nest, we'd climbed a rickety flight of wooden steps to the second floor—the taller members of our party having to duck to avoid hitting their heads on the low ceiling. I had a perfect view of the town square through a tiny, grubby window. Hiero had pointed out the Blood Bank—a grand building that looked like it belonged in Greece, rather than the dank cavern—as well as the Lover's Sanctum, the Nest's most popular 'love chamber'. From the description Hiero had given me, it sounded like a cross between a brothel and a hotel, and given the sexual appetites of the vampires, I wasn't surprised to hear it was always bustling. Tonight was no exception.

"That's where Hiero and the Liege Lady will address us before we cast our votes," Myla said when she caught me gazing out the window again, wrapped up in my own thoughts. She pointed towards an enormous mound in the middle of the square. "We call it Speaker's Rock."

"Seems weird to me that vampires have an *election*," I said. "I thought fighting it out would be more your style?"

"It was once," Myla said ruefully. "Entire wars were fought. But that was a quick way to lose our strongest warriors. And skilled fighters don't always make great rulers. When the Hallows first appeared, changes were needed to ensure our survival."

"Much to my relief," Hiero said. "I'd like my chances of winning far less if I had to fight her."

To my surprise, Red nodded in agreement. "Not that she needs to fight. Given the number of souls she's taken, she could probably just flutter her eyelashes and most would surrender on the spot. Hiero *definitely* would."

Myla giggled. "And she wouldn't even need to use her glamour."

"Ha-ha," Hiero said with a thin smile, his eyes darkening.

"Oh, come on, Hiero," Myla said, smirking. "You can't tell me you wouldn't jump into bed with her at the first opportunity."

"Who says I haven't already?"

Madigan tensed beside me. "I read she fought in both the Hallows War and the Vampiric Civil War," he said, his arm dropping from my chair to my shoulders. It was so unlike him to show this sort of public affection, I was certain it was deliberate, and not the casual gesture he wanted us to think it was. "Do you know if that's true?"

"It is," Myla said with a nod. "She's still got the armour she wore."

"Vampires need armour?" I asked. I'd only ever seen them wear leather in the Battles of Blood.

"Only against the Hallows. They say the Hallows had these weapons with special powers."

"Demonic artefacts," Madigan said, his voice so cold that everyone looked at him. He slowly withdrew from me and stared at a spot in the centre of the table, his eyes distant. "They're called demonic artefacts. They look like normal tools or items. But as you get closer, you can *feel* their power. Twisted and cruel, full of hate and violence. A force so dark it destroys all it touches." His breath hitched as his eyes snapped upward to Hiero.

Hiero's usually charming face was drawn into a grim expression, his jaw set, nostrils flaring. "Master Tobias?"

Madigan nodded.

Hiero slowly rose from the table. "We *will* avenge him, Len." Though his voice was measured, his trembling fists betrayed his building rage. "I swear, if it is the last thing I do, I'll hunt every single one of them down, drag them out of whatever hole they are hiding in, and have them shredded into so many pieces the Devil himself couldn't put them back together."

"His killer is dead," Madigan said, perhaps trying to calm him.

"That doesn't matter!" Hiero slammed his hand down on the table, the bustling inn quietening as heads spun to face him. "The Hallows have one goal: to kill us. Every. Single. One. Of us."

Silence now. Thick. Suffocating.

Hiero seemed to awaken from a rage-fuelled daze, blinking back at the faces turned to his and hanging on his every word.

He straightened himself and cleared his throat.

"I don't know what lies Franziska has spread, but the Hallows *are* real. They *have* returned. And while they live, none of us are safe."

"Well, well," said a voice that sent a shudder down my spine. Silky, smooth, and feminine. Beautiful and dangerous. A voice that had both Madigan and me jumping to our feet.

Franziska stood atop the wooden steps, one white-gloved hand still on the banister. She was dressed in a smart black frock coat, her shiny stilettos clicking against the floorboards as she swaggered towards Hiero, patrons falling over themselves to make way for her.

"Don't get involved," Myla muttered to Red, and the two of them stared pointedly anywhere but at the Liege Lady.

Franziska's glamour was working at full force, the glow of the candles shimmering around her. So strong, I found it difficult to tear my eyes off her and onto something safer.

"What silly, childish games are you playing, Hieronymus?" Franziska asked, the corners of her crimson lips curling.

"No games, Franziska." Hiero's teeth were ground so tight he was almost unintelligible.

"No games, *my liege*."

For a second, Hiero stood fuming, his fists clenched at his sides, shoulders rising and falling with his breaths.

But then, like he'd flicked a switch, he suddenly became a whole new person: his lazy, seductive smirk in place, hands in his pockets. "There's no need to call me '*my liege*' just yet."

A small, nervous titter of laughter rang throughout the room, but Franziska was unfazed. Her blue gaze was locked on Hiero, a sinister leer splitting her scarlet mouth.

"You're funny," she said. "That's why you're popular. You could pose a credible threat if you weren't so naive. It's quite cute, honestly."

"I've been called cute before."

"I'll bet."

"But not naive."

"Then a liar? Because why else would you badger these people with nonsense about the Hallows unless you were incredibly gullible or a liar?"

Hiero traced his tongue over his lower lip, and now faces peered up from the stairs—patrons from the ground floor trying to get a better view—and though I couldn't see the stairs leading to the top floor, I'd have bet my Doc Martens that vampires were spying from above.

"It's not a lie," Hiero said. Without wit or flirtation to fall back on, Hiero's answers were painfully lame. "I've had confirmation."

"From whom? A demon? You trust demons, do you, Hieronymus?" Franziska lowered herself into the lap of a vampire sat at a neighbouring table. His eyes lit up like his wildest dreams had come true as she draped an arm around his shoulders. "You don't believe demons, do you, Mister Greentree?" she muttered to him, like they were having their own private conversation, tracing her thumb across his cheek to his lips.

"N-no, my liege," he said in a throaty whisper. "A-and it's Greenwood. Kevin Greenwood."

"I know, darling." She turned her attention back to Hiero. "Or, when you speak of confirmation, were you referring to the shifter? One tiny, insignificant shifter who you met a couple of weeks ago. A stranger. Do you trust strangers?" She then added under her breath again, "You don't trust strangers, do you, Mister Greenwood?"

"Please," Hiero said with a laugh, though his composure was slipping almost as fast as it had appeared. "There's no need to involve Kev. This is between you and me."

"It may be between you and me. But it is decided by *them*." She swept her arm, gesturing to the room. She raised her voice. "Let me hear if you trust demons."

"NO!" rang around the room.

"Let me hear if you trust strangers."

"NO!"

I don't remember when I'd shuffled closer to Madigan, but I found myself clutching his arm.

Franziska's eyes fell on me, stalling my heart. "I think you have your answer, *shifter*."

Another snicker of laughter throughout the pub—louder than the first—and blood crept up my neck, into my face. Part of me wanted to hide behind Madigan... like a *coward*. In defiance, I stood my ground, though I couldn't help but hate myself for the way my legs shook.

"Then what about Len?" Hiero said. "He's not a demon or a stranger. He is a vampire that lived here for decades. Why don't you trust *his* word? Isn't the Liege Lady meant to listen to her people?"

My stomach gave a horrible lurch as Franziska's smile widened into something disturbing; I knew the expression of someone who had set a trap and watch their prey walk into it.

"Your ex-lover, you mean?"

"That doesn't matter."

"But of course it does." She rose, closing the gap between them with two strides. Even on those stilettos, she had to crane her neck to look at Hiero, but it was Hiero who flinched.

"We've all been in love, Hieronymus," she said softly, almost kindly. But I knew better. "We all know what it's like to pine after a lover who's moved on. You'd do anything to win him back, wouldn't you? Tell him everything he wants to hear? Even that you can become Liege

Lord and conscript our people into a pretend war with an extinct foe. Have them butcher lambs and tell them they've fought wolves."

More laughter. Not just sniggers now. *Proper* laughter. Even from vampires I'd seen Hiero shake hands with before. *Everyone.*

Franziska released a long, exaggerated sigh, her face twisting into a look of sympathy—no—a look of pity. "Bless you. Someone who hasn't seen true warfare couldn't possibly understand how embarrassing this all is."

The muscles within Madigan's sleeve tensed, and I tightened my grip on him. I knew *exactly* which nerve Franziska had touched.

"Aww look." Franziska tilted her head, now looking towards us, placing a hand over the spot her heart would be if she had one. "There he is. Your beloved."

"My liege," Madigan acknowledged her through gritted teeth.

"And the shifter who stole his heart. Seems like an odd choice to me. Barely even a supernatural at all. I suppose there is no accounting for taste. But then again"—her teeth grazed her lower lip as she raked her eyes over me—"I suppose she's pretty in a *human* kind of way."

"Leave her out of this," Madigan growled. His voice echoed eerily, and at first I didn't know why. But when Franziska's eyes darted to Hiero, alight with unmistakable glee, I worked it out. *Hiero* had spoken too. The exact same words.

"Oh, *no.*" Franziska couldn't contain her wicked delight. "Not you too, Hiero. I know you have a reputation for sleeping with anyone, but a *shifter*? You haven't, have you?"

The laughter was almost deafening, and without a word, Hiero pushed past Franziska, shoving through the crowd and down the stairs.

"Have I offended you?" Franziska called after him. "Sorry!" She wasn't.

After one shared glance with Madigan, we both made to follow him, only for Franziska to block my path.

"You've got your answer." The sweetness from her voice was gone now. "No one is interested. Why are you still here?"

"She is staying with me until the end of the election," Madigan said, gripping me by the upper arm. "Good luck with your campaign, my liege." He tried to drag me towards the stairs, but Franziska snatched my other arm, so tight I thought she might break it, and I let out a sharp cry.

"I'll be watching," she said before releasing me.

The room burst into cheers as Franziska celebrated her victory, and vampires from the ground floor barged past us, eager to join the party, as Madigan and I chased after Hiero.

CHAPTER SIXTEEN

I sat at the bottom of the entrance hall staircase, face in my hands, mind spinning with images. Images of Hiero: his pained expression as he stormed from the inn; how close his lips had been to Madigan's; the way his cheeks dimpled and eyes creased when he flashed one of those smiles that made my stomach flip.

I jumped as Madigan sat beside me—I hadn't heard him coming.

"Did you find him?" I asked.

"In his room," he said as he adjusted his cuff. "The butler said he's not to be disturbed."

An awkward silence.

We'd had awkward silences before, but somehow, this one was heavier, stifling with the things going unsaid.

"I saw you in the library." I'd never been able to bottle things for long, my tongue always betraying me.

"I know." He wasn't looking at me.

"I saw how close you were."

"I know."

"If I hadn't interrupted, would you..." It was almost painful to ask. "Would you have kissed him?"

He didn't answer right away, tugging on his cuff until the button popped off, rolling across the polished marble floor. When he sighed, his whole body seemed to deflate. "I would hope not. But truthfully, I'm uncertain."

Well, at least he's honest.

I bit my lip, afraid of the answer to the next question. "Did you want to?"

"I..." He drove his fingers through his hair, hanging his head.

His silence told me everything.

Though I appreciated his honesty, it did little to untangle the knot of conflicting, confusing thoughts running rampant. I thought the truth might bring closure. On the contrary, it made things worse. Should I be angry? Because I wasn't. Should I feel betrayed? Because I didn't. I almost felt... guilty? Sympathetic?

"What about you?" he asked, the question ripping me back into reality.

"What do you mean?"

"I've seen the way you look at him, and the way he looks at you. I can sense the *effect* he has on you."

"Yes, well, I can't help that," I said defensively as heat mounted within me.

He took my hand—a gesture I'd not been expecting—and the gentleness of his touch only confused me more. "That's not what I meant. I am not accusing you of anything. I'm asking if you... If you *want* to?"

"Want to what?"

He gave me a pointed look. "Please don't make me say it."

"What? Kiss him? Fuck him? Be with him?"

"All of the above."

I was going to say 'no', but the word died on my lips. After all, he'd been honest with me.

"I'm sorry," I said, though I wasn't *exactly* certain what I was apologising for. My fantasies?

The corner of his mouth twitched. "Don't be."

"You're not angry?"

"No, are you?"

I shook my head. "I'm not sure how I'm feeling, but I *do* know that..." *I love you.* "I... want to be with you."

His grip on my hand tightened. "I never want to lose you. Never. And if that means I'm never alone with Hiero again, then I'll—"

"No, that's not what I want. I want you to be happy. Whatever that means. Just promise you won't keep secrets. That's all I ask. And in return, I'll promise not to hide anything from you."

He brushed my hair from my face and smiled. Perhaps it wasn't as dazzling as Hiero's, but Madigan's hidden smile was more powerful than any glamour, and before I knew what I was doing, my lips had met his.

Hiero's manor was deathly silent. After waiting an hour for him to emerge, Madigan had grown impatient and decided to visit the Nest's public library to continue his research. At first, I hadn't given the suggestion a second thought, but now I wondered if he was avoiding Hiero's library and the memories it would conjure. He'd asked if I wished to accompany him, and though this was the perfect opportunity to see if the library had a book on shifters, all the noise in my head had quashed my motivation.

I amused myself by wandering through the house, hunting down the secret passages Hiero had shown me, and trying to remember where each of them led. One was at the bottom of the twisting spiral staircase outside our room, and to my delight, it led to the kitchen. Chef had a soft spot for me and let me pinch anything I wanted, which was useful when I was weak from shifting and workouts, but tonight, the kitchen was deserted. Of course. The one time I could use some company, no one was around. Still, solitude was preferable over bumping into Xander or Talia, who were as pleasant as a water infection.

But after a while, even exploring lost its appeal. I'd seen all there was to see.

Except... Hiero's room...

I knew where it was, having walked past it many times now, yet never set foot inside after Hiero's explicit instruction to keep out unless invited. A fair request—even vampires needed privacy.

My heart thumped as I stood a small distance from his bedroom door, listening for any signs of movement. Nothing. Perhaps Hiero was sleeping?

He said he didn't want to be disturbed...

I rocked on my feet, wondering if this was a good idea. It probably wasn't.

I took a step closer, the red carpet muffling my footsteps, soft beneath my feet. And then a second step. And a third. I raised my fist to knock.

The door swung open, and Hiero leaned his forearm on the door-frame. Though he still wore his usual shirt and braces, he'd unbuttoned his shirt to the bottom, his muscled abdomen peeking through.

Fuck...

I dragged my eyes from his chest to his face.

He smiled; the smile that melted me from the inside out.

I grinned back stupidly, heart fluttering, heat creeping through my chest.

He laughed, a low rumble in his chest. "Hello, Ava. What can I do for you?"

"You seem to have cheered up a bit," I said, coughing slightly to re-gain my composure. I fixated on a spot above his eyes, like I was trying to avoid being caught in his glamour, though I knew deep down, it wasn't his glamour that was responsible for the way my mouth grew wet, nor the swirling sensation in my stomach.

Hiero licked his lips. "It was a tough night," he said. He was putting on a brave face: I knew, because I did the same thing, though admit-tedly, *my* brave face didn't include a seductive smirk.

"I'm sorry that happened." What a dumb, cliché thing to say, but it was all I had. "The butler said you shouldn't be disturbed, but I think we need to talk."

"Agreed." A flicker of amusement skittered across his face as he ran a thumb along the underside of one of his braces, catching my eye in the way I'm sure he'd intended. "Would you like to come inside?" He turned his body so I could squeeze past him.

Red candles wafted their sweet fragrance through the doorway, bathing his four-poster bed in a warm, sensual glow.

"N-no, thank you." I knew myself. I didn't have that level of self-control. Walking into that room would be a big mistake. "How about we go to the library?" The image of Hiero leaning into Madigan flashed before my eyes, and from the devilish smirk on Hiero's lips, he'd relived the experience, too.

"Or," I said in a hurry, "somewhere else? Like the lounge? Or—"

"I have an idea. Somewhere with enough entertainment for some-one so bored they've resorted to creeping around the house," he said with a knowing wink.

We wound up in the billiard room, and I instantly poured drinks at the bar—vodka for me, whiskey for Hiero. The walk had been a slow, agonising stroll, making forcefully innocent conversation, while Hiero smirked at me as I became flustered each time he held open a door, or put his hand to the small of my back.

If I'd wanted him to stop, I could have asked.

But I didn't.

And I didn't want to enjoy how his eyes lingered in places that made me blush.

But I did.

"Have you ever played pool before?" he asked, chalking a cue as I knocked back my shot of vodka, then poured myself a second.

"Only a few times at Uni. I warn you, I'm not very good."

"That's all right, I'll teach you." He racked the balls into their starting position, then set up the white cue ball. "Break shot?" he said, holding out the cue towards me.

"You do it. I'll only fuck it up."

He shrugged, then bent over the table, winking one eye and then the other as he took aim. "So, what did you want to talk about?"

I'm not sure what made me jump: his question, or the sharp *crack* as he took the break shot, red and orange balls bouncing wildly around the table, before a red ball was pocketed. He circled the table, searching for the best angle for the next shot.

"About what Franziska said about Madigan."

"Oh yes?" He had his back to me as he took aim once more. Though unable to see his face, I still detected the tension in his voice.

"It's not true."

"Isn't it?" Hiero stood upright, abandoning the shot to face me. He still hadn't buttoned his shirt...

I swallowed. "No. He didn't abandon you. He told you how he got roped into Ivan's coven, didn't he? He's already admitted he shouldn't have joined in the first place and—"

"It was more about you, really. He could have left you behind and returned to me. But he chose you." He turned away, leaning across the table as he took aim, giving me the perfect view of his firm backside. I could have sworn it was on purpose—but perhaps I was making excuses. He pocketed a second red ball, and it was only when he marched to the other side of the table that I released a held breath.

"I saved his life, you know?" I said.

Hiero glanced up at me briefly as he took aim. "A life debt?"

I bit my lip. I hadn't thought of it like that. But perhaps... "I became a shifter to save him. Maybe he *does* feel like he owes me."

"Maybe, but if I know Len—and I do—I don't think he'd be in a relationship with someone because he owes them. Otherwise, he'd have married me already, the amount we saved each other's arse."

Click! He took the shot but missed.

My turn.

I bent over the table, struggling to get the cue into a comfortable position on my thumb as I took aim, then jumped as Hiero took my hips from behind.

"Stand like this," he said, adjusting my position. A shiver ran through my body; a shiver I tried to deny.

It's just chilly in here...

I hit the cue ball, sending it flying into an orange, but the orange ball merely bounced off the cushion.

I straightened myself, turning to face Hiero, expecting him to step back after having stood so close. But he didn't. Instead, he leant even closer, placing a hand on the pool table, trapping me against it in the exact way he'd cornered Madigan in the library. So close I could smell his sandalwood aftershave and whiskey on his breath.

I had to keep talking. "You went through hell together. And so did we. A different kind of hell, perhaps, but still..." I considered telling him how sometimes I awoke drenched in a cold sweat as Ivan haunted my dreams but decided against it. I wanted some secrets, and my recurring nightmare was one of them.

Hiero nodded before picking up his cue and circling the table once more. I'd not realised how tense I'd been until my muscles relaxed.

"Those kinds of experiences shape you," Hiero said. "When we were young, being homosexual was a crime. We witnessed another soldier being flogged by our superior for committing the crime of falling in love. I think Len has been careful about how he displays his affections ever since."

"What do you mean?"

"Well, in public, he's a total gentleman, isn't he?"

I grinned. Breaking down his cold outer shell to make him smile had been one of the things I'd enjoyed most.

"But, in the bedroom…" He paused to chuckle at the memories he'd recalled, an impish sparkle in his eyes. "Has he got you calling him *'Sir'* yet?"

Blood rushed into my face. "W-what did you say?" The way Madigan had teased me, made me *beg* to cum, burned in my memory. "N-no, not exactly."

"It won't be long, I'm sure. But we had to be secretive about our relationship in the human world. Going from that to the other extreme, here in the Nest, messes with his head, I think."

Hiero took the shot, pocketing his third red ball, but missed the fourth.

"Which is a pity," he went on, as I lined up my shot. I felt his eyes on me and became hyperaware of how my skirt rode up as his hands found my hips, adjusting my position. "Because if you ask me, when it comes to love, the more the merrier."

He leaned his body against mine, holding my arm to take aim, but all I could focus on was the soft bulge of his cock against my ass. My breath hitched as treacherous, impure, *filthy* ideas flooded my mind. All of them with me bent over this pool table, and to my shame, I felt the tingle of growing wet.

Hiero's breath was hot against my ear. "As much as I want to hate you, Ava, I just can't. I'm a lover, not a fighter." He helped me take the shot, tapping the white ball into the orange that spun away and into the pocket. "If I had it my way, you would both stay here, with me."

I spun to face him, and like last time, he didn't move. But now he was closer. So close, my body pressed to his. "I-I'd have to speak to Madigan."

"So, that's not a '*no*', then?" Hiero's smile widened as he moved a millimetre closer. I could almost taste the whiskey on his lips.

I swallowed, my mouth suddenly too wet. "I-I've not thought about it..."

Liar...

"Well, perhaps you should have a think. At the very least, speak to Len about it."

Hiero stepped away, and as he did, I heard the slamming of the front door.

"Len's home," Hiero said. "I'll tidy this away." He gestured to the pool table before turning his alluring smile back to me. "And you should probably calm down, or Len will think we were up to something."

CHAPTER
SEVENTEEN

I'd been counting down to Red's final match, but now it had arrived my mind was elsewhere.

The arena looked like a combination of the Colosseum and a rodeo: a circular battleground covered in dirt or sand, and wooden benches for the spectators rising higher row by row. I stretched, my back already complaining. Hiero had arranged for us to sit in one of the front boxes, though I'd rather he hadn't. I didn't need a front-row seat to the bloodbath. Franziska was in an opposite box containing a throne decorated with twisting red and gold metal.

We'd been waiting a good fifteen minutes now, but Hiero had insisted on getting here early, buzzing with excitement. He and Myla were standing, rather than sitting, leaning against the barrier of the box, like they were afraid to miss anything. Madigan sat beside me, arms folded, jaw set. If anyone wanted to be here less than me, it was him.

I twisted my fingers in my lap. It probably looked as though I was nervous about Red's match. I *should* have been nervous about Red's match, but all I could focus on was the conversation I'd had with Madigan following my game of pool with Hiero.

I'd told him everything that had happened the instant we were alone. He'd snorted a laugh and said he expected nothing less from the pair of us—whatever that was supposed to mean.

When I'd asked him if he'd ever been in a polyamorous relationship before, he shook his head. "It's common here, but I never thought it was right for me."

"Do you still think that?"

His answer played around in my head as I stared into the empty arena, my heart fluttering when it should have been pounding with nerves.

"I am yours, Ava, but if it's something you would like me to consider..." His voice had trailed off as his eyes diverted, lost in a memory. A memory that had made the corner of his mouth twitch. "I'm starting to understand the appeal."

My airways constricted as his words echoed through my mind. Sure, I'd fantasised about bedding two men at once—what girl hasn't? But the idea it could really happen...

My sights drifted towards Hiero leaning over the edge of the box, once again displaying his ass to me in tight brown trousers, and I forced myself to tear my eyes from him, back to the arena.

Was that what I wanted? To be with him? He could be insufferable, but then again... That smile... Those deep grooves between his abs...

I shook myself. I couldn't stay at the Nest forever. As much as I was putting it off, I had to return to my coven eventually.

Didn't I?

What would happen if I stayed? Would Latisha come and find me? Demand I return? She'd once told me I was free to leave the coven if I chose, but that was before I'd seen what she really was.

Focus, Ava. Focus... You're here to support Red. Worry about Hiero and Latisha later.

I scoured the arena again, looking for something—anything—to steal my attention, but all I found were rowdy vampires screaming and chanting with impatience, and the scent of ale and sweat. Nothing as horrifying as those wet, ripping sounds as Latisha stripped rotting flesh from bone. And nothing as captivating as the soft caress of Hiero's whiskey-tinged breath against my ear. *Almost* nothing. I shuffled closer to Madigan, inhaling his vanilla scent as I slid a hand through the crook of his elbow, forcing his folded arms apart.

"I wish they'd get on with it," he said through clenched teeth, but his prayers were answered when Franziska rose from her throne, earning cheers from the spectators and a tut from Hiero.

"She's wearing the crown today," he grumbled. "Figures. Never misses a chance to show off."

I squinted, trying to make out the bone-coloured ring among her raven curls. "Is she *using* it?" I asked.

"No. You'd know if she was." But before I could ask what he meant, the crowd hushed into silence as Franziska's silky-smooth voice rang out.

"My people, thank you for joining us for the Battles of Blood finals. It is truly an honour for you to attend this historic tournament, as well as having me—your ruler—be among you tonight."

This earned her more cheers and applause, and Hiero's knuckles whitened as he gripped the edge of the box, perhaps fighting the urge to leap from it and make a charge for Franziska.

"Our youngest vampires may not understand why the Battles of Blood and Souls take place," Franziska said. "We've all made substantial changes and sacrifices for our survival. One of which is to ignore our very nature, and be *gentle* with one another—like humans." I could have sworn I felt her blue eyes pierce right through me.

Boos and jeering rumbled through the spectator stands. Franziska raised a hand for quiet, and this time, it took a little longer for the crowd to settle.

"But," she continued, "this is why we have the Battles. Channel your bloodlust and become a champion. Or, imitate these law breakers and kill in the streets." With a snap of her fingers and a clank of chains, one of the wooden gates leading into the arena clicked upward, Franziska's guards herding five naked figures into the arena with the tips of their spears.

"Oh, here we go," Hiero said with a groan, stepping back from the edge of the box to slide down onto the bench beside me. As Franziska continued her speech, Hiero's mouth wordlessly moved in unison, perfectly lip-synching every syllable.

"I give you law. I give you safety. I give you *justice*."

The five figures knelt before Franziska's box, and though the distance hindered my sight, I was certain a couple were trembling, their heads turned downward.

"Whether you choose to fight honourably in the tournament, or kill unlawfully, either way, you'll end up in the ring. Since you five are such fearsome fighters, please, show us what you've got," Franziska said, her tone dripping with schadenfreude, then added in a hiss, "Last man alive goes free."

The moment she said it, all five had scrambled to their feet and began the bloody free-for-all. No weapons, just their fists and brute strength.

I couldn't watch, leaning back on the bench, my eyes down on my fidgeting fingers.

"What's the point of this?" I asked as my stomach gave a lurch at the unmistakable sound of breaking bones, followed by whoops from the crowd.

"When the arena isn't used for the tournaments, it's used to publicly punish criminals," Hiero said. "But this is the first time Franziska has carried out a punishment before a Battle."

"You know why she's doing it, don't you?" said Madigan.

"Of course I do. Point scoring." He let out a groan, dragging his hands down his face. "Fuck, Red needs to win. Her popularity might be the only thing getting me votes at this rate."

I didn't know what was harder to watch: the bloodshed in the arena, or Hiero unravelling beside me. I settled for my feet, and it was only when the wet sounds of ripping flesh and the snapping of bones had died, I glanced into the arena again. Four broken bodies in pools of blood, and the fifth kneeling before Franziska's box as he received his pardon.

If the spectators had been excited before, now they were positively frenzied, the scent of iron thick in the air.

Once again, Franziska rose to her feet, raising her hands for calm, and this time, the crowd fell silent.

"That was good, wasn't it?" she called out, receiving a roar in return. "Are you ready for more?" Another roar. "I think you have been patient enough."

I covered my ears as they rang with the deafening cheers sweeping through the spectator stands.

"Then let us welcome our first contestant, Maximillian Strider—or as you might know him—Max Morningstar!"

The gate on the left clanked open, and Max strutted into the arena, waving to the crowd as they cheered him on. He didn't smile, instead wearing a haughty expression, like he was above such things. He shifted his weight from one foot to the other as he rolled his shoulders, flexing his arms in such a way I was sure he was flashing his muscles rather than doing any meaningful stretches.

"And on the other side, we have Krysten Wojda, but you all know her as Red!"

The opposite gate clicked open, and Red marched into the arena, blowing a kiss into the crowd. Thunderous cheers erupted from the spectators, a greeting she played up to, placing a hand over her heart and giving a bow.

I noticed Max kicking up dirt like a bull preparing to charge, clouds of dust billowing behind him, his eyes locked on Red as she blew one last kiss.

Meanwhile, Franziska stood with her hands on her hips, waiting for Red's supporters to calm down, but as the cheers continued, her smile became more like a grimace with every passing second.

"If we may proceed?" I caught her voice—but only just—and it seemed not everyone had heard, or if they had, they ignored her. It was only when Red put a finger to her lips the crowd settled. She faced Franziska and gave another deep bow, and though Franziska smiled, I was sure her eyes remained as icy as ever.

"Red's even more popular than Franziska," Madigan mused, only now showing the slightest bit of interest.

"Of course she is," Hiero said. "Why do you think I'm sponsoring her?"

Madigan's eyes narrowed. "Tactics?"

Hiero grinned unapologetically.

"If you're all quite finished," Franziska said, trying and failing to keep the irritation from her voice, "we can get started. You know the rules. This is a fight to the death or until your opponent yields. Unlike previous Battles, where you may request a weapon of your choice, the weapons around the arena have been chosen at random."

It was only now I noticed more of Franziska's guards hauling wooden crates of various sizes into the arena. I estimated some to be my height, while others would have barely reached my knees.

"And you may find other items of use," Franziska said, "but anything used, save the clothes on your backs, must have come from within the arena itself. You have both been searched, but I trust there are no foreign items or substances upon or within your persons?"

"No, my liege," Red called out.

"No, my liege." Max was still shifting on his feet, like he couldn't keep still, staring intently at Red like he was afraid to look away.

Franziska took a white handkerchief from between her breasts and held it out over the edge of her box.

"Then let the final commence!" She dropped the handkerchief that floated down to the sandy floor of the arena. The second it hit the ground, both fighters darted forward, whipping up sand as they dashed.

As hard as I strained my eyes, I could only *just* keep up with the fighter's movements.

Red was a blur, undeterred by the sand, zipping to the nearest crate and smashing it open with a fist. Max mirrored her, but as fast as he was, he was second to reach his crate, slipping in the sand as he ran.

He seized his weapon—a mace—and raised it in a defensive arc above his head as Red brought down the short sword she'd acquired.

I rubbed my eyes, leaning forward in my seat. One second Red had been at the opposite end of the arena, and in the next she'd reached Max, on the offensive.

"Impressive," Madigan said as he, too, leant forward, resting his elbows on his knees.

"Sometimes the smaller, faster opponent can defeat the larger, stronger one," Hiero said.

The clang of metal echoed throughout the arena as the two exchanged blows, Red's lighter but faster, Max's slower but harder. Red fell back under the weight of his blow, stumbling onto her backside. She rolled as Max brought down the mace and the crowd burst into cries of excitement or disappointment.

"And sometimes they can't," Madigan said, his voice as tight as his clenched fists.

I winced at the memory of the gargantuan Ivan catching the smaller and faster Madigan before pummelling him into the dirt, and my heart gave a sudden leap like I was watching the pair beyond a wall of flame again.

Max swung at Red wildly as she danced backward, hopping onto a crate and leaping off again as Max brought down his mace and smashed it into splinters. Seizing the opportunity, Red grabbed something from inside—a heavy length of rope—and hurled it at Max, who fell back in a tangle.

That was all the time Red needed to smash open another crate and find her weapon of choice: a spear. She abandoned her sword, twirling her spear in both hands in a manner that spelled defeat for every opponent she faced.

Without thinking, I jumped to my feet, gripping the edge of the box.

"Come on, Red!"

And I wasn't the only one. Seeing Red with her signature weapon was enough to make others leap from their seats too. Including Hiero, his warm hand closing around mine where I gripped the barrier.

It was only when I glanced at him that he whipped his hand back, redness creeping up his neck, and shouted in a voice that sounded staged, "Come on, Red, you can do it!"

Red jabbed the end of her spear at Max, his body contorting to avoid being punctured. He circled her, catching a blow to his ear, a spray of blood issuing from the side of his head, but he didn't even flinch, continuing his path before unleashing a mighty swing of his mace. Then another. And another. Forcing Red back with the wildness of a berserker. She lost her footing. And another swing of the mace caught her side.

A shriek of pain. A splatter of blood. Screams from the crowd.

I clapped my hands to my mouth as Max brought down his mace once more.

Despite the blood soaking her side, Red nimbly dodged the blow and retreated. But I couldn't ignore how my stomach flipped at the horrible realisation that I didn't need to squint to keep sight of her anymore. She was slowing down.

Max, on the other hand, continued the attack, occasionally deflected by the spear, but more often missing her entirely as his attacks became more frenzied. He picked up Red's dropped sword and continued the onslaught, blades crashing into crates as he went, weapons and decoys scattering in his path.

"What is he *doing*?" Myla gritted out. She'd remained standing throughout the fight, leaning against the barrier, both hands covering her mouth, muffling her words.

"I've noticed it too," Hiero said, putting a hand on Myla's shoulder. "Something's not right."

"She's not trained for this." Myla drove a hand through her curls, knocking loose her glittery hair clip, her hands shaking as she tried and failed to catch it. My throat constricted. I'd never seen Myla afraid. *Never*. And I'd seen her wrestle with Soul Suckers and bench press a small car. "I trained her to fight Max Morningstar. Not... not whatever *this* is supposed to be."

My teeth shredded my lower lip as Max swung the sword, then his mace, smashing through another crate and narrowly missing Red, who grabbed a dagger from the debris and slotted it in her boot.

"Well, she needs to work that out quickly," Madigan said as he abandoned his seat, face whiter than usual, eyes focused on the battle. "She's losing blood, and her current strategy isn't working."

Each time Red distanced herself from Max, he closed in before she could raise her spear, his arms swinging erratically. And with each attempt, Red left a trail of blood in the dirt.

"Only chance Red has of winning is if he accidentally impales himself," I said, as Max let out a roar and bull rushed his smaller opponent, who only just dodged in time.

Hiero's spine straightened, his eyes widening. "It's almost like... he's taken Sacrilegious Strength."

"Taken *what*?"

Hiero raised an eyebrow at me. "Aren't you a witch's familiar?"

"In training," I said dryly.

"It's a potion that gives temporary strength, but with the drawback of a wild rage that drives the user to mindlessly attack... well... anything."

Myla grabbed Hiero by the shoulders, forcing him to look at her. "Are you sure of it, Hiero? Are you *certain*?"

Hiero stared wide-eyed at Myla, then turned his face back to the fight. Red raised her spear in defence as Max brought down the mace, cleaving it in two.

"I'm certain."

"Only Franziska can stop this." Myla released Hiero, turned on her heel and bolted.

I dared not take my eyes off Red, though my knees shook with the fear of what I might witness.

"How did he get potions down here?" I asked, doing my best not to so much as blink.

A brief pause, broken by a yelp from Max as Red used one half of her spear to skewer him through the shoulder.

"The same way as Hiero, I imagine," Madigan said, his tone exuding disapproval.

"Please!" Hiero snapped, his temper flaring. "There's a time and a place!" He gripped the edge of the barrier so tight it groaned under the pressure as he muttered, "Hurry up, Myla."

Max dropped the sword as he wrenched the tip of the spear from his shoulder and threw it aside as Red snatched the dagger she'd stashed in her boot. A mere toy compared to the spiked ball already dripping with her blood.

"There!" Hiero cried, making me jump as he pointed to Franziska's box. Myla stood beside the Liege Lady, her hands braced on her knees as she caught her breath, mouth moving rapidly as she spoke.

Franziska glanced between Myla and the fighters before her lips spread into a smile that turned my stomach, and from Myla's pained expression, I knew her request to stop the fight had been refused.

"You cowardly, cheating, vile sack of shit!" Hiero shouted—to Max or Franziska, I couldn't be sure—his eyes so wild he looked like he was about to leap from the box and join the fight himself.

Max swung again, and Red, in her clumsy leap backwards, fell to the floor. She scrambled back as Max advanced on her, digging in her heels and pushing, her face contorted with the effort as her life drained away in the dirt beneath her.

He brought the mace down as Red clawed herself back—but was too slow. The swing he'd aimed at her chest came crashing down on her shin, spraying blood, shattering bone, as Red let out a high-pitched, terrible scream that sent a shockwave through my body.

"I can't look." I covered my face, peering through the gaps in my fingers.

Max raised the mace once more, an arc of blood spraying upwards. Then the spiked metal came crashing down. On the same spot. And Red stared open-mouthed at the mangled remains. *Horrified*. In shock.

After the third strike, she finally snapped out of her trance and shuffled backwards. All that remained of her shin was fleshy pulp and splinters of bone, and the rest of her lower leg stayed exactly where it was, lying useless. Severed. Gone.

Blood gushed from the tattered stump, pooling beneath her. Gasps and cries from the spectators, along with shouts of "*Kill her!*" from Max's supporters. Franziska's smile widened.

Max needed no encouragement. He brought the mace down.

Red rolled to one side, the head of the mace narrowly missing her, embedding in the sand, and as Max's balance wavered, Red drove upward with her dagger, slicing Max's face from cheek to forehead.

He screamed, dropping the mace as he put a hand to his wound, blood seeping between his fingers.

With her one good leg, Red swept it across the floor, knocking Max to his feet, clambering on top of him. The blade to his throat.

"Yield," she snarled through gritted teeth. "YEILD!"

Max thrashed beneath her, clutching his face, screaming incoherently, but he didn't yield, even when his thrashing caused the blade to draw blood.

The crowd that had been in uproar only seconds ago was now watching in silence, Max's bloodcurdling shrieks the only sound throughout the arena.

Red shuffled, trying to get up, but couldn't. "He yields," she called out to Franziska, her voice strained like it was taking every drop of strength she had to form the words.

"I didn't hear him," Franziska said with a shrug, her pretty face made ugly by the sneer she wore, looking at Max like he was a pile of wet dog shit on a hot day.

"You bitch…" Hiero said, so quietly only Madigan and I would hear. "Discarding him the moment he's no longer of value."

"He yields!" Red repeated, her voice shaking now. "He yields!" She whipped her head back to glance at Hiero. Her face was ash grey, like she would pass out any second.

Hiero leapt up onto the barrier, standing head and shoulders above everyone in the front rows. "I heard him! He yields!" He waved an arm, encouraging everyone to chant with him. "He yields!"

And within seconds, the entire crowd was shouting alongside him. Even I joined in, until Franziska raised her hands for calm, her eyes pinned on Hiero, almost black with rage.

"I give you," Franziska said, so tightly she could barely be heard over Max's screams, "your new champion."

The crowd went wild, all manner of things—flowers, coins, clothing—thrown into the arena, but Red took no notice.

Her lips were moving, addressing the crowd, but couldn't be heard over the din of their celebrations. And my heart shattered as I realised she was trying to make her announcement.

But her words went unheard as her eyes rolled upward and she collapsed on top of Max's writhing body.

The medics rushed in.

CHAPTER EIGHTEEN

I paced outside the medic's tent until my feet ached. My lower lip stung from where I'd been biting it, and yet I nipped away as we waited for Myla to emerge.

The spectators had left the arena, spilling into the streets, but their chants and laughter carried towards me like they were still in the stands. I didn't mind a rowdy afterparty, but when those celebrating could break my bones with an accidental knock, I figured it was best I didn't get involved. Besides, I had little to celebrate. Red might have won, but her victory had come at such a steep cost, I wondered if even *she* thought it was worth paying.

As pain flared through my arches and I considered sitting on the mucky ground, Myla's enormous frame appeared through the flaps of the tent.

My breath froze in my lungs as I waited for her to speak, her expression unreadable.

"She's all right," she said, and relief crashed over me. "She's awake, and her wounds have closed. It's just her... mental state."

Fuck...

"Did they..." I started, but then wished I hadn't. It was a stupid question. But when Myla, Hiero, and Madigan all stared at me expectantly, I asked, "Did they save her leg?"

To my surprise, none of them rolled their eyes, tutted, or laughed.

"They tried. If it had been a clean cut, they could have reattached it," Myla said. "But not with damage like that. There wasn't enough to work with."

"Is she seeing anyone?" Hiero asked.

"No. She wants to be alone."

"Let us know if there's anything we can do," I said, though I had no idea what help I could offer.

Once we'd returned to Hiero's manor, Hiero disappeared into his office while Madigan and I sat at the dining room table, Chef's meals growing cold in front of us. I pushed food around on my plate, but my stomach was so twisted I couldn't have eaten anything even if I'd wanted to. Madigan hadn't even touched his cutlery.

"Why are we here?" I asked after a too-long silence.

"You know why." Madigan frowned at the question. "To recruit—"

"We asked the Liege Lady for help. She said no. So why are we still here? I've tried talking to every sodding vampire in that sodding training ground and Red was the only one who said yes. And now..."

I stopped myself short of saying out loud the blunt, harsh reality. *She's lost her leg. How much help could she offer now?*

"Hiero may yet win." Madigan sounded as though he was trying to convince himself just as much as me.

I let out a loud huff as I slumped back in my seat, my fork hitting my plate with a clatter.

"If you'd rather leave—"

"No," I said more abruptly than I'd intended. "You're right. Hiero is our only shot now. We should stay until after the election."

I eyed the food on my plate, easier to look at than Madigan whose calculating stare roamed over me, and the instant a crease formed between his brows I knew he'd sussed me out. Perhaps at first I'd been avoiding the haunting memories of ripping talons and a spread of wings, but now there was something else anchoring me in the Nest. A bewitching smile I wasn't ready to leave behind.

"Parting is such sweet sorrow," he said.

The following nights dragged. Red still refused to see anyone except Myla, and without them, my personal training had ground to a halt. With newfound time on my hands, I finally got round to scouring Hiero's library, but if he had a book on shifters, he'd hidden it well.

After three long nights of boredom and disappointment, my mood shifted when Hiero announced the Champion's Ball would commence at the end of the week.

"It's a party held at the Champion's manor," he said when he caught me staring at him in bewilderment. "It's usually held the day after the final match but is postponed if the Champion isn't in a fit state to attend."

A party!

My insides fizzed with nerves or excitement—I couldn't tell which.

"Red didn't want the ball so soon, if at all," Hiero said, rubbing his chin. "She's been coerced into having it before the election. Franziska wouldn't want anyone taking the spotlight from her during her moment of triumph." Hiero muttered the last sentence, fiddling with an item on the mantelpiece as he spoke. If *I'd* managed to hear him, Madigan would have too, and like me, he ignored Hiero's negativity. Instead, he gave me a nervous glance, perhaps recalling the discussion we'd had over cold food.

Red's manor was as large as Hiero's, the only difference being the décor.

"She doesn't choose what's in here," Hiero said, as I examined a lewd tapestry in the entrance hall, impressed someone had the patience to weave such intricate detail of the acts on display. "She'll only be here for ten years. Then it's given to the next Blood Champion. Unless she regains her title, of course. But that would seem unlikely given the circumstances..." Hiero's voice trailed off as we took a step further through the queue leading into the ballroom, the tune from the string instruments spilling out into the entrance hall.

I brushed down the front of my dress—a gift from Hiero. Although the word '*gift*' didn't feel appropriate. Gifts were things people exchanged at Christmas. Books, toys, and frivolous tut that ended up in a charity shop two weeks later. The ball gown Hiero had bought me was worth more than a house. Worth more than *several* houses. Hell, if I sold it, I could buy my own manor, furnish it, and still have money left for a chippy tea.

My fingers traced over the pearls and diamonds sewn to the cardinal-red satin, weighing me down. They flowed from the sweetheart neckline, swept down to the red and white silk roses at my right hip, and cascaded down the skirt. Radiant, but not *me*. This dress belonged to a queen. But, just for tonight, I could pretend. No one needed to know I was still wearing my Doc Martens underneath.

Hiero took my hand to stop my fidgeting and kissed my knuckles, his dark eyes sparkling as they peered through his masquerade mask. It matched mine: the same shade of red as my dress; the same glittering diamonds. Something fluttered low in my belly, and I lowered my gaze, but his body was as dangerous to look at as his eyes.

I'd known men's corsets were a thing, but *fuck*, the photos online didn't do them justice. It looked like a waistcoat, but the way it accentuated his broad shoulders, his tapered waist, and the S of his spine, was too much for me to handle, making my eyes linger for far too long. I swallowed.

Stop it...

I peered over my shoulder at Madigan, who stood arm in arm with Myla. Neither of us had received an invite—those were reserved for the wealthiest or high-status vampires—so the only way we could attend was as a plus-one. After some debate, we'd decided I'd go with Hiero, and Madigan with Myla. It was difficult to tell which of the four of us had drawn the short straw.

It was one of the rare occasions Madigan wasn't overdressed. Although Hiero had bought him a new suit for the ball, it appeared much like his others: fitted to his slender frame and jet-black, albeit with silver embroidery to complement his grey eyes. My heart fluttered as his masked gaze met mine, and we shared a smile.

Myla looked as uncomfortable as I felt. She wore a sheer black ball gown speckled with silver to match Madigan. It fit well, but she plucked at it in the manner of someone who felt awkward in a dress of *any* kind, well-fitted or not. She displayed her full sleeve tattoo down her right arm. A collage of mermaids, fairies, and unicorns that was so sickeningly cutesy, I couldn't help but like it. I ignored the ungrateful voice in the back of my mind that said I'd rather have been on Madigan's arm and dressed like the night sky than on Hiero's, adorned in colours of blood and bone.

As a 'Lord Bedgebury' entered the ballroom, his name ringing out as his announcement was made, Hiero and I stepped to the front of the queue.

"Nervous?" Hiero asked, holding his arm out to me. Though Madigan had given his blessing, it still felt wrong to link mine through Hiero's. Even more so when I gave him a sideways glance, only for him to beam at me in response, flashing perfect teeth and those dimpled cheeks.

I looked ahead again. "You've not seen me dance."

"It's all right, I can teach you."

I snorted. "I think I've had enough of your teaching methods."

"Have you?"

I gave him another side glance, not answering as my heart skipped a beat—a skip I tried to ignore—and hoped the others, caught up in their own emotions, wouldn't notice.

One of the city guards greeted us at the door.

"Are you two together?" he asked Hiero.

"No, she's just keeping my arm warm," Hiero said, but when his joke received a scowl, he added with a sigh, "Yes, we are together."

"Names?"

"You know me!" Hiero put a hand to his chest, as though hurt.

The guard continued to glare at Hiero, but then slumped, and said in a lowered voice, "Come on, Hiero, it's procedure. This is demeaning enough as it is. I should be fighting. Bloody brawls, epic battles, you know?"

Hiero raised an eyebrow. "Oh, believe me, I fully understand. A warrior, such as yourself, shouldn't be wasted on guard duty. It is a pity Franziska won't allow you to leave to exterminate the most ruthless killers humans have to offer, but I suppose she knows best, doesn't she?"

The guard didn't answer, his eyes shifting, his jaw locked like he was afraid of what he might say if he let the words out.

"Still, should you change your mind, you know I'd never waste your talents, right? Give me your vote, and I'll give you some action."

Laughter slipped out of me at the double entendre as I heard Madigan mutter, "That was unfortunate phrasing," and I could practically sense him pinching the bridge of his nose.

"*Fighting* action," Hiero corrected, trying to keep a straight face.

The guard's face flushed the same colour as my dress. "Your guest's name?"

"Ava Monroe."

Hiero let loose his laughter the moment the guard hurried into the ballroom to announce our arrival, and after wiping a tear from beneath his mask, he whispered against my ear, "That's a *filthy* mind you have there."

But before I could hit him with a comeback, our names echoed throughout the ballroom, and Hiero ushered me along with him.

I was hit by a wall of sound from the string quintet. Crowds of vampires stood to the sides, creating a path through the middle. At the end, Red sat in a chair that looked more like a throne, her feet—*foot*—covered by the skirt of her red-and-black gown. Hiero led me towards her, and as he did so, it was like she awoke from hypnosis, the vacant, glassy stare she'd worn lifting to give us a small, friendly smile.

Hiero bowed, "Congratulations."

Following his lead, I dipped into a wobbly curtsy. "Congratulations."

"Thank you for coming," she said, then added in a lowered voice, "You're probably the first people I've said that to and meant it."

Hiero took me aside to a burning brazier as Red greeted Myla and Madigan, giving them the same smile she'd given us, but then resumed a blank stare as she continued to welcome her guests. A few more vampires joined the party, and though murmurs were low, everyone fell silent as the last guest was introduced.

"Maximillian Strider."

All heads whipped around.

Max stood in the doorway, pulling on his sleeve in a fashion similar to Madigan, then adjusted his collar, and finally... his eyepatch.

The string music that had been so cheerful and welcoming now felt ominous, cutting through the tension as Max strode towards Red.

He paused for a moment, then inclined his head, so stiff it looked painful.

Red watched him, unblinking, her nostrils flaring. I could almost hear her brain ticking away. Gripping the arms of her throne, she rose, a little off-balance at first, but then steady. Proud.

The string quintet fell silent.

"Thank you for coming," she said to the guests, but kept her sights locked on Max, who returned the stare through his one good eye. "I stand before you, your new Blood Champion."

Applause rang through the ballroom from all but Max, his lips clamped tight, the corners of his mouth turned downwards.

"I hope," she went on, "we can enjoy this celebration without fear of conflict. The fighting is over. Now is the time to honour all who lost their lives... or body parts."

As the guests started clapping again, Max offered her a faint nod, and after a what felt like a lifetime, joined in.

Once Red resumed her seat, servants flowed into the room, drink trays held aloft. Seizing the first opportunity, I snatched two glasses.

I drained the first as Hiero held out a hand expectantly.

"Oh, thank you," I said, gifting him the empty glass before downing the second.

His smile sharpened into something wolfish, making my skin prickle. "Cheeky."

"Where is Franziska?" I asked, scanning the guests in their sparkling gowns and suits, the usual mishmash of fashions through the ages. One wore a French court dress, pink ribbons heaped onto her chest, her hair piled high in curls. Another wore a doublet and ruff.

"She'll be here soon. Always fashionably late so she can make a grand entrance."

No sooner had the words escaped his lips than the doors to the ballroom flew open, and the guard's voice boomed, "Liege Lady Franziska Revay."

Cheers and applause from the guests—even Hiero managed a slow clap—as she entered, dressed in something more akin to a piece of art than a dress. Layers and layers of iridescent fabric gleamed like lapis and amethyst as she passed beneath the hanging candelabras.

"Please," she raised her hands in false modesty. "Tonight is not about me. It's about the Blood Champion." She gestured towards Red and clapped.

Red forced a smile that fell short of her eyes. "Now the Liege Lady is present, let the celebrations begin."

The quintet started up again, and guests took their positions on the dance floor. Hiero pulled me along with him, and a cold rush of dread rippled through me.

"I don't know what I'm doing!" I whispered, barely moving my lips, and hoped he'd read the urgent panic in my eyes.

Hiero took one of my hands in his, the other roamed to my waist, pulling me tight against his body, stopping my breath. "Just follow my lead."

"Wait—" But I was cut off as music filled the room, and Hiero effortlessly whisked me along with him.

CHAPTER NINETEEN

My toes barely scraped the floor as Hiero effortlessly swept me through the air, like it was a puppet he danced with and not a twenty-two-year-old woman.

I clung to him, peering over his shoulder to see Madigan and Myla having far more difficulty.

My mind drifted back to the blood-moon moth field, and how despite my two left feet, Madigan had taught me those four simple steps. How we'd waltzed in silence, moonlight glinting off the moths' wings. The scent of vanilla as his body pressed to mine. The taste of his lips...

His grip had been firm, yet gentle. But Hiero pinched me tight.

Like he knew I was thinking about him—in fact, he probably did—Hiero anchored me against him. Solid, powerful muscle met my softer frame, his sandalwood aftershave almost bewitching.

I glanced over his shoulder once more, praying for distraction from my lecherous imagination. Most of the dancers moved with the same smooth elegance as Hiero.

"You're staring," he said against my ear, his breath a warm caress.

"I didn't realise." I sounded more breathless than I'd have liked, so I cleared my throat, playing it cool. "It's kinda difficult not to, what with Madam De Pompadour and William Shakespeare over there."

Hiero snorted a laugh through his nose. "You shouldn't call them that. Poking fun at someone's era is like racism for supernaturals."

"Really?"

Hiero nodded, smiling in amusement.

I didn't know what to say, taken aback.

"It's all right." His smile was a full-blown smirk now. "Everyone does it at some point. Luckily, it's only me who heard you."

I danced with Hiero for another two songs. I'd have stopped earlier, but no one else had abandoned the dance floor yet, and I didn't want to draw attention to myself.

There were only two vampires not dancing: Red, who remained on her throne, staring deadpan into the crowd of dancers; and her unlikely companion, muttering in her ear.

Max Strider stood at her side, his forearm leaning on the back of her throne, one leg crossed in a figure of four. His lips moved, but it was impossible to hear him over the music, the babble of chatter and laughter, and the thundering of heeled footwear on the marble floor.

I twisted my head to keep my view of Max each time Hiero spun me round until he whirled me into a sudden dip, forcing my attention on him. I stifled a squeak of surprise, gripping a muscled arm and shoulder in case he dropped me.

"I told you to stop staring," he said, his dark eyes meeting mine. "Bit rude not to pay attention to me on our first date."

"What's Max up to? Look. He's whispering away in Red's ear while she has to sit there and—wait—"

Did he just say... first date?

I opened my mouth to correct him—this was *not* a first date—but stopped when Hiero lifted me up. Even with my feet set on the ground, it took a second for the room to stop swaying from the way he'd manhandled me.

"So he is," Hiero muttered, eyeing Max. "Come with me." He seized my hand and led me through the dancers. I flinched each time an arm or flying skirt brushed me as I manoeuvred through them, but we finally reached Red.

"Red, I wanted to congratulate you again," Hiero said, raising his voice over the music. "Hosting the Champion's Ball is such an honour, don't you think, Max?"

Max regarded Hiero with a stony expression. "Indeed."

"Go find yourself a drink. There's a bar in the billiard room. Might not be the sort of drinks you're used to, though. The only *special effects* they have are inebriation."

Max narrowed his one good eye, his lips pursing. He took a step closer to Hiero. And then another. Until they were face-to-face. I shrank back behind Hiero, my breath caught in my lungs.

"Let it go, Max," Red said.

I was surprised to hear her trying to calm him, but the tightness in my chest eased when Max heeded her advice. He shoved past Hiero, knocking into his shoulder as he marched towards the exit, but Hiero barely wavered, standing firm in defiance.

"What poison was he spewing?" he asked, kneeling beside Red's throne, looking up at her.

Red managed a weak smile. "Nothing, really. Don't worry about him."

Hiero raised an eyebrow. "You sure? I might not be Liege Lord yet, but I could make things very uncomfortable for him."

"How noble of you," Red said, a little of her usual banter.

"The offer is there if you change your mind." Hiero stood upright and turned back to me. "Now then, where were we?"

"Actually," I said, "I was wondering if I could speak to Red for a moment?"

"Of course." He took my hand and planted a kiss on my knuckles, gazing at me through his eyelashes, then flashed that dazzling smile. My heart leapt, and his smile grew wider, satisfied with my response.

Smug bastard...

Once he'd disappeared into the crowd, I took his spot at the foot of Red's throne.

"I'm sorry things haven't turned out better," I said and immediately cringed.

"Do you mean, *I'm sorry you lost your leg*?" She wasn't angry, but there was a bluntness to her tone.

"Yes. That."

"Don't be afraid to say it out loud. It's not shameful. It's not offensive. What is done can't be undone. I can only move forward."

I stared into her mismatched eyes, like the secret to her fortitude lay within. "I have no bloody idea how you can be so brave."

"No, me neither sometimes." A pause as she picked the skin around her nails, then said in a babble, "Ava, I'm sorry, but I can't come with you." Her tight expression emphasised the scar down her face. "It's going to take time to re-learn... *everything*. Walking. Running. Fighting. I know I said I'd come with you—"

"I understand." I'd known what she was going to say, but weight settled in my stomach all the same. "Any idea how long your recovery will take?"

She shrugged. "Not really. Faster than a human. Slower than a shifter." She gave me a tight-lipped smile. "But I have ten years to prepare for the next Battles of Blood, so I'm in no hurry."

"You're going to enter *again*?" Surely I must have misunderstood her.

"Damn right I am. I'd rather die in the Battles defending my title than return to the outer ring and end up working in some seedy shithole like the Lover's Sanctum."

Was *that* what Max had said to her? I suppressed the urge to rant about that cheating turd-tosser.

"Well," I said, "when you put it like that, I can't say I blame you. I'll come back to cheer you on." I stood. "Now, did I hear Hiero mention a bar?"

"In the billiard room. Help yourself but go easy. It's strong stuff."

We clasped hands before I weaved through the dancers to the exit. I'd hoped to bump into Madigan or Hiero on the way— literally, given how many times the dancers knocked into me—but still hadn't found them by the time I reached the ballroom's double doors.

I jumped as I walked inside, not expecting to discover two familiar figures: Madigan leaning against the bar, and Hiero sitting on it, swinging his legs.

"Seriously?" I said, planting my hands on my hips.

Madigan pushed himself from the bar, giving me an uncharacteristically wide grin.

"Ava!" He glided towards me and planted a kiss on my forehead. "So glad you could join us." There was something fruity on his breath, and his usually pale cheeks were rosy.

I raised an eyebrow at Hiero and said wryly, "You've drugged him."

They both laughed, and I couldn't keep up the stern act any longer, my face cracking into a grin before I joined Hiero on the bar.

"So, what's this then?" I asked, nodding towards the three glasses containing a peach-coloured liquid.

Hiero handed one to me. "Something special. But you only get *one*. Understand?"

I put the rim of the glass to my lips and sipped. Though the sweet scent within was pleasant, the taste was far stronger than I'd anticipated, and I emerged from my glass coughing as fire ran down my throat.

"Vampires need stronger drinks to get drunk," Hiero said, and drained the remaining liquid from his glass.

"That's not true—I've seen Madigan drink wine."

Madigan topped up Hiero's glass, and then his own. "You've seen me drink. You've not seen me drunk."

"Fair point," I wheezed after another sip, my voice almost failing as I began another round of coughing.

"She's persistent," Hiero said, sounding amused.

Madigan swirled the liquor in his glass, his lips curling into something roguish. "You have no idea."

Normally, I'd have thrown him a dirty look—I hated when they talked about me like I wasn't there—but already the bubbles had hijacked my brain. Instead, a giggle snorted its way out before I could catch it, setting the vampires off again with howls of intoxicating laughter.

Time slipped away while Hiero cracked more jokes, making my sides ache and tears stream down my cheeks.

Occasionally, I caught Madigan watching me, his eyes tender and his lips spread into a relaxed, natural smile that not only made him look younger, but felt like a glimpse of who he might have been without a lifetime of torment.

Heat coursed through me, and those three words that I'd failed to speak were on the tip of my tongue.

I love you. I love you. I love you.

But it wasn't the right time.

"Come on, let's get back," Hiero said once they'd finished the bottle. "They might have moved on to a different dance now."

With a reluctant sigh, I jumped down from the bar; if I could have frozen myself in that moment for eternity, I would have.

I wasn't sure what Hiero had meant by moving onto a 'different dance', but his meaning became apparent the moment we returned to the ballroom. Dancers stood in two lines, mirroring each other's synchronised movements like something from a period drama.

"There's no bloody way I'm doing that," I said. With unsteady feet and a squiffy mind, I'd have those vampires falling like a row of dominoes.

"I understand," Hiero laughed. "But could I ask Len? With your permission, of course."

I wrinkled my nose. "He doesn't need my permission. I'm not his mother. Go on, have fun."

I was content to watch.

Myla was now dancing opposite another of Franziska's guards, and even Red had allowed a guest to carry her bridal style, leaving me to sit alone at the foot of her throne.

I don't know how long I sat there, watching the dancers change their style every few songs. Even the music changed. Vampires with wind instruments joined the string quintet, and another sat at a grand piano.

Madigan's face shone through the crowd, positively beaming at Hiero, who gracefully performed each step with a lazy finesse. The passion in their eyes had the bubbles I'd consumed fizzing again.

I tore my gaze from them as Red returned to her throne, slightly pink in the cheeks, her masked dancing companion disappearing into the shifting crowd. That split second was all it took to lose track of Madigan and Hiero.

As the musicians packed away their instruments and were replaced by a boombox, vampires started vacating the dance floor, and I squinted through the bustle in my search for them.

"Most vampires prefer regency dances," Red explained, more vampires drifting to the sides of the room as a familiar beat pumped out the speakers, my body bopping of its own accord.

"They're missing out. This song absolutely slaps!"

She chuckled. "Of course *you* like modern music."

"*Modern*?" A laugh erupted from me. "My grandma listened to this!" But my laughter died as I spotted Hiero among the remaining dancers. And who should be with him but the living embodiments of prolapsed haemorrhoids—Talia and Xander.

The sight of them turned my blood cold, and I immediately sprang to my feet, searching for Madigan, mentally berating myself.

After a few minutes searching, I spotted him near the double doors, leaning against the wall, arms folded as he watched Hiero. The warmth in his eyes had vanished, replaced by his usual frosty glower.

No... Not his *usual* glower. My heart twinged the moment I recognised the flicker of pain across his face.

A burning surge of adrenaline shot through me, and I was marching onto the dance floor before I'd even realised what I was doing. My fingers bunched into fists, my mind full of fire, and rage, and blood, and...

My stomach dropped.

They're Soul Suckers, you idiot. You can't fight them.

I froze.

The world moved in slow motion as I watched them, dancing like they were in a nightclub. Talia danced between the two men, her back to Hiero, one of Xander's thighs between hers.

Hiero had one hand on her hip, swaying his own to the rhythm of the music. But his spine was stiff, and as much as Talia tried to grind her backside against him, he kept his distance.

A devilish mischief awoke in me as I calculated my plan of attack; the same plan of attack that had led to my discovery of vampires in the first place. I might not be able to *fight* Talia and Xander, but I could still hurt them the same way they'd hurt Madigan. I was going to *dance*.

Summoning every drop, every fibre, every *speck* of confidence I had, I swaggered towards Hiero, relishing how the light danced off the diamonds I wore. I *was* a queen. And this was *my* dance floor.

Hiero sensed me before either Talia or Xander, and the moment he turned his face to mine, his features split into that delicious smile. He pushed Talia off him, marching to meet me.

Our bodies met in a wild, frenzied dance, all inhibitions dissolving. So passionate, so free, that many of the vampires around us whistled or cheered, upping their own energy to match ours.

I grabbed a fistful of my skirts, hoisting them up around my hip as he pulled me flush against him, sweeping a hand up my now-exposed thigh. My free hand gripped his shoulder as he slid one of his legs between mine.

"I thought you said you couldn't dance," Hiero said against my ear.

"I lied."

His hands roamed as I danced, gliding down my back, pinching my hips, cupping my ass with a squeeze. He guided my movements—at least, that's what I told myself. But deep inside, I knew I was the one who'd started rocking my hips back and forth, grinding against his leg in a way that made me feel... *good*.

Over his shoulder, Talia and Xander shot me venomous glares. I grinned at them. I'd won. Or at least, part one of my plan was complete.

But there was one piece missing.

I searched for Madigan. He was still by the doors, but now, instead of scowling, he was staring directly at me. His eyes were wide. Focused. Unblinking. Even from across the room I caught the hunger in them. And the way his teeth caught his lower lip confirmed it.

I beckoned him towards me, but he shook his head.

"He won't," Hiero called over the music. "If it's not a *proper* dance—as he calls them—he won't do it."

"I'm sure between the two of us, we could convince him?" I raised an eyebrow as I walked my index and middle fingers up his chest.

He tilted his head, a naughty glint in his eyes. "I *love* the way you think."

I spun, Hiero's firm body pressed to my back, his hands grasping my hips as I beckoned Madigan once more. And again, he shook his head. But I saw how his jaw tightened.

I chanced a sideways glance up at Hiero, only for my insides to ignite as the alluring essence seemed to pour from him, a seductive aura that highlighted his beauty. His auburn curls, strong jaw, those dimples when he smiled. And then there was the *smell* of him. Sandalwood, alcohol, and something else, a deep, rich, earthy fragrance that was perhaps the very essence of him. He reached out to Madigan, beckoning as I had.

Madigan's hand drifted to his cuff as his gaze flicked between the pair of us, and I could practically see his resolve weakening.

I raised my eyebrows suggestively.

And that was all it took.

In one breath, Madigan had straightened himself, and in the next, he was in front of me, tilting my head up to keep his gaze.

My heart almost stopped as he traced his thumb over my lower lip and said, "I'm not here to dance."

"Then why are you here?" I asked, my voice almost disappearing.

The corner of his mouth curled into a smirk that made my very soul ache for him. "To take you somewhere private. *Both* of you."

CHAPTER TWENTY

Heat from the lounge fireplace licked my exposed arms and shoulders. It was identical to Hiero's, except for the tapestry hanging above it depicting two men and a woman, their bodies twisted into positions I'd only ever fantasised about. Perhaps it was the reason Hiero had suggested we use this room. Or perhaps it was the perfect, low, sensual lighting cast by the dancing flames. Or the fluffy burgundy rug spread before it.

I could still make out the distant buzz of chatter from the ballroom. I should have been nervous—anyone could have walked in—but the idea of getting caught somehow added to the excitement.

Madigan stood in front of me and used one finger to tilt my chin away from the tapestry to focus solely on him, his silver-flecked eyes looking into the very heart of me.

"Give me a word," he whispered. "Any word at all."

I drew a blank, distracted as I became aware of Hiero behind me, his hot breath caressing my neck. Madigan smirked, undoubtedly sensing my body's reaction, which only made me more flustered, my cheeks aflame.

"Fire," I said at last, the only word my useless brain was capable of.

Madigan nodded, brushing the back of his fingers down my cheek. "Say it and we stop. No justification required. All right?"

My heart seemed to swell. "Thank you." He was always looking out for me. And the ghost of a memory echoed through my mind.

"Miss Monroe, I implore you, please be careful should a vampire—any vampire—try to kiss you."

There was no way I would let anxiety ruin this for me. "But no kissing."

Hiero's lips skimmed my neck. "You don't trust me?"

Madigan kept his focus on me as he said, "It's a fair request." His eyes creased as he smiled; his secret smile made just for me. *Mine.* Until his gaze flicked to Hiero, and his expression dissolved into something impish. "Besides, I'm sure you can find parts to kiss other than her mouth. Now that's sorted"—he adopted a strict tone I'd grown all too familiar with—"Miss Monroe, be a good girl and undress Hiero for me."

My breath caught, equally surprised and excited by the command. I twisted to view Hiero, who held out his arms like he was presenting himself to me, the firelight glinting off the diamonds on his corset.

"Undress him?" I said in a small voice, acting coy. *Acting.* It took all my self-control to stop myself from grinning.

Madigan had settled himself on the sofa, long legs spread apart, and picked up an amber-coloured drink from the trolley beside him. "Did I stutter?"

A rumble of laughter from Hiero, and my cheeks grew hotter.

"You can take your time," Madigan said, ice clinking in his glass as he took a sip. "I'm in no hurry. *But*"—his tone was dangerous now, cold eyes flashing—"I hate asking for something twice."

His gaze burned into me as I stood before Hiero, smiling expectantly. My heartbeat thrummed in my ears as I traced a finger down the busk of his corset. Only six clasps, but from the way my fingers trembled, I was surprised I managed it at all. He didn't assist me in the slightest as I pulled it off him, one arm at a time, then tossed it towards Madigan, who, in a blur, snatched it out of the air.

"Careful now, Miss Monroe." A smile tugged at the corner of his mouth, but his eyes remained frosty, like he was daring me. "You wouldn't want to get in trouble."

I got to work unbuttoning Hiero's shirt. The material was so thin I could feel each bulge of the sculpted muscles beneath, firm and tight, my breath hitching as I peeled his shirt away, firelight flickering across the planes of his chest. Without thinking, I traced my fingers along the defined slopes and valleys down his stomach, his skin smooth and searing.

"Keep going." Madigan eyed me over the rim of his glass as he took another sip, the front of his trousers straining upward, the outline of his erection visible. It was sweet agony to tear my eyes from him, but worth it when I fumbled with Hiero's belt to discover he, too, was hard.

My mouth grew wet as I unzipped his fly, manoeuvring him out of his trousers and letting them drop to the floor. As he kicked them aside, I paused to admire his powerful thighs. Then the V of his hips, pointing down to what I wanted to see most.

I hooked a finger over the waistband of his boxers, coarse hair brushing my fingertip. My heart pounded with anticipation, almost painful, but I wouldn't rush this. I'd savour every second.

Slipping my hand inside was easy, his erection tenting the fabric, and I brushed a palm up the inside of his thigh. Close. *So* close... Then skimmed my fingers over his hip to his firm backside.

"You're a worse tease than Len," Hiero said in a low hiss, his expression tight, like he was in pain.

"I'm not *that* cruel." I was done torturing him. And myself.

With one swift movement, I dropped his boxers. He loosed a low moan as I cupped him in one hand, full and heavy.

"Very good," Madigan said, and when I shot him a glance, I saw him massaging the front of his trousers, like they had become uncomfortably tight. "Now, Miss Monroe, it's your turn. Take off your clothes."

My skin tingled as I faced him, both his and Hiero's eyes already undressing me as I tugged at the ribbon at the small of my back, tied into a bow at the bottom of my corset. And as I did so, Madigan unfastened his trousers, freeing his erection and stroking as he watched me.

My breath became constricted, the heat in the room stifling as I prepared to present myself to them, each with their cock in their hand, my mind whirring too fast at what was happening.

I tugged on the ribbon again, only for it to lock into a tight knot, the blaze within me shifting into a cold panic.

But Madigan's eyes sparkled with wicked amusement. "She appears to be stuck," he said to Hiero. "Care to help her out?"

Hiero came up behind me, his fingers climbing the ladder of my corset to the very top. I was about to ask what he was doing—the knot was at the bottom—but the question caught in my throat when his hands roamed to the front of my dress, fingertips teasing the swell of my breasts as they slipped beneath the sweetheart neckline.

"W-what are you—?"

A sharp *rip* cut through the air as Hiero tore open the front of my dress, diamonds and pearls scattering. I gasped as the air struck my skin, my breasts spilling free. I don't know what aroused me more: that Hiero had exposed my body, or the blatant disregard of the expensive piece of art he'd destroyed to do so.

Madigan's eyes widened, the grip on his cock tightening. "You appear to be missing your bra, Miss Monroe."

"I didn't... The straps would have... They'd be visible... And I didn't need..." I couldn't string the words together as Hiero cupped a breast, his thumb almost brushing against my nipple. Close enough to make it stiffen, aching with the need to be touched.

With his free hand, Hiero pushed my skirts to the floor, falling in a heap at my feet.

Madigan sighed, slow and exasperated. "And what, Miss Monroe, have you got on your feet?"

I'd almost forgotten my Doc Martens. I'd have answered if it hadn't been for Hiero pinching my nipple, turning my reply into a soft moan.

"Do you think that's appropriate footwear for a formal occasion?" Madigan asked, but when I didn't reply for a second time, he barked, "*Answer me.*"

"N-no," I spluttered. "I'm sorry. I'll take them off."

"No." He got to his feet, slowly unbuttoning each of his layers, presenting his slender, toned abdomen peppered with those scars so tragic and beautiful. "You'll keep them on. But your knickers will have to go. Hiero, would you do the honours?"

And with a snap of lace, Hiero ripped my panties away just as Madigan dropped his trousers, and he beckoned me towards him.

I stepped out of the tattered remains, heading towards Madigan with Hiero close behind, the heat from his body blazing against the coldness of mine.

Madigan tilted his head as if in thought, tracing a fingertip across my collarbone with a torturingly featherlight touch. "You know, Miss Monroe, one is usually punished for violating social customs so brazenly."

"It wasn't *brazen*. You didn't know until now—"

"And answering back, too?" He arched an eyebrow, grey eyes meeting mine. Unblinking. A challenge.

I never back down from a challenge.

But Hiero's fervid hands found my waist, pinching the soft flesh of my hips, grinding his erection against my ass, and instead of the comeback I'd wanted to unleash, all I managed was another soft sigh as one of Hiero's hands crept over my hip, sliding down to the wetness between my legs.

Madigan smirked. "Good girl. You're learning. But you're not off the hook yet."

He spun me to face Hiero, before once again settling on the sofa, taking me by the hips and pulling me onto his lap. His hands were everywhere, gliding across my stomach, squeezing my breasts, sweeping up my thighs, as his hot mouth found my neck, planting kisses until I melted inside.

My eyes met Hiero's. And he stared back. Ravenous desire in his grin.

In a sobering moment, I suddenly felt vulnerable. Exposed. Weak. And I wondered if I should stop everything. Say my safety word and let Madigan shield me, as I knew he would. *Safe*.

I didn't want safe.

I bit my lip as Hiero sank to the floor, his hands on my thighs. His dark eyes never left mine as he kissed the inside of my right knee. One soft brush of his lips. Then the left. Right knee again—higher this time. Then the left. Climbing. Slowly. Slowly. So that I gradually parted my legs for him.

Madigan supported my weight as he shifted his hips beneath me, and I gasped as the tip of his cock parted me before sinking inside in one, slow, fluid movement. He didn't thrust. Just held me. Filled me.

But I let out a ragged, raw cry as Hiero's tongue swept over my clit, and my walls twitched around Madigan. Behind me, laughter vibrated in Madigan's chest. He'd felt it. Felt *me*.

Hiero's tongue flicked again as Madigan squeezed my breasts, plucking my nipples into stiff peaks. From the shuddering gasps in my ear, I knew it wasn't just *me* Hiero was attending to, and with a glance, I saw him massaging Madigan's balls in his palm.

The visual was too much.

I unravelled, my hips bucking, back arching, unable to stifle the groan of pleasure, knowing others might hear. My body was electric. Quivering. Eyes tight shut. Lights bursting before them. And then I sank back against Madigan, gasping for breath.

Another rumble of laughter, his lips against my neck.

"Oh, you're not done yet, Miss Monroe," he said, his voice a deep purr. He lifted me off his lap, Hiero holding my hand for support. Just as well—my legs had turned to jelly. "You're not going anywhere until you've cleaned up the mess you've made."

With a grin that teetered between carnivorous and seductive, he rested his hands behind his head, thrusting his hips slightly as he got comfortable, his cock glistening. Blood burned in my cheeks as I realised what he meant.

"You're *filthy*," I gasped.

Madigan's lip curled. "Is that a refusal?"

"No," I said, surprising even myself at how quickly the word slipped out.

Madigan grinned. "No, *sir*."

Goosebumps rippled over my skin as Hiero gave a self-satisfied chuckle beside me. I couldn't bring myself to meet his eye, knowing a smug grin would be plastered over his infuriatingly beautiful face.

I sank to my knees at Madigan's feet and said in my most sultry voice, "No, sir."

His cock looked enormous in my hand, slick with my arousal, throbbing in my grip. The moment I flicked the bridge between the head and shaft with my tongue, I felt Hiero's hands take my hips, manipulating my body into the position he wanted, allowing him access to the core of me.

I moaned around Madigan's length as I wrapped my lips around him, making him inhale sharply through his teeth. And all the while, Hiero's fingers swept back across my pussy, coating me—and him—with my arousal. At least, I'd thought it was his fingers, until I felt the tip of his cock press against my entrance, and then painfully slowly, sink into me. Inch by inch, I took him to the hilt.

He felt wrong. Forbidden. An invader I'd surrendered to. And the deepest, darkest, most depraved corners of my heart sang with delight. He rocked his hips gently, adjusting to me as I was adjusting to him.

And I was perfect—*perfect*—between them. So very, very, *full*.

Hiero withdrew, then plunged his hips against me, before starting up a slow, steady rhythm, forcing me forward with each thrust and take Madigan deeper into my throat.

"That's it," Hiero said, gradually building momentum until the obscene slap of his skin on mine echoed throughout the room, too loud to ignore. One hand drifted from my hip, his fingertip circling my clit, swollen and sensitive. "I want you to cum on me, Ava. I want you to cum on this cock—*my* cock."

Oh fuck...

There was no holding back the moans vibrating through my lips and around Madigan's length. And now he was moaning, too, his head tilted back, running his fingers through my hair. His sighs of pleasure almost pushed me over the edge, and my insides threatened to contract around Hiero.

It's wrong, said a voice in the back of my head. *I shouldn't...*

Hiero's fingers stroked me so expertly that the building pressure threatened to peak once more. His thrusts became sharper, shorter, the head of his cock pressing into the spot that made me lose control.

I should, I said back in defiance.

Hiero squeezed my hips as he drove into me, his cock throbbing as he let out a long, loud groan.

I stopped fighting it and closed my eyes.

Shockwaves ravaged me as I came, my body quivering, sweat coating my skin. Too powerful to control. And that my involuntary moans were muffled by the thickness in my mouth made each pulse stronger.

I was only vaguely aware of words being spoken. Words of encouragement. Slightly teasing.

And I could no longer tell whose hands were whose as they played with my body. There seemed so many, fondling, kneading, stroking. Like they wouldn't let me stop. Just a toy. A plaything. *Theirs.*

Something wet trickled down the inside of my leg.

Madigan let me up for air as Hiero's grip slackened, sliding out of me, his breaths as ragged as mine. For a moment, all I could do was gasp for air, my legs too weak to move.

Madigan wiped my chin with his thumb, smirking as he joined Hiero and me on the fluffy rug.

"You're doing such a good job," he said in a breathy whisper, as his eyes raked over me, lingering at my heaving breasts and then the wetness between my thighs.

I'd never felt so debased but honoured; defiled but worshipped; submissive but powerful.

"Are you ready for more?"

My eyes snapped up to meet his, a devilish grin creeping across my face. "Yes, sir."

We tried every position imaginable, putting those figures in the tapestry to shame. The three of us tumbling on the rug. Or one of us bent over the sofa—me first, then Hiero. I was on top. Beneath them. Between them. And it would never be enough. Their hands. Their lips. Their cocks. I could have stroked, licked, caressed them for eternity, with nothing but the fire, and their heat to warm my bare skin.

I don't know how long we were tangled together, or for how long we lay on the fluffy rug afterwards, my body aching, muscles screaming, inside and out. But it was a *sweet* ache. An ache I'd chase again if I could.

I rested my head on Madigan's chest, listening to the ebb and flow of each breath.

Hiero was on the other side. His hand crept across Madigan's chest to meet mine and interlocked our fingers. He smiled as our eyes met. Not the usual smug grin I was used to, nor that gut-melting smirk. Just a slight crease at his eyes. Genuine. Peaceful.

"Do you think anyone would have heard?" I asked. It was the first thing anyone had said since collapsing in front of the fire.

"Probably," Hiro said. "But it's not a big deal. That's your human sentiments talking."

I managed a sleepy smile in return, my eyelids growing increasingly heavy. "Well, we should probably be more private next time."

"Next time?" He cocked an eyebrow. "Already planning the next one? You're keen."

Madigan managed a chuckle, his chest vibrating beneath my head, perhaps unable to form words.

"I'm too tired for mind games," I dismissed, breathing in Madigan's scent, both mine and Hiero's mingled with it.

"We should probably think about getting back," Hiero said.

"I'm just resting my eyes," I said, the ache of my eyelids becoming too much to bear. "Ten minutes."

A pause, and then the sound of Hiero shifting his weight, settling down. "All right. Ten minutes."

CHAPTER TWENTY-ONE

*C*RASH!

I jolted upright, my face peeling from Madigan's chest, a string of cold saliva running down my chin. Then a sharp twinge pierced through my temples to a spot behind my eyes, so intense I flinched.

Shit... How much did I drink?

A second *CRASH*—louder than the first. Madigan and Hiero snapped awake.

"What's that?" Hiero asked, rubbing his eyes. I rather enjoyed seeing his auburn locks dishevelled, stray waves and curls poking up at awkward angles. But my moment of amusement was interrupted by high-pitched screams that turned my blood to ice.

Then a shout. And a screeching, non-human cry. Familiar, but unlike any animal I'd heard before. Realisation slapped me as colour drained from Hiero's face, his eyes widening as we reached the same conclusion.

"Brain Eaters," he said in a whisper.

Still naked, he leapt over the sofa to the double doors. He gripped the door handle, squeezed it downward, opened the door a crack, and peered through the gap, allowing a beam of light into the room. Then slammed it shut.

"Get dressed! Quick. We need to leave. Now!"

"What's happening?" Madigan began sifting through the heap of clothes, tossing Hiero his trousers.

"Brain Eaters. Lots of them."

A shiver ran through me at the memory of needle-sharp teeth and hot, putrid breath. "What are Brain Eaters doing here?"

"How am I meant to know? Just get dressed. Quick!"

I gaped at the pile of shredded satin and scattered diamonds, my heart dropping to my navel, cold and heavy. "I can't!"

Hiero let out a snarl of annoyance, as though it was *my* fault. "Wear this, then." He flung me his shirt.

After scrambling to make ourselves decent—or as decent as possible in a too-large shirt, boots, and *nothing* else—we joined Hiero at the doors.

He opened one—only a fraction—barely wide enough to see through, but what I glimpsed had my stomach roiling. Bloody smears on the polished floor. Shredded tapestries. Broken glass.

"Let's get out of here. We'll head straight back to mine," Hiero said in a hushed voice.

"What about Red and Myla?" I asked.

"They can take care of themselves."

"*Can* Red take care of herself?"

Hiero glared at me, but I stared back in defiance.

"We'll stop by the ballroom to see if she's there," Madigan said. "If not, we'll leave. Got it?"

"Got it," I said.

"Fine," Hiero said with a roll of his eyes. "Let's get moving."

Madigan seized my hand as we slipped through the door and into the hall, following Hiero towards the ballroom. The screams were dying, but crashes clattered about the house like an infestation.

I held my breath as we drew closer to the ballroom, carefully placing one foot after another, straining my ears for the slightest movement... then jumped out of my skin as a deafening screech pierced the air. I looked up. A Brain Eater, dangling from the chandelier, pounced. It landed on top of Madigan, sending him crashing to the floor and breaking my hold on his hand.

Rage flared in my chest. Without a thought, I raised a fist and smashed it into the Brain Eater's head.

Crack!

I cried out as pain reverberated through my knuckles and into my wrist. The Brain Eater absorbed the blow as if it had been a cushion I'd thrown instead of a punch. It spun its head towards me and screamed, revealing its jagged teeth and the abyss of its gullet.

Hiero, body trembling and eyes wild, drove his fist into the Brain Eater's head from the other side. With a wet crack, its skull caved in, brains and blood splattering over me and Madigan. An eyeball popped from its socket, pointed teeth clattering as they rained onto the marble floor. Its body slumped.

I stood frozen in shock, hot blood soaking through Hiero's shirt, making it stick against my skin. The smell made my stomach clench, and I shuddered as a trickle ran down my face.

"How did you do that?" The question barely escaped my throat as a whisper.

Madigan shoved the body off him and got to his feet. He tried wiping the blood from his face, and then his hands on his trousers, but it stuck to his skin, making him jittery, one of his eyes twitching.

"How?" I asked again when Hiero didn't answer.

"I... don't know." His eyes were wide, blinking, his lower lip trembling. He looked as horrified as I felt. "Adrenaline?"

"I've spent the last month watching vampires throw fists at each other, and not one of them caved another's head in with a *single* blow."

"Can we discuss this later?" Madigan snapped. "We have slightly more pressing matters at hand!"

Without another word, we darted across the entrance hall to the ballroom. The doors were closed, and for a hopeful second, I thought we'd open them to find the ballroom deserted. But then a screech rang from within. A smash, a grunt of exertion, and time seemed to slow as Hiero placed his hands on the doors and pushed them open.

My mouth went dry.

No less than fifteen Brain Eaters. Maybe twenty. Each of them charging, leaping, pouncing at the group of three up the other end of the room. Max, Myla, and Red.

Max and Myla each gripped a brazier, swinging them like a bat each time a Brain Eater attacked. One after another. A relentless bombardment. And Red was behind them, leaning on her throne, shaking and lopsided, but it was her expression of unadulterated terror that formed a lump in my throat.

I gasped at the sea of white bodies, writhing like one ravenous entity, and that single sharp intake of breath was all that was needed for the nearest Brain Eater to turn its bald head and focus its pearly-white eyes on us.

"Shit!" Hiero grabbed the nearest brazier and swung it at the Brain Eater, spraying it with coal and embers. It shrieked in pain and outrage, and more Brain Eaters turned their heads towards us.

"Where is everyone?" Hiero shouted across the room. "We need a Soul Sucker here!"

"Party is over, mate," Max called back, his voice strained as he swung at the Brain Eater launching itself towards him. "*You're* a Soul Sucker! Do something!"

Hiero shot me a nervous glance that mirrored the icy dread unfurling in my stomach. He *wasn't* a Soul Sucker. And now his secret had come back to bite him.

"I can't!"

"Fat lotta good you are!" Max snarled, smashing the face of a Brain Eater pouncing towards Red, a shower of blood splattering the ground.

"Find Talia or Xander," Hiero said to Madigan, stopping only to swing the brazier at another Brain Eater as it lunged. "Bring them here. We need them to take control of these bastards."

I glanced at Madigan as his face twitched with scepticism. He must have been thinking along the same lines as me. Would Talia or Xander help? Or would they be their usual stuck-up selves?

"I'm not going anywhere without Ava," he said.

"GO!" Hiero averted his sights from the Brain Eaters for a microsecond, eyes pleading. "She'll slow you down. We need a Soul Sucker right NOW!"

Madigan's eyes flicked between Hiero and me as he took a step back towards the door. Then another. But then froze, staring at me, like I was anchoring him.

"Go," I said, but as I uttered the single word, a pale body flew towards me.

My scream caught in my throat as I dropped to the floor, covering my head with my arms, screwing my eyes tight shut.

But the impact never came.

I opened one eye. Then the other. Lowered my arms.

Hiero shielded me, blood dripping from one end of the brazier, the Brain Eater sent sprawling across the floor. He hadn't caved in its head like earlier, but I didn't have time to dwell on the mystery as the onslaught continued.

"GO!" I shouted again, and with one last parting glance, Madigan disappeared in a blur.

"Stay behind me," Hiero said, holding the brazier lengthways.

Any Brain Eater that tried to jump us, Hiero smashed away. I couldn't help but be impressed. For someone who identified as '*a lover, not a fighter*', he was more nimble and powerful than I'd imagined.

But Max and Myla were having more difficulty, Brain Eaters launching themselves at the pair. All I could do was keep my distance, *useless*, and gasped as a Brain Eater almost penetrated their defences, hurling itself towards Red.

"Ava! Watch out!" Hiero screamed.

In my split second of distraction, a Brain Eater slid past Hiero, and crashed on top of me, pinning me beneath its wretched, skeletal body.

"Hiero!"

But Hiero was caught up with another Brain Eater.

The one on top of me screeched as it bore down.

Shift!

The thought was barely an echo inside my head before I plunged into pain, then darkness, hidden among the folds of Hiero's bloodied shirt.

A second of relief.

It won't find me now.

Then something long and sharp like a sword stabbed downward, almost skewering me. I scuttled away, but my hooked feet got caught in the fabric. More stabbing. Clawing. And I realised these swords were the Brain Eater's nails, hunting for its lost prey.

My stinger twitched as killer instinct surged through me, a mix of fear and fury, but without skin to pierce, I might as well have struck the open air.

And then I was weightless, tangled up inside the cloth as those sharp nails shredded it to ribbons.

Falling.

Landed at the monster's clawed feet. It wasn't the first time I'd almost been trampled. Bracing myself for agony, I shifted again.

The Brain Eater's mouth spread into a monstrous leer as I scrambled away—not fast enough.

Then it pounced.

Its gaping jaws froze mere inches from my face, its breath full in my nose.

I shuffled back.

Hit a wall.

But the Brain Eater didn't pursue. Locked in place.

It was only now I registered the pain of my raw throat as I drew ragged breaths, my chest too tight. And yet I *was* breathing, each gasp a reminder I was alive—a crash of relief that made my eyes sting.

The room was motionless except for Hiero, who swung at the static Brain Eater and splattered its brains across the ballroom floor. I drew my knees up to my chest, crossing my feet to cover myself as best I could, the remains of Hiero's shirt nothing but a tattered mess.

"Ava." Hiero dropped the brazier and hurried to my side, putting his hands to his chest to remove a shirt that was no longer there. He scanned the room. "Max, give me your shirt."

But Max ignored the request.

"Red?" he said in a soft voice that sounded foreign to him. He put a hand on Red's shoulder, but she didn't seem to notice. Her eyes were on the surviving Brain Eaters, their heads turned down, eyes open but vacant, emitting a low, groaning noise. "Red"—he gave her a shake—"snap out of it."

"Whoa, whoa, back it up, Morningstar," Myla said, now turning her brazier on Max. "Lay off."

Max's single eye flashed. "You have a weird way of thanking someone for saving your life," he said, his usual, haughty tone returning.

"I never asked you to stay."

"No, *Red* asked me to stay." His eyepatch only made his sneer more withering. "Jealous?"

Myla opened her mouth as though to bellow in response, crimson flushing across her nose. But she never had a chance to utter her defence.

"If you're all quite finished," drawled a cold, feminine voice, "I'll accept your thanks at any time."

All heads turned to the doorway.

Franziska stood, hands on hips, her normally pretty face warped with smudged makeup and an expression of irritation. She was wearing the same dress she'd worn to the ball, though it was slightly askew and rumpled, like it had been removed and hastily thrown on again. But it wasn't her dishevelled appearance that had me staring. It was the crown upon her head, a line of blood running down her forehead and dripping from her eyebrow and onto her cheek, dark against her porcelain skin.

"I don't know where these infected monsters came from," Franziska's crisp voice echoed throughout the still room, "but I'll have them exterminated immediately and we'll speak no more about this. I'll not have our people panicking." Then, feigning a casual air, she added, "You know how they love drama."

"Wait—" Hiero said, but in the time it took to blink, Franziska had vanished from the doorway and reappeared in front of him.

"Don't turn this into political point scoring, Blackford," she hissed, her temper bleeding through her façade.

"I wasn't!" He raised his hands defensively. "I was going to say, don't exterminate them—I'll take them to the factory."

"What?" Franziska wrinkled her nose like he'd said something idiotic.

"Talia needs bodies."

Franziska tilted her head, eyeing him suspiciously. "A single Soul Sucker couldn't control this many Brain Eaters without the crown. Not unless they are taking a soul every day, and even I can't manage that, as hard as I try."

"She doesn't need servants. It's their blood she wants. Don't ask me to explain her science-y shit. She asks. I provide."

Franziska shifted her weight from one heeled foot to the other. "Fine." She turned her sights downward, noticing me huddled on the floor. "Ava Monroe." The use of my full name made me flinch, reminding me of Ivan.

"Forgive me for not rising," I said, keeping my knees to my chest.

"Ava!" Madigan, who'd arrived with Franziska, only now spotted me and rushed to my side, removing his shirt as he went and draped it over my shoulders.

I felt Franziska's ice-blue stare on me as I got to my feet, buttoning Madigan's shirt that *just* kept me modest, then pulled on my boots that thankfully remained untouched by the Brain Eater.

"Ava will come back with me, and I'll find her some suitable attire," Franziska said, her expression tight and unreadable.

"I'm coming too," Madigan said.

"No. You go back to... whatever hovel you're staying at... and I shall return your sweetheart once we've had a little chat."

My stomach lurched.

"Len, I told you to get Talia or Xander!" Hiero hissed.

"That's where I was going!" Madigan snapped back. "I was near yours when I bumped into Franziska."

"Oh yes?" Hiero said, rounding on Franziska. "Expecting the attack, were you?"

Franziska snorted with laughter. "Lord Tonbridge witnessed another attack on a different house. Once finished, they moved onto this one. Who knows how many would have died if Lord Tonbridge hadn't found me? You're welcome, by the way."

"I'm not going anywhere without Ava," Madigan said hotly.

"You're in no position to argue."

"An attack on another house?" Hiero cut in. "Which one? What's Lord Tonbridge doing snooping about?"

I toyed with the hem of Madigan's shirt as they shouted over each other. Red, Max, and Myla also watched on, occasionally glancing at each other or towards the open doors, perhaps calculating a way to escape unnoticed.

"For fuck's sake!" Franziska stomped her foot, and both Hiero and Madigan fell silent. "I'm taking Ava to the Shadowfort, and I'll return her! If you continue to argue, I'll have you both executed! I'm your fucking Liege Lady! Show me the respect bestowed by my title!" Her voice squeaked as she reached an almost inaudible pitch. Her shoulders were tense, fists balled, nostrils flaring. She'd lost it. But in such a way that made me feel almost embarrassed for her.

"If you hurt her—" Madigan started.

"If I hurt her, you can't do a single bloody thing about it," Franziska snarled. "I could have her chopped up and fed to my people if I wanted. I could drain her of blood, bathe in it, then force feed it to you. But you'll have to trust me, won't you? Because I'm your Liege Lady, and you are *nothing*." She snapped her fingers at me as a second trickle of blood dripped from where her crown touched her forehead, running down the side of her nose. "Monroe. With me. *Now*."

I tried to give Madigan a reassuring smile, but my insides were squirming so much I probably looked like I was trying not to hurl. I stepped towards Franziska, trying to keep my legs from shaking.

"Thank you," she said with a heavy breath.

I followed her out of the ballroom, and the instant we passed through the doorway, Hiero's and Madigan's voices rang into a heated argument, followed by Max's, and then Myla's.

CHAPTER TWENTY-TWO

Franziska guided me through the twisting corridors and stairways of the Shadowfort, a maze that made Hiero's manor look like a cute cottage.

Her heels clicked on the black marble floor as she led the way, each echo cutting through the silence. No paintings or tapestries decorated the stone walls. Just the sconces made of the same twisting black metal I'd seen throughout the Nest, candles flickering within. Even the air felt colder here.

Occasionally, we'd pass a guard standing to attention in silence, not looking at Franziska as she marched, like they were not worthy to do so. I suspected servants flitted about unseen, their only traces the patter of rushed footsteps or the flutter of a cloak whipping around a corner. The Shadowfort was as barren of life as it was décor, and became scarcer the deeper Franziska led me, the corridors becoming darker and narrower the further we went, until we rounded a corner to a wooden door.

"In," Franziska said, jerking her head into the pitch-black room.

I came to an abrupt halt. "I don't fucking think so." Going into a blacked-out room in a stranger's house was stupid; going into a blacked-out room of the Shadowfort with the Liege Lady of all vampire-kind was suicidal.

"I forgot humans fear the dark. Sorry—I meant *shifters*. My mistake. They're so similar, I forget."

I pursed my lips. She hadn't insulted me as much as she thought she had, but that she *tried* made my muscles tense.

She headed into the darkened room. With a scrape and a hiss of a struck match, she began lighting oil lamps. "Better?"

As more of the room flickered into existence, my mouth fell open, and without thinking I stepped inside.

Rows upon rows of outfits on hangers, the room so vast the lamps only illuminated the first few. Beyond, who knew how many racks there were? A walk-in closet on steroids.

And these weren't any old outfits, either. Like the vampires themselves, these were a range of fashions throughout the years. A sea of different fabrics, patterns, styles, and colours. I touched the nearest before I could stop myself—a gorgeous, black-and-white polka-dot dress. Vintage. Lace sewn around the hem and square neckline. Black glass buttons down the middle of the skirt. Too small for me—pity—but looked like it would fit Franziska perfectly. The fabric was softer than I'd expected—this was made of cotton, rather than the polyester replicas I was used to. And the *smell*: a musty fragrance that reminded me of an old haberdashery Grandma used to visit.

"You're impressed," Franziska said. A statement, not a question.

"Sewing is a hobby..." I managed, though my voice was lodged in my throat, making the lame words sound even more pathetic. It was only now I realised how much I missed my sewing machine, making those costumes for the theatre society, and having *time* to do it. No trials, no fights to the death, no monsters. What wouldn't I give for a day of peace?

But Franziska's next question cruelly wrenched me back into my new, harsh reality. "Why are you still here?"

I dropped the hem of the dress I'd been caressing, whipping my head around to face her. She was holding something out to me. Small enough to bunch in her hand. I reached out, tentative, and my heart skipped a beat when I realised what it was. A red-and-black lace thong.

"What the actual fuck?!"

Suddenly Franziska was up close to me, so close I took a stumbling step back and my back slammed against the nearest wall. But she pursued, pressing one hand to the wall beside my head. In her heels, our eyeline was level.

She inhaled, her eyes fluttering closed as she did so, before snapping open to stare into mine. I could have sworn flecks of silver danced in the pools of cerulean.

"You're nervous," she said, her scarlet lips twisting into a smirk. "Don't worry, Ava. The panties are to wear. You only need to worry if I ask you to *remove* your undergarments."

Despite myself, blood rushed to my cheeks, my skin tingling.

Fuck her fucking glamour! I hated it. I *hated* it.

"Don't you have anything more... modest?" I asked, my throat dry.

"You didn't strike me as a modest kind of girl. You were quick to leave Krysten's party with not one but *two* men, weren't you?"

The burning in my face intensified, blazing beneath my skin, spreading through my body.

"In fact," she continued, "you were the first three to leave for that *particular* reason. Not the last, by any means, but you certainly didn't waste time."

"All right, all right!" I snapped. "What do you want? What's the point of this... interrogation?"

She released a short huff of laughter through her nose, pushing herself from the wall and turned to flick through the outfits on the nearest rail. I took a breath, only now realising how tight my chest had been.

"I've already asked you," Franziska said. "Why are you still here?"

"And I've already told you. I'm recruiting—"

"Right," she said, glancing at me over her shoulder with a smirk, then nodded towards the thong still clenched in my fist.

With an exasperated sigh, I slipped it on, as Franziska began swiping through the outfits again and said, "The only person you recruited was Red, and now she's incapacitated. No one else will join you—I've made sure of that. So, I'll ask again. Why are you here?"

"If Hiero wins the election, he'll help me."

"Have you ever seen a vampires' election before?" she asked, holding out an outfit still on its hanger towards me.

I rolled my eyes as I took it. "You know I haven't."

"Ever heard about them? Read about them?"

"I'm sure you'll get to the point eventually."

"They get ugly." Her smirk had gone, replaced with a furrowed brow; she was serious. "Scheming. Conniving."

"That's standard in politics."

"People get hurt."

"Is that a threat?"

"More of a warning."

I doubted that. "Oh, I'm sure you have nothing but my best interests at heart."

Franziska folded her arms, her icy stare shifting between me and the outfit in my hands, then raised her eyebrows expectantly.

Irritation prickled through me, but once again, my mouth dropped open as I examined it more closely. It was made of a stretchy, synthetic material—perhaps Lycra—and had thin, metal plates attached. It was impossible to tell what it would look like in its current state, but I could guess, and once I'd pulled it on, my suspicions were confirmed.

Those plates looked and behaved like the plates covering my body in my scorpion form, wrapping over my shoulders and across my breasts like armour. The material clung to my body—around my throat, down my arms, hugging my ribs—as though it were a second skin, until it reached my hips and floated down to my mid-thigh. I hated how much I loved it.

Franziska twitched her head towards a full-length mirror, her eyes never leaving me as I admired myself. If I didn't know any better, I'd have thought the dress was made specifically for me. And as much as I loved my reflection—perhaps for the first time in my life—I blushed as I spotted a purple bruise peeking beneath the high neckline. A badge from either Hiero or Madigan, and the fact I didn't know which had my stomach twisting with a clash of shame and pride.

"There's one week left until my people cast their votes," Franziska said, cutting the crap now she'd bribed me. "I think it would be best for *everyone* if you were gone by then."

I turned my back on the mirror, narrowing my eyes. Why did she care if I was here? "I'm harming your campaign, aren't I?"

Her lips twisted to one side, perhaps wondering how honest she should be. "I've recently had more requests for deployment than I have in decades. I mean, I *always* get requests for deployment—vampires love a good fight—but not on this scale."

"So let them! If that's what they want, why not let them fight? Then I'll leave and we both win."

She folded her arms. "No."

"Why not?"

She gritted her teeth, nose wrinkled, lips tight, like she was containing what she wanted to say, but still an intelligible, grunting noise escaped her. "Because—"

"Are you scared of the Hallows?"

"Scared?" Her eyes flashed, her wild stare boring into mine, but when I didn't back down, she sighed. "I'm not scared of the Hallows. I'm *terrified*. Let me show you something."

She grabbed a lamp and carried it aloft as she led me towards the back of the room, weaving through the rows of clothes until I was utterly lost within the labyrinth of fabrics, and finally stopped in front of a glass display case. Inside was a suit of plate armour.

I squinted as I looked closer. At first, the metal shimmered an ethereal blue, but the longer I looked, the colour shifted into teal, then to purple, to pink, and back to blue. And what's more, I could *feel* magical energy buzzing from it, even behind glass.

"This armour saved my life more than once when the Hallows fought us," she said, the shifting colours reflecting in her eyes as she stared at it. "It's enchanted, more durable than regular armour. Lighter. Easier movement. But most importantly, immune to most magic—including the curses within demonic artefacts."

She traced a finger along the glass, looking up at the armour almost lovingly. "I wasn't even Liege Lady at the time. Just a general. But the Witch Queen thought me worthy enough to enchant my armour. One of only five to receive such a gift. My lover and children were not so lucky."

"You had children?"

"*Had* being the operative word. But yes. I did once. Of course, they were adults when they died. But they were still mine."

Part of me wanted to ask how she and her family had become vampires in the first place, but it didn't feel like the right time, so instead I watched her, waiting for her to continue.

She stared at the armour like she was talking to *it* instead of me. "I am the last vampire at the Nest who survived the Hallows war. The other survivors either never returned to the Nest, or found an immortal life after witnessing those atrocities such a heavy burden that they... unburdened themselves."

She faced me now, all her theatrics and flair gone, replaced by a stony seriousness that could have rivalled Madigan's. "Vampires relish violence. It's in our nature. But my people haven't seen the things I've seen. They don't understand the horrors they'll face if they fight the Hallows."

"You're not the only one who's been to war—"

"This is not war as you know it, Ava," she said, her voice rising. "The curses their artefacts are capable of repulsed me. Made me sick. Do I strike you as someone squeamish?"

A heartbeat of silence. "No."

"They made me *sick*," she repeated. "Curses of living-decomposition, parasitic worms the size of rats, turning people inside out—" She had to stop, doing her best to hide how she retched, but I heard the thickness in her throat. "I'll never put my people through that again. *Never.* They don't know what they're signing up for. This isn't the Battles of Blood where vampires fight and die with honour. This would be a slow, painful slaughter. My people are too young to know better. Too naive. And so are you. Do yourself a favour and go to Havoc with all the witches and shifters. If the Hallows have returned, the world you know is already dead."

I glanced at her armour. It was easier to look at than her; it wasn't staring at me pleadingly.

"I can't."

"By supporting Hiero, you're sentencing my people to a fate worse than death." There was a harshness to her voice now.

"Then why haven't you killed me? You could if you wanted to, right? Or at least have me thrown out. So why haven't you?"

She made another of those incomprehensible noises, her face scrunched in annoyance.

"As it turns out," she said, her lips pursed and teeth ground so tight I had to strain my ears, "I owe your mistress a great debt. If you were anyone else's familiar, I'd have taken your soul by now. But as you are Latisha's,"—she took a sharp inhale, her nostrils pinching before giving me a cold, sarcastic smile—"I'd better be a gracious hostess."

I couldn't help the smirk that spread across my lips. She was talking of Latisha in the same manner she spoke of the Hallows.

"You're afraid of her, aren't you?"

But my smugness died the moment her features twisted into a sneer.

"So are you."

CHAPTER TWENTY-THREE

My heart weighed heavy as I trudged back to Hiero's. I couldn't get my head around the weird exchange with Franziska, but it didn't fill me with optimism, and the sense of doom worsened when I reached Hiero's house to find one of the front doors ripped clean off its hinges.

I crept forward, straining my ears to make out the voices coming from within, holding my breath and praying my heartbeat wouldn't attract attention.

"You have a problem—seriously. I told you it was too many," hissed a voice I recognised as Talia's, distorted in the whispered shout.

"Fine, no more," Hiero answered in the same whisper. "Just one more week, Talia. We're so close now. *So close*!"

I skulked behind the remaining door, out of sight. There was something... *off* about their whispering. They'd been happy to talk about the election freely before. Why so secretive now?

"What will you tell your friends?" Talia asked. "Where do they fit in? You know the shifter can't stay."

I bristled at her words, the desire to storm in and say I can come and go as I please—thank you very much—almost overpowering. But I bit my tongue, taking slow, shallow breaths to catch every word of their private conversation.

"Can't she?" Hiero said, filling my chest with a smug satisfaction. "We're on the same side, fighting the same enemy. That's all that matters."

"And Leonard? What about him?"

A beat of silence.

"I will convince him to stay," he said at last.

"And the same rules apply to him as they do everyone else? You promised everyone would be treated the same. *Everyone*. That includes him."

Another agonising pause—longer than the last.

"Yes," Hiero said at last. "Conscription is something he's faced before, and I... I hope he'll do what's right."

"Why not ask him now and be done with it?"

"Because if he disagrees, he'll tell Ava, and I don't think she's ready to know yet. She might never be. I'm waiting for the opportune moment. Once I'm Liege Lord it won't matter what she—or anyone—thinks. It will be too late."

Could I have heard that right?

I frowned, Hiero's words chasing themselves around my head as I tried to make sense of them. It sounded like Hiero planned on conscripting vampires into his army—but why was he keeping it a secret from me and Madigan? Something wasn't right...

"I don't understand why you're obsessed with the Hallows when they didn't even kill him in the first pla—"

My heart stalled as a loud crash and a clang of metal cut Talia off, followed by a hiss from Hiero, so full of venom it could have been a different person speaking.

"*Stop* talking about Len. I'm not letting *anyone* undo twenty years of work. Twenty. Fucking. Years. This fight is bigger than me. It's bigger than Len. And it's certainly bigger than you. If you want to be a part of the new world I'm building, then I suggest you stop questioning me and do the job I pay you for."

A gasping breath. A scrape of something heavy on the marble floor. Hurried footsteps growing quieter. And then a long, drawn-out sigh.

I peered through the doorway, gawking as I surveyed the carnage.

Like Red's manor, Hiero's was in a state of chaos. Thankfully, there was no blood, but broken glass and splintered wood littered the floor.

Hiero had his back to me, head bowed, bracing himself against the table in front of the framed floor plan. The golden bell that usually sat upon it rolled across the floor, only stopping once it hit the debris of a destroyed painting.

I knocked to announce my presence before crossing the threshold, my boots crunching against glass.

Hiero raised his head, frowning through narrowed eyes, but then smiled.

"Ava," he breathed, his whole body relaxing as relief washed over him, and the bundle of nerves forming in my stomach fizzled out. "Len! She's back!"

"Ava?" Madigan's voice rang from a nearby room. He emerged from the library, his hair sticking up from where he'd run his fingers. He darted from the doorway, nothing but a dark blur as he rushed across the landing and down the stairs, coming to a standstill in front of me and cupping my cheek in one hand. "What did she do? Are you all right?"

"She *dressed* me, Madigan," I said in mock horror. "Do you think I've grounds for a lawsuit or...?"

Hiero stifled a laugh behind his hand, while Madigan's look of concern became one of annoyance.

"I forgot how you can be," he muttered.

"To be fair, Ava, he's got a point," Hiero said, still smirking. "What did she *really* want?"

A grin slowly spread across my lips. "She's not doing as well as we thought."

Hiero's eyebrows jumped so high they almost disappeared behind his locks.

"She said that since I arrived, loads of vampires have been asking for deployment. She sure as hell isn't mentioning that when she makes a scene at the Lucky Lantern."

"Of course..." Hiero said, his smile widening as he rubbed his chin, speaking to himself more than us. "It all makes sense. That's why she ordered the attack. I'm becoming a threat."

"What?!"

Hiero's smile became wry. "I've been thinking it over, and it's the only plausible explanation. As you can see"—he gestured towards the damage—"it was *my* house Lord Tonbridge saw the Brain Eaters attacking. Franziska said it herself: only the crown can control that many Brain Eaters. It was *me* they were after. And when they couldn't find me, they attacked Red's."

I nodded slowly. It was advantageous to Franziska if Hiero died in a tragic accident.... and yet...

"Wouldn't Franziska have known you were at Red's manor?" Madigan asked. "She saw you at the party."

"Actually, no," I said, heat rising into my face. "She saw us *leaving*. She probably thought we'd come straight here."

Silence followed. A flash of skin, sweat, and panting breaths burned through my mind, and from the way Madigan tugged on his cuff and Hiero grinned, I guessed they had experienced the same.

"Speaking of which," Hiero said, a slight pink tinge in his cheeks. "There's something I need to talk to you about. Both of you. About what happened at the ball…"

I lay beside Madigan, staring up at the canopy of the bed, one hand resting behind my head, replaying Hiero's words.

"Last night was… amazing. And I don't want you to think I don't care about you, or that I didn't enjoy it. But with the stunts Franziska is pulling, I can't afford to be distracted. She's already tried to use you to get to me. And if something happened to either of you, I could never live with myself. Which is why I ask, could we wait until after the election before discussing our… our… arrangement?"

"What did he mean by *'our arrangement'*?" I asked Madigan. "Does he mean a relationship? Like the one he has with Talia and Xander?"

"I believe so." Madigan's eyes were closed, attempting to sleep, and though I knew I should let him, I couldn't switch off my brain, replaying Hiero and Talia's hushed conversation.

"How do you feel about what Hiero said?" I asked.

"Fine, honestly. It makes sense from a logical point of view. Better to wait until after the election to discuss it."

"No, I mean about being in that sort of relationship. Is that what you want?"

Madigan opened one eye, glancing at me before closing it again. "I gave myself to you because I desire to be with you—not because I want to bind you to my side. I would not begrudge you the affections or touch of another, but if you wanted a relationship with *Hiero*, I hope you wouldn't begrudge me the same?"

I rolled onto my side, propping myself on one elbow. "I've not been with more than one person before. Not in a relationship. Or the bedroom."

Madigan now opened both eyes, turning to mirror me. "Were you uncomfortable?"

"No—I was *very* comfortable," I said. "A little *too* comfortable. I just never thought I'd have to consider something like this, y'know?"

He took my hand. "Well, you've got time. And no matter your decision, I shall support you." A second passed where we gazed at each other, warmth radiating from him and into me. Through my chest. Around my heart.

I love you. Say it!

He was perfect. The silver in his grey eyes. The curl of his lips. A smile so secret and beautiful.

But then, his usual, serious expression returned.

"Now, if you don't mind, I'm exhausted. Please, let me sleep?"

"Go on then, as you asked so nicely."

He lay back and rolled over with his back to me. I wanted to sleep too, but my mind was still racing. And somehow, I had this strange feeling it wasn't my muddled relationships that had my brain ticking. It was something else. Something I'd pushed to the back of my mind. Something that didn't make sense. An odd puzzle piece.

And then there was that strange conversation between Hiero and Talia.

"Madigan, what are your thoughts on conscription?"

But only soft, almost silent snores responded.

The sense of something being off hung over me for the rest of the week. I often headed to the training ground to pass the time, but with Myla dedicating herself to Red's physical therapy, all I could do was muddle through the regimen she'd planned out for me.

Red recovered faster than any human could, but it was still a slow process.

"I'm walking alone now," she said, showing me her prosthetic leg when I'd gone to visit. "I want to try jogging, but Myla said it was too soon."

"You'll get there," I said. "I have no doubt. Are you coming to the speeches before they open the polls tomorrow?" Hiero had been practising his debating skills with Madigan, the two of them shut up together in the library. Part of me wondered if I should be worried, but I pushed my insecurities to the side, Hiero's words repeating through my head like a mantra.

Wait until after the election before making any decisions...

"Yes, I'll be there," she said, frowning with determination. She'd been avoiding public appearances. "Myla and Max are going an hour early to walk down with me. We're grabbing a table at the Lucky Lantern to get a good view of Speaker's Rock. You're more than welcome to join us."

"Oh, Max is coming, is he?" I asked, raising an eyebrow. I'd not yet asked how the man who'd destroyed her leg was now refurbishing her manor, or what he'd been doing in Red's manor after the ball.

Red smiled, blushing, but said without shame, "Yes. He is."

"Forgiven you for cutting his eye out?"

"He is more pissed about being defeated than about his eye," Red said. "He's a true warrior."

"True warriors cheat, do they?"

She focused her mismatched eyes on me, expression tight, and for a second, I thought she was about to snap at me. But she sighed and said, "Honestly? At first I was mad he disrespected me and made a mockery of the Battles of Blood. But I think losing an eye is a fair price. But since then, he's... kinda changed."

"Seems legit." I wasn't buying it. Probably spying for Franziska, most likely. Or maybe trying to get close to Hiero. As if it wasn't bad enough having thoughts of Hiero robbing me of sleep, now I had Max to worry about, too. But I wouldn't have to fret much longer. Tomorrow, the vampires would cast their votes. And the following night, the winner announced.

But this didn't help my restless mind, and once again, I found myself staring up at the canopy of my bed with Madigan snoozing beside me.

I sat up—far too alert—and scanned the room, like the reason for my insomnia hid in the shadows. But my eyes settled on a fluffy, maroon dressing gown.

Cold air sparked a chill over me as I darted out of bed, seized it, and wrapped it around me, its pleasant, earthy scent in my nose as I brought the hood up over my head. It was too big, but that only made it cosier.

Sadly, there were no slippers, so my toes tingled as I crept from the room, leaving the carpeted floor of the bedroom to the chilly stone staircase and secret passage to the kitchen.

I'd done this trip a few times now, and left myself matches and a candle to make the journey through the dark passage easier—a suggestion from Chef after leaving me secret stashes of snacks.

The soft orange glow of the candle danced against the walls as it lit my path. I took care, my free hand against the stone wall, its rough surface passing beneath my fingertips, until I found the hidden door to the kitchen and unfastened the latch. A small wooden panel swung open. One step at a time, I climbed into the kitchen and closed the panel behind me. From this side, it looked like an oil painting of a bottle of liquor.

"Ava?"

I jumped, dropping my candle. Engulfed in darkness.

"Who's that?" I asked, blinking into the gloom.

"It's Hiero. What are you doing?"

"I'm just... I couldn't sleep..."

"Hang on... let me..." With a scrape of a match, Hiero lit a lamp, filling the air with the scent of sulphur and oil.

He looked like he'd just rolled out of bed, his hair dishevelled, and dressed only in a pair of well-fitting grey pyjama bottoms that left little to the imagination. And the light flickering from the lamp highlighted every groove of his sculpted abdomen. I swallowed, my mouth growing wet.

He smiled knowingly as I avoided eye contact, focusing on his forehead... his nose... his lips...

Oh no...

"Why are you sitting in the dark?" I asked, noting the wooden stool he'd risen from and the amber liquid in what looked like a short wine glass.

"I can see in the dark, remember?" His smirk widened.

"Sorry. Stupid question."

"Flustered?"

I gave him a withering look. *Yes... But you won't get me admitting it...* "No, just tired."

"I thought you said you couldn't sleep?"

"Do you always have the last word?" The heat in my cheeks spread to the rest of my face, my temper bubbling.

"Naturally." He pulled another glass from a cupboard and poured more amber liquid. I tilted my head to read the label.

"Oh, you like cog-nac, too? Madigan drinks that stuff."

Hiero laughed. "It's *ko-nyak*, and yes, I know he does. That's why I have it. I was going to wait until after my victory to share it with him, but..." His voice trailed off before he hung his head, sighing. "I'm having trouble sleeping, too."

I pulled up another stool, letting its wooden legs scrape against the floor before taking a seat and giving the *ko-nyak* a sniff. Its scent burned my nostrils just like when I'd tried it before. I wasn't a fan, but it might help with the insomnia, so I sipped, shuddering as it went down.

"Nervous about tomorrow?" I asked. Another stupid question—of course he was.

"No," he said with a wry smile. "I just have a drinking problem. What about you? Why can't you sleep?"

"I've a lot on my mind," I said, toying with the idea of asking what he and Talia were discussing before I'd walked in on them. "Hiero, what are you going to do when you win the election?"

Hiero took another sip, tilting his head in thought. "Well, first, I would take the crown and send a telepathic message to all the vampires—Soul Suckers, Blood Drinkers, even Brain Eaters—that I am their Liege Lord. Then I'd choose my council. I'd need a new Blood Lord or Lady to replace my position. And I think Lord Tonbridge needs to go—I can't trust him—so that would mean a new Gold Lord—"

"And once you've chosen your council, then what?"

Hiero raised an eyebrow, giving me a calculating look before saying, "I'd summon every vampire to the Nest to be recruited into your army."

"Would they have a choice?"

His eyes narrowed, like he was looking for a trap I'd laid.

"It's all right," I said. "I'm not bugged, or anything. This won't go beyond this room if you don't want—"

"Yes, they would have a choice."

I took another sip of the burning liquid, shuddering again.

"And what about you?" he asked. "What will you do when I win?" He drained the rest of his glass, then turned on his stool, facing me, so my knees were between his. I kept my eyes focused on my glass, praying for my heart to calm down.

It didn't.

"I guess I'll stay until you have the army, and then..." Then what? I'd been so caught up in finding the recruits I'd not thought what I'd do next.

"Yes?"

I glanced at him. He was staring at me, unblinking, leaning forward in anticipation. "Well, I suppose I'll have to take them to Kinwich, or wherever the coven is."

"And then?"

"And then, what?"

He leant closer, his thighs pressing against my knees. "Will you come back?"

I swallowed, able to smell him now; that earthy fragrance I now realised was also on the maroon dressing gown. "I... don't know..."

"You *do* know," he said, his voice low, husky. "I'm sure someone else could escort them to your coven." His breath was warm on my cheek.

Closer. Closer... His lips were inches from mine...

My mouth was too wet. I just needed to lean forward and my lips would be on his...

With every drop of willpower I had, I turned my face. "I-I'd need to think about it." My heart was thumping so hard it reverberated through my body. I cringed, knowing Hiero could hear each and every thump as blood rushed through my veins.

"You *still* don't trust me?" he asked, like he could read my thoughts. The irony that I'd been happy to let him fuck me but not kiss me wasn't lost on either of us.

"No, it's not that. It's just..." I closed my eyes, as though it might switch off my desire if I couldn't see him. But his scent rolled over me, and heat seemed to pour from him, seeping into me until every cell of my body yearned for him. "Please don't use your glamour on me," I said in a whisper, my throat too tight.

"I'm not." I could still *feel* how close his lips were to mine, and it almost hurt not to close the gap. To feel his warm skin. To taste him.

I opened one eye, focusing only on his mouth. "You are."

"All I am doing is showing you my old face," he said. "Before the explosion. I'm not using it to seduce you."

"How can I be sure?"

"Because if I was, you'd be *begging* me to fuck you."

His words sent a spasm through my body, my womanhood clenching. And from the way he smirked, I knew he'd sensed it.

"I'd already have you bent over this bench," he said, his voice a warm caress, "just like I had you bent over that pool table. And I'd already have my cock deep inside your tight little cunt, fucking you until you cum all over me—*again*."

My breath hitched in my throat. If I didn't stop him now, I would submit to him; I knew I would.

"Would you... show me your real face?" I asked.

He didn't answer, and for a heartbeat, he hovered in front of me, his breath mingling with mine. All he had to do was lean forward and claim me.

Slowly, he pulled back. "Ava." His voice was heavy. "The man beneath the glamour is... not me. Or at least, it used to be. But no longer."

I took a breath, the tightness in my chest easing, a sobering chill washing over me. Relieved... and yet... disappointed. "Perhaps after the election? When we discuss our *arrangement*?"

A smile tugged on his lips. "Perhaps." He didn't sound convincing.

I drained the rest of my glass, easing the adrenaline I only now registered pumping through me. "We should probably go to bed. You'll want to rest for tomorrow."

Hiero nodded, smiling, but not his usual grin, unable to hide his obvious disappointment. "Would you like me to escort you back to your room?"

"I'll take the passage," I said, nodding towards the painting. "It would probably be safer... for both of us."

"Very well."

He made to leave, but paused, leaning against the doorframe, one thumb hooked around the top of his pyjama bottoms, drawing my eye.

"Sweet dreams, Ava." And with one last satisfied smile, he closed the door behind him, leaving me in silence, though the sound of blood rushed in my ears.

CHAPTER TWENTY-FOUR

The Lucky Lantern was even busier than last time. Although we'd arrived an hour before Hiero and Franziska were due to address the vampires at 10 o'clock, we still had to squeeze through the crowds. Fortunately, having the Blood Champion with us meant vampires practically fell over each other to give up their seats, and we nabbed a table with a perfect view of Speaker's Rock.

I was opposite Max, who sat with his blind side towards me, as though trying to block me out, his good eye on Red.

"I can't stay," Myla said after bringing a tray of drinks to the table and knocking back her pint in one go. "Franziska wants me with her at the Rock. Said something about it *getting ugly*. But I'll be back as soon as it's over."

I shared a nervous glance with Madigan as she left, vampires making way for her brawny frame as she bulldozed through them. The inn was packed now, vampires spilling out into the town square. And it wasn't just the Lucky Lantern bursting. The Lover's Sanctum was also rammed, vampires leaning out of windows—some dressed, others not so much—to get a clear view.

Within minutes of settling at our table, it became apparent that word of the Brain Eater attack on Hiero and Red's homes was the hot topic.

"Trashed both of their mansions hunting Lord Blackford. That's what I heard," a vampire from the neighbouring table said.

"Why? Franziska doesn't need to kill him. She's more popular by a mile!" their friend replied.

"I'm not so sure. I heard Cassius telling Edward about the shifter girl trying to recruit fighters. I don't know about you, but I've been waiting for an honourable war, and now the chance has arrived, Franziska is telling us it's all a hoax. No glory in lying, is there?"

"No glory in sending Brain Eaters to attack your enemy, either. I heard the armour she has is all for show and she's never seen a real battle."

"Oh no, that can't be true…"

I could have listened to the gossip all night, but I had something more important to address, and he was doing his best to ignore me. That is, until Red nudged him with her elbow and he twitched his head in my direction.

"Not yet," he said through a stiff jaw.

"Just say it," Red said.

"Say what?" I asked, and with a slump of his shoulders and an exasperated sigh, Max swivelled in his seat to face me.

"I'd like to ask you something," he said, though he was talking to my hands, rather than my face.

"Well, that's convenient. I would like to ask *you* something."

His eye snapped upward, narrowing with suspicion. "What?"

"What's your obsession with Red?"

"Ava!" Red's voice rose to an almost inaudible squeak.

"It's a fair question!" I said, refusing to look away from Max's good eye, even as uncomfortable heat pricked my skin. "You were a dick to her in the training grounds. You betrayed her when she was your teammate. You cheated during your match. And now you suddenly want to be besties?"

"Ava," Red said again, this time low and soothing, but Max and I continued our staring match, clenching his jaw so tight his teeth crunched. But he didn't answer.

"Got nothing for me?" I asked, raising an eyebrow. "Shame." I finally broke eye contact to look at Red. "Sorry to sound condescending, but I think you've forgiven him too easily—"

"I've *always* admired Red," Max cut in with such force several vampires turned their heads. "Trash talk is all part of the Battles. And yes, she was my teammate in the semi-finals, but ultimately, we were rivals."

"And the cheating? The potion that made you go mental and grievously wound her? Yeah, sure sounds like you admire her."

"Grievous wounds are the whole *point* of the Battles of Blood."

"And is *cheating* the whole point, too?"

His nostrils flared, his mouth a tight line, and I thought he was about to lose it. But then he sighed. "If you really want to know..." He glanced sideways at Red, who nodded, encouraging him to continue. "I was afraid."

"Um-hmm," I said with a roll of my eyes. "Sounds legit."

His nose wrinkled with annoyance. "Well, if you won't listen..."

"Ava." Red reached across the table to me. "Please. We talked during the Champion's Ball—"

"Yeah, I saw that."

"—And you should hear him out. I didn't believe him at first either. But if you do, you might find him helpful."

I raised a sceptical eyebrow. "Helpful?"

She nodded. "What's the point of cross-examining him if you won't listen?"

Damn... She's got me there.

I slumped back in my seat, folding my arms. "Fine. Go on then, *Morningstar*. You were afraid, were you?"

He glared at me, before answering, "Yes, actually." He shot Red another glance, then took a breath, like he was mustering the courage to elaborate. It was a brilliant performance. "I'd been watching her previous matches for a while. And her training. The way she moved. Her skills. Everything. She was the only competitor that made me nervous. Then Franziska approached me, saying if I didn't knock her out in the finals, she'd stop my funding."

"So, you did it for *money*?" I said witheringly.

Max slammed his fist on the table, making me jump as our drinks went crashing to the floor. "Do you have any fucking idea what it is like living here without it?"

I didn't answer, my heart still thrumming from his outburst.

To my surprise, it was Madigan who answered him. "I do."

"Would you have done the same?" Max asked him.

Madigan's tongue traced his lower lip. "Perhaps," he said fairly. "I certainly wouldn't have ruled it out."

Max returned his sights to me, a smug *'gotcha'* smile on his face.

"Really?" I asked Madigan.

He shrugged. "He has a point, Ava. You *don't* know what it's like living here without money. Hiero has done an excellent job of sheltering you from that. But before he became a lord, he was a rat catcher. We barely scraped enough money together to feed and clothe ourselves. Fortunately for us, we didn't need to buy blood since we had a familiar." He shot me a meaningful glance. "Until we didn't."

My stomach twisted.

Roz—the familiar he lost at the Blood Bank. Torn apart by frenzied vampires.

Madigan was right. I couldn't judge Max's motives. But, he *had* still cheated.

"I suppose Franziska gave you the Sacrilegious Strength herself, did she?" I asked.

"Actually, no. It was a fluke I got it. I found some old hag wandering through the streets. She looked lost and like she was about to keel over, walking with this strange limp, skulking in the shadows with half her face covered. When I asked if she needed help, she said she was trying to leave the Nest, and in exchange for my assistance, she'd give me a potion of my choice. She had a few on her. Witch's Tears. Some sort of age accelerant. She said the Sacrilegious Strength was for herself, but that was the one I wanted. In the end, it didn't matter. Before we could reach the exit, we ran into Lord Blackford, who took her away. Fortunately for me, I'd already received the potion—"

"Wait—*Hiero* took her?"

"Yes. Said he was looking after her. Not that he was doing a decent job. As I said, she looked ready to drop. Probably starving herself of blood. Some of the oldies do that when they've had enough of this long, *long* life."

"Did he say anything else? Who she was? Anything like that?"

"No. Why does it matter?"

"I don't know..." I turned to Madigan, who was frowning. "Did Hiero mention anything to you?"

Madigan shook his head, his frown deepening.

I drummed my fingers on the table, thinking. Something was wrong.

"Now, if we're finished with my interrogation," Max said, his tone dripping with forced politeness that didn't suit him at all, "could I ask *you* a question?"

I'd almost forgotten he had something to ask me. I nodded, bracing myself for the worst.

"When you leave the Nest, would you allow me to accompany you?"

"Uhhh... what?" I must have misheard him. "What do you mean?"

"Take. Me. With. You. I have brought great shame upon myself, and if I am to bring myself honour, I must fight for a noble cause. I will take Red's place in your fight against the Hallows. Perhaps then I can redeem my actions and find peace and glory."

I opened my mouth to respond, but no words came, still certain I must have misunderstood him.

"He means it," Red said, perhaps reading my puzzled expression. "I offered him a room in my mansion so he doesn't have to live in one of those shacks, but he said he didn't want my charity."

"And I still don't," Max said, his fists clenching on the table. "Please. I need this."

I blinked at him, my mind refusing to accept what I was hearing, then at Madigan, who gave the slightest nod.

"This isn't some sort of trick?" I asked.

Max shook his head. "All I ask is to spill Hallow blood and restore my good name."

I didn't know what to say. He was almost as popular as Red, so having him join us might encourage others, but I didn't trust him, even if Red did.

But I was spared from answering when the vampires outside erupted into cheers and applause, the sound carrying inside, and everyone made a rush for the nearest window.

Hiero and Franziska stood on Speaker's Rock, elevated above the crowd. Franziska was as radiant as ever, looking every part like a vampire queen, clothed in a red-and-black dress, her waist cinched with a corset and an enormous ruby glittering on her choker. Hiero dressed as he always did, but at least he'd buttoned his shirt to the top.

"Thank you all for coming," Franziska's voice rang out, a little more simperingly sweet than usual. "In a moment, you will cast your votes at the polling station. But first, Lord Blackford and I have one last chance to speak to you."

The crowd was restless, muttering, jostling, a contrast to when they'd listened to her at the Lucky Lantern, still and silent, hanging on her every word.

Franziska spoke first, and I found my mind wandering as she discussed politics. It was boring in the human world, and boring in the Nest. Boring, that is, until Hiero cut in.

"She *says* you'll earn more gold," Hiero's voice was as condescending as Franziska's had been when she'd humiliated him. "She *says* you'll have better jobs. But how many of you are still in the same position you were in twenty-five, fifty, seventy-five years ago?"

Murmurs among the crowd, and now I spotted Myla, inching closer to Franziska, who, to my surprise, didn't reprimand her guard for joining them on the Rock.

"That's how it's always been, right?" Hiero continued. "Soul Suckers were worshiped as gods until we realised they are just like us, but with a different diet. Still, we keep electing them because they're the most powerful of our kind. But does that mean you should slave away in the dirt and dark, while they live the highlife in their mansions?"

Franziska snorted. "Everyone has an opportunity to join us. Look at you, Hiero. Once you lived in some rundown little cabin, but now you're running for Liege Lord. This is the world I created. A world where everyone has a chance. All they need to do is put in the work."

Hiero grinned. But it wasn't the grin I was used to. It wasn't the grin that sent heat rippling through me. But a sly, serpentine leer I'd seen

Franziska wear herself when she'd laid that trap for Hiero and watched him walk into it.

"'*Put in the work*,'" he said. "Our Liege Lady doesn't think you're working hard enough."

"That's not what I said—"

"How much work is needed, Franziska? You weren't interested when I caught rats."

"Just how important is rat catching?"

More unsettled whispers from the onlookers, and Franziska must have realised her mistake, her smile slipping.

"'*How important is rat catching*?'" Hiero said, once again using Franziska's own words against her. He faced the crowd. "Perhaps one of you can tell me? How important *is* rat catching? Tell me, when a rat becomes infected with our blood and rips through our city, eating our food, killing our familiars, how important are rat catchers then?"

The muttering in the crowd grew louder.

"See the contempt she has for you? For *us*? She doesn't deem you or your work important. Whether you catch rats like me, or make our clothes, bake our bread, keeping our city running. It's not important enough for a decent wage or living conditions. And what's worse, she lies to you: put in the work and you can live in the inner circle. How much *more* do these people need to do, Franziska?"

She spluttered to find an answer. "I don't... That isn't... That's not how it works."

"You're right. It *doesn't* work. You've broken the system. A system so corrupt you resort to cheating to maintain it."

"Excuse me?" There was no hiding the edge of panic in Franziska's voice now, no matter how hard she tried.

"Sent some Brain Eaters after me, didn't you?"

"What are you blathering about?"

"Where is Lord Tonbridge?" Hiero called out into the crowd. The vampires moved, swaying in place as they looked for Lord Tonbridge. Soon, heads and fingers pointed to a window of the Lover's Sanctum.

"You saw the Brain Eaters attack my home, correct?" Hiero called out to him.

"I saw them attack your house, yes," Lord Tonbridge called back. "I never said they were sent after *you*."

"Then they attacked Red's house, which is exactly where I was. Do you think that's a coincidence?"

Lord Tonbridge opened and closed his mouth, looking for an answer that didn't come.

"But there's someone who can control Brain Eaters, isn't there? Someone we saw controlling them later that night with the crown."

"You're not suggesting I sent them to attack you, are you?" Franziska didn't even try to stay calm, instead looking at Hiero with such disgust you'd think he'd not washed for a year.

"That's exactly what I'm suggesting," he said. "Deny it all you like. We all know you're lying. *Again*." Hiero turned his back on Franziska. "And she lied about the Hallows, too. The Hallows War was the greatest our people have ever seen! Hunters died in their thousands. More blood was spilt in Kinwich in a single night than any other battle in our history. Kinwich: the very place the coven is recruiting. And she wants to rob you of the opportunity to spill Hallow blood!

"Join my army, and not only will you see the blood and glory you deserve, but I'll pay for your efforts in gold. It won't matter who wins the Battle of Blood or Souls anymore. You will fight *real* battles. No longer will it matter if you're a Blood Drinker or a Soul Sucker. There will be one people. *Vampires,* who shall strike fear into the hearts of any that threaten our existence!"

Cheers and applause rang out, followed by boos from some of Franziska's supporters. Then jostling. Pushing.

"Uh oh…" Max clenched his fists.

"What?" I asked.

"This is going to get nasty. I can tell."

"Agreed," Madigan said. "Ava, we're leaving."

"What? But it's getting interesting!" There was an electric excitement in the air as the vampires grew restless.

"Ava, please?" It was a request, but the crispness in his tone matched his frosty eyes.

I glanced out the window once more. Hiero continued his accusations, while Franziska's expression shifted between mortification and fury. And the crowd became more restless.

"Fine," I said with a sigh.

With a scrape of chair legs, we gathered up our things, other vampires almost knocking us out of the way to claim our vacant seats. Until Red drew in a sharp intake of breath.

"Someone threw something at Franziska!"

Everyone rushed to the window.

Franziska's jet-black hair was dripping wet. She put a hand to her face, wiping liquid from her cheek, examining it for a second, before turning to a vampire within the crowd.

"Franziska, don't—" Myla said, hand outstretched, but Franziska had already marched into the throng. A moment of unease as the vampires rippled to let her pass. Then a torrent of blood erupted into the air like a small volcano, spraying upwards and raining down. Screams pierced the air as my heart gave a sudden jolt, white-hot panic shooting through my veins.

"Let's move," Madigan said, holding out a hand to me. I seized it, and he closed his iron grip around me.

I caught one last glimpse of Max assisting Red before Madigan swept me away. My feet could barely keep up with his long, fast strides. I stumbled, but he yanked me upright before my knees could hit the ground, gliding through the other vampires crammed in the pub.

But it was even harder to keep pace with Madigan once outside, the vampires even rowdier. I had to contend with bodies knocking into me, either shoving to get past, or being jostled by others. Feet trampled mine, elbows digging into my ribs. Something struck the side of my head, and for a second I saw stars.

Madigan's hot grip on my hand tightened, but my palm was sweating.

A sudden wave of vampires crashed into me as Franziska's guards marched into the crowd. I still grasped Madigan's hand, though my arm was pulled tight, and I could barely see him among the bodies blocking him.

"Madigan!" I shouted, but my voice was almost inaudible over the shouts and screams. My hand was slipping. "Don't let go!"

He looked back at me, eyes widening as they flicked to our clasped hands, colour draining from his face.

More bodies piled into me. I was slipping. Slipping…

I gripped harder. So did he. Crushing my fingers together painfully. Tighter. *Tighter…*

I winced as the pain intensified with his grip, my bones threatening to snap, and I let out an involuntary, strangled cry.

"I'm… I'm sorry…" he said, grey eyes glistening, and my heart dropped into my stomach as I realised what he was about to do.

"Don't!"

He released my hand. And he was swept away, while I hurtled into cold, wet mud.

CHAPTER TWENTY-FIVE

My fingers went numb, plunging into mud as I braced myself, only then to be trampled by a vampire in front of me.

Crunch.

I screamed as the crushing pain lanced through me, but the vampire couldn't hear me over the shouting, and it wasn't until I head-butted the back of their knee that they lifted their feet.

Wrenching my hands back, I cradled them to my chest, afraid to glimpse the damage. But in that second, someone else collided with me, legs crashing into my side, driving me down, ice-cold mud rushing to meet me, slamming into the side of my face.

A foot on my back. Then another. Expelling air from my lungs.

I scrabbled in the mud, raising my head. *Gasped* for breath. Then someone fell on top of me.

Darkness. Cold. Heart raging. Body squirming. Muscles screaming. Getting weaker. And *fear.*

I'm going to die... I'm going to die!

The weight lifted.

Another *gasp* as I pulled my face from the mud. It clogged my nose. My eyes. Bitter in my mouth.

Broken fingers forgotten, I heaved myself off the ground, my vision blurry, my throat burning, my legs threatening to give way.

Someone slammed into me, pinning me against another body. Both were taller than me. As were the next two, boxing me in.

My lungs were too tight.

Gritting my teeth, and snarling with the pain in my fingers, I reached up, one hand grabbing a vampire's shoulder, the other taking a fistful of someone's shirt, and I hauled myself upwards, my head bursting free from the scrum and drinking in a lungful of air.

"Madigan!" I screamed as loudly as my raw throat would allow and squinted at every face surrounding me. He wasn't here.

Rough hands on my shoulders, pinching tight through my clothes.

"Get off me!" The vampire whose shirt I'd grabbed shoved me forward with such force, bodies fell like dominoes into a heap.

I tried to scrabble to my feet, but the vampire I'd fallen on knocked me back. Fighting for what felt like a lifetime, vampires threw me about until I lost any sense of direction, getting tangled in a group. They carried me along with them, the bark of a guard ordering them forward.

Screams nearby.

I twisted to see a fountain of blood spurt from another group. Acid rose in my throat, my stomach tightening, but I *forced* it back down.

"Move!" someone from our cluster shouted, and they carried me along until we arrived at a structure I recognised.

The city wall. And we'd reached a gate.

"Let me through!" a vampire near the front demanded. "I'm staff."

"The inner circle is in lockdown," said the guard.

"Please, you must let me through!"

A terrible moment of pause as each waited for the other to act.

I knew what was about to happen... and braced myself for the impact. The group surged forward, piling into the guard who held their staff across their body in defence. Outnumbered.

I was crushed between two vampires, suffocating between their bodies. The cloth of their shirt in my face, their body odour thick in my nose. Lost my footing. Slipped. Dropped to my knees as another group crashed into ours.

I covered my head with my arms.

I can't take this anymore!

Screwing up my eyes, I steeled myself for the agony... and plummeted into darkness as my bones reformed into exoskeleton armour. Then a weight from above crushed me into a tangle of clothes and mud. Completely submerged. Unable to breathe.

My stinger twitched as a bolt of panic shot through me, thinking of Madigan as I prepared to drown.

The weight lifted.

Only for another to take its place. Then another. Over and over again.

I waited.

There'd be an opportunity to rise for air. There *had* to be.

Feet continued to thunder down on top of me.

And I waited.

The vibrations were like a jackhammer. Unrelenting.

And I waited...

Soon, I realised I *didn't* need to come up for air. Not at all. The urge to sting lessened, my heartbeat steadying.

Feet continued to hammer away, and awful as it was to be trapped among twisted fabric, coated in mud, frozen, wet, and alone, the realisation that I wouldn't drown calmed me.

I shut down my senses, picturing Madigan.

I will find you. As soon as this lot has calmed down, I'll find you, and you will be safe. We'll meet back at Hiero's house, and everything will be fine...

Hiero's house...

I lost myself in my own thoughts, concentrating with every drop of willpower I had, shutting out the surrounding bedlam. I'd no idea how much time had passed—it felt like hours—but eventually, the vibrations softened. The crowd above was dispersing. Then disappeared. All that remained was the pulse of someone above shifting their weight from one foot to the other, tapping their staff on the ground.

Mud clogged the fine hairs over my body as I wriggled free from my restraints, making it difficult to make out my surroundings. But I could just sense the guard stood above me, the wooden gate, and the small crack beneath it—large enough for a scorpion to squeeze through.

Flattening myself to the ground, I slipped undetected through to the inner circle, and unearthly silence. The inner circle had always been quiet, but it was never... *dead*.

It was now.

Screams still echoed throughout the outer ring—muffled by the mud coating me and the wall dividing us—along with the marching of feet as guards rounded up civilians. Who knew what had become of Hiero or Franziska? Surely the guards wouldn't have stopped *them* coming through the gates? Hiero might have made it home safely already, and if Madigan freed himself from the swarm he'd been caught in, he'd head straight for Hiero's.

My innards twisted as I recalled the guard's words about the inner circle being in lockdown—whatever that meant. Did it only apply to staff? What about residents? But without a better plan, I made a beeline for the manor.

I scuttled towards Hiero's until my eight legs ached, not daring to take on human form in case I was stopped by a guard and thrown out—not that I met a single soul along the way.

It was easy to climb up the side of his house and creep through an open window, and it was only when I'd dropped onto the chilly stone floor of the kitchen I returned to my human form.

Like shifting post-workout, the aches and pains I'd sustained from being battered through the horde of vampires vanished—even my broken fingers had repaired themselves—but the gnawing ache in my stomach was too much to ignore. Especially with Chef's peanut butter cookies sitting on a plate in the middle of the working top, like he'd put them there especially for me. Maybe he had. My stomach knotted at the thought. Had Chef been caught in the riot, too? Probably. We weren't exactly close, but he was *nice*. Too nice to live in the Nest, that's for sure.

My mouth was so dry it made munching on cookies difficult, but I forced them down. I'd have pocketed some if I had any. Only now did I acknowledge my nudity, something I'd always been painfully aware of before. Latisha once told me it was something I'd get used to, but I'd never believed her.

Another lurch in my stomach.

I wish you were here...

When the flashback of wings and feathers shot through my mind, I prepared for the shudder. But it never came. Whatever she was, whatever form she took, whatever she'd done, I'd been an idiot not to trust her when she's shown me nothing but love and support.

I'd seen enough of the Nest. Enough of politics. Army or no, it was time for me and Madigan to leave. It was time to go *home*.

Hiero's house was as silent as a tomb, my voice reverberating throughout the entrance hall as I called his name, my echo the only reply. I checked his office before heading to his bedroom, knocked... and waited.

I pictured him opening the door, like he did last time. Shirtless. The deep ridges between his muscles. The memory usually stirred a fire in my belly but now left a weight of guilt instead. Yes, it was time to leave, but I didn't want to leave *him*.

Would he help us escape, like I trusted him to?

I knocked again.

"Hiero?"

No answer.

I closed my hand around the doorknob and twisted, expecting it to resist, but to my surprise, it gave way and clicked open.

"Hiero?" I called again, pushing the door open and poking my head inside.

No one. Just Hiero's four poster bed, and extinguished red candles. The rest of the room looked worse for wear—the most noticeable damage done to a vanity table, deep claw marks in the woodwork, and the mirror smashed—like all the other damage during the Brain Eater attack.

"Fuck..."

I turned to leave. Then stopped. Glanced over my shoulder into Hiero's room. And sniffed.

Yes. There was a sweet fragrance wafting from Hiero's candles. But there was something else, too. A smoky, almost chemical scent. The unmistakable fragrance of a candle that's *just* been blown out.

I marched to his bedside table and picked up the nearest candle. *Yes.* The wax on top was liquid, dripping onto my hand at the sudden movement.

"Hiero!" I called, whirling on the spot, almost expecting him to jump out with a cry of *'Surprise!'*.

Still no answer. But he'd been here recently. He was close.

I searched under Hiero's bed, behind his curtains, in his closet—grabbing a shirt and boxer shorts in the process. It was only when I pulled on a pair of socks I thought of my Doc Martens laying in the dirt, abandoned with my clothes, and it was a sign of my desperation that, despite the heaviness in my chest, I wrote them off without a second thought.

Hiero must be somewhere else in the house.

I scanned the room one last time and turned to leave before doing a double-take. There was *one* other place for Hiero to hide: behind a tapestry even more detailed than the one at Red's.

Of course, he has an erotic tapestry in his room.

I reached out to sweep it aside but froze as the tapestry seemed to let out a low, soft groan—so quiet, no wonder I'd missed it before when frenziedly rummaging through the room. Blood pounded in my ears, my every instinct telling me to run, but my legs were locked in place. Even my arm was paralysed, my hand—now shaking—hovering inches from the tapestry.

Somewhere in the corners of my mind I knew it wasn't the *tapestry* making that noise but accepting it would mean facing the truth. There was someone behind it.

Closing my eyes and taking a steeling breath, I flexed my fingers, working up the courage to face what Hiero had been hiding.

I wrenched the tapestry aside with such force I nearly ripped it from the wall and swallowed the scream that was desperate to escape.

A figure stood in an empty doorway. Though hidden in the darkness of the secret passage, from the way they hung their head and continued to groan without acknowledging me, I knew exactly what they were.

A Husk.

Perhaps... it's one of Talia's? That's the only explanation... Talia or Xander. But why are they stashing their Husks back here? Or maybe this one is lost? Can Husks even get lost?

My mind raced with questions, but I may as well have posed them to Hiero's claw-marked vanity for all the good it would do.

Behind the Husk was a spiralling stone staircase. Steep. Unlit. One wrong step and I'd land at the bottom with my head cracked open.

I glanced back only once, biting my lip, fighting the urge to flee to the safety of my bedroom, but the thirst to explore the passage was overpowering. Besides, it might lead me to Hiero. I grabbed a candle, lit it, and with a deep breath, crept past the Husk and into the darkness of the spiralling steps, down, down, to who knew where.

Just as I wondered if this staircase would ever end, I set my feet down on an uneven, rocky floor within a tunnel not unlike the passageway to the Nest itself. Still in darkness, I couldn't see how far this tunnel stretched.

Time became meaningless as I shakily crept through the tunnel, placing each foot with care, one hand on the wall for guidance. When my heart ached from beating too hard, I pretended I was in the passage to the kitchen, but I couldn't lie to my senses. The air was different down here. Almost humid, leaving a funny taste in the back of my nose and mouth.

I stopped when I discovered something that stalled my heart as much as the Husk had.

A fork in the path.

"Fuck..." My candle was burning low, the wax softening in my hand. How long had I been down here?

The safest option would be to turn back. I glimpsed over my shoulder, and into the black abyss. No. I had to keep going.

But which way? Left? Or right?

The left path appeared to continue straight with a slight decline, but the right path dropped sharply. Since I didn't know which path Hiero was hiding in—assuming he was down here at all—it seemed smart to take the path least likely to break my neck.

As more hot wax dripped onto my hand, I prayed he was close, and took the left path, resuming my slow, steady march into the unknown.

My candle flickered, the flame dangerously low in the pool of wax as I came upon a wooden door set into stone at the end of the tunnel, over six feet tall, thick, with what looked like an iron handle and hinges. Unlike Hiero's house, this door looked new, the metal shining, and on the ground were tools, presumably left by whoever had put the door here.

I couldn't be lucky enough to try a second unlocked door, could I?

I tried the handle, and yet again, it opened.

I really am lucky!

But as the door swung upon its hinges, my mouth dropped open, and I realised I couldn't have been more wrong. I clasped a hand over my mouth as my stomach spiralled, and I pinched my nose at the putrid stench from within.

My candle could barely illuminate five feet in front of me, let alone the entire cavern, but it revealed the swarm of bone-white, gangly, naked bodies of the Brain Eaters within. Too many to count. Beyond the nearest, I could only make out their vague outlines, shifting among themselves like one unit

I should be dead... Why aren't they attacking?

The fact that they paid me no mind was unsettling, especially as my heart was raging so hard it was impossible for them not to hear it, let alone smell the blood pumping through my body.

But now wasn't the time to question it. Now was the time to get the hell out of Dodge.

I stepped back, keeping my eyes fixed on the Brain Eaters, afraid they'd jump me the moment my back was turned. Perhaps if I'd not focused all my attention on them, I might have noticed the footsteps of the person now standing behind me.

I backed into them, and my heart that had once been pounding so hard, stopped, as a hot, firm grip squeezed my shoulder.

I turned my head, slowly, somehow knowing who it was before I laid my eyes on him.

Hiero...

CHAPTER TWENTY-SIX

I recoiled, wrenching my shoulder from his grasp. The candlelight flared. Wax splattered—down to the last inch—searing my hand, but I gripped it tighter.

Meeting his stare, I planted my feet, caught between the instinct to flee and the urge to confront him.

Through the open doorway behind me, the Brain Eaters shuffled mindlessly, letting out those deep, haunting groans and raising the hair on the back of my neck. But Hiero didn't move. Didn't give me space to step away from the doorway. And gave me the unmistakable feeling of being cornered.

He was dressed as I'd last seen him, only now covered in mud from the knees down, and a streak of red across one cheek. His hair was unkempt too. But he stood with one hand in his pocket, head tilted to one side, like he'd returned from a stroll in the park rather than a riot.

"What are you doing down here?" His voice was steady but crisp, so unlike the jovial Hiero I knew. As was his smile: a crooked curl of the lip instead of his warm, wide grin.

"I was looking for you," I said, my voice weak. "What is all this?" I waved my hand in the general direction of the Brain Eaters, as looking at them made my insides roil.

His brown eyes bore into mine, flicking from side to side, and I could practically hear babbled, clumsy arguments tumbling inside his head.

"The Brain Eaters, you mean?"

"No, the fucking doorway. Of course the Brain Eaters! And the Husk." I wanted to sound brave, but unshed tears burned my eyes. I wouldn't blink. I wouldn't. "It's not Witch's Tears that grants your glamour, is it?"

"Ava," Hiero said, forcing a laugh, like I'd said something ridiculous, but he straightened from his casual stance, rubbing the back of his neck as he cast his eyes away, looking anywhere but at me. It was an unconvincing act.

"You're a Soul Sucker." And despite my efforts, the tears spilled as I spoke the horrible truth.

He returned his gaze to mine with a heavy sigh, an almost apologetic look on his face. His beauty still shone through his expression of melancholy, but it was a sorrowful beauty. "I didn't want Len to know." That was as close to a confession as was needed. "He never would have approved."

I shook my head. I didn't *want* to believe it. But all those oddities that were so out of place now made sense: how he'd overpowered that rapey Soul Sucker, Boris, in the Lucky Lantern; how he'd smashed open a Brain Eater's head with only one punch. He said he took potions but always changed the subject when someone asked how he got them, or how much they cost.

"Where is Madigan?" I demanded. "What happened after the riots?"

His tongue swept across his lower lip. "The inner circle is still in lockdown. Only a select few have been granted permission to enter, but Len is safe. Of that, I can assure you."

"Take me to him."

"That will depend."

"On what?" I stepped closer to Hiero, squaring my shoulders.

A pause.

His gaze flicked over me—up, then down—as his mouth curled into a slow, sly smirk. A glint in his eyes.

Then, in the time it took to blink, he seized my arms, twisted me, and slammed me against the open door.

A squeak of surprise escaped my throat. The candle's flame wavered. Shrinking. Dimming. Almost out...

Then slowly... slowly... burning brighter.

My chest heaved with ragged breaths, my body tingling with adrenaline.

Hiero let out a huff of amused laughter through his nose at my loss of composure. "It will depend on your cooperation, but in answer to your first question, '*What is all of this*?'"—he released an arm to gesture towards the Brain Eaters—"this is your army."

"*What?*"

"I promised you an army, didn't I?" He released my other arm, instead placing his palm on the door, leaning in close.

"Well... yes. But this isn't what I had in mind."

"Blood Suckers are a waste of resources," Hiero said, a slight edge to his voice. "We've had to resort to blood farming just to keep them alive down here, but all they're interested in are street fights, fucking, gambling, and wasting the precious gift of immortality. You've seen them yourself, Ava. The wasters in the streets. Drunkards in the taverns. Whores in the love chambers."

His cruelty stung. Not just the way he spoke of his friends and supporters, but the way he spat the words.

'*Wasters*'.

'Drunkards'.

Spoken with that same venom—same *disgust*—everyone used when talking about my father. It had always prompted a clammy sweat to lick my skin. It did again now.

"But... isn't that what *you're* like, too?" I asked.

His expression became tight. "That's what I *used to* be like. Back when Len lived with me. When everything made sense. Life was hard, but simple. And then... Len died."

"But he didn't though!"

"He may as well have! Twenty years I thought he was dead! *Twenty years!*" The low candlelight reflected in his glassy eyes as he pressed his other hand to the door, stooping so we were level, and forcing me to stare into endless portals of darkest brown and flecks of bronze. Hypnotic. "When news of his death reached the Nest, I knew I had to do something meaningful and destroy the *fuckers* that did that to him. It doesn't matter that Len survived. They *still* killed Master Tobias. They are *still* roaming the Earth. And they *still* need to be eradicated.

"I don't begrudge my brethren their vices, but to suggest they're not wasting their immortality—as I was—is living in denial. Even the best among us, like the warriors in the Battles of Blood. How many of them volunteered to join you?"

"Franziska stopped them—"

"They were cowards. Whether they were afraid of the Hallows or Franziska—it makes no difference. But you're not a coward, are you, Ava?" He moved a fraction closer, keeping his hands on the door on either side of me. Boxed in. "You stood up to Franziska. You defied her orders. And you're here because you're prepared to fight the Hallows. Who do you want at your side? A handful of bottom-of-the-barrel vampires, or an army of Brain Eaters whose primary purpose is to kill, and all at my command."

"How are you controlling them?"

"I'm a Soul Sucker, as you have already worked out. I have a psychic link with them."

"Right. And as Franziska said, to control this many, you'd need to drink a soul a day. And you're not doing that, are you? Or *are you*?" My guts twisted at the accusation. The Hiero I knew wouldn't have done that. But he *wasn't* the Hiero I knew—he wasn't even the Hiero Madigan knew.

He pressed his lips together, and once again I could sense his inner quarrel before saying, "That's why I need the crown. I am certainly not lax in maintaining my diet, but I've felt my grip on them slipping for a while now. That's why you found me at the Halfway House, actually. A few had escaped and I was tracking them down. I only stopped at the pub for a pint and a *moment* of peace."

I ignored as he muttered something about *'nagging'* and *'baggage'*.

"The Brain Eaters from the cave," I said, a chill making my spine stiffen as I put the pieces together. "They were the ones you were tracking."

"And I thought adding one more to my army wouldn't hurt, especially as I had to waste so much time out there. But when I tried to liberate your friend, he went berserk and destroyed the campervan. Almost burned the whole farm to the ground."

I didn't bother to correct him—Dominic was *not* my friend—focusing on keeping my temper, my body shaking with the effort.

"And I lost control *again* during the Champion's Ball. You could say I had"—a slight smirk traced his lips as he gave me a pointed look—"a lapse in concentration."

Heat crept up my neck, flooding my face, making him smirk even wider. My nails cut into my palms, my knuckles cracking. "You mean... when we..."

"You should be proud of yourself, really. I've been fucking Talia and Xander for years and never lost control. That's why I put this door here: to stop them escaping."

"Oh sure," I said, the words barely escaping, my teeth clenched tight. "Most powerful army in the world stopped by a fucking wooden door."

"I thought that attack was the end of the road for me," he continued, as if I'd not spoken. "But I used it to my advantage, suggesting Franziska was trying to kill me. Many believe it, and it could be what swings the votes in my favour."

"And what about Madigan?" Right now, I couldn't care less about his stupid election. "He's a Blood Drinker. Is he a waste of resources, too?"

His smile dropped. "Len is... different."

"Sure," I said, though my mouth had gone dry. "The Blood Drinker you crush on is the one exception. How convenient for you."

"What do you care? I'm offering you an army!"

"At *your* command!"

"What's wrong with that? Don't you trust me?"

"No, I don't! You lied about being a Soul Sucker! You've had these monsters living beneath your house this whole time! You're willing to pin the blame on Franziska after they escaped! All you have done is lie!"

"I'm not your enemy, Ava." He moved a fraction closer. So close I could feel the heat of him. Not as tall as Madigan, but brawny. *Powerful*. Making my heart skip as it always did, but there was also this cold, uncoiling fear deep in my belly. "Don't forget who your *real* enemy is. The Hallows."

"Fuck the Hallows." Though I'd meant to shout, it came out little more than a whisper. His face was still close to mine, and even among the dampness of the tunnel and the putrid odours from the Brain Eater's cavern, I still caught that waft of sandalwood.

"Fuck the Hallows? They're the reason I did all of this! They want to kill us all—you included now you're a shifter. The whole reason you came here was to recruit for the upcoming battle. I'm offering you an army on a silver platter and you say, '*Fuck the Hallows*'?"

My head was spinning. Was he right?

"I... I don't know what to say..."

"Say you'll help me." He pushed himself off the door, standing upright, but kept his body close to mine as he traced a finger along my jawline, tilting my face up to his, and whispered close to my lips, "All you need to do is keep quiet until I have the crown."

"From everyone? Even Madigan?"

"*Everyone*. Len cannot know I'm a Soul Sucker. At least, not yet."

A comforting essence radiated from him and into me, his mouth so close his breath caressed my lips. Heavy breaths. His chest rising and falling as he awaited my answer.

Just agree. Just agree. Just agree...

I don't know what had corrupted my common sense, whether it be fear, or the sudden desire to please him and receive the kiss his lips were promising. But with the sobering sounds of the shuffling Brain Eaters, I tore my eyes from Hiero and onto the swarm. It was almost impossible to believe these had once been unique individuals. Now they all looked identical, save for those with battle wounds, missing limbs or...

"Dominic..." The name caught in my throat.

"What?"

"That one there." I nodded to one of the closest Brain Eaters, three distinct claw marks down its face—the scars from his struggle with the werewolves. "That's Dominic, isn't it?"

He had already looked terrible. Now he had completely turned. All monster.

"The effort to capture him was barely worth it," Hiero said. "But I suppose it was a small consolation after losing the other three."

The comforting heat flowing through me sparked into a raging inferno. Another lie he'd spun. "How did you capture him without us noticing?"

"I didn't." His eyes darkened. "I have help, remember? Though in the end, it turned out to be blessing in disguise. I needed an excuse to get them out of the house for a while, after your... awkward introduction."

I'd heard enough.

"I can't keep this from Madigan," I said, my temper boiling over. "If you love him enough to raise an army to avenge his death, you should love him enough to tell the truth."

For a second, we simply stared at each other.

Silent.

Until Hiero loosed a heavy sigh, his shoulders slumping.

"I was afraid you would say something like that."

A filter seemed to lift from his eyes, and all that warmth and desire vanished as quickly as it had come. And I sucked in a breath at the horrifying realisation that I'd made a terrible, terrible mistake.

With the slightest effort, he shoved me into the cavern, sending me hurtling into the Brain Eaters. The candle flew from my hand, landing with a splat of soft wax, and plunging me into total darkness.

The Brain Eaters screeched, but continued to amble about, uninterested in me, but before I could scramble to my feet, Hiero slammed the door shut.

"Wait!" I got up and fell upon the door. The moment my skin made contact with the wood, a sharp, stinging pain flared through my palms, and I yanked my hands back with a yelp.

Magic... I didn't have time to contemplate how Hiero had enchanted the door, but I *knew* it was magic. I could feel it, like it was a part of me.

"You can't leave me in here with these!" I shouted, my voice echoing off the cavern walls.

"Don't worry," Hiero's muffled voice came from the other side. "I'll keep them in this docile state, and when I have the crown, I'll have total control. You should be fine. But I can't let you go ruining everything when I'm so close to victory. I'm... I'm sorry, Ava." His voice broke as he said my name.

"Hiero! Please!" And now my voice was breaking too. "Don't leave me here!"

But the last sounds I made out were Hiero's footsteps growing quieter and quieter.

CHAPTER TWENTY-SEVEN

I stood frozen. Blind in the darkness. Heart pounding. Blood throbbing in my ears, so loud it almost drowned out the Brain Eaters ambling and groaning.

My chest ached with held breath, afraid to make the slightest noise, until I had no choice but to release a slow exhale. But the Brain Eaters didn't seem to notice, nothing but dark shapes writhing in an even darker abyss.

I don't know how long it took my eyes to adjust.

The Brain Eaters kept their heads hung low, taking the occasional step forward, dragging their clawed feet. All except one, and though I couldn't see him clearly, I'd have wagered it was the Brain Eater with three scars down its face.

Dominic.

He stood as deadlocked as me, head turned in my direction, and I imagined his soulless pupils fixed on me.

Why?

Brain Eaters had no mind. Had Hiero commanded him to do this to keep me under control?

It was only when my legs cramped I dared to move, shifting my weight to one foot, and then the other, biting back the sharp pain.

No good.

I sank to the floor. Squatting. And still, the Brain Eaters ignored me. Even Dominic remained fixed in place. Finally, I sat down, my legs thanking me as I massaged life into my calves.

I'd lost track of time, my mind constricted by terror, but even my brain was exhausted now.

What if Hiero doesn't free me? How long will he keep me down here? Days? Weeks? Would I last that long?

Yes, said a calm inner voice that sounded like Latisha. *Scorpions can last months without food or water...*

Oh great, I'll become a scorpion and live down here with the Brain Eaters, I argued back.

I'm sure dying as a human is a far better prospect? retorted the inner voice.

I pressed my lips together, forcing back the tears. *I'm so sorry, Latisha. I wish you were here. What would you say if you were?*

I pictured her smiling face. Imagined her kind, soothing voice as she said, *I'd tell you to keep calm. I'd tell you to trust yourself.*

Yeah—okay, I answered. *Got anything more specific?*

This was a harder request. I closed my eyes, ignoring that death stood on the other side of my eyelids, and concentrated with every-thing I had, until Latisha's voice rang so clearly maybe she really *was* speaking to me.

Find Len. But first, you'll need to escape this cavern.

How?

One of the dangerous things about scorpions is that they fit through the narrowest of gaps.

My cheeks felt tight as I grinned.

The next instant, I was hurtling into agony, my exoskeleton form-ing, pulling my skin tight. New limbs. New lungs. New everything. Shrinking. The world expanding. And the Brain Eaters that had al-ready been monsters were now nightmarish behemoths.

If scorpions could hold their nose, I would have. The stench of stale faecal matter and urine left by the Brain Eaters had already been vile. Now, it was positively overwhelming.

But I could *see*.

I inched closer to the door, flattened myself, creeping closer, squeezing through the gap. Pain flared as the hairs on my body grazed the door, but I pressed onward, even when an intrusive memory of trying to squeeze through burning branches flashed through my mind.

Until I was on the other side. *Free.*

But I didn't have time for celebrations. I had to find Madigan, and I suspected I knew where he might be. I'd taken the left path when I'd come across that fork in the tunnel. What was down the right path? It wasn't a stretch to believe it held another cavern, and my concerns about the steep climb in the dark were nothing to a scorpion.

It was a long scuttle down the tunnel on tiny legs, but I reached the divide and descended into the unknown.

My heart gave a sudden leap—an odd sensation now my heart was somewhere in my back—as another door came into focus. Metal this time, more incongruous than the wooden one. No matter. It still had that gap between the door and ground.

Once again, I pressed myself as flat as possible, squeezing through the gap. It was narrower, but luckily there was no enchantment. Nothing but the cold metal against my hairs as I passed beneath.

I'd been expecting a holding cell, but I found myself in a narrow corridor. Man-made. Or rather, vampire-made. Though admittedly it *looked* more human. Cold and clinical, like a hospital corridor, lamps issuing a harsh, white light. More magic. I knew it like I knew my own name. It was all oddly jarring in the Vampires' Nest. Too modern. Too bright. And that's when it hit me: I'd seen something that clashed with the Nest before.

I was in Hiero's factory.

Shit...

So much for my theory.

I scuttled down the corridor, squeezing beneath yet another door, and into a stairwell.

Which way?

I could go up, down, or there was another door. Labelled. Illegible from down here.

What should I do? Shift and read the sign? Crawl under the door? Or climb up the stairs?

The factory entrance was on the surface, so it made sense to go upwards to escape. Should I climb as a scorpion, or as a human? Being human would be far quicker.

No sooner had the thought crossed my mind than the cells in my body vibrated in response. I was human, naked and shivering.

I headed straight for the stairs, hand on the banister, foot on the first step, cold and firm beneath my sole. Ready for the climb. Ready...

But a nagging curiosity rooted me, and with a slow turn of my head, I read the sign.

'Holding: Specimens Delta.'

Holding? A bolt of excitement shot through me.

'Specimens' could mean anything, and I have no idea what 'Delta' means. But I do know what 'Holding' means, and if there's a chance that Madigan is in there...

It would only take a second to check. I doubled back, grabbed the door handle, wrenched it open, and slapped a hand over my nose and mouth as the putrid stench from within slammed into me.

The blinding, white light from the stairwell illuminated the first few feet of the darkened room, but part of me wished it hadn't. It was lined with holding cells, iron bars separating me from the Husks within. Groups of men and women looking downwards, their faces vacant, dead behind the eyes, standing in puddles of their own making. But it was the *children* that made my eyes brim with tears. Some no older than maybe four or five.

Hiero... What the fuck have you done?

I closed the door with a soft click. Leant against it. Mind spinning. Feeling smaller now than when I'd been a scorpion. A sour taste in my mouth.

What have you done? What have you done?!

I closed my eyes, tears spilling. Heart breaking.

Then Madigan flashed through my mind. I didn't have time to dwell on what I'd seen. I had to find him and escape this pit of Hell.

Without looking back, I bolted to the staircase and climbed, not stopping when my thighs burned and my lungs itched. I climbed several floors—each with its own door labelled *'Holding: Specimens Delta'*, and each time I read the words, my stomach gave a threatening lurch.

I couldn't have imagined it would get worse, yet Hiero managed it.

As I reached the next few floors, panes of glass separated me from a single enormous room, and on the other side, more Husks. But these were hooked up to metal contraptions, tubes issuing from their bodies, red liquid flowing through them. Rows upon rows. Level upon level. And upon one wall, a sign read *'Production'*.

My already broken heart shattered into dust.

I should have asked Hiero how his operation worked. I should have asked how he made human blood so easily available.

Why didn't I ask?

Why?

Why?

I climbed higher, staring at my bare feet instead of through the windows at the human blood farm. And now, as much as I wanted the tears to come, they wouldn't.

My palm was sweaty on the door handle as I turned it. Another corridor with those too-bright lights, and on one wall, a floor plan. I couldn't make sense of the basement levels and whatever cryptic bullshit Hiero had named them. Different *'Specimens'*. Alpha, Omega and the like. Whatever that meant. It didn't matter. All that mattered was finding the exit, then Madigan.

There were two ways out. One was the main entrance—it would be best if I avoided that one—but there was another option. An exit labelled *'Disposal'*.

Memorising the route, I took a sharp turn down another corridor. Through a door. And again found myself in darkness. This corridor wasn't lit like the others. This corridor contained metal carts down each side, and though I willed myself not to look, I couldn't help my wandering eyes. But I regretted it when the sunken, rotting flesh of a woman's face stared back at me. Dead. Drained of everything Hiero needed and discarded.

The tears still wouldn't come.

I fixed my eyes on the last door—the exit—and focused on that.

Beside it was a heap of ragged clothes, and I winced as I pulled some on. But the dead didn't need them anymore.

I gasped as I stepped out into the air of the Vampires' Nest. It had never been fresh, but it felt colder, crisper, and cleaner than ever.

The inner circle was silent—presumably still in lockdown—so I headed straight for Hiero's manor and tore it apart in my search, telling myself I'd find Madigan, and we'd be long gone before Hiero discovered the carnage.

Except, I *couldn't* find Madigan. Not in our room. Not in Hiero's room. Not in the library. The billiard room. The kitchen. *Nowhere.* And I found myself panting with exertion in the lounge, curtains ripped down, sofas toppled.

"Where *are* you?" I grit out, facing my reflection in the window as I stared out into the Nest.

Though the inner circle was lifeless, smoke issued from chimneys in the outer ring.

Was he out there? Perhaps the Lucky Lantern. Or knowing Hiero, the Lover's Sanctum. My stomach twisted at the thought, and I shook myself before images of their bodies intertwined invaded my mind. Images that once made my body tingle, but now made me feel sick.

I can't believe I slept *with him.*

But I didn't have time to wallow in self-pity. If there was a chance that Madigan was in the Lover's Sanctum, or the Lucky Lantern, or *anywhere*, I'd look.

As soon as I stepped through Hiero's front doors, the clock tower was in sight. Quarter to ten. And the moon symbol.

I frowned. I must have read it wrong.

That can't be right... They had the speeches at ten... Perhaps it's been twelve hours?

I squinted at the moon symbol again, but there was no mistaking it. If it had been twelve hours, that symbol should have been a sun.

How has it been so long? It must be a mistake.

Sure, I'd spent hours searching for Madigan and exploring the tunnel and factory. And then I'd lost track of time while locked up with the Brain Eaters, but it couldn't have been *that* long. Could it? But my blood turned cold as I recalled my trip to the Nest, tucked away in Madigan's pocket... and how, to a scorpion, time became meaningless. And I had shifted *twice*.

But then... that would mean... Shit....

If it *had* been twenty-four hours, that would mean the votes would have been cast, counted, and...

"Shit!"

I took off, running as fast as my feet would allow on the cobbled path, suppressing grunts of pain. I'd never find Madigan while the streets were packed full of vampires, but perhaps I could stop Hiero from getting his hands on the crown. Or maybe Franziska would win, and I knew *she* would help me escape. She'd probably kick me out of the Nest herself.

I reached a gate of the city wall, took hold of the iron ring and pulled, but the gate barely twitched in response.

I slammed my fist. "Let me out! Is anyone there? Please, let me out!"

A heavy clicking noise, and the gate opened.

"All right, calm down," the guard on duty said, giving me an impatient huff. "No need to shout."

"Has the winner been announced yet?" I asked, panting from my run, ignoring the guard's withering expression.

"It should be any minute now," he said. "You'll have to hurry, though. Hang on..." He tilted his head to one side, looking at me sceptically. "What are you doing within the inner wall? And"—he wrinkled his nose as he scanned me up and down—"what are you *wearing*? Where are your shoes?"

"No time!" I said, brushing past him.

"Wait!"

But I was already off.

I almost lost myself down the narrow passageways through the houses and shops, most of them identical, but I didn't stop to think about it. Just kept moving. Even when I reached the grotty end of town and I waded barefoot through mud and waste, ignoring the usual pressure in my stomach and the acidic tang in my mouth.

No... No time to worry about that...

Steeling myself, I pressed onward, disregarding what I was walking through and focused only on where I was going. Soon, I caught the buzz of voices.

I was close.

I kept going. Turned a corner. And another. Then slammed straight into the back of someone, falling flat on my arse in the muck, filth splattering up my back, coating my hands.

"Watch it!" They held out their hand, but when I raised my own with filth dripping from my fingers, they seized me by the upper arm instead and helped me to my feet.

"Chef!" I couldn't believe my fortune. "Have they announced the winner yet?"

"You're welcome," Chef said, quirking an eyebrow. I only now realised how rude I must sound. But it didn't matter.

"It's an emergency," I said. "I need to know."

"They're just about to, but you won't get a good view. We'll probably have to wait for the news to reach us back here."

I looked past Chef, down the narrow passage, but vampires blocked my sights.

Do I become a scorpion to get through this crowd?

My heart was already racing so hard my chest ached, and my limbs hurt too. I was running off pure adrenaline—like during my fight with Ivan—exhaustion threatening to overpower me.

No... You won't get there in time.

I gave Chef a tight-lipped smile. "Wish me luck." And slipped past him, crouching to weave through the legs of the vampires ahead.

"Miss! What are you doing? You're crazy!" he called after me, but I was on a mission, and I wouldn't let anyone distract me. Soon I was within the square, lost within the thick crowd.

"Ladies and gentlemen," a voice called from Speaker's Rock.

I stood upright, perching on my tiptoes. Nothing but a wall of shoulders and the back of heads. So I jumped, trying to glimpse them.

It was Lord Tonbridge, a red velvet cushion in his hands, and the crown displayed on top.

"The votes have been counted, and our leader chosen."

The crowd jumped and cheered, buffeting me as Hiero and Franziska took their spots on Speaker's Rock. But I forged ahead. It didn't matter who'd won. I *had* to get the crown before Hiero.

Dropped to my knees again. Scrabbling forward. Sliding through legs. As fast as I could.

"It is a great pleasure to announce that for the next twenty-five years—"

I could see them now. Near the front. Pushed to my feet. Drove on. I had to move faster.

"—the leader of the vampire council shall be—"

Hiero's eyebrows jumped as his eyes met mine. My cover blown. And he smiled a wide shark-like smile.

"—Lord Hieronymus Blackford."

"MOVE!" I forced the last vampire aside. Scrambling up Speaker's Rock. Reached out. Fingertips inches from the crown...

Until Hiero whipped it from the cushion and placed it upon his head.

"Nice try, Ava," he said, his voice sombre despite his predatory expression. "Guards!"

Hands seized me before I could see who they belonged to. They forced me down. Knees first. Then my face. Squirming. Helpless.

At Hiero's mercy.

CHAPTER TWENTY-EIGHT

Mud coated the tip of my tongue, its fetid, sour-bitter flavour assaulting my taste buds. I spat, but that just made more muck splatter into my face. Into my nose.

Someone yanked me to my feet, and I gasped for air, spitting mud, shaking my head to flick it away.

"Wipe her face," Hiero said to the guard holding me. "Gently."

A soft cloth brushed over my face. Over my mouth. My skin felt tight, like it was *too* dry, dirt still marking it, but at last I could breathe.

Myla and another guard held Franziska. Or at least, they each had a hand on her shoulders while she stood with arms folded, not the least bit fazed, glaring at Hiero.

"I'll sort you out in a moment, Ava." He turned his attention to Franziska, flashing that sinister smile. "You first. As per tradition, I ask: do you choose death or exile?"

Franziska's eyes narrowed, her scarlet lips tight, like she was holding back what she *really* wanted to say. Although she didn't struggle against the guards, her anger seemed to hiss out of her like steam. In fact, both Myla and the second guard—a male of the same height and width as Myla but twice as hairy—shared a nervous sideways glance.

"Exile," she said at last.

Hiero hung his head, letting out a sigh. "I thought you'd say that. I'm afraid I cannot honour your request."

A murmur through the mass of onlooking vampires who I'd almost forgotten were standing behind me. I turned my head as much as the guard holding me allowed, and spotted Red, her eyes wide, mouth open. Max stood beside her. Far more stoic. But his good eye was barely blinking, an intense stare on Hiero, his jaw set.

But I couldn't see Madigan. Not *anywhere*.

Hiero strode towards Franziska, straightening his back and puffing out his chest, looking down at her with the utmost contempt. "I'd hoped you'd choose an honourable execution, and I could keep up the pretence of maintaining the status quo for a few more minutes. But I can't allow you to leave. You're too dangerous."

Hiero gave Myla and her colleague a nod. A silent command the hairy guard understood. His biceps bulged and the veins in his forearms fattened as he grabbed Franziska's arm and tried to drag her from Speaker's Rock. But Franziska didn't so much as flinch, standing firm, like it was a soft breeze trying to move her instead of a six-foot-something beast of a man.

Myla didn't move either, instead keeping her hand on Franziska's shoulder and her sights on Hiero, a crease forming between her eyebrows.

"Myla," Hiero said in a tone that was no doubt a warning. "That was a direct command. I'm your Liege Lord now, and you are my guard. Aren't you?"

"Giving the choice between death and exile is the law," Myla said, still frowning, but her voice was soft, almost sorrowful, like she couldn't believe what she was hearing.

"I *am* the law."

A sudden shriek from the back of the crowd pierced through the air, and all heads spun in its direction, towards an alleyway. Another scream. Then a roar of anger. Growing louder. And louder. The vampires started shifting, panic rippling through them at the unknown disturbance. My stomach dropped. *I* knew what it was, and the answering, high-pitched non-human screech that raised goosebumps over my skin confirmed it.

"Here they are," Hiero said as white, skeletal bodies ripped through the alleyway and into the throng of vampires. The Brain Eaters had arrived, but not the mindless killers I'd encountered before. Now, there was a sense of purpose in their movements, seizing their captives, their pinprick pupils focused with intent.

I faced Hiero, a bead of blood dripping down his face from where the crown cut into his forehead. He was in complete control, and he'd not exaggerated their numbers. It was difficult to count them as they swarmed through the vampires, but they really *were* an army.

They tore through the crowd, several rushing Franziska. Even the former Liege Lady knew when she was in danger, and bolted, breaking the hold on her with ease, vanishing for a split second... Only to reappear in focus, pinned on the ground, no less than eight of the pale, gangly monsters on top of her, thrashing in their clawed hands.

"Take her away," Hiero said with a lazy wave of his hand.

"I'll kill you for this, Blackford! I'll fucking kill you!" Franziska screamed, still clashing with the Brain Eaters. Each time she almost broke free, another Brain Eater grabbed hold of her, and slowly, they dragged her away, still cussing Hiero as she went.

"Hiero." I could barely hear Myla's voice over the chaos. "What are you doing?"

"Making some changes," he replied before calling out to the vampires once more. "We have become weak. And now, the Hallows are coming for our heads. If we remain as we are, they'll eradicate us. But not if we fight back. Not if we become stronger. As you can see, I have built an army." He held out his arms, gesturing to the Brain Eaters, all with their eyes on Hiero, waiting for a command. "But it's not enough. Which is why"—his eyes flicked from the vampires to me—"*I am recruiting.*"

I clenched my fists so tight my knuckles cracked as he bastardised the words I'd spoken over the last month.

Hiero faced his people again. "I need Soul Suckers to command troops on the battlefield with their telepathic abilities. But we don't have enough. Not *nearly* enough. Which is why I've decided all Blood Drinkers will become Soul Suckers. All who refuse will be made into Brain Eaters. You can either go to my factory for conversion willingly or be *assisted.*" The Brain Eaters hissed as one, understanding their orders.

A heartbeat of silence, like the vampires couldn't comprehend what their Liege Lord had said. But then, uproar.

Bodies smashed into each other as the vampires went berserk, and the Brain Eaters responded, seizing them, dragging them away.

"E-even us?" asked the guard holding me, and the tightness around my arms slackened.

Hiero looked at him, nose wrinkled. "Of course, even you. You're a Blood Drinker, right?"

"Yes, sir."

"And *all* Blood Drinkers will become Soul Suckers. Take yourself off for conversion, or"—a Brain Eater appeared at Hiero's side, its wide, soulless eyes staring unblinking at the guard—"my friend here will assume you're to become one of them. Either way, you'll be going to the factory."

"You... you don't have enough human souls for all of us." Although the guard's grip was loose, my body vibrated as their hands trembled.

"Don't I?" Hiero asked, an eyebrow raised, as though daring the guard to call his bluff. He marched up to us, thrusting out his chest in the same manner he'd done when standing up to Franziska.

Without warning, the guard released me, knocking me down in his bid to flee, but the Brain Eater tackled him to the ground and dragged him through the mud towards the factory, kicking and screaming all the way.

I didn't run. There was no point. Hiero held out a hand to me, but I smacked it aside, rising unaided despite my sore muscles.

He looked at me with a pained expression. "I'd like you to return to your coven and tell them I offer an alliance in the upcoming war."

"Where's Madigan?" I asked, ignoring his request, the words almost disappearing behind my clenched jaw. It took everything—*everything* I had—not to launch myself at Hiero. All teeth, and nails, and fists, and feet. He might be taller than me. And infinitely stronger. But I bet he had the same weak spot all men had. All it would take is one well-aimed kick...

But if I was unsuccessful, he might lock me up with his Brain Eaters. Or would he hook me up to those machines in his factory? My blood wasn't as effective as human blood, but Hiero might take it anyway, just to spite me.

He didn't reply right away, staring at me with his head tilted to one side, hands in his pockets, casual as ever while chaos raged around us.

"He's a Blood Drinker," he said at last, his voice cold.

"Let him leave with me, and I'll do whatever you want."

"If he becomes a Soul Sucker, he is free to do as he—"

"No. I mean, let him leave with me. *Now.* As he is."

Hiero swallowed. "I can't do that."

"Why not? No one would know you let one Blood Drinker go. Besides, there's loads of Blood Drinkers in the human world running about."

"And all of them given the message to return to the Nest at their Liege Lord's request." He tapped his crown with a finger, another dribble of blood running down his face as he did so. "Not that they know what awaits them, of course."

"I... I don't care about your politics. Or your army. Please, just let Madigan go and you'll never hear from us again." I didn't want to beg. But I would. I would get on my knees and kiss his feet if that's what it took.

"It's not about politics. The condition of Talia's and Xander's assistance is that everyone is treated the same—including Len—and I *need* their help with my operation."

"Fuck your operation! What if he doesn't choose to be a Soul Sucker? Don't you love him?! He's the whole reason you started all this!"

Hiero's face twitched. I'd struck a nerve. His eyes glinted as he opened his mouth, and for one glorious second, I thought he'd tell me where Madigan was.

But then he pursed his lips, eyes darkening as he put his face close to mine and hissed, "Leonard Madigan died twenty years ago, and the man who returned—*with you*—just looks like him."

I glared into his eyes. Eyes that once seemed so warm. Now, they were flinty, staring back into mine, his handsome features twisting into an ugly expression. My heart slammed against my ribs with such force my chest ached, heat searing through my veins like my blood was on fire. From my peripheral vision I saw Brain Eaters smashing into fleeing Blood Drinkers, carrying them away. Only a few were spared the onslaught: those who didn't resist, slowly heading towards Hiero's factory. But all my focus was on glowering at Hiero, my jaw clenched so hard I thought my teeth might break.

"You've been fixated on your vendetta for so long you've forgotten your reason for starting it," I said.

"And you've forgotten we're on the same side!" He stepped up to me, his composure gone, a tear tracking down his face that he hastily wiped away—so quick I almost missed it. "I'm giving you what your leader asked for! What would she think if you returned home with Len instead of an army? Which does *she* want?"

Latisha's face flashed through my mind. Her large, kind eyes. The security her smile offered. Followed by a spread of wings and the sound of ripping meat—a memory that once chilled my blood. But now...

"She'd want me to return with Madigan. A member of *her* coven," I said fiercely. "I know the lengths she'd go to keep him safe. And if you think I wouldn't do the same, you don't know me very fucking well. I'll send Latisha your regards, but I *will* find Madigan, and he *is* coming home with me." And with one last glare of defiance, I shifted.

"No!"

I scurried from my rags before Hiero could catch me, scuttling through mud and stones until I scrambled onto someone's foot.

"Where is she?" Hiero's voice vibrated through the din of noise. "Don't let her get away!"

The boot I'd clung to flew through the air before smashing down to the ground. And again. And again. Whoever I'd attached myself to was running, but I was flung aside as Brain Eaters tackled them. The elongated, clawed feet of a Brain Eater smashed down either side of me, and I scuttled away before it noticed me.

"Stop!" Hiero shouted. "Forget that last order. Continue with your original command. Take the Blood Drinkers to the factory."

"Let me look for her," said another voice.

"Not now, Boris. Just help me get the rest of the Blood Drinkers to the factory. After all, that's where she'll go to save her *dearly beloved*." The high-pitched, mocking way he said the final two words made my stinger spasm.

"Now, what about you two?" Hiero asked.

"We'll go voluntarily," said a vampire stood above me. I hadn't realised how close Hiero was—how quickly he'd caught up to me. I scrambled onto the heel of the vampire's boot, hiding from Hiero's gaze. "Won't we, Red?"

Red?

"That's right. I'm not winning any races on this leg," said Red. "Max and I will gladly become Soul Suckers for your army."

My world seemed to shatter. How could she? Red, of all people. A fighter. A *friend*.

"I knew I could count on you to make the smart choice." Hiero's smug tone made me want to sting him even more. "Perhaps you can convince Myla. She'd be wasted as a Brain Eater. But unless she complies..." He shrugged.

"We'll get on it," Red said. "Come on Max." And as she spun on the spot and started walking, I realised it was *her* boot I'd clung onto, her every other step heavier than the first.

"What's the plan then, boss?" Max asked in a lower, darker voice. The hairs over my body prickled as I focused on their every word, trying to block out everything else.

"We have to find Myla," Red answered in the same tone. "Convince her to come with us, and once we're inside the factory, we make our last stand. Whatever shit Hiero is pulling, we're stopping it."

My insides squirmed with a mix of relief and guilt for doubting her.

"Last stand?" Max said. "You can barely walk."

"I know. Thanks for that."

"If I'd known we were days away from being ruled by a lunatic, I wouldn't have done it! But if this is what you want—"

Red stopped, and high above, I sensed her grab hold of Max. "It is. I'm not being dragged in there to become a Brain Eater or Soul Sucker. I'd rather die first."

Silence—except for the continued screams of others, of course.

"You know we *will* probably die, right?" Max said at last.

"*We?*"

"That's what I said."

Red's grip on Max's arm slipped down to his hand. But then dropped it, pointing towards a mess of bodies I couldn't make out. "There's Myla. Help her!"

Max dashed away from us, crashing into a pile of Brain Eaters and pulling Myla from beneath them, her leather tunic slashed and mud caked in her curly hair.

"Wait!" Max said, raising his hands as the Brain Eaters got to their feet, their heads turning towards him, eyes wide. "We're going willingly!"

"Are you insane?!" Myla hissed as she joined Red, Max following her, but after a hurried explanation in lowered voices, Myla slammed a hand down onto Red's shoulder, almost making the smaller vampire buckle. "That's my girl."

Part of me longed to regain my human form, to tell them I would battle alongside them. Fight the power. Vive la révolution, and all that.

But no. This was my third transformation, and I'd be exhausted and useless. I'd let them do the heavy work. In fact, they'd provide the perfect distraction for my plan: find Madigan and get the hell out.

CHAPTER TWENTY-NINE

It took everything to keep my stinger from accidentally lashing out and striking Red's ankle, my survival instinct going berserk as she carried me closer to the factory. I'd seen enough to last me a lifetime of therapy.

I couldn't deny the rage burning within me, not just at Hiero, but at myself. If I'd explored a little deeper, I might have found Madigan and we'd already be making our escape during the chaos. But I pushed these thoughts aside. Red had already carried me to the back door of the factory—as per the instructions from the guard at the city wall.

"The Brain Eaters are using the main entrance," he'd told her. "Go through the back and head to Conversion."

'Through the back'. That's an unfortunate way of saying 'Through the corridor of dead bodies'. Or perhaps the guard didn't know?

"What's that *smell*?" Max asked before he'd even opened the back door, gagging as he pulled it open.

"Bodies," Red said, her voice muffled as she put a hand over her nose and mouth, taking a tentative step inside. "Rotting. Who knows for how long."

"This one's fresh," Myla said, peering inside a cart.

"This one isn't." Max looked inside another, retching again.

I had to get out of here. The stench was almost blinding, overwhelming my olfaction until my other senses were rendered useless.

It appeared Red was of the same mind, her pace quickening. But before she'd reached the end of the corridor, the next door swung open with a bang. That horrid, white light streamed in as someone pushed a cart on squeaky wheels. The figure had their head lowered, and from their body language—or lack of—I knew they were a Husk, not so much as acknowledging my friends' presence.

Great. Another body. I wonder how quickly they get through them.

Before I could give it much thought, my heart stopped. A familiar scent wafted from the cart.

The scent of vanilla...

No! It can't be...

I leapt from Red's boot, almost getting myself run over, but climbed onto the wheel bracket as it passed, and scuttled upwards, the scent of vanilla getting stronger.

Venom oozed at the tip of my barb as I peered inside, petrified of what I might see.

But it was nothing but a heap of old clothes.

But... how? I can smell him in here. I'm sure it's him...

I dropped into the pile of clothes and explored the maze of fabrics until I discovered something that froze my blood. A material I recognised. Black, thick, with fancy embroidery around the cuff. A cuff that Madigan almost ripped off every time he was flustered. This was Madigan's tailcoat, in with the other bloody rags.

He's... being processed... into a... into a...

My brain refused to accept it.

No—it wasn't real. Whether he was being forced to become a Brain Eater or had volunteered to become a Soul Sucker... It didn't matter... It wasn't happening. It *wasn't* happening!

I had to find him *now*.

I cried out as my body freed itself from the scorpion's form. The sudden force of the transformation made the cart topple over with an echoing clang, and I kneed myself in the face as I tumbled out.

"What the hell?" Red's voice echoed up the corridor. She, Max, and Myla had bypassed the Husk and were about to enter the next room, only to hurry back.

"Ava?! What were you—?"

"They've got Madigan here!" The words spilled out, echoing through the corridor the same way they echoed through my head. I scrambled to my feet, untangling myself from the clothes, and seized Red's arms, staring into her face. She had to know. She had to help me. She *had* to!

"They've got him!" I cried, my voice thick, my mouth suddenly too dry, and hot tears burned my cheeks. "Hiero's got him! I need to save him. I need to—"

I gasped as Red's palm smacked my face, the sting blazing on my skin.

"Cut that out," she said. "You'll save no one freaking out like that."

I put my hand to my face, my cheek still burning, my chest aching with panting breaths. The tears continued to flow.

"Where did you come from?" Red asked.

"I was on your boot," I said in a small voice. "I've been here before. The things Hiero is doing down here... It's... It's..." My face crumpled. So did the rest of me. And Red caught me before I could fall to my knees.

"We don't have time for this," Max hissed.

"Fuck, Max! She's in shock! Give her a break," Myla snapped at him, but I steeled myself, wiping my face on the back of my hand.

"No, he's right," I said with an undignified sniff. "We don't have time. Madigan is in here."

Red stared deep into my eyes, her face close to mine, like she was trying to block out the nightmares surrounding us. "We'll find him, Ava. That's why we are here. This ends tonight. Understand?"

I nodded.

"You said you were here before?"

I nodded again.

"Can you show us where he is?"

"No. I don't know where he is exactly. But there's a floor plan through that door. We might find something on there."

A ghost of a smile pulled on Red's lips. "Are you with us?"

"I don't know what good I'll be. I used my last transformation. I'm weak and I—"

"You're here anyway. You stood up to Hiero. You're braver than Hiero's lackeys. You're braver than Hiero. *Are. You. With. Us?*"

I swallowed. And nodded again. "Yes."

"Perhaps... you could put some clothes on too..." Max said.

I'd never cared less about being naked in front of strangers. It was the least important thing in the world. As I got a grip on my panic, the gnawing ache in my stomach settled in. No more shifting. I was fortunate not to contend with a pounding headache, too, but I'd not escaped the all-consuming exhaustion, my limbs sluggish, and I was clumsy as I pulled on a ragged t-shirt, leggings, and Madigan's tailcoat—several sizes too big. But I didn't care. I pulled the lapels up to my nose and sniffed. Creepy, perhaps, but right now *he* was the only thing giving me strength.

I led my friends to the floor plan, squinting against the harsh light as I traced a finger down it.

"*'Holding: Specimens Alpha'. 'Beta'. 'Delta'.* I think Delta means the Husks. So we can rule out that one. Perhaps Alpha?"

"What's going on in here?" Red asked, pointing at the bottom levels.

I shrugged. "It just says *'Basement'.*"

"Right. So why isn't it labelled properly? Everything else is. What is Hiero hiding down there?"

A screeching cry from a Brain Eater nearby.

"We need to choose quickly," Myla said. For a moment, Red and I stared at each other, as though expecting the other to have the answer.

"We could wait for the next Brain Eater to bring someone in?" Max suggested. "Follow them to wherever they are keeping them?"

Red's eyebrows sprang upward. "That's a good idea."

"And risk getting caught and imprisoned ourselves?" I shook my head. "I still think we should check where they are holding the Alphas."

"Doesn't Alpha mean the strongest?" Max folded his arms. "You might walk into a room full of Soul Suckers."

Another screech from a Brain Eater. Getting closer. But from which direction?

"Right." Red clapped her hands. "We go down to the basement." But before I could protest, she continued, "If my hunch is correct, Hiero is hiding something important down there. If we can stop his operation, it doesn't matter where he is hiding Len, or any of the other vampires. We can find them afterwards. Right now, the priority is stopping Hiero."

I almost argued back. But the longer I thought about it, the more sense it made. As much as I hated the thought of Madigan being locked up somewhere, knowing I could stop him from being turned into either a Brain Eater or Soul Sucker gave me hope.

"All right. But you will help me find him afterwards. Okay?" I stuck out my little finger, like a child making a pinkie promise. Pathetic. But her word was all I had.

She wrapped her pinkie around mine. "I swear it."

We hurried to the stairwell, Max leading the way, followed by Myla, Red and I struggling at the back. Although she could walk, Red was still getting used to her prosthetic, and exhaustion weighed me down, only my stubborn determination fuelling me.

I kept my eyes on the floor as we passed through the blood farm, shutting out the words of disgust and horror from the others as best I could as they echoed my sentiments. Even they hadn't questioned how Hiero had fixed the blood shortage.

We passed '*Holding: Specimens Delta*'. Down another level. And another, passing '*Specimens: Alpha.*' '*Beta*', '*Omega*', and '*Neutralised*'.

"Only a few more floors," Red said, gripping onto my hand, ignoring how sweaty my palm was.

As we reached the lowest levels, the lighting dimmed, and I found the muscles around my eyes eased as the lamps were replaced with burning torches. But my relief was short-lived as we reached the basement.

Two doors.

And it quickly became apparent why Hiero hadn't labelled these rooms on his floor plan. He might have given the other rooms stupid names, but these were self-explanatory.

"'*Breeding*'," Myla read, her voice strangled. "And..."

"'*Maternity*'," Max finished for her when she couldn't bring herself to say the word.

"No... no no no," I said, gripping onto the banister for support, my legs threatening to give way beneath me. "I'm not going in there."

"What does it mean by maternity?" Max wondered out loud.

"What do you think?" I said, icy dread filling my body until my head swam. "Hiero needs souls. He needs blood. Where do you think he's been getting them from?"

Max slapped a hand to his mouth, appalled.

No one moved. Max hovered by the '*Maternity*' door, while Myla and Red stood beside '*Breeding*'. I was still on the bottom step, as though afraid to set my feet on the ground, like it was the lowest circle of Hell, and if I took that last step, a part of me would be lost down here forever.

"Let's go," I said at last. "There is nothing down here that can help us stop Hiero."

"I'm going in," Max said, gripping the door handle to the maternity room.

"Stop!"

But he wrenched it open and stepped inside. Myla and Red remained with me, unwilling to enter, until Max let out a bloodcurdling scream that pierced my soul.

"Max?" Red hurried after him. Then Myla.

With a deep, resigned breath, I took that last step into Hell.

I lurked in the doorway, torn between following the others and running back up the steps to put as much distance between me and the maternity room as possible.

"Oh... oh my God..." Red's voice sounded thick, like she was trying not to cry.

"You're an idiot, Ava Monroe," I muttered to myself as I stepped into the room. "An idiot. A one-hundred-per-cent, twenty-four carat, absolute..." My final word died on my lips as I took in the scene that broke me.

On one side of the room, several babies lay sleeping in their cots. Though it was only when I drew closer, I realised the babies were not asleep; their eyes were wide open, staring at nothing. Husks. And yet, that wasn't the worst of it.

Women at various stages of pregnancy lay on stretchers, all as empty as the children. The mother in the farthest bed looked like a shrivelled corpse, her bones visible beneath withered skin, though she too was heavily pregnant, perhaps the furthest along. I thought she was dead until she let out a soft groan, trying to raise a hand, but falling short of energy.

Just like the room holding the Husks, it stank of stale bodily fluids, so strong, the air itself tasted bitter.

"Can Husks feel pain?" I whispered, almost afraid to ask the question.

"I... didn't think so," Red whispered back. "They never complain or—" She was cut off when the Husk groaned again, high-pitched and more urgent.

"Yes, they can feel pain," said a croaking voice from behind us, making me jump.

I spun to see an old woman hidden in the shadows, sitting on a wooden stool in the corner of the room, chained by her ankle. She was difficult to make out in the darkness, one side of her face obscured. The other side had deep-set wrinkles, her eye watery and a little cloudy. Wild, grey curls peeked out from under her hood.

"Who are you?" I gasped, stepping behind Myla as a shield.

"My name is Desdemona, but they call me the midwife."

"They?"

"Hieronymus and Xander."

Just the sound of his name set my teeth on edge.

"I know you!" Max stepped towards her. "You're the old woman who gave me the Sacrilegious Strength."

If the warrior vampire intimidated Desdemona, she didn't let it show, simply gazing up at him and a wry smile making her cheeks wrinkle.

The last piece of the puzzle.

"Max," I said. "Who did you say stopped you from helping her escape? Who said they were looking after her?"

"Fuck..." Max ran a hand over his cornrows. "Fuck!"

The heavily pregnant Husk groaned again, an eerie, hollow noise, sending a chill down my spine.

"Why are they like this?" I asked, emerging from behind Myla, inching closer to Desdemona.

She tilted her head, her visible eye narrowing with suspicion. "Who are you?"

"We are putting a stop to this," Red said. "That's who we are. You?"

"Hieronymus's slave. He's kept me down here for years—I don't know how many. Detached from the human world, my demon, and—"

"You're a witch," I said—a statement, not a question. "You're responsible for the lights and the enchanted door."

"Hieronymus is responsible. I'm simply the tool he used. We don't blame the dagger for the wounds it inflicts."

"You don't look like a witch," Max said, folding his arms. "Aren't witches meant to be... prettier?"

"Am I not pretty enough for you?" The witch got to her feet, stepping as close to Max as her chain would allow, until illuminated by the nearest torch and making us all gasp. In place of her right eye, she had four, black, beady orbs. And instead of a right leg, two long, pale, hairy spindles poked out beneath her rags.

"You're a spider," I said, my skin prickling with the realisation.

"And how would you know that?" she asked.

"I had a friend," I said, my chest feeling tight. I didn't want to say any more on the matter, Billy's cheeky, smiling face burning into my mind's eye and turning my heart to lead.

"I used to be a spider shifter. My glamour doesn't work here," she said. "Hieronymus kidnapped me a long time ago. With my powers weakened, I couldn't escape, and the only ingredients he gives me are the ones required for specific potions."

"Like Sacrilegious Strength?" Max asked, counting on his fingers.

Desdemona smiled. It wasn't a reassuring smile. If anything, it made her look scarier. "You have no idea how resourceful I had to be to make that one."

"Witch's Tears?"

"Technically not a potion. You'd cry too if you were locked down here."

"And an age accelerant," I finished for Max, the weight of the words sitting in my chest. "Now we know what it's used for." I turned my head, glancing at the corpse-like mother. "How far gone is she?"

"She'll give birth any day now," Desdemona said. "But she's been pregnant for the last week or so."

"Fucking hell." I drove my fingers through my hair, grabbing a fistful and clenching tight, a feeling of ineptitude creeping over me. All this time, *this* had been going on under my nose.

"This is how Hiero acquires blood and souls," Red said, her voice as hollow as I felt.

"Poor little things." Desdemona looked at the soulless babies. "Still, better they're unaware their life amounts to nothing but being aged, harvested from, and then bred."

"That's all I needed to hear." I clenched my fists, shaking with righteous fury. "*Let's kill that motherfucker.*"

"Ava—" Red said calmly, but I wasn't having it.

"There's nothing down here to stop Hiero. We can free the witch. Maybe even the Husks. But that won't *stop* Hiero. There is only one way to do that. Kill the bastard."

"She's got a point," Max said.

"I agree," Myla joined in, and we all looked at Red.

But before she could answer, a silhouette appeared in the doorway, making me jump.

"Oh dear," Xander's voice echoed throughout the room. "It would seem my volunteers are lost. But not to worry. *I've found you.*"

CHAPTER THIRTY

Even the Husks groaned in fear at Xander's arrival, weak limbs flailing, like they were trying to scramble away. They might have lost their souls, but their bodies had learned what a monster he was.

"Where's Madigan?!" My voice rang through the room, my blazing fury mimicking bravery. I wanted to hurt him. *Break* him. Destroy him for what he'd done.

His dark eyes roamed over me, his pointed features scrunching into a sneer. "If you're looking for your beloved, you've come to the wrong place, but I'll happily take you to Beta Conversion. He's being processed as we speak."

My body shook with the effort of restraining my temper, my fists balled so tight my nails cut crescents into my palms. I had to kill him. I had to *kill* him. "You..."

Keep it together... Keep it together....

"You..."

He's a Soul Sucker, Ava. Don't do it. Don't do it!

"You son of a whore!"

I charged. Blind to my surroundings. There was only his face. His pale, weaselly face that longed to have my fist punch through it. I'd break his nose. Smash his teeth and puncture his eyes. I'd feel when they pop. Just like Ivan's. *Just* like Ivan's. And when the flashback of blood and pulp shot through my mind, so vivid my thumbs felt sticky with Ivan's blood, instead of filling me with dread and nausea, I felt… *excited*…

Max grabbed me, his firm grip pinching into my arms as I tried to break free. Xander was close. Still sneering. I could still kill him if Max would just fucking let go!

"Xander," Max said, his voice as icy as when he'd trash-talked Red in the training ground, so calm, so cold, even my bloodlust cooled. I stopped fighting, twisting my neck to look at him. His good eye glared at Xander with a pompous contempt that, while Max-like, didn't fit with our perilous situation. The things Xander had done were *evil*. Yet Max had the face of someone who wanted to speak to the manager.

"Red, Myla, and I came here under the impression we could become Soul Suckers. Except, when we arrived, there was no one to greet us."

Xander's eye flicked from me to Max, his thin lips still curled, but the faintest crease formed between his eyebrows. "*What*?"

"I said," Max gritted out with the air of someone trying to keep their temper in check, "There was no one here to greet us."

Xander's sneer faltered, his frown deepening in genuine confusion.

"*US*!" Max released one of my arms, gesturing towards Red and then himself. "The finalists of the Battles of Blood, you absolute fool! You made us wait!"

My limbs tingled as I clocked what Max was up to.

Oh shit—he does want to speak to the manager!

"Why are you down here?" Xander asked guardedly.

"Looking for you? Looking for Hiero? Looking for whoever runs this dump? Whoever is in charge. Fifteen minutes we were in that damn corridor. Standing around like fucking peasants. Where is Hiero? I'm telling him about this, you know. This is not what I expect from our Liege Lord's staff."

Xander's frown eased as a flicker of fear crossed his face. "We don't need to tell Hiero," he said, raising a hand. "I can take you to Omega Conversion now."

"No!" Max threw me to one side—so forcefully I lost my footing and fell to the cold, hard floor—and marched up to Xander. Bending down so they stood eye-to-eye, he hissed in a vicious voice, "I want to speak to your superior. Right. *Now.*"

Xander swallowed, but never broke eye contact. "Careful," he said quietly. "You might be finalists, but if I need to defend myself, I will."

"There's no need for that," Red said. "Max, stand down. Xander has generously said he will take us for processing. We won't have to wait around anymore. Xander, lead the way."

Xander glanced between Red and Max, nodding slightly, like he had been convinced, and turned to leave, only to pause at the doorway and squint over his shoulder. "What's *she* doing with you?"

Max rubbed at his eyepatch, his lips twitching with the search for an answer. Nothing. He stared at Red, whose mouth hung open.

"We brought her here for Hiero," Red said at last.

Xander didn't move, eyes darting between each of us, visible doubt creeping across his face.

"Damn it," Max snarled, before throwing caution to the wind, and in a blur, rammed into Xander. Xander shoved Max off him with ease, but not before Red had joined the fight, darting forward and clumsily landing on top of him. Myla was the last to crash into the bundle with a frenzied battle cry.

I strained my eyes, but their speed combined with the darkness made it near impossible to make out what was happening. Blood splattered across the floor—who it belonged to was anyone's guess—each of them merely grunting at each thump of connecting blows.

"Do it now!" Myla shouted... and then all four of them went still.

Myla and Max had Xander pinned either side, Red on his chest. She was the first to move, swaying as she stepped aside, the hilt of a dagger protruding out of the soft flesh of Xander's neck, the blade buried up into his head. His eyes rolled up, his body twitching, blood gargling in his throat and pouring from his gaping mouth. I saw the moment his light extinguished, and it was *good*.

I waited as the vampires recovered, wheezing for lost breath. Max lay on the ground, one elbow draped over his eyes, his chest straining with each breath. Myla turned her back, bracing her hands on her knees like she was fighting the urge to be sick.

Red plopped herself on the ground to adjust her prosthetic. "I can't... get used... to this wretched thing."

"You did... great." Max hauled himself up to put a hand on her shoulder. Red ignored the compliment.

All the while, I watched them, my body twitching with increasingly restless energy, and the words spilled out of me before I could stop them. "Xander said Madigan is being processed. We need to go now."

All three shot me a dark look, and for the first time, a shiver of fear ran through me.

But Red's expression softened. "She's right. We can't afford to waste time."

"What about me?" asked Desdemona. I'd almost completely forgotten about her after Xander's arrival.

"We should bring her with us," I said. Max's eye rolled. "Or we can leave her down here to make potions for Hiero. That would be a *great* idea."

"Who the hell do you think you're talking to?" Max snarled with the same pomposity as before, but now he wasn't acting. "I just saved your life. What do you think you were doing charging at a Soul Sucker? Are you thick?"

"Would you give it a rest?!" Red had clearly had enough. "Myla, snap the witch's chains. You'll have to carry her. I don't think she'll keep up otherwise. Max, cut it out with all the arguments. We need to stick together. And Ava," she stepped toward me and said in a lowered voice, "I understand you're worried about Len, but we need to be smart. Keep your head. All right?"

I looked up into her eyes, just able to make out their mismatched blue and green in the gloom, her glare of determination calming me. "All right."

She smiled, making the scar down her face stretch. "Then let's go get him."

We headed back to the stairwell, Myla carrying the witch over her shoulder as we climbed upward—an infinitely more arduous task than the climb down—and my legs seared with the effort.

Soon I was squinting against the piercing glare of Desdemona's magic lights, my hands trembling as I reached for the door labelled *'Conversion: Beta'*. I held my breath as I squeezed the door handle downward with a soft click and winced as hinges squeaked.

This room, like the hallways, had that cold, clinical appearance. Sterile. It looked more like a hospital than ever, six metal beds in a row against one wall. But those weren't IV drips beside them. And those weren't wires and cables for tracking vitals. Beside each bed was an upside-down bottle—like those you find in water coolers—reddish-brown tracks dripping down to the bottom.

My legs carried me to the nearest bed on their own, and I gazed into the face of the vampire strapped down. Not Madigan. Neither were the other four vampires. The sixth bed was empty.

My stomach churned as I brushed my fingertips over the bottle, like I was making sure it was real, and not some fucked up hallucination. It was real, all right. As was the thick tube protruding from the bottom, leading to the mask locked onto the unconscious vampire's mouth. My insides gave a threatening crunch that forced me to take a deep, slow breath to keep it in check.

"I think we've discovered how they're being converted," I said, my voice stifled by a thickness in my throat.

My stomach crunched again, and I tore my eyes from the contraption before I vomited, heading to the opposite end of the room to a desk strewn with papers while my friends tried to free the trapped vampires.

"It's no use," Myla said, her voice strained. "I don't get it. I should be able to break these restraints."

"It's magic," I said. "I can feel it crackling in the air."

"Correct," Desdemona said, sounding impressed. I might have cared under different circumstances. "Only the key can open these. I wove this spell particularly well, if I say so myself."

"Can't you undo it?" Red asked.

"Only the key can open them," she repeated.

"No prizes for guessing who has the key," Max said.

My eyes scanned over the papers, looking for something—*any-thing*—that might help.

I was drawn to a chart tracking each 'dose' the vampires received until they were '*Neutralised*'—whatever that meant.

"I guess some have better tolerances than others." I dropped the chart, my hands suddenly weak, and was about to turn from the desk when a sparkle of silver caught my eye.

"Madigan," I gasped as I snatched the silver pendant from the desk. This was *his*. I recognised its mismatched chain.

They must have taken this from him when they captured him.

I pulled Madigan's tailcoat around me tighter, breathing in his scent like it was some sort of calming sedative, before putting the pendant around my neck and tucking it beneath the shirt I'd borrowed.

My heart gave a jolt as someone seized me by the back of my shirt, dragging me back through the room.

"Quick!" Red hissed—it was her hand grabbing me. "Someone's coming." She dragged me behind a bed to join Myla, Desdemona, and Max already hiding there. I still couldn't hear anything but held my breath all the same.

Soon, I made out the distant noise of shouting, too muffled to comprehend the words, but as they grew closer, my blood froze in my veins.

I knew that voice...

A door burst open, and Talia shoved Madigan into the room. He was dressed in the same rags as the unconscious vampires.

"He'll be here shortly," Talia said.

"What the *fuck* is this?!" Madigan's voice cracked, stifled with terror I'd never heard from him before. Not even when he'd fought Ivan. *Never.* And it cut through my heart like a blade.

"I have to get to him," I whispered to Red, who still gripped me tight.

"Shh, she'll hear—"

"I already know you're in here, Ava and Red," Talia called out. "And who's that you've got with you?" She sniffed the air. "Myla, is that you? And others too? Why don't you come out and play?"

Colour drained from Red's cheeks. And she sighed in defeat. The instant she relaxed her hold on me I wriggled out of her grasp and crawled out from the hiding spot.

"Ava?" Madigan blinked in disbelief, his voice hoarse from where he'd been shouting. He looked paler than usual. Dark circles around his eyes. Yet he found the energy to dart towards me in a blur, swaying slightly when he reached me. He took my hands in his, but as soon as we'd made contact, I threw my arms around his neck and squeezed him tight. So tight I could feel his heart crashing against mine.

"How touching," Talia sneered. "So, what's this then, Ava?" She gestured to my friends. "Your band of Merry Men here to save Maid Marian?"

But before anyone could respond, the door slammed open again, the sound of it making me jump, as Hiero staggered into the room, freezing on the spot the moment his eyes fell upon us.

He leant heavily on the door frame, looking up through streaks of blood pouring from where his crown sat on his head.

Madigan's grip on me tightened, but his attention was on Hiero. "What is this, Hiero? What the fuck is *any* of this?!"

Hiero opened his mouth to answer. Then his face scrunched into a grimace of pain, letting out an anguished groan as more blood poured down his face, flowing faster and thicker. But gritting his teeth, he addressed Talia.

"I told you to get me when it was *his* turn."

"You wouldn't have gone through with it," she hissed under her breath. "I was trying to spare you grief."

As much as I wanted to listen in on their whispered squabbling, I had greater priorities.

"Madigan," I said, tilting my head upward so my lips were close to his ear. "We need to get out of here."

"We can't fight him," he whispered back.

"They're outnumbered," I said, recalling how Red, Myla, and Max had killed Xander.

"Hiero's taken so many souls, Ava. S-so many..." He held me tighter as his body shuddered with suppressed sobs. "I've seen how they do it. I've seen *who* they take souls from. And when I w-wouldn't do it..." He pulled away, eyes roaming over the five unconscious vampires before settling on the sixth, vacant bed.

I tugged him back into an embrace just to keep him from looking. "We know. We've seen how... how Hiero gets them. Downstairs there's a... a..." I couldn't say it.

"So call for reinforcements!" Talia's voice rose, stealing my attention. "We've spent years getting you the crown. Use it!"

"I am!" Hiero didn't even bother keeping his voice down. "Do you have any fucking idea the price to pay for controlling this many with such complex demands!?" His knees gave way, and if it hadn't been for Talia catching him, he'd have fallen to the floor. His whole face was now crimson.

"It's all right for you, hidden away in here," he said, jaw clenched in pain. "Outside is—"

The door slammed open a third time.

Franziska Revay, soaked in blood, stood in the doorway like something from a horror movie, the spine of a Brain Eater—head attached by flesh and tendons—in one hand, a severed leg in the other. Her eyes, wild and bulging, fixed on Hieronymus.

CHAPTER THIRTY-ONE

No one moved. I gripped onto Madigan, eyes flicking between Franziska panting in the doorway, and Hiero, still supported by Talia, blood pouring down his face.

"You *bastard*!" Franziska charged at Hiero like a rampaging bull, barrelling into him and knocking him and Talia to the ground. They moved too fast to watch, appearing only as blurs, debris of Hiero's desk and papers sent scattering in the chaos.

"Time to go!" Red said, appearing at my side.

"But what about Franziska?" I asked, just as she became visible for a microsecond, smashing into a wall with a groan. She was powerful, but Hiero must have had almost God-like strength with the number of souls he'd taken. And Talia was with him.

"You want to stick around to help?" Max asked. He was already at the door, Myla with him, carrying Desdemona over one shoulder.

"Go!" Franziska screamed during her blurred tussle with the other two Soul Suckers. "I'll catch you up!"

Madigan grabbed my hand and bolted, following the others into the stairwell. A high-pitched screech rang from above.

"How long until Hiero finishes Franziska and sets his minions on us?" Max glanced up to the higher levels. "We'll never make it to the top."

"We don't have to," I said, my heart giving a sudden leap. "We only need to make it halfway. There is another exit that leads to a secret passageway beneath Hiero's manor."

Max almost smiled. "Which level?"

"Opposite where they're holding the Husks. Or specimen Delta."

Another screech.

"Then let's get going."

Madigan grabbed my hand again as we climbed the stairs, pulling on me each time I lagged, my legs threatening to give way with each step, my lungs so tight I thought they might collapse. I stumbled a few times, unable to keep pace with the vampires—even Red was faster than me—but Madigan yanked me back to my feet before I could hit the floor.

"I... can't... keep up!" I said after stumbling a fourth time, my arm nearly popping out of its socket as Madigan tugged on me.

"Right." He stopped, swept me off my feet and lugged me over his shoulder. Dread crawled up my spine as I noticed that, with my added weight, he now matched Red's limping speed. All I could do was hold on and grit my teeth each time he jostled me, his shoulder digging into the soft flesh of my middle, and I forced myself to focus on the pain instead of wondering when Madigan had last drunk blood, or how long Red could keep hobbling.

As we climbed, the screeching got louder.

With a scrape of clawed feet on the hard floor, a Brain Eater clattered down the stairs, mouth wide open, needle-like teeth on display, screaming its high-pitched shriek. Max raised a fist, and with a feral roar, drove it into the Brain Eater's head with a crack.

The Brain Eater collapsed, and before it could recover, Max brought down his fist again, smashing its skull until all that remained was a bloody pulp.

"Let's keep moving!" he shouted back to us, flicking blood from his swollen knuckles. "I can hear more on the way!"

We were almost at the exit. But dread coiled in my stomach at how Madigan's breathing was becoming more ragged, and his hair slick with sweat. And then—I saw it.

"There! That's the door!"

Max led the race down the corridor, wrenching the final door open and darting into the pitch-black tunnel, just as another bone-chilling scream rang from behind us, echoing throughout the stairwell.

"Great," Max said as we reached the steep slope of rocks.

I could have cried. The slope had been easy to climb down as a scorpion. But now? Climbing *up* with limbs that could barely function?

A clatter of claws echoed from the corridor, the Brain Eaters almost upon us.

"Myla, help get everyone up. I'll hold off these mutants." Max dashed back to the door, his growls of exertion ringing in my ears as one-by-one, we clambered up the rocky slope.

Madigan first, reaching down to grab my hand as Myla seized my waist, hauling me up to him. I snatched his hand, slippery in my sweaty grip, my feet flailing for support until I connected with one rock. Pushed against it. Muscles tearing. And scrambled onto solid ground.

I drank in lungfuls of air as Madigan assisted Red, then Desdemona, Myla making her own way up the slope. And finally, Max, now almost as bloody as Franziska had been.

"Keep going," he wheezed. "More are on their way. *Many* more by the sounds of it. Looks like Franziska bought us all the time she could."

Despite the all-consuming fear ensnaring me, somewhere deep in my soul, I felt a pang of guilt, but there was no time to linger on it. Madigan had already seized me again and flung me over his shoulder.

"Want me to carry you, Red?" Max asked, his eye flicking to me, then to Myla as she hoisted Desdemona over her shoulder again.

"Pfft, I'm not that desperate." She managed a thin smile before an echoing screech wiped it from her face.

We half-sprinted-half-stumbled through the tunnel, and I squinted through the darkness for any sign of Brain Eaters following us. Then twisted my body to look ahead at the distinct sound of a low groan, followed by the splatter of blood and brains as Max caved the enemy's head in. A Husk. Then another, leaping from the shadows.

I wasn't sure if Hiero was controlling them, or if the crown's power was so intense his orders had bled through to them, too.

It didn't matter. The cracking of bones echoed through the tunnel as Max charged ahead, attacking anything he encountered.

And then, the rapid thunder of footsteps from behind, the Brain Eaters hot on our tail. *Lots* of them. Not yet visible in the blinding dark, but getting closer with every second.

"Stairs!" Max shouted from the front.

"That's it!" I called to him. "It leads to Hiero's room!"

Another climb up the stairs, Madigan's hold on me tightening as his breathing laboured harder, his pace slowing...

With a rip of threads, Max tore back the tapestry, and we tumbled into Hiero's room.

"Where now?" Myla asked.

"Out of the Nest," I said. It was the only option. "You won't hide from Hiero or the Brain Eaters. If you don't want to be converted, you'll have to leave." I squeezed the back of Madigan's neck. "That's where we are going, right?"

He nodded. "We'll need their help to escape." He looked at Myla through desperate eyes. "We can't get through the portcullis without help."

Myla nodded. "Got it. We're all going. Right, Red? Max?"

Red nodded in agreement, massaging her leg, wincing. Max pressed his lips into a thin line, but even he didn't have any sniping remarks.

"Let's move," he said shortly.

We tore through Hiero's manor. Red kept up despite her limp, but she couldn't hide the strain, her face contorted into a grimace of agony.

"Sure you don't need a hand, Red?" Max asked as he wrenched open the double doors. I'd have thought he was mocking her if it wasn't for the deep lines across his forehead.

"I'm fine," she said through clenched teeth. "Keep going."

The Nest was eerily quiet, though distant shouts and screams beyond the wall still carried towards us, and now there was the smell of smoke in the air.

We dashed to the city wall, encountering more Brain Eaters carrying vampires over their shoulders. All they could do was scream at us in frustration—their captives their priority—though some stalled, as though their conflicting orders confused them.

Myla slammed her great fist on the gate. "Let us through!"

"Myla, is that you?" the guard called to her, then opened the gate. His eyes narrowed as they scanned over each of us.

"Hiero's orders," Myla said, unable to hide how out of breath she was. "I'm to escort these—"

"I've heard no such order." The guard folded his arms across his broad chest. "Have you been converted yet? Where's your glamour? And who is *that*?" He scrutinised Desdemona.

"You think our Liege Lord has time to inform you of every minute detail?" she asked, bypassing his questions. "I'm still a member of his guard, and I still outrank you."

But I could tell from his stony expression that he had already deduced exactly what we were doing. He opened his mouth—to argue or to call out to a Brain Eater, we would never know—as Max rushed past him in a blur. In the time it took to blink, Max had whipped a dagger from the sheath on the guard's hip and slashed it across the man's throat. The guard dropped to his knees, clutching his neck in a futile attempt to stop the blood flow, and we shot past him through the open gate... only to freeze upon seeing the hellscape of the outer ring.

I felt Madigan's muscles tighten as we drew a breath in unison.

"Now, this is more like it!" Max cried out, excitement exuding from him.

The Blood Drinkers were fighting back. Some had found weapons. Bodies of Blood Drinkers and Brain Eaters alike lay in dark puddles. Several buildings were on fire. And every sort of noise imaginable—screams, cries, roars, and snarls—rang throughout the Nest, a dreadful cacophony of pain and anguish.

I gripped Madigan tighter as I recalled the riots and how easily I'd been ripped from him.

"I've got you," he said, holding me tighter, like he knew what I'd been thinking. "I never should have let you go."

Max had already claimed a morning star from a corpse and was smashing down a Brain Eater barrelling towards us. "Let's go!"

Max led the way again, destroying Brain Eaters with the morning star as they charged at us. Myla followed him with Desdemona. Then Madigan and me. And Red brought up the rear. I kept a look out, shouting to Red each time a Brain Eater dared to attack from behind, who'd stab at them with a sword she'd acquired.

Our pace slowed as we wove through the narrow streets, keeping to the shadows, slipping past Brain Eaters preoccupied with other victims.

"Stop!" Max raised a hand, backing up from a corner he'd been about to turn. "The other way! Quickly! Move!"

Madigan's grip on me slipped at the sudden halt, and he hoisted me up again, my stomach lurching at the jerking motion.

We turned, taking a different route, Red now leading, but at a slower rate, her limp getting worse.

Madigan almost dropped me again as Max barged past him.

"What are you—" Red asked, but Max had already grabbed her, heaving her over one shoulder.

"No time!" he said and began running.

Madigan's breaths became raspier, and I could practically feel the rawness in his throat and lungs.

Myla must have noticed too, calling, "Not far to go! We can make it!"

Madigan struggled to keep up with Max as he clambered up the steps towards the portcullis.

"Myla!" Max shouted, dropping Red and seizing the winch to open the gate. "I need your help!"

Myla set down Desdemona and together, they opened the portcullis. Madigan put me down too, hunched over, hands braced on his knees as he gasped for breath, sweat dripping from his sodden hair, face flushed crimson.

A high-pitched scream set my hair on end.

A Brain Eater charged up the steps towards us. Eyes wide and focused. Teeth bared.

My body acted on its own. I shoved Madigan out of the monster's path. Dropped to my knees. Covered my head. Waited for the end to come... and was doused in something hot and sticky with the scent of iron.

Dead.

I had to be.

I opened one eye…

Gasped.

Red stood above me, a blade jammed through the monster's skull, a shower of blood raining down. Its body twitched. Then dropped.

I whipped my head back to check on Madigan. On the ground—where I'd pushed him. *Alive.* His eyes widened as he stared at me, mouth gaping, like I'd risen from the dead.

Before I could process what had just happened, Red grabbed me by the arm, yanking me to my feet. "Come on! Let's go! The gate is open!"

More Brain Eaters spied us from the bottom of the steps. Some were preoccupied with other vampires, but at least five charged, and I could have sworn their wide mouths split into monstrous grins.

I grabbed Madigan's hand and bolted.

"Go!" Myla shouted, her voice strained and legs shaking as she held the first gate open upon her broad shoulders—the only way to keep it open now Max had released the winch and slipped beneath it.

Red, Desdemona, Madigan, and I ducked after him before Myla dropped it with a *slam.*

"Again!" Max said, his hands on the winch of the second gate, his arms trembling with the strain. We all dived through, except for Myla, who once again braced it on her shoulders as Max darted after us, then let it drop, the floor of the tunnel vibrating with the force of it.

A moment of silence. All except everyone's wheezing breaths and a groan of pain as Red massaged her leg.

More torches lined the walls since the last time I was here, but it was of little comfort. The flames flickered in a way that made the shadows dance, like monsters were hiding within and ready to pounce.

"You think this will hold them?" I asked, pressing an ear to the gate, listening out for the slightest noise.

Slam!

I jumped back from the portcullis.

"Don't count on it," Max said through a locked jaw, as the Brain Eaters started battering down the first gate.

Slam!

"Keep moving," Myla said, hauling the witch back up onto her shoulder.

Slam!

Max picked up Red, who, despite her earlier protests, now allowed him to carry her without complaint.

I glanced at Madigan. He looked dreadful: his eyes sunken, dark smudges beneath them. His breathing was more like a death rattle, but he took hold of me and lifted me into his arms.

Slam!

"You can't," I said. "Let me run. You won't make it while carrying me."

"Never," he said, and managed a weak smile before darting off behind the others.

CRASH!

They'd breached the first gate.

The sounds of smashing echoed through the tunnel as we sped off. We'd barely made it a few feet before the crash of the second gate rang in my ears.

I peered over Madigan's shoulder at the white, monstrous forms clambering over each other to reach us. Their eyes blazing. Teeth gnashing. Claws spread.

Madigan stumbled but regained his balance.

"I can see moonlight!" Max shouted from up ahead.

"We're nearly there," I said, trying to encourage Madigan to move faster, but the gap between us and the Brain Eaters was closing.

He stumbled again.

"Please keep going!" I cried, my voice breaking, eyes burning.

But they were getting closer. And again, they seemed to grin.

This was it. I was going to die here, in this tunnel, torn to pieces. With Madigan.

I inhaled, his sweet scent calming me. There was no one else I would rather die with. And a strange sense of acceptance washed over me.

It was time.

"Madigan," I whispered against his ear. "I lov—"

"Myla!" he shouted.

What?!

Myla turned and reached out a hand.

Before I knew what was happening, Madigan tossed me through the air to her. She caught me, grunting with the strain of carrying both me and the witch. I didn't acknowledge the crushing pain of the impact—just focused on getting my bearings. Under Myla's arm. Facing Madigan.

He raced behind, faster without me weighing him down, but the Brain Eaters were still getting closer... and closer...

"We're here! Red, get up there! Move!" Max's voice called from ahead.

Madigan closed the space between us, the stampeding Brain Eaters hot behind him.

"Keep going!" I reached out a hand.

The Brain Eaters closed in. Mere inches from him.

"Madigan!"

He reached out towards me. Our fingertips connected.

And...

The Brain Eaters swarmed around him, slamming him to the ground, engulfing him, and he disappeared beneath a sea of white bodies.

"No! Myla, let me go! We have to save him! Let GO!"

"Take her!" Myla shouted, tossing me just as Madigan had done, but this time Max caught me, who immediately shimmied up the rope.

I thrashed in his grip. "Let me go! Madigan is still down there! Let me go!" But he held me fast, tighter than Myla or Madigan had done, his grip pinching my flesh.

He hauled me over the edge of the well. But I spun on the spot to dive back down.

Red seized my arms, wrestling me to the ground. I thrashed. Thrashed with all my might, until mud and leaves stuck in my hair, small stones shredding my skin. I'd fight her. I'd fight them all. I just *had* to get back down there!

Max emerged, single eye blazing as he knocked Red aside, grabbed me, and slammed me into a tree. "What the fuck was that?! You could have got me killed, you little shit bag!"

"Let me go! Save Madigan! Let me go!"

Myla appeared over the top with Desdemona. "Shut up, both of you!" She peered into the depths of the well. "They're not following. *Why?*"

"Orders?" Red suggested.

"Or maybe they're too busy feasting on your boyfriend?" Max snarled at me.

I let out a wild, heartbroken scream and slammed my forehead into his face. Pain blazed through my head, almost blinding me, but Max released his grip on my arms, covering his nose.

"You fucking little bitch!" He smashed his fist into the tree—right where my head had been—but I'd already made a dive for the well.

"Stop!" Red caught me, and shook me so hard it made my stomach writhe. "Don't you fucking go down there, Ava Monroe! Is that what Len would want?"

But I couldn't hear her. Her words meant nothing.

"Let me go! Madigan is down there!"

She sighed. "I'm sorry to do this." She twisted me into her body, and the next thing I knew, she had an arm around my neck and braced my head with the other.

"*What are you—*" but I couldn't even get the words out, my jaw locked shut by her choke hold. My vision was getting foggy. And so was my brain. I grabbed at her arm, trying to wrench her off me, but she didn't budge, and my limbs grew heavier with every passing second. And my joints stiffer. Until I couldn't move.

Couldn't even... see...

Shift, Ava... Shift...

But it was no use. My energy was spent.

Darkness...

CHAPTER THIRTY-TWO

B *lood poured from Ivan's empty eye sockets as he laughed at me. I lay on the floor, scooping my innards up, trying to put them back inside the hole in my stomach, and all the while, his laugh rang through my mind.*

I looked up. Madigan was lying nearby, too far to reach. I stretched out a hand.

"Madigan!"

He looked at me, his face a mask of sadness as he mirrored my movement, reaching out. I brushed his fingertips with mine, but no sooner had I done so than a tidal wave of Brain Eaters crashed down on him, obscuring him from my sight.

And all the while, Ivan's laugh grew louder and louder, until almost recognisable.

I faced him, only now it wasn't Ivan standing over me. It was Hiero, his once beautiful face contorted into a sickening leer. And he laughed. He laughed, and he laughed. Cold, cruel, and evil.

I looked back to Madigan, but the pile of Brain Eaters hid him from me, each of them letting out a hiss from their wretched throats, until blood sprayed upwards. Outwards. Every direction. And the Brain Eaters screeched in delight as they held his severed head aloft.

"Madigan!"

I jerked awake, one hand reaching out, soaked in a cold sweat.

For one blissful moment of confusion, I thought I was still in Hiero's manor, tucked up in the fourposter bed, and frowned as I blinked into the darkness, wondering why it smelt of damp straw. My eyes adjusted, taking in the crumbling walls and decaying roof of the hut. Then I caught the voices of Red, Max, and Myla carrying through the wooden door.

I shivered against the night air, pulling my coat around me tighter.

But it wasn't my coat. It was Madigan's tailcoat. Tattered and dirty, but unmistakably his.

And the recollection of what happened in the tunnel crashed over me like I'd been doused in ice water.

I put a hand to my chest, my fingers closing around the pendant, and reality set in.

"No, no, no, no, NO!" The last word erupted from me as a shout. I sprang to my feet, making a bolt for the doorway, only to slam into Red.

"Calm down or I'll knock you out again," she said, wrapping her arms around me and pinning my arms to my side. I immediately wriggled to free myself, my heart giving a small leap when somewhere, in the back of my tormented mind, I noted how her grip wasn't as strong as usual, and she had the telltale dark rings around her eyes from blood starvation.

But Myla stood behind her, thick arms folded; she didn't need blood to overpower me. And Max stood at Red's side. He didn't look at me—the front of his shirt still splattered crimson from where I'd head-butted him—and I knew he wouldn't hesitate to use force. In fact, he was probably waiting for a good reason to pay me back.

"We need to go back," I said, my voice raspy, and only now did I realise how raw my throat was.

"That would be suicide." She spoke the truth, but I wasn't willing to hear it. Nor did I care.

"We survived them once."

"No, Ava."

"I'll shift and sneak in."

"NO, Ava! Don't test me, I'll knock you out again, I swear—"

"FINE!" I turned my back on her, my heart pounding, adrenaline puppeting me, but somewhere in the back of my mind, a tiny, rational voice told me this was not the way to save Madigan.

"Fine," I said again, forcing myself to keep my voice low, and faced the trio once more. "Sorry, I'm... not thinking straight."

Red regarded me with a calculating expression. "You know we can't go back."

"Yeah, yeah, I know." I nodded. She needed to believe me, and it wasn't difficult to pretend I'd lost the will to fight, my genuine exhaustion doing most of the acting for me. "Where are we?"

"About one night from the farm rest stop. Hopefully, we can jump-start a car and get to the Halfway House. We can rest there for a bit, get some food and a hot shower. How does that sound?"

I nodded again, pinching false tears from my eyes, and said in a broken voice, "Sounds good."

One night from the farm. That's further from the Nest than I'd expected.

"Could I have a moment alone, please?" I asked, turning my face upwards and blinking like I was trying not to cry.

Red's expression softened, and my hollowed-out soul sparked with a glimmer of hope. She was buying it.

"Of course," she said. "Sunrise will be upon us soon, but we'll leave you until then."

"Thank you…" I turned my back again, covering my eyes with one hand, shoulders tensing with fake sobs while listening to their every movement as they left me inside the hut. As the door squeaked on rusted hinges and closed with a soft thud, I emerged from behind my hand.

Though I'd never tried to sense Latisha's whereabouts, somehow I knew what to do. I sat crossed-legged, and closed my eyes like I was meditating, thinking of my mistress like I was seeking her soul with mine. Within a second, I knew where she was. Some town up north with a name I could barely pronounce. And I could *see* her—laughing at something Trevor had said as he handed her a cash box, the funfair's bright, colourful lights reflected in her eyes as the showmen closed their attractions. But my stomach turned to lead as I felt the distance between us, like there was an invisible string connecting her heart with mine, pulled so tight it might snap.

I opened my eyes, and the heaviness inside me only worsened, the shepherd's hut feeling more like a prison than a sanctuary.

My mind raced as I chewed on my lip. The farm was a night away. And *if* we jump-started a car, it would take another night to reach the Halfway House. After that, who knew how long it would take to reach Latisha? Three nights? Four? Too long. And that was just the journey to Latisha, never mind the journey back again.

If I was to rescue Madigan in time, I was on my own.

The door swung open.

"Sun's coming up," Max said, not looking at me as he marched in, followed by Myla and Red.

"How are you doing?" Myla asked, but I didn't answer, keeping my head hung low as I walked past them and stepped outside.

I shielded my eyes against the harsh glare of sunrise, unaccustomed to its brightness, and squinted as I looked around; nothing but fields, forests, and valleys. But I couldn't admire their lush green hues, nor the sweet and earthy scents on the wind. I'd miss them once I'd ventured back down, down, down into the endless abyss of darkness, blood, and monsters. Rank air and rotting bodies. A pit where evil was born.

"I wouldn't search for the Nest again, if I were you," said a voice, making me jump. It was Desdemona, sitting beside a campfire, an infuriatingly smug expression on her face.

Except she didn't *look* like Desdemona. If it hadn't been for the rags she wore and her spiralling curls—black now instead of grey—I wouldn't have known it was her. Gone were the deep-set wrinkles, replaced by soft, plump, rosy skin. But most noticeably, all her features were one-hundred-per-cent human. No spider legs. No black, beady orbs. Just a pair of slightly narrowed forest-green eyes.

"I'd forgotten about you," I said, unable to hide the bitterness in my voice. We'd rescued *her*, while Madigan had been left behind.

She held out a scrap of meat she'd been roasting over the fire, and though my stomach ached with hunger, I had no interest.

"Where are we?" I asked.

"Wondering which direction the Nest is?"

"No."

Her smirk widened, and I resisted the urge to shove her headfirst into the fire. "Good, because you'll never find it again on your own."

"And I don't suppose you'd be willing to help me?"

"I think I'd rather set myself on fire."

That makes two of us.

But the rage I'd projected onto her fizzled at the realisation that she was right. I couldn't find the Nest on my own, and the only person who would help me was too far to reach. By the time I found Latisha, it would be too late. Madigan would be...

I flopped beside her, taking the scrap of meat to keep my hands occupied, picking at it, popping pieces in my mouth and chewing, but it didn't taste of anything. I couldn't register the kiss of the sun, the smoky scent of the fire, or the coolness of the breeze. There was nothing. And I wondered if this was how Husks felt.

Once the moon had risen and the vampires awoke, we set off again. I followed behind them, dragging my feet, knowing each step I took was a step further from Madigan. The *wrong* direction. He was, of course, still alive. The idea that he was gone was incomprehensible.

"Look, Ava, through the trees," Red said, pointing. Narrowing my eyes, I glimpsed a red field that seemed to ripple as the moonlight shone down on it, glittering crimson and silver. The moth field. The moth field in which I'd danced with Madigan.

My face contorted with ugly tears, and whatever had kept me going—be it adrenaline, willpower, denial, or even magic—vanished. I bawled until my tears ran dry, my eyelids swollen and my face hot and itchy. Even my chest felt heavy with pain, and I wondered if hearts really could break.

If it hadn't been for Red putting an arm around me, I couldn't have taken another step. My brain shut down, no longer registering the ache in my muscles or the passing of time, and I only awoke from autopilot once we reached the farm.

Max and Myla started examining abandoned vehicles, trying to find one that might be of any use.

"Where's the storeman?" Myla asked. "Was anyone here when you came this way, Ava?"

I shook my head.

The three vampires discussed their options, Desdemona listening in. But I wasn't interested. Instead, I trudged towards the burnt-out remains of the campervan, recalling the days Madigan had spent working on it. The nights we'd travelled together. The warmth of his hand on my knee.

Until Hiero came along...

The hollow feeling inside me changed as something scalding hot awoke within me. An all-consuming hatred. A fiery need to *hurt* Hiero. To have his bloody remains in my hands. I'd do to him what I'd done to Ivan.

You'll never be strong enough, said a small inner voice.

I screamed, kicking the metal frame of the camper, dirt scattering and ash wafting up in a cloud as the raging fury pulsed through me, bursting free. But that was all the strength I could muster before depression consumed me, and I dropped to my knees.

I stared dead-eyed at the camper's remains. A hollowed-out shell. Just a vessel for ash and ruin. An urn, of sorts. Dead inside, like me.

Moonlight reflected off something shiny, half-buried in ash.

And somewhere, deep inside my soul, the last traces of curiosity sparked within me.

I reached into the ash pile, seizing the small object...

...and my heart...

...stopped.

A flower made of rubies and gold, a crimson eye in its centre, not so much as a scratch on it.

Mischievous...

I recalled his parting words as he'd pressed the trinket into my hand.

"There will come a time when you realise what you saw tonight wasn't so bad, and when you do, call on me. I'll be there to help."

"He *knew*..."

I slowly got to my feet, my sights fixed on the flower, and the flower stared back as my mind spun with memories, questions, and wild, impossible ideas.

"I'll be there to help." He can make you a witch.

But wait—Lascivious said I wasn't ready. He even questioned why Mischievous wanted to see me. But then... what was it Mischievous said?

"You never could think outside the box."

What did he mean?

How do I summon him?

"I'll be there to help."

"What's that?" Red's voice made me jump; I'd not even heard her approaching. She stared at the trinket in my hand that seemed to grow warm in my palm. My last hope. My only option.

"A gift. From a demon."

"A demon?"

"Yes," I said the single word without hesitation. I wasn't afraid of demons. Not anymore.

"What does it do?"

"I think it will help me contact Mischievous."

"And he'll find your coven?"

"No." I grasped the flower tight in my shaking fist, bringing it to my chest—over my heart. "He'll help me get my man back."

End of Book Two

The story continues in:
Book Three of the Blood and Venom Saga

If you enjoyed this book, and would like to support an indie author, please consider leaving a review so others might discover and enjoy it too!

More From The Author

The Blood and Venom Saga

FREE Prequel: *Out For Blood*
(Sign up to my newsletter to download! QR and link below.)
Book One: *The Vampire and the Scorpion*
Book Two: *The Vampire Lord*
Book Three: *Title TBC*

For updates on future instalments, and other projects, follow me on
social media and sign up to my newsletter!

linktr.ee/k.e.beale

About the Author

Hi, my name is Kat.

After I published *The Vampire and the Scorpion*, a writer friend of mine asked why my 'About the Author' section was so short. I guess I don't really enjoy talking about myself! But here is my attempt at doing so.

It's hard to remember when exactly I started writing, but I can tell you that when I was in primary school, I was always excited when the teacher would hand us a lined sheet of A4 paper, and tell us to write a story. Now, I grant you, my early work was... questionable. Very often, it would be my take on the cartoon I watched that past weekend and had been silently obsessing over. But occasionally, I would come up with a story I fell in love with, or a character I felt was a friend.

At about age ten, I started writing 'books' for my mum. They were pieces of plain printer paper I'd folded and slotted together. It was a series about a court jester who had been sent by the king to fight various monsters. Looking back, I'm not sure why the king didn't send—oh I don't know—a soldier? Clearly not a smart king, that's for sure. I believe my mum still has these books somewhere.

But I soon moved onto writing my stories on a computer. While this meant I could start writing longer stories (yay), it also meant that, after leaving my computer unattended, my cousins were able to 'modify' some of my work.

Now, the sad thing is, I shall forever remember that work as 'The Great Coral Love Story'. What was it really titled? Couldn't tell you. But it wasn't very good, anyway. No, really. It was shockingly bad.

My next three books were pretty interesting. Not good. But interesting. It was the first time I created an outline. After playing some sort of 'let's pretend' game with one of my cousins (yes—one of the cousins that murdered my book), I became obsessed with the character I'd created. I planned a three-book series, each consisting of ten chapters at about two thousand words each. I didn't realise it at the time, but fifteen-year-old me had created her first writing habit. To this day, I aim for about two thousand words per chapter in my first draft. I don't always reach it, and sometimes I'll go over it. But that's always the target.

Now, as I said, those books weren't great. I queried the first, which adult me is slightly mortified by. Luckily, those who responded were very kind—after all, I was only fifteen.

But that was a knock to my confidence, and so, while I still created outlines, I never finished the projects. With that said, my outlines and early chapters improved as I started taking an interest in story structure and the craft of writing. In fact, creating an outline and doing some basic world-building got me through one of the darkest periods of my life. I may well revisit that particular story one day.

I reached a point where I was bored with planning and never finishing a book. I don't know exactly what it was about *The Vampire and the Scorpion* that captured me so. Perhaps it was because Ava was my first protagonist I had anything in common with. While our personalities and appearances couldn't be any more different, neither of us dealt with heartbreak particularly well, and both have a love of gaming (and vampires).

So, there you have it!

Acknowledgements

As always, my first thank you goes to my husband and children for your love and support.

Thank you to my family—my parents, siblings, grandad, aunties, uncles, cousins, and all my in-laws, for being my earliest 'fans' before I had any. And an extra special thank you to my sister for your stunning artwork.

Thank you to my beta readers and critique partners, Chloe, Katie, Nichola, Mikaela, Belle, and Emma. Your feedback and critiques were invaluable, and this story wouldn't be what it is without you.

Thank you to my writing bestie, Chachi, for supporting me throughout my writing journey.

Thank you to Bridget for always being there and sharing your wonderful stories with me.

Thank you to all my followers, subscribers, and dare I say... fans? The bookish community has welcomed me into their space, and I couldn't be more grateful.

And finally, reader, thank you for giving me and my mad little story about spicy vampires a chance!